WISH
UPON THE
STARS

WISH UPON THE STARS

A Superhero Cultivation LitRPG

Book 7

MALCOLM TENT

Timeless
Wind

First published by Timeless Wind Publishing LLC 2025

This novel is entirely a work of fiction. The names, characters and incidents portrayed in it are the work of the author's imagination. Any resemblance to actual persons, living or dead, events or localities is entirely coincidental.

Malcolm Tent asserts the moral right to be identified as the author of this work.

First edition

Editing by Lorne Ryburn.

Cover art by Brian Flores.

Recap of Book 6

Following the Walking Silence Auction's sabotage by the Black Sorrow Cult, Shane and his team leave Doomtown to enter the Moonsong Glade Tournament.

The team performs well in the team matches, with Abel seemingly unbeatable, even against other Master Candidates. The group balances networking and information-gathering with competing and reunite with friends made in Doomtown. They also collaborate with Shane's cousin, Natalie, since Shane and Nat previously agreed to share Moonsong Glade spots should either side win the tournament.

They soon discover the involvement of foreign powers to manipulate the tournament's outcome. Concerned about the Empire's involvement and potential threats, Shane and Callie seek a meeting with Frostbite, a powerful Unity executive and a rival of Callie's father, Midknight. They secure an alliance and learn of an information leak within the Unity.

During their investigation, they learn that Benny's girlfriend, Celine, was involved with a mercenary attack orchestrated by her sister, Nalia, an E-rank elf from the Faerieland. Celine warns them about escalating faction tensions and urges them to withdraw from the tournament. Benny reels from her betrayal.

The solo part of the tournament kicks off, pitting team members against each other. Shane and Callie face one another in a tense and emotional battle where Shane emerges victorious.

His next opponent is Abel. To prepare for his hardest fight yet, Shane merges his Enchanting and DS Mastery Skills, achieving Intermediate Path of the Doom Sovereign.

Before they compete, Shane discovers that Natalie and her guards, Perit and Valk, have been attacked by the Black Sorrow Cult. They find Celine injured and learn about the Cult's escalating attacks on other factions, including the use of multiple E- and F-rankers.

When Shane and Abel meet in the ring, Shane puts up an excellent showing with his upgraded DS Mastery, but Abel emerges victorious, moving forward. He ultimately wins the final round of the tournament against the spear-wielding Lament, securing ten slots for the Moonsong Glade.

The victory is interrupted by Kix, an Arch-Bishop of the Black Sorrow Cult, who declares the Cult's intention to seize the Glade slots and annex Callus. Two B-rank cultists accompany him.

Zeke intervenes, revealing his own B-rank status and summoning powerful masked figures through his Voltomancy ability. After a brief but brutal battle, Zeke defeats the cultists, capturing their souls and sending a stark warning.

With the tournament concluded, the team prepares for their journey to the Moonsong Glade.

Between Shane's team and Nat's, they have one Moonsong Glade slot open. The teams decide to offer the final slot to Celine, officially forgiving her for her reluctant involvement in her sister's schemes.

Finally, the team departs Callus through a Waywalker teleporter, stepping into the wider universe.

Chapter One

When Zeke had mentioned the bazaar, I had assumed we would be attending some small gathering of stalls. Maybe some tents, a few blankets on the ground. The word invoked images of a temporary market that contained equally temporary sales locations. What we actually ended up walking into was… not that.

For one thing, I felt heavier, like I was under pressure, suffocating even as I took a deep breath. Once I realized I was panicking about nothing and forced myself to calm down, the choking sensation went away, though the weight remained.

Pressure aside, the place we'd ended up was *amazing*. The night sky I saw on the other side of the portal made much more sense now—we were literally in space. It looked like someone had torn a city (a very large one mind you) out of the ground and let it float among the stars. Buildings extended for as far as the eye could see, all of varying shapes and styles.

"This is… temporary?" I said in shock. The bazaar was supposedly a random camp set up to wait for the glade's opening, but it looked like it had taken centuries to build.

Zeke snorted. "They've probably got a high-ranking Architect around somewhere. I've seen variations of an ability that can make entire countries with a snap of their fingers. There are a bunch of ways to do it, though out in space like this they either had the rock shipped out or they hired one of the Fantasy based variants. The latter would be pretty damn expensive, though."

Someone cleared their throat, and we turned to see a short, burly man with curly dark hair and horns. His eyes were horizontal like a goat's and he had a small patch of facial hair that somehow paired well with his annoyed expression. He held out a hand. "My tip?"

Rolling his eyes, my uncle started muttering something about Waywalkers, and fished out a chit he flipped to the goat man. The other ascendant caught the chit, then made a show of biting it while staring at Zeke, before nodding and vanishing into thin air in a blink. I was guessing since Zeke had been transported too, tipping wasn't a breach of contract, but I wasn't going to ask in case he'd just managed to slip that by the geas by not thinking about it.

"So... we're here," said Callie slowly. "Wherever here is. Does this place have a name?" She looked around excitedly. "Actually, I can find out on my own. I should try out my new powers here. I can use them to spy on everyone nearby to figure out all the important info. Learn the ins and outs of the city."

She stepped toward a wall, but Zeke held up a hand. "Don't!" he said quickly. When she stopped to give him a confused look, he just sighed. "Don't forget that your ability, while amazing, is Perception based. Anyone with a sufficiently high Perception can detect you even in the shadows. This place is full of random elders and faction management. Given the low standard of the cluster, I'm guessing that there won't be many B-rankers, if any, but a C or D-ranker is more than up to noticing you."

Wincing slightly, she stepped away from the wall. "Ah. And you can't protect me because I'm not your charge. Speaking of, D-rank is the new level of protection you can offer, right? If we run into any E-rankers and piss them off we're screwed." She sounded about as worried as I felt.

Zeke just waved it off. "Oh sure, but there won't be any here. Sending an E-ranker to this place would be stupid. Everyone else would be stronger, or weaker, depending on if they were entrants. With the Glade blocking anyone below or over F-rank, and any protectors being notably powerful, most of the people will be C-rank. Only lower middle class factions will send B-rankers. Strong enough to have them but weak enough not to trust their reputation to protect their people."

2

That seemed to put Callie back on balance. "That makes sense. This whole thing is its own kind of challenge. The chaperones will be seen as expressions of both power and confidence. Won't having you here make us seem weak though? You're *way* overkill for this place."

"Nah," my uncle said casually. "I'm his sole protector, technically speaking. Stuff like this tends to be a gray area for candidates. If anything, having a protector like me is bound to impress. Most candidates get rookies like her." He jabbed a thumb at Selka, who was standing next to my cousin, Nat.

The other guardian bristled. "I'll have you know that I'm a talented combatant. You don't get chosen to be guardian unless you can handle yourself. Don't treat me like some punk kid."

Zeke just grinned maliciously. "Awww, it thinks it's dangerous. How cute. Here's the thing though, you *are* some punk kid. It becomes exponentially harder to rank up as you climb. You may never reach B-rank, and even if you do it'll take you absurd amounts of time to reach the point I'm at. By that time I'll probably be an A-ranker." He paused. "Or dead. I might just be dead. Either way, respect your elders, kid."

Her glare was almost funny, until I snickered and she turned it on me, at which point I shut up. "Anyway," Callie interjected, "where are we going? Do we have some sort of... faction safehouse here? Are there other WCP branches? Can we trust them if there are?"

"There are, and we can't," my uncle said firmly. "I don't know if there are other candidates, though if there are I would wager not many. Regardless, the WCP isn't cohesive, and there are too many people for me to keep track of, so I can't tell if there's a branch worth visiting. Not that my geas would allow me to find it."

Callie scowled. "Maybe we should find a hotel or something, then. Do we have the money for that?"

I hadn't paid much attention to joint funds lately, but I knew I personally was just short four and a half E-rank coins. I was betting that wouldn't be enough.

Zeke just gave her a pitying look. "Did you forget we're traveling with a pair of Wishmaster candidates? They're basically walking piggy banks. You can trade wishes for nearly anything." He pointed over at me and Nat, and I scowled at him in annoyance.

3

"Hey!" I said loudly. He just raised an eyebrow at me. I looked away, grumbling to myself. "You could be nicer about it, you know. I'm not just some asset to pay for things."

"You're a *pain* in my asset," he drawled. "But we can figure out where to go with an easy trick of the trade. I wish we had the location of a safe place to stay."

I blinked at him. Zeke had never wished for anything from me. I could see how it was within his geas, though, since he needed a place to stay too. He paused as the words flowed across my vision. "Oh, payment." He pulled out a chit and flicked it to me. An F-ranked chit, which was pretty decent.

Wish detected. Grant wish?

I confirmed, accepting the point cost. It was an easy wish, as evidenced by the much lower stat requirements than what had become typical. There was a flash of electricity, revealing why there had been Creation points folded in. A piece of paper covered in a spidery scrawl flashed into existence, bearing a map that showed all the nearby areas, including a single neatly marked X off to one side with a caption over it that said, "Daylight Dreamer Inn."

I grinned at him. "I take it you want me to get more used to using my Wishes as an asset now that I'm stronger?"

He nodded amiably. "Yup. There will probably be another candidate or two around here given the sheer scope of a Cluster-wide search. Even candidates who don't travel horizontally among similar scale worlds like Natalie probably got swept up in this mess."

Clapping me on the shoulder, he chuckled lightly. "More candidates means that your Wishes are both more and less valuable. You can use them more freely, but they aren't quite as limited a commodity as they used to be. You'll need to adjust to the new environment. Granted, it's pretty specific to places like this, but the Ruined Soul Temple will be one of those locations as well, so it's something to get used to."

I nodded, following Callie as she grabbed the map from Zeke and set off. Benny stepped up next to me. "This place is nuts, right?" he said, gesturing around us. "Because I thought Rajak was big, but this place has to be, like, half the size, and they put it together short-term as a place to hang out and wait? Architect or no, that's insane."

"Yeah," I murmured back. "I feel that. I think I feel... slower here. Weaker maybe? Which is nuts because my stats are higher. This must be a higher-level area than our planet. Probably just D-rank though—if it were more than a rank-up away, I assume it would be more obvious."

Zeke, who was ahead of us, turned to nod. "Yeah, D-rank. Since your planet is a pseudo D-rank world anyway, it's less difference than you would expect. It won't have much effect at this level. Just a bit of suppression and a change to the strength of your abilities. Nothing too noticeable with all the recent upgrades."

"It's true," Celine said solemnly. "I've been on higher-ranked planets before. Your combat efficiency doesn't drop much, considering it's a linear change across the board. The one difference is that the surrounding environment tends to be harder to damage. I doubt it would be a simple thing to destroy a building here, if we were even capable of doing so."

Which seemed like a big change from our pseudo D-rank planet, but then again, this place was much smaller. Maybe the Impact was more condensed here. Suffice to say I could understand why they didn't let anyone under F-rank off the planet. While this was only mildly stifling for us, I got the feeling that with twenty less Impact it would be much more difficult to bear with.

Finally we came to a stop in front of a large, tower-like building. With cream-colored walls and red tiled roof, the place looked more like a vacation destination than a run-of-the-mill inn, and it was definitely upscale enough to be a feasible place to stay. Zeke looked it over carefully before nodding. "Decent security and top-notch stealth. Probably a high C-ranker running the place. Not perfect but more than enough for our purposes."

I was curious how it had top-notch stealth when we found it so easily, but I didn't dwell on it. Zeke said it was fine and I trusted his judgement.

We stepped inside, strolling up to the counter. The girl behind it had black hair in a ponytail, pale skin, and dark lips with a hoop piercing. Her eyes were ringed with dark liner, and she mostly ignored us as we approached, engrossed in a leather-bound book.

Knocking on the counter, I cleared my throat. She looked up. "I'm hoping to talk to your boss about accommodations."

She pointed above her head at sign with pricing on it before returning to her read. Must be a fascinating story. I scanned the values and sure enough, *way* too many chits.

I grinned, knocking again. "Tell them we're from the WCP—and that we're willing to trade wishes."

It was satisfying how quick she slammed the book shut.

Chapter Two

THE OWNER of the Daylight Dreamer Inn was not what I expected. Though to be fair, that was probably more my issue than his. He looked younger than I'd thought, but then again, Ascendants were almost always young looking. Sindar was more the kind of person you'd expect to see at a club than in the office of an inn, though. A handsome guy, with dark skin, dark eyes, and long wavy black hair. He had on an expensive looking suit (which for an Ascendant meant it was enchanted) and had an easy smile that was belied by the coldness in his brown irises.

I could tell he was trying to give off the impression of a friendly, amiable guy, and I could *also* tell that if I believed that impression I was going to get badly ripped off.

Which was interesting, because he was at least at the peak of F-rank (probably one of the entrants), and he really should have had a Skill that would make it harder for me to spot that. It took me a second to realize that I'd picked it up through the bond, and that Callie, with her high perception stat, was the one who had noticed. It was a bit jarring how smoothly that had come through, honestly.

"I'm told you have a precious resource you're seeking to barter with," Sindar said, folding his hands in front of him as he smiled at us cooly. Then he did... nothing. Damn it. He was waiting for us to make the first offer. I tried to consider who would be the best fit for this situation. Benny had the haggling Skill, but it was Minor, and there was no way it would be useful here.

To my relief, Celine stepped forward, offering a cool smile. "Mr. Wyndham is interested in safe lodgings until the Glade fully opens, but we have some concerns. We need a few questions answered before we can decide if your establishment is right for us."

I had to stifle a sigh of relief, and Callie felt the same, as we both turned to stare at Celine. Because *of course* being a noble meant she knew how to negotiate. I was suddenly extremely glad that we'd brought her along, because she clearly had a much better handle on this situation than any of us.

What came next was a master class in diplomacy. I learned enough to almost pick up a Skill just watching her. First, she turned the tables on him with that initial reversal, forcing him to go on the defensive instead of waiting patiently for us to respond. Once she had him off balance, she pretty much tore him apart.

Every comment Sindar made was taken in the worst possible light, every open-ended statement was looped around to be a negative. It was almost beautiful watching the character assassination of his inn, and by the time she was done, I don't think even *he* considered the place worth staying at. She finished the negotiations with a one wish per day payment schedule over a single month, and he looked confused and almost nauseous when she was done.

As we headed up to our rooms, each of us with our own room key, we all turned to stare at Celine in horrified fascination. She just gave a small but smug smile. "Negotiations are an important part of diplomacy. As a noble, I'm naturally quite experienced in the art of discourse. I hope that was helpful?"

Callie burst out laughing. "You smug ass, of course it was helpful, and you know it. I appreciate the save, and I'm glad we decided to bring you along. You're officially in charge of haggling and negotiations." As she saw Celine's smile grow, she countered it with a savage grin of her own. "I wouldn't be so happy about that if I were you. We're going to an inter-stellar market—you're about to get a pretty sizable amount of work."

The elf girl's expression fell as she realized she'd basically just been upgraded to a personal shopper for the foreseeable future. Benny snickered at his girlfriend's dismay, only for her to whirl on him and shoot him a surprisingly expressive glare. "Oh, I wouldn't be laughing if I were you," she said sweetly. "I know you have the haggling Skill, and I plan to train you up so that we have more options in the future. You're coming along everywhere I go."

His eyes widened in panicked horror, but sadly for him, his fate was sealed. Celine grabbed him by the wrist, wished us all luck with finding our rooms, and dragged him off down the hallway. Callie was smirking as she watched them leave, a thoughtful look on her face I didn't really like. The last thing I needed was my girlfriend deciding she needed to take a firmer hand in our relationship.

"Oh hey," I said desperately. "I forgot to ask you what you think about my weapon. I'm about to replace it. Zeke was talking about possibly picking up the staff so I could learn a martial art. What do you think?"

She was startled out of her thoughts by the question, which was about weapons and therefore *basically* loot. Helping me shop would keep her distracted, and I also really wanted her opinion.

The others scattered to their rooms, leaving the two of us alone to find ours, and she looked pensive as we walked. "That's a good question. I could see how a staff might work, but it seems... off. The length is wrong. Maybe I just got used to you with a cane, though. If you think it would work, I could see it. Maybe take it further, try for the spear? Having a blade on the end of your weapon might be nice."

I shook my head firmly. "Hard pass. A lot of my Skills increase flat impact damage. A blade would mitigate some of the advantages, and it just feels wrong. Not like me." Pushing through the door to our room, I looked around in surprise and enthusiasm, stopping the conversation so I could take in the new digs.

The hallways of the inn had been well appointed but small. About five feet across, with thick carpets, smooth painted walls and the odd bit of bric-a-brac or a painting hanging at eye level. I expected similarly meager sizes for the rooms, but when we stepped inside, I was blown away.

If the room had been some gymnasium sized palace with tons of marble and beautiful gold accents, I'd have been pleased and amused but not shocked. Ostentatious and huge was what I'd come to expect from Ascendant places. To my surprise though, this place was pretty homey. It wasn't a small room, fifteen feet by fifteen or so, and painted in dark earth tones.

The furniture was plush without being showy, looking a bit beat up but supremely comfortable. The only nod to traditional over the top Ascendant decorating was the absolutely massive bed, large enough for me to lie sideways and not have my head or feet stick out. Callie bolted across the room, throwing herself bodily through the air to land with a loud *whump* on the mattress with a giggle, making comforter angels as she groaned in appreciation.

"Okay," she said in a voice of utter bliss, "we're buying this bed, or we're sneaking it out when we leave. We'll have spatial rings—we can pull it off. I demand we carry this with us everywhere now. What rank is this?"

I glanced down at the bed, surprised based on how happy she was that it was only G-rank. I didn't see enchantments or anything, but for all I knew it was an Invention, some random interaction between materials making the perfect bed. I dropped my bag and put my mask on the dresser as I walked over to climb up onto the absurdly comfortable mattress.

Callie's earlier groan was completely understandable—I made one of my own as I pretty much melted into the cloudlike softness of the bedding. "Okay, deal. I'm never letting anyone else sleep in this bed. It belongs to us and there's nothing anyone can say to convince me otherwise."

She rolled over to cuddle up next to me. "My hero." She stayed like that for a bit, and I was about to bring up the weapon again when she finally spoke up. "Doesn't this feel weird?"

With the bond and my own knowledge of her, I could tell exactly what she meant. "It does. Being on our own like this. Like, we were living on our own anyway basically, minus Zeke who doesn't count as an authority figure, but being out in the wider universe together like this... it feels like a big deal."

She looked up at me, bottomless blue eyes boring into mine. "Big in a bad way? Are you having second thoughts about us?"

Leaning down for a quick kiss, I shook my head, laughing. "Hardly. It just makes me amazed at how far we've come. From dancing around each other until you finally asked me out. I spent a while just dragging my feet and it makes me wonder if we'd have had more time together if I had just had the guts to ask instead of bringing you on dates until you broke from the frustration."

That got a giggle. "It's okay sweetie. I don't mind that you made me work for it. Besides, I like where we are. We were friends before we got together and I think it made us more comfortable with each other. Without all those dates you probably would have been a squealing fanboy still." At my offended noise she grinned at me. "Oh please, I remember the first time we met. If your jaw dropped any faster it would have broken the sound barrier."

"I have no idea what you are talking about," I said with dignity. "I admit I always found you attractive, but I certainly never let it unbalance me."

Rolling her eyes, she kissed my cheek. "Owning my merch would say otherwise, but whatever you need to tell yourself, love." She paused. "You as excited about this whole Moonsong Glade thing as I am?"

"Probably not," I said mildly. "There's loot in them there woods. I'm surprised you're even lucid. I half expected you to be floating along a golden scent trail into the void with giant credit signs flashing in your eyes." Her glare was adorable, and I ignored it. "But... I am kind of pumped about all the new enemies. Not to mention my new earth- and plant-based divination skills will come in so much handy here."

She lit up. "That's true! Oh, I can't wait to get mountains of treasure and then sell some of it. I want a giant vault filled with chits with piles of magic items strewn throughout. Maybe we can drag the bed into the vault and sleep on piles of money." Her high-pitched squeal of delight made me chuckle as I tried to imagine her as a dragoness sleeping on a hoard of treasure.

"Well," I said with a yawn, "I think we'll have plenty of cool treasures to see in the bazaar. You can have as much fun out there as you want. For now, this comfy bed is making me tired. We should take a nap, then we can figure out our next move after."

Snuggling into my side, she let out her own yawn, glaring at me for getting her started. "I guess we can do that. I am feeling a little sleepy."

I closed my eyes, letting the warmth of the bed and someone I loved lull me to sleep on a floating city in space above an alien world.

Chapter Three

I WOKE up to the sound of pounding on my door. Not urgent pounding, granted, but someone wanted me to wake up. It was annoying and I tried to ignore it, but it was insistent and I eventually dragged myself out of bed, ignoring the whine of my extremely clingy girlfriend as she burrowed into the covers.

When I threw the door open with a glare, I was mostly unsurprised to see Benny waiting for me, Celine looking mildly uncomfortable behind him.

"What?" I snapped, knowing it wasn't anything serious by the smug look on his face. I'm not a morning person almost ever, but being woken up before I've finished sleeping puts me in a bad mood every time. Even for naps, premature wake-ups are the best way to piss me off if there's no special reason for it.

He just raised an eyebrow, long since immune to my bad moods. "You've been sleeping for like four hours, and I'm bored. We want to go to the bazaar now."

"I'd like it noted that this wasn't my idea," Celine said, raising a hand to get my attention. "Also, hi Shane. I told him to let you sleep, but he's quite excited about shopping, despite how scared he was earlier when I told him that he'd have to learn to haggle."

Benny glared at her. "Don't tell him that! Now he's going to think I'm a huge pushover."

"Oh, please—that ship sailed years ago." I blew out a breath in annoyance. "I… guess we could go out. I'm up now so I guess it doesn't matter." I looked over my shoulder. "Hey, Cal, you up?" My girlfriend's only response was a hand with the middle finger out poking through the covers. Celine actually giggled at that, and I turned back to Benny. "Yeah, she's up. I wouldn't expect much civility from her for a while though."

There was a series of muffled words croaked out from under the blanket, and Celine went red. Benny blanched. "You can't say that to someone!" he squeaked. "Where did you even learn to talk like that?"

Her hand snaked out again and pointed to where I was standing.

My best friend glared at me. "You're a bad influence."

I gaped. "I didn't tell her to say that," I snapped indignantly. "She's got an even worse mouth than I do sometimes when we're alone." Sulking a bit, I huffed. "Go get ready or whatever, we'll be out in a bit. You check with the others yet? Do they want to go?"

He shook his head. "Mel and Abel already left to explore, Jessie is cuddling with the animals, and Natalie is in her room. Cass decided to follow in your footsteps and take a nap, and Cark is hanging out reading some book Zeke gave him. Seems pretty into it. I bet it'll just be the four of us."

I hadn't seen a spot to put the animals, but this place was an Ascendant inn, so they probably had a basement for it or something. Shutting the door in Benny's face, I walked over to grab some clothes. There was an attached shower behind a hanging tapestry on the wall that I'd only just noticed.

I poked Callie as I went by. "You want to join me?" There was some muffled muttering and I winced. "Not only is that not anatomically possible, but even if it was I wouldn't do it. How about you wake up a bit while I shower and we can talk later." Her response was a grunt that may or may not have been a four-letter word.

By the time I came out, Callie was awake, albeit wearing the blanket like a hood. She'd managed to scrounge up a cup of coffee from somewhere and was sipping it, staring blankly into the distance. I snickered because I'd seen this before. When Callie was really tired, especially after partial naps,

13

her brain kind of overloaded itself after waking up. She would stare into space while her thoughts ran for a few minutes, letting her mind catch up.

Despite that, when I walked in wearing my armor, her eyes snapped up to me. "Shower," she croaked. I laughed and gestured that it was all hers. She downed the coffee like a shot, shook her head back and forth like she was trying to shake-start it, and then stumbled into the bathroom, grabbing her clothes on the way. After she left, I grabbed my mask off the dresser and popped it on my face. I started stretching to loosen myself up after that absurdly comfortable nap.

The hot water from the shower had relaxed me a ton, too, and the combination meant I needed to warm my muscles up to really feel like I was awake. As I was stretching, the tapestry pushed aside and steam billowed out of the bathroom. "Oh gods," Callie groaned as she emerged. "I'm going to punch Benny in the throat someday when he isn't looking."

I snickered. "Don't be so grumpy. Napping longer would have messed up your sleeping schedule. I'll cook breakfast to make it up to you. In return, make sure he *is* looking when you punch him in the throat." She giggled at that as she dried her hair with a towel, not worried about normal water damaging her armor or anything. "Anyway, aside from the spatial rings, you planning to browse for anything?"

She gave a hum of consideration. "I think I might look into some weapons myself. I raided the Pavilion coffers before we left so we'd have enough for rings, but I should have some chits left over for a dagger or something. My personal stash I'm saving for wishes, but I think it's about time for me arm up. If you remember, I can imbue my darkness into items and control them like shadows. I did it with my bike, though it took years of imbuing and special materials."

"Ah," I said, understanding her point. "You've improved. Your new rank and all the stats will make it easier. Plus I bet having a smaller target would help too. Will you need to find a dagger with special materials, or can you just brute force it with anything darkness related?" I wasn't sure even a market this big would have her weapons if they were too rare.

She grinned at me. "The latter. I just… Gods Shane, I never thought I'd be this strong at this age. It would have taken me *years* in Valen to get to F-rank, if I ever did. I might have been able to do it in Rajak if I'd left with my dad originally, but I'd have basically been selling my soul. Now not only

14

am I an F-ranker with a *terrifying* new ability, I also have a whole team of friends and I'm *still* growing. By this time next year, I might be at E-rank!"

I wanted to tell her not to jump the gun but... she wasn't wrong. I didn't think it would be quite that fast, but I could see her point. "So... you're happy then?" She gave me a flat look and I held up my hands. "Okay, forget I asked. I know we just talked about this. I just worry. I don't want you to regret coming with me."

She rolled her eyes. "You're such an idiot about some stuff. You're lucky you're so cute. Not much in that giant head of yours."

It was my turn to flip her off, to which she giggled. After she finished brushing her hair, she dragged me out of the room. We met up with Benny and Celine in the downstairs entryway, and then the four of us set out to explore the city. As a cheat, I reached into my pocket and pulled out the map that led us here, but it didn't actually help. Lots of streets and buildings, but nothing was labeled.

"Nice try," Zeke's voice called out from behind me. I nearly jumped out of my skin, whirling to find my uncle leaning against the wall behind us. He gave a lazy wave.

"What are you doing out here Zeke?" I asked. "You're usually pretty hands off. Do you have something you wanted to pick up?"

He sighed. "This place has way too many C- and B-rankers. I can cross a planet in a blink, but that only matters if my abilities are leagues above everyone else. If two equally strong B-rankers are attacking someone, the closest wins. Don't want to risk you pissing off someone who might be a genuine threat."

That hadn't occurred to me, but it seemed like a sensible precaution. "The mask won't work on high rankers. Right." I paused for a second. "Wait... is this mask made from a person? I know your other ones are."

He snickered. "No. I have a limit to how many greater masks I can make. I can add little buffs to them with my Voltomancy easily enough, but soul binding a mask is complicated and time consuming, and I can't sustain too many of them. Thirteen at a time, give or take. I can make as many lesser masks as I want from lower-ranked Ascendants, but I usually don't bother."

"That's a super creepy power," Benny said matter-of-factly. "Just in case you didn't know. At least they're masks made of porcelain and not, like, actual faces."

Zeke nodded solemnly. "Even I have limits. Anyway, you're all looking for the marketplace. What specifically were you hoping to find? I know spatial rings, but I also know Shane wanted a weapon. What kind did you settle on? I can point you in the right direction. Since I'm with you and don't feel like wandering around for hours, it's only really helping myself."

I nodded. "I've been waffling, but I decided on a specific type of staff that has the properties I like. It's called a Bang. Some crazy Ascendant with a monkey trait used to use one a long time ago. It's a short staff made of wood with long iron caps on both ends. Small, heavy, and with good spin, plus it's compact and easy to carry on my back. There are some martial arts that use that kind of weapon, so I can pick up some new Skills with it and keep a similar style of combat."

He nodded thoughtfully. "I know the guy you mean. Way before my time obviously, but I think the original Wishmaster knew him. Gods don't age at all as far as I know, and he's been around a *long* time. Not that I can swear to it—I've only met the old man a few times. He likes to spoil the grand-kids, but attendants aren't usually allowed near him. Me and Eli were close, so he got an exception made."

I stared at him in shock. "You... met the Wishmaster? The *original?* What was he like? I always figured he'd be really scary."

"He wasn't," he said simply. "But because of that... he was. Being a god and being able to hide your presence so thoroughly you seem like a normal old man? He looks to be in his fifties probably, and the one time I met him, I couldn't tell. Not based on the way he moved, or talked, or even his senses. He just felt regular. It was extremely jarring, because I knew he could atomize me with a strong thought."

He trailed off, seeming distracted, so I focused back on the task at hand. "Let's see if we can find my weapon, then. I assume you have a place in mind?"

The grin he gave me in response made me a bit worried, honestly. I got the feeling this was going to be a wild kind of place.

Chapter Four

"WELL," I said uncertainly. "I wasn't expecting… this."

Zeke smirked as we stood on stairs leading down into an underground chamber filled with tables and stalls. The whole individual vendor thing wasn't a surprise, since this city was supposed to be a bazaar. No, the surprise was the fact that the entire setup was built on a giant sword sticking out of the rock of the cavern.

Below us, I could see a yawning abyss, and off far in the depths, a few shining lights that had to be stars. The hole we were standing in dropped out the bottom of the city into fucking *space*. Weirdly, the air here was fine, and I wasn't too worried about freezing to death or my lungs exploding, but even knowing that empty space was within sight was seriously freaking me out.

My uncle took in a deep breath, inhaling the smoky, metallic-smelling air. "Titanblade Emporium. The whole giant sword thing is a bit of a gimmick, but the family that runs the place are weapon fanatics. They're a Unity-wide organization and have branches like this all over. I knew someone would have set one up here."

Benny raised a hand cautiously. "Um… what the hell is big enough to use *that?*" He pointed at the sword. "Or is it just a platform made to look like a sword?"

Zeke chuckled. "Nope. Every Titanblade Emporium is built on an *actual* titanblade. Giant swords forged for the elders of the Kyros family. They're size shifters, some of the very best. Dakken Kyros, the S-ranker who founded their clan, is known as the Worldhurler because he literally gets big enough to throw planets. Pretty high-rank ones too."

I stared down at the massive sword and gulped, but Zeke just patted me on the back. "Don't worry so much. That thing is a push pin compared to one of Dakken's blades. I've seen the main branch of their emporium before. The sword is stuck in the side of that planet like a dart in a dartboard. The hilt reaches the atmosphere. I'd imagine this thing probably belonged to one of the C-rankers the family sent over."

Thinking of a blade that size was terrifying. Especially since that emporium was probably on a high-ranking planet, and they got bigger as you ranked them up. It was part of the reason for the gravity increase. Some of it was the weight of Impact, but massive planets had a stronger gravitational pull. You could probably fit a hundred Calluses lengthwise in whatever world that blade was stuck in.

Walking down the steps, we made our way along a crystalline energy bridge that extended from the bottom of the steps, leading us out onto the metal platform created by the huge blade. I expected the floor to shudder or make a hollow clang, but it was like stepping onto a normal metal floor. The only strange thing was that I could feel some of the sword's Impact. It was much higher ranked than I was, though it seemed to be suppressed somehow.

Since my uncle didn't seem to know more about this place than where it was, it took some wandering around to find the shop we needed, but find it we did. An old man sat on a blanket before a squat red tent, his hands folded in the sleeves of a long, gold-trimmed red robe. A literal pile of staves rested next to him.

We approached and I started browsing. Since some were buried under the others, I eventually got sick of trying to differentiate with just my eyes. "Hey, I was wondering if you have a short staff with iron caps on the end."

The old man, white hair hanging in a braid down his back, sighed. "There's always one." His eyes focused on me. "Yes. I have a Bang you can buy."

"Perfect," I said with a grin. "I'm looking for and enchanted one that—"

"Changes size." He cut me off with annoyance. "I know. Like I said, there's always one. I don't have a size-changing staff—they're pointless and not cost effective. You wouldn't be able to handle the increased Might requirements when using it, and even if you could, without some kind of specialized Skill or a staff that was indestructible, it would either be impossible to control or just break under its own weight."

This had the air of a rehearsed speech, but despite how direct he was, I felt the need to point out the obvious. "We're standing on a *giant sword.*"

He groaned. "We're standing on a giant sword made to *be* a giant sword. It doesn't change size. It's a huge blade made with the express purpose of being used by a huge person. That's why Titanblades are made like that. I can't sell you a size-changing weapon, and if I could, I wouldn't because it's stupid."

I just stood there and blinked at him for a second before sighing. "Okay, fine. What does the staff do? And what rank is it? I was hoping for an E-rank weapon to future-proof my layout a bit. Do you have a bang that's E-ranked?"

Shoving his hand into the pile, he fished around for a second before withdrawing... power. The staff was E-rank, and I could tell it would be tough to get used to. I knew that people could use weapons and armor one rank above them, but I'd never asked what was required to actually do it. Judging from this sensation, I was going to need to train with this thing for a while just to be able to hold it.

The shaft of the staff was a deep, rich brown wood, the grain seeming to form enchantment symbols on its own, though the symbols shifted when I stared for too long, preventing me from studying them. The caps on the ends were made of a greyish black iron, and I could see screaming faces in the metal, their empty eyes pleading for release in a truly chilling way.

"Ghost iron and infernal ash wood. Enchanted by an elven master. They have a peculiar way with wood-based enchantments. The weapon can pass through solid objects if you focus. The ghost iron also has the interesting effect of absorbing minute traces of life energy on contact. The energy can't exist inside the necrotic metal stably, so it's stored and corrupted, and can be released in an explosive burst of death damage."

He offered it to me, and when I took it, I almost staggered from how heavy it was. Not physically, but... in other ways. The Impact of the staff weighed on me, making it feel like I was standing under a great burden. I loved it. "It's perfect," I whispered as I ran my hands over it. "How much?"

He squinted at me calculatingly. "That's a lower-end E-rank weapon, but it's made from the finest materials. I'd say fifteen E-ranked coins." I winced, since there was no way I could afford that, but when I went to argue, I was cut off as Celine stepped in.

I'd forgotten she was our go-to for haggling so I backed off as she issued her counter offer, and when it was rejected, tore into the old man. She started making weirdly accurate deductions about his social standing and effectiveness based on his placement in the market and the condition and organization of his wares.

Sadly, despite my hope that our terrifying negotiator would be able to get him down low enough, he stopped at ten E-rank coins and refused to go lower. He wasn't an amateur like Sindar had been, and Celine's skills (or possibly Skills) weren't enough.

"Alright," I cut in once the haggling stalled. "How about this?" I wrote down a few lines on a piece of paper I was carrying and passed it over, and his eyes widened in shock when he saw them, then narrowed in suspicion.

He glanced from me to the paper. "How many?" I held up three fingers. "And you want me to throw in six rings?" I nodded. His eyes gleamed with avarice. "I can use them as the actual payment, yes? Because if these are compensation I'm not paying twice."

"Yes," I said firmly. "If you have somewhere private nearby, we can do the trade there." I poked a thumb at Zeke. "Though be warned—if you decide to try anything funny, I'm not without protections." Even if Zeke couldn't intervene most of the time, there was no need for him to know that.

Zeke met his eyes, and there was a frisson of pressure, too fast and focused to jar the sword or alert anyone else. The old man's eyes went wide again, this time with fear. He was an F-ranker, which meant he was old as hell to look like he did. Like thousands of years old. Even then, feeling what Zeke really was obviously scared him shitless.

He led us back into the tent, closed the flaps, and touched a few runes that lit up with contact before nodding at us. I'd carried the staff in, but he plucked it out of my hands and dropped it on a pillow in the middle of the tent, fishing in a pocket and pulling out six spatial rings. "As agreed, three wishes—one for the staff, two for six rings." At my nod, he grinned. "Good. I wish to be young again."

Wish detected. Grant wish?

I was positive this wouldn't work like he wanted, and sure enough—

Insufficient stat points to restore youth to target. Requirements: NA reversing thousands of years or Ascendant aging beyond the capacity of Intermediate Wish ability.

"That's not going to happen," I said bluntly. Before he could argue, I cut him off. "As in, I don't have the stats to do that. You're too high ranked and it's too much time. I'd suggest shooting for something a bit more feasible." I didn't suggest a wish, because I was paranoid about them not working if they knowingly benefited me too much, but with the hint I was confident the old man would think of something.

He looked annoyed but then thought it through. "I wish for ten biological years of my youth restored to me," he said confidently.

I shook my head—same message as before. Ten biological years might not sound like a lot, but Ascendants aged slower because of Impact. Ten years was around ten percent of his already lengthy lifespan. "Too much, scale it back further."

He snarled out a curse and then snapped. "Fine! Three years. I wish for three biological years of my life back." He paused, waiting to be let down, but... huh. That actually worked.

When I told him, he brightened a bit. Three years multiplied by 32 Impact (the normal amount at F-rank) amounted to almost a century. He repeated the wish twice, recovering almost 300 years.

He passed over the rings and the staff. He looked sprightlier, albeit not to an insane degree. He'd probably been biologically in his mid-nineties (albeit in extremely good shape because of Vitality), so taking him down to his eighties wasn't a huge physical change. It was still noticeable, especially with my Perception being what it was.

I weighed the staff (apparently it was a Stygian Branch) in my hands, grinning madly at my new weapon and how much fun it would be to use it, and thanked the old man before we moved on.

We had more shopping to do, looking for a weapon for Callie and possibly something for Benny to integrate alongside the new inventions he'd apparently just finished. Besides, I still had all my money to spend. This would be so much fun.

Chapter Five

AFTER THE TITANBLADE EMPORIUM, I bought a giant bacon-wrapped turkey leg from a street cart vendor, a small plush doll from Cass's favorite cartoon that would dance if you said its name and had a self-repair function, and a hat with ears from some weird animal called a kangaroo. I was positive it didn't exist on Callus, but Callie lit up when I put it on.

None of this put too big a dent in my funds, obviously, but it was nice to just walk around and do dumb shit to enjoy myself with friends. Benny had conned me into paying for food for him and Celine as well, which meant I had to pay for Callie, of course. They got some strange cloudlike candy made of spun sugar (Callie let me have a bite, which for her was pretty much a declaration of undying love) and we just walked around, enjoying the variety of people.

There were stores for everything I could imagine. I'd expected plenty of weapons and armor shops, but there were magical foci, ingredients, inventions, and crafting of both the artistic and practical kinds. Plus dozens of street performers and interesting musical acts.

"Why is this place so lively?" I asked Zeke.

He just shrugged, biting into his own turkey leg. "It's mostly an excuse to blow off steam. Dungeons can get pretty nuts, especially ones that are closed for a long time. The locals can be a big surprise, and it's pretty hostile in there. This is a big excuse to party before getting serious. Plus there are the smart ones winding through the crowd, listening for information. I think your girl is doing that as we speak."

Glancing over at Callie, I saw her eyes were kind of blank, like she was distracted. I took her arm to make sure she was okay and grinned at Zeke. "Guess so. It's still pretty neat. Is the dungeon really going to be that bad? I figured it would be like the scavenger hunt."

He waggled his free hand, stopping for a second to suck turkey grease off his fingers, then resuming the motion. "It is and isn't. One thing to remember, no matter what, is that you aren't there to win. The hunt was a competition, but this won't be. It might *involve* competition, and don't shy away from that, but at the end of the day the Glade is huge. There are more than enough resources for everyone in your limited timeframe. Don't get sucked into petty power game bullshit. Work the mission. Ascendants will turn anything into a pissing contest if you let them."

That did sound pretty on brand. It was a surprise to hear Zeke advise me not to pay attention to the power games, though. He seemed to pick up on that, because he just smiled. "Let me guess, you're wondering why I didn't tell you to crush your enemies like bugs and cackle over their corpses?"

At my slight nod, he just shook his head. "Do you know the most important trait an Ascendant can have for progressing and getting stronger? Flexibility. Recursion is the change killer. It'll turn you into a static parody of yourself if you let it. Sticking with your legend is one thing, but you need to find the break points, the parts of you that people don't talk about where your story gives you flexibility. Losing your ability to adapt is nearly always a death sentence."

"Why tell me this now?" I asked. "Why not ages ago?" I mean, he'd kind of hinted at it, and Callie had circled the point, but information this important should just be directly stated.

He just shrugged. "Because you didn't need to know. Callus may have seemed big, but it was a tiny corner of the sky. The recursion from that level of renown wasn't likely to be enough to warp your personality much. Now we're getting out into the wider world. You'll be getting more attention, enough to actually get some points despite your constant improvement with your wishes. It seemed important you know what's what."

"You're saying that I *shouldn't* fight everyone," I said slowly, "because people will assume I'm fighting anyway, but that I'm just too sneaky to detect? It's like a loophole."

That got me a wide grin and a nod. "Exactly. And things like that will boost your renown too when others hear about it. Having a reputation for being unpredictable not only makes more people pay attention, it also grants you more freedom within your recursion."

I nodded thoughtfully, not feeling the need to respond.

After walking a while longer, I got a text. I read over it and blinked in surprise. "Hey guys," I said, causing everyone to stop. "Nat and her guards left a bit after us. I guess they've been walking around and were hoping to meet up. Anyone down for dinner?"

Callie, of course, snapped her head up. "Food?" Benny and I both started snickering and she just glared. "Shut up you idiots, I'm just hungry." Her eyes narrowed at me, her tone becoming sickly sweet as she asked, "Or are you implying I eat too much?"

Rolling my eyes, I snorted. "I feed you most of what you eat. If I thought you needed a change in diet I'd cook you something different. You can't intimidate me with your cliche girlfriend terrorist tactics, woman."

She looked pretty skeptical of that, but I moved on. "Anyway, there's a high-end restaurant around here that serves F-ranked steak." I grinned at her. "I believe I promised someone that I would find a way for her to try dragon again after she traded the memory. I bet a place like this would have it."

My girlfriend literally squealed with joy and hurled herself into my arms, and I was sure I'd have gotten a pretty enthusiastic kiss if I didn't have my mask on. She squeezed me so hard I felt like my spine would break. She let me go, grabbed my hand, and started hauling me off in a random direction. She was so excited she didn't notice she had no clue where she was going until seconds later.

I followed the location ping my cousin had sent me and we arrived at the steakhouse within a few minutes. Apparently Mel, Jessie, and Abel had gotten the same text, because they showed up just after we did, and my mentor gave Callie an excited high five while Mel and I rolled our eyes at our gluttonous significant others.

The good mood lasted until we got inside and were seated at Nat's table. It was derailed by her guard, Valk, who looked terrible.

"What the hell happened to you?" Abel asked in appalled fascination. "You look like you fell out of a sickness tree and hit every branch on the way down. I can kind of see your bones under all that sallow skin."

He wheezed out a laugh. "It's temporary, I've been assured. I made the mistake of picking a fight with a fucking Vampire. Drained off literally twenty points of my damned Vitality. Perit pulled it off me." He nodded gratefully to the tall blonde woman, who gave a placid nod of her own.

Zeke's head had snapped up when he heard that. "You met a Vampire here?" We all turned to stare in shock at the tone of caution in my uncle's voice. Zeke didn't worry about people. Definitely not F-rankers. But after hearing about the Vampire he seemed unsettled. Not afraid (I wasn't even sure Zeke could feel that emotion anymore), but he sounded unhappy all the same.

"Yes," Valk confirmed. "Trust me. You don't mistake that for anything else. It felt like she was tearing out a piece of me. Like she ripped out part of my soul. It's fading, and I'm healing as we speak, but the sensation." He shuddered violently. "It was the most horrifying thing I've ever experienced. The helplessness, the weakness. I'd rather die than feel that again."

Zeke nodded. "I got bit once. It's not something that fades with time. If there's a Vampire here, you need to be careful. Do you remember what I told you about Vampires?"

Callie nodded. "Yeah, you said they're stupidly rare. All from the same family. I was surprised because Vampire stories are common enough. Seemed like there would be tons of them."

"There used to be," he said emphatically. "Morgan Lark fucking *ate* them. This was centuries ago, back when he was still young. He started hunting down all the Vampires his own rank he could find. He drained them all dry. Some people think that's how his ability became what it is, that he drained some sort of vampiric power from them one by one. Regardless, no one takes Vampire racial traits anymore, and if you get one, you fucking *change* it."

"Are you scared of this guy?" I said in surprise. "Because he can't be that much stronger than you are. And even if he is, he's not going to fuck with the family just for fun, right?"

Zeke's eyes pinned me to the spot. "Morgan Lark is the strongest S-ranker in the universe. He is widely considered the being closest to godhood. He's so powerful he literally fought the Unity in direct combat and survived. This was *after* the Unity attained his divinity. The Vampire is a monster of the most terrifying kind, and anyone who isn't afraid of him is either stupid or very insane."

He let out a long breath, calming himself down. "That said, he's also a hands-off parent. He isn't likely to pick a fight with us over a little dustup with one of his spawn. He doesn't have that many of them relatively speaking, but he's old as dirt, so relatively speaking doesn't mean much. His kids are in the triple digits, and I'm guessing this one is a baby. Don't kill it if you can help it, maybe make friends, but it shouldn't be a problem either way."

I tried to imagine what The Vampire would be like, someone who would scare Zeke. Scare my dad. Scare the terrifying S-rank grandfather I hadn't even met yet, and the image was not a nice one. I breathed a sigh of relief as I saw Jessie plant a hand on Valk and start pumping life energy into him. It helped, and I was glad to see the man filling back out from the living skeleton he'd been turned into.

Looking around the steakhouse, I took in the intimate design. Dark wood walls, candlelight, rich plush tablecloths. I nodded at my cousin's taste and made a mental note to bring Callie back here for a date. Speaking of my girlfriend, the waiter had finally made it over, and Cal was thrilled to learn that dragon steaks were on the menu.

She ordered, and I smiled as I removed my mask. I was at dinner with my team, my family—I hardly needed it right now. Zeke was here personally, and besides, it wasn't like anyone could recognize me by my face out here.

Callie leaned up for that kiss from earlier, and didn't pull away until Benny started loudly clearing his throat to be annoying. We both grinned like loons as he did.

Chapter Six

THE DRAGON STEAK WAS FANTASTIC. Callie actually gave me a bite of hers (I got something called Infernal Lobster, which was huge and absolutely delicious) before she finished. Once we were done, we got cheesecake to wash it down. As we ate, we caught up with the others about what had happened over the course of their day.

"Now that you're feeling better Valk, what the hell happened?" I asked. "Like… was the Vampire just waiting in an alley to jump you? How did you even get her attention? Or is she just like some crazy monster who attacks anyone nearby?"

Perit snickered at that. "He wishes." The tall woman didn't talk nearly as much as Nat or her partner, but she clearly felt more comfortable with us now that we were on the same team.

"I— Well, I was showing off a bit in the street," Valk said with a grimace. "One of my whips clashed with an opponent's attack and a bolt of energy slipped free. It didn't hurt her but it kind of burned a hole in her dress. She wasn't pleased." He sounded more embarrassed than upset, despite having twenty points of his Vitality sucked out. It seemed like an overreaction to me, but then I didn't care much about clothes. I could understand being pissed about being randomly attacked by a stranger though.

Nat rolled her eyes. "This moron shouldn't have been doing party tricks for a crowd on the street. I can return the points, so no real loss. Even if losing twenty is a bit of a waste. That's almost a day of wishes."

Benny blanched. "Wait... is that enough to take him under a thousand? He's not going to like... die from that is he?" I hadn't actually considered that myself, but when he mentioned it, I glanced to Zeke worriedly. Valk was a member of the team even if I didn't know him well, and he seemed like a decent guy.

"No," my uncle said. "Stat milestones let your soul know when it can handle more Impact, which lets it then handle more stats, but once you rank up your Impact and soul both qualitatively improve." He gestured to me. "Your soul is orange now, about fifteen percent of the way to yellow, like it was fifteen percent of the way to orange before. Losing stats won't change that. And it won't change your Impact, so you'll be fine."

That made sense. "What about losing Impact though?" I asked cautiously. "What will that do?"

"Kill you," he said bluntly. "Losing a point of Impact kills you unless you have some to spare. It's part of why you don't see people trading Impact with wishes at lower levels. Until you hit S-rank and have Impact beyond the baseline, even a single point of it will bring most people below their threshold. Wishes require fair compensation—what's fair compensation for dying? Not just normal death either. Your soul will shatter."

I blinked. I knew that Impact wishes existed and could work, but I hadn't really tried it except for with Benny and Amelia. Though that brought up another question. "Wait. I've given mortals abilities before. They didn't have any Impact and I gave them a point of it, so can I give someone Impact just from my power?"

"Not possible," he said. "Impact isn't like other stats. It's more *primal.* You can't *make* Impact. You can take it, hold it, trade it, but you can't make it. A mortal does have Impact, like they have other stats, it just isn't a full point. When you awaken someone as an Ascendant you're giving them a PORTION of a point of Impact. It works the same way Enchanting does. You can recover that over time. It pushes them to a point and then the universe does the rest."

Nodding slowly, I thought over everything I knew about Impact. "That explains why the WCP isn't mass producing gods. I know Impact has some-thing to do with godhood, so aside from soul strength, the need for Impact is probably a limiting factor. I guess stuff like the Moonglow Dew is an exception, right? If you have more than the rank limit in Impact, you could trade it safely."

He waggled a hand. "Safely is a bit of an overstatement. Trading Impact *hurts*. It's painful and diminishing. Finding someone willing to do it is difficult, and the cost is astronomical. You need extremely high stats to arrange an Impact trade for the most part. Theoretically though, yes, if you can afford the cost of the wish, someone with more than the baseline Impact for their rank could survive trading it."

Nat didn't look surprised by any of this, though Selka (who hadn't really spoken since we showed up here, presumably out of fear of Zeke) seemed intrigued that he'd mentioned all that to me. It was probably touching on secrets that candidates weren't allowed, though he hadn't crossed the line based on his lack of excruciating pain.

Gesturing to Valk, I asked Zeke my last question. "What about The Vampire? Can he consume Impact? Can other Vampires?"

Because that seemed incredibly broken. I wasn't sure why they wouldn't all be gods at that point. As expected, he shook his head. "No. Or at least, not most of them. Whatever Lark is, people believe he can drain Impact, though judging by how long he's been at S-rank, not fast or reliably. Might be something to do with all the Vampires he ate when he was younger, or at least that's the prevailing theory. Regardless, the others only do stats, and the number of them varies based on both Vampire and target."

Nat finally had enough of the remedial nonsense and groaned aloud. "Oh gods, enough." We all looked at her. "I'm sorry, but I can only take so much of 'baby's first cultivation journey.' No offense little cousin. But spiraling over how scary the boogeyman of all S-rankers is won't accomplish much. If you want to meet a Vampire, I can introduce you with an apology as a pretext. I'll just offer her a wish in exchange for her dress. Now can we please get back to some proper dinner conversation?"

Abel started snickering around his own steak (some kind of shark or something). When we all looked at him, he swallowed, looking around innocently. "What? It was funny." When we all kept staring, he just sighed. "Alright, I guess I can share what we did during our day out." He adopted an air of gravitas and suspense. "I... got in a fight."

Something about the delivery, his serious expression, and the wait mixed together broke me, and I cracked up, joined by Mel, Callie, Jessie, and Benny.

"What my idiot means to say," Mel cut in, still chuckling, "is that we went out exploring and met up with some of the other contenders. Abel hit it off with some big burly guy with curly red hair named Craygen, and after yapping for about an hour they decided to mix it up in public."

Abel nodded. "It wasn't that weird of a call—there have been a lot of street fights here based on what I saw. People just clear out a circle and throw down in the middle of the road. Craygen was a pretty tough guy with a material shifting power. He turned into some kind of gemstone. Super durable. It was a solid fight. He's much further into F-rank than I am, so I was able to really cut loose a bit."

I was about to ask how that was possible given the tournament requirements, but then I realized I was making assumptions. We brought Celine even though she hadn't been in the tournament. Granted, Celine was much closer to our rank because she had basically bribed Nat to grind her up to F-rank in that one-month gap like I had done for Jessie. It made sense that the other winners would bring F-rankers who were stronger than the contestants.

"Anyway. Craygen lost, obviously, and he invited us to some crazy party tonight. All the other contestants will be there. Craygen's tourney winner got the invite from some imperial Ascendant who made it through their own tournament. It sounds like fun to me but I wasn't sure if you wanted to go."

It was a strange reminder that even though I was the legacy and Callie was the leader, Abel, for all his lack of care about it, was the real winner of the tournament. He was still our muscle, despite breaking through, and being able to take on a higher-level F-ranker from this crowd just proved it. This party would be a damn good opportunity to meet some more of the people around here that were like him.

I looked at Callie. "I think that's a good idea." She seemed poleaxed by the statement, knowing my hatred for parties and social gatherings, and I had to laugh at her expression. "Zeke said that we shouldn't treat this like a competition. These people aren't our enemies, even if they think they are. The mission is what matters. If we can make friends and be on good terms with the other entrants, it could end up being a huge help later."

31

She giggled at my impassioned speech. "Oh I know. I'm just shocked you're willing to go to a party. I think it's a good idea too." She glanced at Jessie, Benny, and Celine. "You guys in? You too, Nat—you're part of the team and we'd love to have you along."

My cousin smiled but waved her off. "Nah, I appreciate the invite, but we've had enough excitement for today." She jerked a thumb at Valk. "Besides, dipshit over there needs to recover. Even if he looks better after Agria topped him up, losing twenty points of Vitality isn't something you brush off. He needs bed rest."

I could have sworn I heard the bald, red bearded man mutter, "Yes *mom.*" But if he did, he did it so quietly even my Perception barely caught it. I guessed Nat heard it fine though because she whirled to glare at him. He looked away innocently, actually whistling as he avoided her gaze. She scoffed, but I could tell she thought it was funny by her smile.

Benny cut in, answering Callie's question from earlier. He'd been whispering to Celine, though they must have used a Stealth Skill to talk silently. "We're in. I want to check out some of the other entrants, see what we're dealing with. Plus it'll give me an excuse to stock my new artifacts. I made replacements for a few of my more outdated pieces of gear—I can't wait to show you guys."

I'd been wondering about that. He'd mentioned working on some inventions, but I wasn't sure if they were done. I never wanted to bring it up. Now that he was volunteering the information, though, I was excited to see what was coming.

We decided to invite Cark, though I doubted he would come with us. Nat offered to watch Cass if he did, though—my cousin was becoming just as enamored with the little girl as the rest of us.

As we finished dessert and headed back to the inn, I couldn't help but glance around the restaurant one last time, making sure to remember the details for our next date. Callie adored that dragon steak, and while the place was a little pricey, it was worth it to see that smile light up her face like it had when she tried her dinner for the first time.

Chapter Seven

Since this party was a semi show of force, we weren't wearing gaudy formal wear. Instead we wore our costumes, which was nice. I was more comfortable in my gear than in most outfits, and not just because of my badass coat. The sense of security from F-ranked armor was unbeatable. I was also glad we'd haggled to get a set of F-rank armor because it meant our gear wasn't already out of date.

We convened outside the building where the party was, and I had to admit, I was impressed. Rather than a normal building with square floors on top of each other, this place seemed to have been made to resemble a stone whale. It was huge, and the open mouth was covered by a single pane of F-rank glass.

Even for Ascendants, a giant stone animal as a building was kind of novel, and I spent a moment just taking it in when we arrived. I was cut off by Callie, who stopped us all to give a warning. "Alright everyone, just remember, these are elite combatants. The contestants in the tournament were tough, but every one of these people *won* their own tournament or was brought along as backup by someone who did. Be careful out there."

I grinned at her cheekily. "Now, why do I feel like your warning is more specific than most people would expect? I take it you found some way to effectively use your spying abilities? I thought Zeke said it was too dangerous here?"

She returned my grin with a proud smirk. "Only that first day. There was some paperwork I needed to do that he mentioned to me after our nap. I filled it out on my scan ring and submitted it over the network. I was okayed for spying up to a certain range. Apparently long-term bans on powers like that is too much like coddling the juniors. You just aren't allowed to do it without restriction because while any sufficiently powerful Ascendant would sense it if they looked, there's an off chance you might accidentally hear important elder business before they notice you."

Which probably meant they had some kind of countermeasure to her power on a personal scale, and since they knew she was there they could work around it. It also implied a substantially more cohesive leadership behind the place than I had suspected. I turned to Zeke, who was following us in a blank porcelain mask of his own design. "Who is running this anyway? I don't think I ever asked."

Zeke chuckled. "See, she's such a good influence on you. You didn't ask. But it's the Lakedeep Clan. They're pretty powerful in the Unity's galaxy. The founder is a top executive in the Unity itself, Salara Lakedeep. I'm guessing your girl has heard of her. The higher up you go the more widely known an executive is. All of the Unity's S-rankers are pretty famous in this galaxy."

Callie's eyes were wide. "I do know her. Even in a backwater like Callus we've heard of the Kraken. Her summon is supposed to be able to pluck stars from the night sky and eat them. She's so in tune with it she can manifest its traits herself and use them at will."

Zeke nodded. "She's an S-ranker, so she can probably do both of those things, and she can definitely manifest traits. It's one of the more common high-rank summoner ability variations. While abilities are highly customizable, there are some basic directions that usually have more benefit. With weapon masteries, manifestations are a common path to take. Summoners usually make up for lack of individual combat potential by learning to harmonize with their summons. Not that a party trick like that is the end of the line for an S-ranker. She undoubtedly has much scarier powers."

I shuddered, thinking about how terrifying the fight between the B-rankers had been. "So, the Lakedeep Clan is running things and you got permission to use your ability from them. I take it you managed to find out the identities of some of the people we're meeting tonight?"

She grinned, pulling her focus back to the matter at hand. "Yup. Most of the others were talking about a few particularly scary standouts." Stopping her recitation, she hurled herself forward, gripping me tightly as she squealed. "Oh, I love my new power so much! I spent most of the day in the shadows whenever I had a spare moment. It took a bit to get used to filtering through so much input, but with my Focus I managed it just fine. I learned so much!"

I laughed, squeezing her back and grateful she was controlling her strength better. "I'm glad to hear it, but that was all you. Most I did was help you get one extra Skill and focus your stats."

Laughing, she pulled back. "Yeah, because those are such inconsequential aspects of how I got my ability. Not worth mentioning." She rolled her eyes at me, but her smile stayed wide and happy, just how I liked it. "Anyway, there are five people we need to watch out for, that Vampire being one of them. Her name is Bethany Lark. She's apparently the baby of the family, which isn't shocking considering how low rank she is. She's considered mostly stable and sane for a Vampire, though she's extremely touchy about her clothes. Has quite the reputation for it."

I winced. People with a reputation for one specific kind of behavior tended to be heavily obsessive about that particular trait. It was actually something some people did on purpose, because weird and quirky people were more interesting, and it helped focus recursion in one direction. It also explained her draining those stat points from Valk for burning her dress.

We could work with that. Callie picked up on my emotions over the bond and came to the same conclusion I did. "I figure we can wish for a really nice dress she would like and offer it as a meeting gift. If having the idea first messes with your ability to do it we can just ask Nat."

Having my cousin around was damn useful, even if we couldn't engage in any wish looping after forming our alliance because of the family rules. She provided an easy source of wishes to work with even if she wasn't willing to be as creative with payment structures as I was. Sadly she charged points for points almost exclusively, so none us had really availed her of that service, but for utility wishes like this she was a perfect second option.

Callie waved me off. "We can think about it after, or just offer Bethany a wish and let her decide for herself—you still have three for today right?" I nodded. I'd traded three for my new staff and the six rings, one of which

I'd slipped on immediately after filling it with all the odds and ends we'd kept in the magic box we'd found in the Necropolis.

"Good. Now, the other four standouts," she said, moving on. "One of them is a member of your family, Alistair Wyndham. His branch of the family is different as far as I know, so I doubt you're more than distantly related. I asked Nat but she doesn't know anything about him. Sadly most of the gossip about him is absurd nonsense about Wishmaster Candidates in general, about three quarters of which we know isn't true, so all I got was a name."

That was still plenty—it was good to know about the only other candidate around. I doubted I'd be lucky enough to meet two friendly ones in a row, and Nat was my literal blood cousin which I think had helped. Plus, if he was from another branch, he might not be as scared of Dad, so I made a mental note to watch out for him.

"Flicker and Blink are twins," Callie continued. "One of them creates clones and one of them teleports, and they seem to be able to share powers, which gets… obnoxious. They're higher-level F-rankers with a Fantasy focus, which means their fate sense is pretty absurd." My girlfriend sounded a bit wary of those two, and I could see why, but hopefully we wouldn't need to fight them.

She sighed as she moved on. "The last one is a Crusader for the Red Revenant Church. That's the fourth Job advancement in their warrior caste. Gabriel Brightlaw. He's more than halfway into the F-ranks, and he's supposed to be terrifying. He's a Master Candidate with the lance, and a summoner who can call up some kind of Celestial Charger he rides into battle. He's also an Adamant cultivator."

Zeke whistled. "That's… rough. Not a lot of those make it that far in a Cluster this remote." At my confused head-tilt he shook his head. "You know, you should do *some* research. Your girlfriend is not a walking encyclopedia and neither am I. An Adamant cultivator is someone with a reputation for being unbeatable. Adamants become stronger, more skilled, and more in tune with combat the longer they last."

"So…" I said slowly. "Like Abel? Abel never loses."

"No," Zeke said flatly. "Abel *rarely* loses. Plus he's too quiet to be an Adamant. It takes a serious reputation for that kind of thing. You have to be in the spotlight from day one and win every fight with ease. I suspect

Abel would find the idea of being an Adamant pretty boring. He doesn't need the help. And the idea of losing doesn't bother him." He shot a glance at my mentor, who nodded confidently.

I got his point, but it was worrying. "Can recursion make someone harder to beat? I know it kind of alters reality, but it doesn't actually *make* him unbeatable, does it?"

Zeke shook his head. "Adamants can and do break all the time. They become functionally useless once it happens, which is why it's not a path people take often. Mostly that kind of thing gets purposefully derailed early on. The higher they go, the more precarious it is. They aren't invincible, though they are in kind of a zone all the time. Their recursion keeps them at peak form constantly, which—combined with fast advancement because of their impressive skills—makes them a pain in the ass to fight."

"The point is," Callie cut in, "we don't want him to be an enemy. It might be worth telling him about your mother. The Star Queen is apparently a legend in the Church, and your grandfather being the Radiant Pope will earn you plenty of points too." She looked at me with a slightly jealous expression. "Having S-rankers for both grandfathers is pretty damned useful."

I laughed bitterly. "Yes, I particularly enjoyed the constant murder attempts because of my mother's side of the family. Nothing like having a cult of bloodthirsty shadowy lunatics out for your blood to make you count your blessings." My voice was... perhaps a bit more biting than I'd have liked, and combined with the bond, she actually flinched a bit. "Cal, I didn't mean—"

She held up both hands. "No. You're right. That was insensitive. Your family is a sore spot and bringing it up like that was shitty. You've had a lot of problems because of them. I should have remembered that." She leaned in for another hug, this one much gentler, and I felt the apology through the bond, no words needed between us. I squeezed her back so she knew I forgave her, but we were interrupted by the sound of a throat clearing.

"This is sweet, but can we maybe do it another time?" Abel said mildly. "We have a party to get to. And I kind of want to fight this Adamant guy." We groaned aloud, and the rest of the trip inside was filled with the sound of Mel berating her boyfriend for being a battle maniac and an idiot. My friends could sometimes be morons, but they were the best.

Chapter Eight

THE INSIDE of the whale building was less whale and more building, which was nice since it meant we didn't have to walk down a stone throat or something, but was disappointing because I'd been hoping for something more interesting. The smooth marble floors and intricate wall carvings were a lot more generic than the external facade.

I was still pretty impressed by the sheer size of the place, with the whale interior all forming one huge room. The ceiling seemed to be a wide-open sky, and miniature floating islands drifted among the clouds, containing hot tubs or small bars with different kinds of food. Loud music pumped through the room as the sky above flashed a variety of shifting colors.

As we entered, a massive man with curly red hair who I didn't recognize strode up to us, throwing his arms wide in effusive greeting. "Apollyon! My friend! Good to see you," boomed the friendly, accented voice of the large man I assumed to be Craygen. "I wasn't sure you would be coming tonight." He turned his head, calling to someone we couldn't see. "Cady! Come meet my opponent from earlier today. A mighty warrior who bested me in single combat."

The crowd shifted a bit and a girl appeared. Short and athletic, with pink hair pulled back into a ponytail and wearing a stylish hat over a pair of shorts, a t-shirt, and a brown leather vest. She looked mostly annoyed. "Cray, we've been over this. You need to slow down in crowds this size. I'm short enough that I can't see which direction I'm going if we get separated."

Callie gave a groan of frustrated empathy. "Oh my gods I know right? I don't mind being short most of the time, stats make up for it. But crowds are the worst. It's so easy to get turned around." The pink-haired girl turned, raising an eyebrow at my girlfriend, who grinned and held out a hand. "I'm Nightstrike. Apollyon is my teacher." She hip-checked me without turning around. "The big lug in the long coat is my boyfriend Solomon, and that's Starbreaker, Agria, and Clockwork."

Zeke was around, I knew that somehow, but he also... wasn't. I couldn't see, hear, or really detect him anyway except somehow knowing he was nearby. I suspected even that last bit was him allowing me to notice him so I didn't go looking. His Stealth Skill was undoubtedly much more sophisticated than mine or Callie's.

The rest of our group waved to the newcomer, who grinned widely. "I like her." Taking the offered hand, she gave a firm shake, pulling back and then sweeping into a sophisticated curtsy that should have looked ridiculous in shorts, but that she somehow pulled off. "As you may have heard, I'm Cady. Craygen is my older brother. He got all the height in the family, and I got all the brains."

The red-haired giant scoffed. "She just tells herself that because she's not any good in a fight. She has a support ability, and she's jealous I have the strength to face my problems head-on."

"You keep telling yourself that, you drooling thug," she said loftily. "Anyway, come on in, you guys just got here and we would be terrible hosts if we chatted with you at the entrance all night. We want to introduce you to a few friends of ours then leave you to mingle."

Leading us into the crowd, we followed close behind, making sure not to lose their forms, despite Craygen's massive size being an easy enough way to find them again (for me at least). It made more sense to keep our eyes on them, and luckily we didn't have far to go.

They dragged us to a group of people standing under one of the miniature islands. There were four of them, a short brunette girl, a blonde guy with his hair sticking up and a handsome face, and two dark-haired men with identical faces who seemed to be twins, one standing on the shoulders of the others as he groped around the top of the island for food without being able to see what he was doing.

Cady pinched the bridge of her nose. "What are you idiots doing and where are the other four? We wanted to introduce you to our new friends."

"Hungry," grunted the lower twin. "Trying to get food." His voice wasn't strained, he was just lifting one person, though I didn't know how this place's thirty plus Impact affected the difficulty. Still, he sounded gruff and not very personable.

Cady glared. "You have *superpowers*," she said scathingly. "You could just teleport up there and get the food yourself!"

The top twin (who was still busy scrounging blindly on top of the barely-in-reach island) withdrew a hand and pointed off to the side where we could see a shattered pile of rock and debris in an empty spot on the floor. "Tried that. Couldn't support my weight."

"I don't..." She just rubbed her temples. "It hurts being around you some-times. How are you both so good at fighting and so fucking stupid at the same time. If not for the dramatic difference in size and hair color, I would think you were related to *my* brother." She sighed and turned to us. "Sorry you had to witness that. I can feel my Focus points dropping every time I talk to them, but I assure you it's just an illusion. I've checked."

"Rude," said the top twin, appearing next to her without moving. "We're always so nice to you—why do you say things you know will hurt us." He nodded to our group. "I'm Blink, that's Flicker," he said, jerking his thumb at his twin. "The girl with the dark hair is Alice, and the guy is Chad. We came over from the Boundwave System. Chad was the winner in our tour-nament, but he lets Cady run things." He pitched his voice a bit lower, making sure it was loud enough to be heard even at a normal whisper. "It's less trouble that way."

Said pink-haired girl slapped him upside the back of his head. "I don't want to hear about trouble from you layabouts. I'm shocked Chad even managed to win the tournament." She pointed at the blonde. "Our hunky champion over there works out with my useless brother and these two menaces at one of the more upscale gyms on our planet. He didn't know who else to invite along so he extended us an offer."

I noticed Alice looking annoyed at Cady's description, and she stepped closer to Chad surreptitiously, putting herself in his personal space. He didn't seem to mind, giving a stoic, relaxed impression that reminded me a bit of Norman. Still, despite him being the winner, Flicker and Blink were among the five we were told to watch out for, so they were probably stronger. I didn't get the impression of terror and oppression that I did from Abel, but that was true of most people.

It was hard not to suspect that the more intimidating parts of Abel's personality and bearing were recursion based. The result of the terror and anguish of his enemies over literal decades. The only person I'd met with an aura like that was Lament, and she walked a similar path of fanatical bloodshed. On reflection, it might be something similar to being an Adamant. I'd have to ask Zeke about it later.

Craygen, meanwhile, took over introductions. "Chad is pretty scary. He charges up from damage, and can burn it to fuel his strength. Alice's power is even cooler, though it's kind of weird. She can absorb attacks into a specially prepared box. The box holds one hundred attacks. Every time she opens it, a random attack comes out, if she guesses which attack it's going to be and gets it right it triples in power!"

I blinked, looking at the diminutive girl. "That's... really interesting actually. Can you absorb any attack? Because that sounds powerful."

Alice flushed a bit, clearly embarrassed to have her abilities praised in a public setting. "It's not like... unbeatable. The box has to be made of materials that can withstand the attack. Plus I need to see it coming and activate my power with the box open. It doesn't work on surprise attacks or anything too strong."

"Still," Callie said in an impressed tone. "That's a fascinating ability. I just have shadow powers." Despite the self-deprecating tone I could feel her satisfaction at having more useful powers now. She was playing the game, but Callie loved her new ability. Abyssal Infiltration was pretty much her dream power.

We all chatted for a while longer, trading stories about our planets. They'd actually been out into their system and checked out a few other planets. Their own planet was C-grade so they had a bit of an advantage, and when they found out ours was only pseudo D-grade, Craygen was even more blown away by how strong Abel was.

Cady whistled. "A Master Candidate on a pseudo D-grade planet? That's pretty damned impressive. It must have been excruciatingly slow going

41

training your soul to that standard in such a backwater place." She seemed almost appalled by the amount of work, which, having made it a ways into my soul strengthening before ranking up, I could totally understand.

Abel just shrugged. "It wasn't easy, but I wouldn't call it hard. Just took time and focus. One fist in front of the other, so to speak. For the most part, it was just battle. You want to get better at fighting? You fight. Training is great, but it can't beat the rush of single combat with your life on the line." He clenched his fists and I felt a bit of that murderous, stifling aura he emitted sometimes leak out. "I love being able to test myself."

That got a grin from the red-haired giant, who held up his fist to bump Abel's. "Hell yes! I hope one of us gets picked for the random exhibition bout tonight!"

We all froze. As one, we turned to Abel, who was agreeing vehemently with the big man, and talking about all the powerful opponents they might come up against. When he realized we were staring, he turned to look at us. "Oh… Did I forget to mention those?"

Mel's orange eyes were blazing… literally blazing, as in they were on fire slightly, her irises shifting color like flickering embers as flames spit from the eyeholes of her mask. Abel looked, for one of the first times in my memory, genuinely scared. "I swear honey, I just got excited and forgot. I didn't mean to trick you all. I promise!"

Before she could react, though I had no clue how that would go. The sky shifted from bright colors to pitch black, stars coming out as night fell. The moon, full and round, emerged and cast a spotlight across the crowd, falling on one person, and then a second.

As the booming voice came echoing from the dark, I winced as I processed what had just happened. I closed my eyes, pinching the bridge of my nose, and exhaled slowly. After a second, I opened them and looked across the crowd to where the other partygoers were pulling back from the first person chosen, just as my surroundings were being cleared by revelers to let me pass.

I turned to glare at Abel, who had the good grace to look sheepish. "Well, shit," he said sourly. "I was hoping I would get picked. Oh well—good luck kid. You're going to need it."

Chapter Nine

I STARED BLANKLY at the other person under the light. A small, doll-like girl with onyx black hair and ruby red eyes, wearing a fancy old fashioned ball gown and smiling gently at me. Smiling just wide enough to show me the fucking *fangs* she was packing.

Despite having never seen her, it was easy to figure out who she was, especially with Nat standing dumbstruck right next to her. She'd decided to extend the wish herself, since Valk was at fault, but it apparently didn't matter at this point. Because of *course* I had to fight the Vampire. I swallowed hard, grateful for my mask since it would hide the look of absolute terror on my face.

"Hey, um... Apollyon?" I asked hoarsely. "How... mandatory, are the exhibition matches?" I wanted to give up. It would leave a bad impression, but then, so would having my spine snapped before a Vampire sucked out my marrow as if through a straw.

He hissed in discomfort, scratching the back of his head. "Completely mandatory? It's one of the conditions for entry. Everyone agreed to it when they arrived, at least from a rules standpoint." I turned to glare at him, and he gave an uncomfortable laugh. "Oh come on. What the fuck are the chances of this happening? You can't possibly blame me for this."

I didn't say anything, just glared harder. We were Ascendants. Everything was always dramatic and unlikely. Fate sense might not be reliable, but

43

most Ascendants had some small amount of it, and the pileup of all those different vaguely precognitive intuitions created a mess of complicated and dangerous nonsense that would take a literal god with all their points in Focus to make sense of.

Sighing, I turned to Callie. "Well, upside is I get to test out my new staff. If nothing else, combined with my own abilities I should be able to put up… some kind of fight. Vampire is a racial trait right? I'm guessing tons of modifiers and a couple of subskills? What should I be expecting here?"

To my shock, Zeke appeared next to me, seemingly out of nowhere. "Pretty much. Individual powers can vary. Lark himself apparently has tens of them, but the kids usually pick up one or two. That one probably has some kind of hypnosis or something. She looks like the type. That said, *do not* blitz her head-on. She'll crush you in a straight fight. Her sheer stat totals will be high into the F-ranks by now."

I winced. I'd been hoping he wouldn't say that. Nodding my thanks for the information, I stepped away from my friends and headed into the crowd. The other guests pulled back, creating a circle of empty space for us to meet in, and the tiny girl with the fanged smile practically skipped out to meet me, seemingly oblivious to any tension. She might have been a bit shorter than Callie, to be honest, though if so only barely, but somehow that only made her scarier. Like a little porcelain doll come to life to murder me. The thought made me shudder.

"Hello," she said brightly, her voice high and pleasant. "Looks like we'll be facing off against each other. I don't suppose you would mind waiting a moment while I change into something a bit less formal? I do so hate to ruin any of my dresses. Blood never washes out." I fought the urge to wince, especially when I noticed she didn't seem to be trash talking at all. She was really worried my blood would stain her clothes. Charming.

At my nod, she snapped her fingers, and a pair of twins with black hair and black dresses, both about five foot ten, melted out of the crowd. They pulled a pair of screens from their spatial rings (or conjured them I guess, but that seemed like a stretch) and set them up around her, touching a series of runes on the things so they became some sort of isolation field, then waited.

After about two minutes, she pushed the thing aside, stepping out in a set of dark leather light armor, her long hair up in a ponytail. "Thanks!" She said cheerfully. "I'll try to go easy on you for the favor." That was actually nice of her. I took up a position across from her while her attendants took away the screens and cleared the way for us to fight.

"Alright," I said when we were facing each other. "Do we wait for them to tell us to start? Or is this something we decide ourselves?"

Before I could actually get an answer, I heard a voice boom out the start of the fight from above. My eyes went wide, and almost on reflex I triggered Moonlit Night, State of Grace, and Double Trouble. I did *not* attack her from behind when I arrived, using State of Grace to bound backwards in case she spun to attack me.

That didn't turn out to be necessary, because the Stealth aspects of Moonlit Night hid me well enough not to be noticed, especially since she wasn't standing in the same spot by the time I finished moving, having blurred across the intervening space to my illusory clone where she was currently shoving her clawed (where had *those* come from?) hand into its guts.

Apparently 'going easy' meant something different to me than it did to her. Sure, that wouldn't have worked on me because of my gear, but it still would have *hurt*. Plus she didn't know I had protection against sharp force trauma.

Deciding that I absolutely did not want to attack this woman head-on, I triggered Pit of Despair, actually earning a squeak as the ground beneath her turned to a hole full of silt. Before she could drop all the way in, though, there was an explosion of movement as she *dissolved into fucking bats.*

I gaped as the winged rodents congregated in a spot five feet left of my pit and reformed into an annoyed Bethany. Okay, I was starting to understand the fear everyone treated Vampires with. How did that even work? Fantasy probably. Was that a Skill? Her red eyes scoured the fog fruitlessly, lips peeled back from razor sharp fangs in an unconscious snarl of annoyance and frustration.

"I hate the sneaky ones," she snarled, stalking forward slowly to try to find me. I slipped my staff free, nervously passing it from hand to hand like a baton. My Stygian Branch was a pretty interesting weapon, and I was eager to try it out. I focused and poison fire crackled through the wood. I stacked a Mercy Kill on just in case. Flurry of Blows and a Marked for Death were next, and I went ahead and stuck on a triple strength tranq blow for good measure.

I waited patiently until Bethany stopped stalking around and triggered Double Trouble, appearing behind her, staff already whirling as I brought it down on the back of her skull. I wasn't fucking around here—I was sure she'd be fine, but I absolutely couldn't hold back against someone this strong. Sure enough, she seemed to sense the blow and juked to the side, causing the impact to smash into her collarbone instead of her head.

Between all the boosts, the weapon's power, and Heavy Hands, the blow landed hard enough that I heard bone cracking, and she howled with rage and pain as it did. I dashed away as fast as I could, knowing she would retaliate and desperately wanting to avoid being gutted by those claws.

Sadly, that was about all that happened. The poison fire was barely spreading, the tranq had done nothing at all, and from what I could see from how she carried herself, the collarbone was already mending. Her Vitality must be high, which was kind of ironic for a Vampire.

"You know," she said conversationally, "not many people manage to injure me when I face them."

I gripped my staff tighter as I circled away, feeling a slight hum of energy inside it. Life energy had been absorbed, though not much. I wondered what a death energy burst would do to a Vampire, but I decided against trying it. This was an E-ranked item—the attack might kill her, even without much buildup. While that was unlikely, I did *not* want her family pissed at me, so it was better not to take the chance.

My arms were also starting to get tired. This damned thing was heavy, and I wasn't used to maneuvering it yet. I hadn't had time to train. I triggered Double Trouble again, deciding to try to finish this as quickly as possible. As I expected, the move wouldn't work twice. She'd twigged to the feeling of my presence last time and was waiting for it. Whirling on me with claws extended, she was completely staggered when I spat a Steam Arrow into her face.

She screeched, hurling herself backwards to bat at her face, and I followed, raining down blows as hard as I could, praying it would be enough to put her down. It wasn't. I managed about ten hits before she did… something. Her eyes became brighter, the red overwhelming as it flooded my vision, drowning my world in bloody light.

When it cleared, I was standing on a dark, foreboding mountain, staring up at a terrifying dark castle under a blood red moon. I looked around slowly, not moving. This… was probably that hypnosis thing Zeke mentioned. Concentrating hard, I used Eye of Revelation, focusing my soul on pushing the skill to reveal the truth of my situation.

My eyes burned as the scene around me blurred, a ghostly outline of the party returning and revealing that my surroundings were just some kind of illusion. It was a jarring feeling, trying to overlap the two radically different realities I was currently viewing. Of course, that was when I realized that I'd apparently been standing there longer than I had realized, because I suddenly noticed that Moonlit Night wasn't active anymore.

As soon as I realized the skill had ended I spun, trying to find any trace of Bethany. Sadly, I was too late. Her form appeared in that strange outline in front of me and tackled me to the ground. I felt the smashing concussive blasts of her punches as she pummeled me into the floor, but I don't think she was going all out.

Finally, the whole thing ended, and she let the illusion drop as a loud voice announced my loss. I groaned, happily noting none of my bones were broken at least, though several were bruised. Not my ribs, luckily. I didn't know why but I tended to break those far too often.

Bethany stalked up and loomed over me, arms crossed as she glared down. "You're sneaky," she said judgmentally. She rolled her shoulder to loosen it up. I'd dropped the poison fire when the battle ended, so she'd probably healed it all the way by now. Suddenly, her pout turned to a grin and she stuck out a hand. "I like sneaky."

I grabbed her seemingly delicate wrist and she grabbed mine (her grip was disturbingly strong) before yanking me bodily up out of the me-shaped dent she'd left in the marble. State of Grace was still active, so I did *not* stumble as I landed like an idiot. Thankfully.

Callie hit my side a second later, squeezing me tightly and burying her face in my side. Through the bond I could feel worry, relief, and… jealousy? I almost laughed. Clearly Callie had taken Zeke's warning seriously and knew Vampires were a threat. She was nuts if she thought I'd be attracted to that monster though. Bethany scared me shitless. I still thought it was kind of cute though. Callie was by far the more attractive of the two of us (though I wasn't bad to look at), so it always secretly thrilled me when she got jealous.

Something she seemed to pick up through the bond as she pulled back and glowered at me. I just chuckled and pulled her back in for a quick hug before letting her go. Bethany was talking, and I figured ignoring the terrifying monster who could almost definitely kill me if she wanted was a bad idea.

"That was a decent fight for someone so weak. I can tell you're not far into F-rank. Impressive. You guys want to come hang with us?"

Huh, well, that was one way to make an introduction.

Chapter Ten

"That was WILD," chirped Bethany as she dragged me over to where her friends were waiting. Callie was clutching my other arm despite the Vampire girl not seeming romantically interested at all. I was a bit worried I might get torn in half until Bethany let me go, spinning back to me. "How did you see through my Mesmeric Gaze Skill? Daddy says I'm the best at that one for my age. I was just like, 'zap, your mind belongs to me' and you were like, 'pow, as if, this is my brain!'"

I blinked. "Um… I have a skill to see through illusions." I didn't, really, but it *could* do that. I was more thrown off by her demeanor. How had I possibly been afraid of this girl? Sure she was strong as fuck, but she was like a bouncing shimmying puppy. She'd changed back into her dress, which she was whipping around as she spun back and forth, clearly fond of the swishing.

"Wow," she said, eyes wide. "That's crazy. You have so many Skills. That's pretty cool." She stopped, thinking back over her previous statements, and smacked her forehead with her palm. "Duh, Bethy, rude. I didn't introduce myself. I'm Bethany Lark, but my friends call me Beth or Bethy." She narrowed her eyes at me, making the irises glow a bit. "Never Bessy though. I ate someone for calling me that. Who are you? Sorry about before by the way, Daddy says I need to have the proper 'gravitas' as a Vampire when I talk to strangers, but we fought so we're not strangers, yeah?"

My eyes were glazed as I stared at her worriedly. If she wasn't a Vampire I'd have been scared she might suffocate because she hadn't paused at all during that.

Callie, far from being threatened now, was trying to hold back giggles, and held out her hand. "Nice to meet you Bethy. I was impressed with your... gravitas, by the way."

Bethy nodded sagely. "Of course." Her voice took on the semi-formal cadence from earlier. "My dark father insists his children comport themselves with the utmost dignity before the masses." Then she winked. "But, like, now we're alone and my Vampire stealth means we can say whatever. Like, 'whoosh, total secrecy.'" Smiling smugly, she tapped her chest. "I'm pretty cool." Then she jumped again, her insane all-over-the-place train of thought bringing her around to face her handmaids. "Oh wow, rude again! I didn't introduce you to Aida and Tracey. They're my besties. They're also my thralls!"

One of the twins (I decided to call left twin Aida and right twin Tracey) chuckled. "They don't know what that means Bethy." Her eyes, a sort of reddish chocolate brown, fixed on us. "Thrall is a job that you can unlock serving a Vampire. It's like the Knight job that some nobles can give. Thralls get bonuses based on their Vampire and can learn unique abilities."

Bethany rolled her eyes. "That's super boring Aida—they don't care about that." I was pleased to see I'd called which was which right. The Vampire girl turned back to me. "That was so fun though. I was expecting you to be super weak—I can kind of feel that stuff and you feel... spread thin. But then you totally put up an awesome fight!"

I grinned at her. "Well, glad I could oblige. Personally, I'm just happy you decided to change into the leather armor. I heard you don't take kindly to people ruining your clothes. How screwed would I have been if I had damaged that dress?" I asked teasingly, figuring I'd get some throwaway comment about her beating me up.

Instead, her face closed off, becoming cold and remote as her eyes blazed a lambent red. "I'd have ended your life on the very spot." Then she blinked, and she was suddenly all smiles again. "Which would have *so* ruined the party!" She turned to Callie. "Oh, and speaking of outfits, I *love* yours! That weird shadowy effect is so cool, you *have* to tell me where you got it. I want to get a dress made like that. It would be like I was swooping around garbed in shadows!"

My girlfriend, still slightly off balance from the terrifying death threat, shook it off pretty fast, introducing herself and filling her in on the details of her costume. Of course, the Vampire wasn't remotely concerned about affording something like that. She just looked over to where a crowd of people was standing nearby.

"That sounds so cool. Taylor!" she barked. A woman stepped out of the crowd, and Bethy pointed to her. "This is my tailor, Taylor. She goes *every-where* with me. Tay, come look at this girl's clothes."

The tailor in question looked... normal. A tall, athletic girl, with a pretty face and a blonde ponytail. She was dressed in a black cocktail dress and heels, looking more party chic than most of the people here, who were almost all in costume. It was interesting that she was a tailor instead of a hero. I wondered how much renown she got just from being around Bethany.

She looked over Callie with an interested smile. "Oh hey Bethy. Wow, I *do* like that. Some kind of conceptual filtration effect keyed to a static enchantment structure? Mental component maybe? Fascinating. Subpar materials, but put to excellent use." She hummed consideringly. "I'd say this came from a lower-end planet. Maybe D-rank? No, pseudo D-rank. Someone put a lot into learning their craft but was hamstrung with poor materials."

We all blinked at her in complete shock. Bethany didn't seem surprised. "Well, I want a dress like that. It would be so cool. You could work the fabric so it would like... float or something. Then I'd be swishing around clad in darkness. Daddy would be ecstatic to see me 'embracing my role.'" She rolled her eyes. "He never stops going on about that. 'Fashion is a hobby Bethany, not a lifestyle. Vampires need to inspire terror.' Ugh. Like, Vampires are all chic and beautiful now. He's so behind the times."

It was hard not to be swept up in Bethy's massive personality. The tiny Vampire was easily one of the most energetic and cheerful people I'd ever met (aside from brief moments of being murderously terrifying). I couldn't reconcile her with the image of the Vampire monster that Zeke had described. I honestly felt almost stupid for being so afraid (though the threat of murder if I'd messed up her clothes helped) and I was curious about her family. "So… Bethy. Tell me more about yourself. You seem like an interesting person—are all Vampires like you?"

She snorted. "No. Most of my brothers and sisters are wannabe posers. Daddy is the real deal, and everyone is scared of him for it, but they all grew up wanting to be just like him." She put a hand beside her mouth as if to block the view of her lips and whispered conspiratorially. "I think that's why I'm his favorite. I don't suck up like the rest of them." Then she giggled. "Get it? Suck up? Because we're Vampires." She burst out into peals of laughter, almost doubling over at her own joke.

Aida and Tracey, who were standing stoically nearby, sighed, Aida pinching the bridge of her nose in exasperation. To my surprise though, she wasn't the only one laughing.

"That was hilarious," said the cheerful voice of Jessie, her face lit up with a wide smile. "You're awesome." She held out a hand. "I'm Agria."

Bethany took her hand, pulling it to jerk my teammate into a hug. "Oh wow I love your outfit! Are those like… leaves?"

Jessie, who was normally the most cheerful and enthusiastic person I knew, looked poleaxed by the speed with which that all happened. Bethy pulled back, chattering happily about the construction of Jessie's costume, which my blonde friend enjoyed immensely, not having really been able to show off since getting it. She'd been wearing it around, sure, but she wasn't in the tournament, and we'd all gotten new costumes.

I remembered how excited she'd been to show off when she got her first costume. How happy she was about it. It was nice she found someone so enthusiastic now.

I heard a throat clearing and looked over to find Nat, Perit, and Valk all waiting politely to one side, my cousin shooting me an annoyed glare. I smirked smugly behind my mask at the expression. Nat was more experienced and confident about all this than I was. It was nice to come out ahead here without really trying.

Before I could comment though, or Bethany could respond, the entire party started shaking. Not in a figurative sense but literally shuddering in place. Everyone in the hall looked off balance, in the literal and figurative sense both, and we all looked around worriedly to try to figure out what the hell was going on.

"What's happening?" I called loudly, worried we might be under attack.

Abel was staring up at the ceiling, eyes looking past the sky and off into the distance. "Spatial ripple. Like someone dropped a giant ass rock into a pond. Something just changed in the nearby space, something big. This place is just floating around in the void so it got shaken up."

"It's opening," Zeke said from behind us. None of us jumped, too distracted to care much about my uncle's theatrics. We all turned to look at him questioningly, and he rolled his eyes. "The Moonsong Glade is opening. We've been waiting for the space to stabilize so you could all enter, and that's what that was. It's stable enough to allow F-ranked passage now. Slightly more than F-rank, honestly. I'd say anyone with under fifty Impact could get through."

That meant we could actually use the Moonglow Dew if we found it. E-rankers had sixty two Impact, so none of them could get in, but it made me wary of the interior of the dungeon. How many people there had more than a normal F-ranker's Impact value? Zeke had said the Dew wouldn't reveal itself to those inside normally, but there had to have been *some* of the stuff. Were we going to be fighting people halfway to E-rank? What would that even be like?

I felt that old fire start to burn in my gut again. Excitement. I'd been… floundering a bit since I lost my fight to Abel. It had been my first real defeat and it derailed me something fierce. Now, though, we were going to be competing for resources, and Abel was on my side.

"Alright," I said firmly. "So we need to go. Bit short notice, but we're already good on supplies and stuff, right?" We all had our rings, I had my weapon. "Also… how do we go? Because you said it's F-rank only. Will there be a portal or something?"

Zeke grinned, gesturing for us to follow, and we all did. Every one of us walked out of the party, followed by dozens more people, and as we exited we stared up into the darkness of space over the city. It was covered with a series of rivers of celestial silver light, shimmering and twisting around the floating city.

"Why do you think the Lakedeeps picked this spot?" Gesturing up at the rivers theatrically, he announced, "Presenting the entrances that flow through the unstable space: Starlight Slides. There's a special song you

have to play to call them, but the process was started when the space solidi-
fied enough to support the slides. That's concentrated moonlight, and it's
where the Glade gets its name." He turned toward the city. "Now, let's go
find you a musician and get you your own. You don't want to be the last
ones to arrive."

Chapter Eleven

We were running, desperately trying to get to a musician before anyone else. As we ran, I saw dozens of others scattering in all directions. Not everyone. Some of these people either weren't here to enter the Glade or didn't care enough to try being early, because they just watched everyone else barrel around with smirks on their faces. Zeke wasn't leading, exactly —he'd just gotten us going. Nat pulled ahead to show us the way to the nearest person who could open a slide.

We turned off into an alley and bolted into a small run-down shop with a door hidden under an overhang. Nat slammed the door behind us, barricading it before she informed Celine we would be contracting the old man behind the counter as our ride and to get us a decent rate. She shoved a bag of chits into her hand, probably because we were in a time crunch, and the elf girl sighed and got to work negotiating.

Callie pulled me aside, activating her Stealth Skill as we stepped into a dark corner. "You know," I said with a grin, "if you wanted to pull me away for some alone time, your timing could be better. Honestly, I think Stealth will make our absence *more* noticeable, not less."

She gave me a wan smile. "Sadly not where my mind was at. Shane... we need to talk." I blinked at her. That sounded... bad. I'd never had someone tell me that and mean anything good by it. I could feel discomfort, uncertainty, and fear through the bond, and I had a sinking suspicion I knew what this was about.

"Right," I said slowly. "Talk about what? Did something happen? Is this about the whole Vampire thing?" I wracked my brain for what she might want to talk about. We'd been pretty solid up to this point, and I hadn't felt any unhappiness through the bond. "Like if I did something wrong, we can talk it out right?" My stomach was in knots. Was that what this was? Was she breaking up with me?

Staring at me uncomprehendingly, she seemed to notice my creeping dread through the bond. Her own unhappy feelings evaporated like snow on a summer day as she finally realized what I meant and... burst out laughing. She was doubled over cackling at me, and my own fear was mitigated somewhat by annoyance. It wasn't *my* fault she'd been so damned vague.

"I'm sorry," she wheezed. "I just realized what that probably sounded like. No, sweetie—I'm not breaking up with you."

I threw my hands in the air. "Well, hell Callie, maybe don't lead the conversation so ambiguously next time. The bond was sending me tons of signals. If you aren't breaking up with me what the hell is this about? If it helps, just know that whatever it is will pale in comparison to what you just put me through, so thanks for setting the stage."

She had to try to staunch her giggles. "Right. Sorry, love. No, I wanted to talk about the group. Specifically, I wanted to talk to you about leading it. I think you should take over as leader."

Blinking in surprise, I cocked my head. "But... why? You're amazing at leading. You always have a plan, plus you have way more experience. Your years as an Ascendant—"

She cut me off. "Mean nothing anymore. I was a G-ranker in a tiny city on a tiny backwater planet. Sure, I spent some time learning how things worked, but my experience is so far behind where we are now that you couldn't spot it with a telescope. It's apples and elephants, Shane. This isn't my world anymore. Literally. It is yours though. And you'll be expected to do more as we go on. To make your own faction. To lead."

"But." I floundered. "What about the others?" It wasn't just my decision to make.

She smiled. "We're all on the same page. It's not like this came out of nowhere. We've all been waiting for you to take over for a while. Considering you're the reason we're all here, it just makes the most sense."

I hadn't expected this. "I'm not... leadership material. I'm a thug. I just hit shit. I don't know politics and backroom deals and tactics. That's you. You're amazing at that stuff, it's one of the *many* things I love about you. Everyone is safer with you in charge."

Flicking my forehead through the mask with a dull thunk, she glared up at me. "You are not an idiot. You are not an animal. You are a smart, capable man with admittedly *some* impulse control issues. You *can* make good decisions. And I'll still be here to help and handle things if you can't. We're partners, remember? But the things we'll be involved in going forward will be all on you. Your family, your enemies. You need to learn to lead."

It was hard to argue that. But I just... didn't want to. I didn't want to be in charge, didn't want all that pressure. I wasn't just a thug because of my reputation, I was a thug because it was *fun*. Turning off my brain and hitting shit until it left me alone was *easy*. It also let me ignore what I'd known for a long time. I needed to make a goddamn decision about where my life was going.

Putting it off for so long had been convenient because of the messes we'd been in, but I needed a direction. I wanted to become the Wishmaster, but that was almost too big of a goal. It was easy to write it off as an overarching path and just ignore the trees for the forest. I needed a direction. We were entering the Moonsong Glade to grow stronger and gain a leg up on strengthening our souls, but for what? Just to keep trying to prove ourselves to the family?

"And if I take over the group," I said quietly, "you'll be with me, whatever I decide we should do? No matter what?" I needed to know she'd be by my side, because I was pretty sure my new direction was going to be a bit more dangerous than the current one, at least in the short term.

She snorted. "Baby, if you don't know I have your back by now I don't know what to tell you. Barring you going insane from recursion and taking up a career punching babies, I'm with you no matter what."

I grinned, triggering the 'eating' function of my mask as I leaned down to pull her into a deep kiss. She grinned back against my lips, until we finally finished and I pulled back, panting slightly. She gave me a wink and I laughed. "Alright," I said breathlessly. "I'll take over. And I know what to do. It's not going to be a short-term goal mind you—we have to finish this mess and then get through the trials at the Ruined Soul Temple, but... I want to find my mom."

She raised an eyebrow at me. "Really? I never got the impression you were too curious about her. She left even before your dad right?"

"She did," I agreed grimly. "But she might have had to. Zeke implied Dad forced her, and even if he didn't... I need to know. I've spent a ton of time brooding about the parent I know, but I want to meet the one I don't. I barely remember my mom, and I want to see her again. It's probably going to be a big deal tracking her down. Somehow I doubt I can just roll up to the Church's backyard and ask to see her."

My girlfriend shook her head emphatically. "You can't. First off, A-rankers are the pillars of the main factions. Their locations are closely guarded secrets, and they change constantly. At least when they aren't locked up in the central stronghold of their factions. But there's no way we reach your mom in the Holy Dominion. I've been reading up on this stuff since we found out we were leaving, and I can tell you that for sure. Luckily your mom is a combat caste A-ranker, and they aren't known for cushy desk jobs. She's *probably* out and about."

I nodded, smiling at the news. "That's awesome. So we just need to find her. I even know who to ask—we can talk to that Brightlaw guy. He's a Crusader for the Church, right? I bet he knows a ton about the combat caste. We can talk to him during our trip through the Glade."

"We can," she said cautiously. "But don't expect finding him to be easy. The Glade is a dungeon, one big enough to support local factions. F-ranker factions too, but most of the big names will have ingested Moon-glow Dew. We're going to have our hands full." Seeming to notice her error she put her hands up. "Not that I'm saying to give up. Finding your mom is a good idea. If Brightlaw doesn't know, I bet someone at the Ruined Soul Temple will. The elites of the factions will be there for the trial—she might even show up."

I grinned at the thought. She was right. I had a direction to go in now. Somehow, having a plan, a short-term plan that mattered to me, made this seem... less daunting. I could do this. I'd track down that Crusader and ask him what he knew, and if it was nothing I'd keep looking until we found my mother and I could finally ask her what had happened. I could finally get an answer from at least one of my parents.

Smiling sweetly, Callie leaned up to kiss my cheek and pulled away, letting the Stealth drop as she walked over to where Celine was negotiating with the musician. "Well," she asked loudly, "how are negotiations going?"

Celine turned to glare at her, or at least give her a mildly disapproving frown, which was the Celine version of screaming and falling on her like a ravenous chimpanzee. "Poorly. This... person"—the way she said that made it clear she wanted to say a much less neutral word but wasn't willing to sully herself with such vulgarity—"is insisting on overcharging us. He thinks he has leverage and refuses to compromise."

The old man grinned, exposing several missing teeth (though the rest of them were perfectly straight and white, so I suspected they'd been knocked out in a fight when he was younger or something). "S'right," he said smugly. "I want thirty F-rank chits for the lot of you. Three apiece."

Callie grimaced, turning to me. "Well boss man? First decision as group leader."

My friends all spun, and a grin split Benny's face. "Yeah, *boss man*, what should we do? Are we going to eat the cost?"

My ears reddened a bit. They... really thought I could do this, huh? Still, their faith in me didn't mean I had to make this decision on my own, so I looked to Callie for guidance. I could tell from the bond she didn't think we should accept, and I didn't either. If this musician was overcharging us, I'd rather go look for someone else.

"Two," I said flatly. He opened his mouth and I held up a hand. "Nope. This isn't a negotiation. I'm not bartering, I don't have that Skill. You'll take two or we'll take our leave. I'm sure you can find someone else who wants to head down there. Of course, the chances are good that you'll run into someone a bit less... civilized than I am, and that their guardian might be less circumspect. You might end up getting threatened into taking nothing."

His mouth snapped shut. He glared at me, but I just stared him down. I didn't know if two F-rank chits per person was a good rate, but it was a better one, and close enough to the full amount that it wasn't *too* onerous to accept. Finally he sneered and nodded, and Celine smugly counted out the chits.

Callie gave me a proud smile and leaned up to kiss my masked cheek. I grinned, then turned to the old man, who had taken a pan flute out of his pocket. He played a note, and the window blew open, then he began to really cut loose. The speed and complexity of the song were astonishing, and with each new note a moonbeam streamed through the window twisting in on itself. I watched in stunned amazement as the moonbeams wove themselves into a bridge, or rather, a slide.

"Okay," I said aloud as I stared, "that was pretty cool."

Chapter Twelve

THE SLIDE that materialized was mesmerizing to look at. Whirls of shifting silver moonlight woven into intricate spirals and shifting symbols I could barely understand. Some looked like runes, some looked almost like pictures, at least for a second, and some I had no words for. "That's... amazing," I murmured, reaching out to touch the silvery substance.

Zeke reached out and smacked my hand away. "Not yet. If you touch it you'll get sucked in. Make sure you have everything prepared before you make contact." I shook my fingers, glaring a little, but nodded.

"So... what is this anyway? Did he make this just now?" The music had woven the slide, but something about it seemed too profound to have been made by the old man. Not in terms of Impact (it was only F-rank like we were) but in terms of complexity. It was like I was looking into an absurdly deep puddle. Even if it was the same size as other puddles in terms of width, the depth was leagues deeper.

Zeke shook his head, looking at it with interest. "No. More like... called it? He gave it a place to connect. The slide is part of the Glade. An important part." He shook off the faraway tone. "Doesn't matter. You need to go— the slides don't connect for long, and someone will have noticed." He patted my shoulder. "Be safe kid. I'll be keeping an eye out, but I won't be any good out here." He looked at the others. "Watch his back."

I looked around. "Hey, where is Jessie? We can't leave without her." Our healer was a key member of our group, especially in a place like the Moon-song Glade, which would be full of wild animals and nature.

Callie pointed out the door. "She's outside waiting for the animals. You didn't think she'd leave without Randall and the wolves did you? It was the whole reason we brought them. It's fine, though—she texted them as soon as we got here, and if she went out to meet them they should be arriving any second."

I turned to Abel. "Can you help her get them to the slide? They're too big to fit through the door, but your spatial lubrication should help get around that. Once they touch the silver they'll be snapped up."

He just shrugged and went outside to help. I looked back at Zeke. "Alright. Once that's done, we're leaving. Don't drink too much while I'm gone, keep up with Cass's training, and teach Cark a few things too." I paused. "And tell them I said goodbye and that I'll see them soon enough."

I debated telling him about my decision to look for my mother, but I knew he couldn't do anything in the Glade anyway, and I was worried he'd try to talk me out of it. I decided not to mention it. There would be time later. Unless I was dead, and then I wouldn't care.

Giving my uncle a quick hug that surprised me almost as much as it surprised him, I stepped back and took up a spot near the silver slide. I saw the air warp as the spatial lubrication created a path to the slide, Abel leading it in so Randall could reach the stream of energy. With one last look around, I reached out, touched the moonlight... and fell.

That's the only word that worked for it—falling. Despite the slide going straight up for a bit and then curving slowly, as I rocketed up it I felt myself picking up speed. It wasn't anything as simple as gravity reversing because I didn't feel like I had a body at all. It was like my soul was being sucked down a tube, but the tube had a million curves and twists and turns yet was straight as an arrow at the same time.

Every inch I traveled felt like I'd gone through a maze, but at the same time I not only didn't slow down, I picked up speed. Like someone was shoving the impression of having traveled a winding path into my head every inch I moved, but they were all different winding paths, and my brain was having trouble keeping up with them, and then, suddenly... I wasn't.

I was just standing in the forest. The trees were swaying, the leaves were rustling, and I was trying my best not to vomit. There was a flash of moonlight and Callie was there. I had barely enough presence of mind to step in and catch her before she toppled over. Abel was fine, oddly, and it made me wonder if soul strength made it easier to adjust. Benny seemed to do relatively well too.

Nat and her guards looked sick but managed to stay standing, and Jessie landed still on Randall's back. Having four legs presumably helped, because none of the animals fell over. Jin, Rellia, Lily, and Rolf, our wolves, all looked energetic and excited actually, and I felt bad that we'd been keeping them cooped up in the city. Randall would want to stay with Jessie, but I would have to consider possibly leaving the wolves if they wanted to stay. We were lucky they were able to come along at all—it had been a relief to find out animals didn't count towards our slots. Sapience was a big thing in this case apparently.

"Alright," I said with a rasp, my voice not working right yet, "is everyone okay? No one hurt?"

"Only mentally and emotionally," moaned Benny. "I feel like I fell out of an existential dread tree and hit every branch on the way down. That was awful. I'm not sure if I feel like less than when I went in or more, or which of those things is worse because they're both somehow terrifying to me right now."

I grimaced. "Don't think about it. It sucked but it's over, and chances are we won't need to do anything like it again anytime soon."

"Speaking of being over..." Jessie said from her perch on Randall's back. "Does anyone know where we ended up? Because I feel like the whole danger thing might just be getting started. The puppies don't look comfortable here, and they have pretty solid instincts."

Staring around us, I took in the trees. We'd ended up in a clearing, natural from the looks of it. Part of me secretly hoped there would be some Moonglow Dew conveniently sitting around here, but there wasn't. Just darkness, shadow, and foreboding thick between the trees. Which was when my brain caught up to the fact that we had our own expert on shadow and foreboding.

"Cal," I called, my girlfriend looking up at me as she tried to shake the cobwebs off of our entrance. "We're in a deep dark shadowy forest—think you could take a listen and get us an idea what we're walking into? See if there are any people nearby, or civilization maybe."

Shaking her head to physically rattle something loose, she grinned at me. "Sounds good. Give me a second." She knelt down, hand pressed to the shadow, and I saw her sink into the darkness beneath the tree, vanishing into the empty shade. I hadn't seen her do that exactly. I'd known she could, but it was still kind of crazy to watch.

As she slipped out, she shot me a frown. "Okay, there isn't much within my range aside from animals, but I did catch the very edges of a conversation somewhere nearby. Just at the edge of where I can listen, which means not close but not far enough for my liking. They're coming this way too. But since they're out of range I just got some noise and voices in a language I didn't know. Can't even give you a number. What do we do?"

I paused. We could run, but we didn't know where we were, and we could easily end up even worse off. Being solidly in place as well as having the numbers and power to protect ourselves meant this was as good a time as any to run into another team. Worst case we could run away.

"We wait," I said firmly. "Callie, if you have the materials, maybe set a few traps nearby, something we can avoid and lead them into if we need to get away." Just because we were going to make contact didn't mean we had to be stupid about it.

She nodded, pulling some materials from her ring. Nothing too fancy—her Trap Skill wasn't high enough anyway. She turned and got to work, and I prepared to greet the other team, whoever they might be. It would be nice to assume we'd know them, but we couldn't count on that.

I half wanted someone to make an escape wish, but I might need the ones I had for bargaining.

I started hearing them pretty soon after. Breaking branches and crackling leaves heralded the approach of... I froze. Too many people. More than ten. More than twenty. I panicked, getting ready to tell everyone we needed to go, but as I triggered Eye of Revelation, I realized we were already surrounded.

A man stepped out of the trees. Pale with dark hair, in plate armor. He glanced around at us for a minute, before speaking in, surprisingly, completely understandable (if heavily accented) common, the language of the Conglomerate (and from what I'd seen, most of the universe). "Outsiders. How... unpleasant." He sniffed disdainfully, and I decided I didn't like him much. While I'd have liked to mouth off because of that, I was the boss now, which meant everyone's safety was my responsibility.

Sadly, that didn't make me a politician or diplomat, but it did mean I needed to be responsible enough to keep my damn mouth shut. I glanced to Celine, giving her a nod, and she stepped forward politely.

"Pardon our intrusion sir. Might we impose upon you for our location? If we've trespassed on sovereign territory we heartily apologize, and would be happy to remove ourselves from your land."

The man's lip curled under his hawkish nose. "Remove yourselves? Why would we allow this? You expect Ladrigan to be the only kingdom without outsiders? Pelegar has already acquired four groups. We will not allow ourselves to be bested. You will come with us. The awakening approaches, and outsiders are the best possible source of the god Dew. You're all drawn to the stuff."

That... wasn't what I expected. Any of it. I knew there were locals, but not that they had fucking *kingdoms*. Not that they knew we'd be coming and wanted to use us as Dew detectors. I forced myself to calm down. We were safe, and if they needed us they wouldn't hurt us if we played along.

"That sounds fine," I said cheerfully. "We'd be happy to help our new hosts, and we appreciate your hospitality. We're quite lost, so it's kind of you to offer us a place as your guests."

His eyes widened, and then narrowed, his face contorting as he presumably started to contradict me, when a musical voice cut him off. "What amiable intruders," a girl said, stepping from the trees. She had long, cascading aqua hair and pale blue skin, as well as ears as pointed as Celine's. "But very well, if it will smooth things over, guests you shall be." Her eyes turned to the pale man. "Drakov, escort them to my carriage. I'll bring them back personally."

Her accent was much milder than his, barely noticeable, and somehow much fancier. She gave us a warm smile, her completely blue eyes (no iris at all) glinting like spheres of ice blue metal as she stared at us. Then she turned and strolled away, expecting us to follow.

Chapter Thirteen

I DID NOT ASK why the woman who picked us up was blue. It was tough. I was pretty sure she was some kind of elf, and I really wanted to know more about her. Luckily, despite my politeness, I did get those answers, because Celine was kind enough to bring it up. "I find it astonishing to meet one of my water-touched cousins," our diplomat said, sweeping back her hair on one side. "Are you a Naiad?"

The blue woman smiled. "I am. At least on my mother's side. Our people are rare here—my father became quite entranced with my mother and decided to take her to his bed." She smiled bitterly. "Sadly, my siblings are far less enthused about my heritage, as none of them share it."

Celine winced. "Ah, I presume your line is... expansive?" Her voice sounded sympathetic. More so than I'd heard it before.

"Of course." The Naiad smiled, her voice dripping false sweetness. "Father has to find an heir worthy of the crown. An inborn racial trait is quite a coup, though sadly my gifts don't lie toward combat. Are you a wood elf? I've never seen one before."

"Yes," she replied simply.

I was intrigued. I knew Celine was an elf, but I didn't know there were subspecies of elf. I also didn't know you could be born with a racial trait, though given Celine was from a family of elves, I probably should have guessed that. I wondered how that worked, since the racial trait took the spot of an ability.

Sadly, now wasn't the time to ask about it, even if I was curious. Celine was our diplomat, but I was in charge now. Which meant I needed to at least make an effort to improve our position, especially since it was my fault we were in it. I wasn't entirely sure I'd made the wrong call making contact, but still.

"The crown?" I interrupted as politely as I could. "You're a princess of this kingdom?"

She smiled at me widely, and I learned that Naiads apparently have razor sharp rows of small, jagged teeth. "I am. Anna-Maria Deville. Fifteenth princess of the kingdom of Ladrigan. Daughter of Salara Vorenas, whose loyal subjects have termed 'the fishwife' behind her back." Her tone had a bite to it, and I got the impression that she didn't care for her 'loyal subjects' overly much.

"They sound like dicks," Benny remarked matter-of-factly. Celine sighed, pinching her nose, but Anna-Marie burst out into giggles. My best friend just shrugged. "What? Racist peasant farmers aren't exactly top of my 'to hang with' list. I'm just saying."

Anna-Marie's smile at Benny was much warmer, despite showing nearly as much teeth. "That is nice to know. I too find them objectionable company." My best friend preened a bit but was treated to a merciless pinch from his girlfriend and jerked back with a yelp.

Celine kept a calm and pleasant expression on her face, but her eyes locked on Benny for a minute, and he crossed his arms, hunching down in annoyance to entertain himself without talking. I didn't think Celine was jealous or anything, more that Benny wasn't a diplomat, and while I had seniority to give me an excuse to talk, he was just saying random shit and messing up her dialogue.

Still, her face was sympathetic when she turned back to the princess. "It sounds like you are having quite a difficult time. Might I be so bold as to ask how we might aid you with that? You seem to have some use for us."

"To be frank," the Naiad princess said, "we all do. The awakening happens very rarely—the last one wasn't even in my lifetime. My father was able to procure some of the god Dew from a prior awakening, and it enabled him to claim the throne of Ladrigan. Should one of us acquire the treasure, our chances of securing the crown when he passes will be nearly assured."

I still didn't get it. "So... just go look for it? I was told that it exists here all the time, I'm sure you guys have plenty of opportunities to find it."

She shook her head. "The Dew requires energy from the moons." She pointed out the window up at the massive silver sphere hanging in the still daylit sky. "The moons can only be seen during the awakenings. The amount of the material increases exponentially then, but sadly, natives do not seem drawn to this substance like the outsiders are. Therefore, whenever outsiders arrive, the royals all scramble to recruit as many as possible."

"This is some kind of... inheritance test?" I was obviously familiar with the concept. "But why doesn't the king just gather the Dew for himself. Actually, will we even get any? He could just take all of ours away."

Her eyes went wide as she shook her head, aqua hair bouncing furiously. "Oh no. We would never do such a thing. There have been dynasties in the past who tried such tactics. They flourished for a few centuries, but upon the next awakening terrifying outsiders fell upon them in droves to exact retribution. As for my father, god Dew becomes less effective the more you use it. He's ingested several drops already and has reached his limit."

That made sense—couldn't have the locals killing people from major factions. The limit made sense too, otherwise everyone powerful here would just grind right up to the edge of E-rank and stay there. "Okay," I said firmly. "You want to use us as your... what? Champions? To find Dew?" I wasn't sure why they couldn't find it themselves—maybe something about being around the stuff their whole lives made their fate sense ignore it?

"Yes," she said with relief. "Other outsiders will no doubt be courted by my siblings. Though some will attempt other methods for finding the Dew. As you saw earlier, not all of the natives are enthused about outsider visits. Drakov, for instance, had two reasons to act as he did. First is prejudice, which I tend to shy away from for obvious reasons, and second is because while he is nominally a castle guard he owes allegiance to my brother Mulciber."

I winced, happy I had my mask on. I really didn't like politics, and while I was up to being in charge, this sounded like it would be a lot of that. I looked at Celine, giving her a nod so she'd know she could take over from here. My elven companion folded her hands in a businesslike manner and gave a practiced smile. "Well, that certainly sounds like a tricky situation. So what exactly can you offer us to side with you?"

Anna-Marie chuckled. "I suppose it was foolish to hope it would be that easy. Honestly, I don't have much to offer other than the same things my siblings could. Protection from our citizens, supplies where needed, my own support as well as those of my guards and other allies. I'm hardly the favorite for the throne, and my retainers aren't exactly numerous." She sounded depressed just talking about it, and I could see why.

Callie reached out and grabbed my hand, squeezing it and looking at me beseechingly. My girl had a heroic streak, and poor Anna-Marie was in a bad spot, if she was being truthful.

My gut said she was, and I trusted that if Anna-Marie were blatantly lying, Celine would have noticed it and reacted accordingly.

Honestly, I wasn't against the idea of helping the Naiad. We had no real reason to accept teaming up with anyone, but if we had to go with some-body, a person who seemed like she would have our backs if needed (out of necessity if nothing else) wasn't the worst option.

Agreeing to help her might be a bit premature, but I knew that sometimes, doing something subpar was better than waiting fruitlessly for a perfect option. It was unlikely any of the royals would be perfect allies, so we might as well go with the devil we knew.

"Alright," I said, surprising her and Celine both. "We'll help you."

The others all looked perplexed, except Callie who beamed at me with such approval and pride I actually blushed.

It was strange to see a pair of eyes that were just blue metallic orbs 'shine,' but they did. Anna-Marie looked ecstatic as she literally cheered. "That's amazing! Thank you so much—I promise I won't let you regret this. I'll do everything I can to support your group!"

I believed she would, though I still had my own means of gathering support and materials. My wishes were a perfect method for that. "That sounds good, because I am absolutely exhausted. It's been a long night for us and we could use somewhere to rest." The party had been in the evening. Combined with the adrenaline of bolting for a musician, the ride here, and the rest of the day's activities, this had been one of the longest days I'd had, and that was saying something.

My thoughts were cut off, however, as I felt a lurch in the carriage. Looking out the window I saw that we'd come to a stop. The massive box of dark shining wood was even larger on the inside, a large, comfortable sitting room lined with bench seats that comfortably fit all ten of us, the princess, and even the wolves. Sadly, Jessie and Randall had to ride outside, because even bigger-on-the-inside Ascendant shit wasn't built for giant bears.

Luckily this carriage was pulled by horses, horses who were also F-rank like Randall, and not nearly as high into it as he was, so the bear didn't have trouble keeping up. Sometimes it was easy to forget how fast and strong F-rankers could be, even being one myself. Animals like horses or bears who were naturally predisposed to physical power tended to accrue lots of Might, and that high stat made crossing long distances a matter of minutes rather than hours.

I assumed this planet was relatively big, given that the gravity here felt heavier than on Callus. So we must have covered a ton of ground for the trip to take fifteen to twenty minutes. I tensed up, making sure that I was prepared for all of what was to come. We could run into other teams at any minute, and that was without the whole 'locals hate you sometimes' thing.

Climbing out of the carriage, I was taken aback by the newest building we saw, an absolutely monumental castle... kind of. I turned to the princess. "Did you guys... carve this out of a mountain?" It was hard to describe, but it looked like the castle was all one piece of dark stone, from the towers and parapets to the tall imposing base of the building. It was big obviously, given it was made out of a mountain, and I was betting a whole city worth of people could live there. Not a small city either. Especially given the almost inevitable larger internal space.

Anna-Marie beamed at me happily. "We did. My great grandfather was an earth-singer. He found this mountain in his travels and discovered it to be some of the toughest F-rank material in the kingdom, and so decided to found our dynasty here. It is the Ladrigan seat of power. Blackrock Spires."

Despite not being a fan of her people, she seemed enthused and excited about kingdom history. Clearly she loved some parts of her homeland. I also noted she'd said F-rank. Aside from some of them speaking another language, it was clear higher-ranking people spoke the same tongue as us, and they had similar methods of defining power.

Anna-Marie's smile dimmed slightly, and her eyes became a bit cautious. "Now, I'll be happy to get you rooms to rest in, but first, we must make a stop. All outsiders must meet the king. We need to go see my father."

Chapter Fourteen

I'D BEEN EXPECTING to be escorted to the king directly by a bunch of guards, but we only got a retinue of four armored figures. They closed in around us, silvery armor clanking as they formed a sort of guide box, forcing us to move in a specific direction and not to deviate. The armor was shimmery to an absurd degree, but more than that, it was also seamless over their whole bodies. It had lines to give it shape like normal plate but seemed to be made of one solid piece in reality.

"I wonder if they need can openers to get undressed at night," I said conversationally to Callie, who snickered as one of the guards stumbled slightly, then tried to pretend it hadn't happened while the others huffed in annoyance.

Stepping up next to Anna-Marie I pitched my voice low, using Stealth through my bond with Callie. "What do we need to know here exactly? I'd rather not get executed because I used the wrong spoon for soup."

That got a giggle. "Etiquette is formal and respectful. Address my father as your Majesty, don't speak unless spoken to, and be polite. He'll tell you what he wants—just agree respectfully and you'll be fine."

Annoying because I'd hoped to possibly bring up wishes, but it sounded like that would be impossible without risking offense. We walked for about twenty minutes before finally stopping at a pair of massive double doors.

Next to them, a single smaller door opened, and a man came out to meet the guards. They whispered to each other for a minute, then spoke to Anna-Marie, all without me hearing. I supposed the man had a Stealth Skill.

Then he went back inside and the double doors began to creak open. I stepped inside onto a long, plush brown aisle carpet, at the end of which sat... a man. The inside of this place was big enough for Jessie and Randall to walk in side-by-side with us. Which is to say that when I said the king looked like a shaved bear, it was definitely accurate because I had an *actual* bear to compare him to.

The man from before stepped up beside us. "Introducing Solomon of the Starchaser Pavilion and Retinue! All kneel for his Majesty Crighton Deville, fifth king of Ladrigan, Mountain Crusher, Lord of Cracking Bone, Fist of the Kingdom, and Bearer of Unyielding Force." The man who was apparently a crier bellowed at the top of his lungs.

Crighton, for his part, just stared at us coldly. Huge and blocky, with broad shoulders and a stocky build despite being tall, he had coal black eyes and long silver hair. There was a crown of beaten black iron adorning his brow, making his gaze all the more eerie, and his large protruding jaw made him look like he might bite into me at some point, his eyebrows thick and pulled down in displeasure.

We knelt, obviously. Because one look at this guy and I knew he could fucking murder all of us. Not only was he obviously at the peak of F-rank, but he'd used several drops of the Moonglow Dew, as his Impact was much higher than ours. I had no real way to gauge it, but I'd have pegged him at somewhere near forty Impact. Which meant he was chronologically prob-ably close to four THOUSAND, because this guy was very obviously incredibly old.

Most old people I'd seen tended toward being just grizzled versions of their younger selves, Vitality keeping them in good shape until the very last minute. Crighton was no different. He looked like a really buff old man, an aged version of who I assume he'd been as a youth. I could very well imagine the huge, bearlike man towering over his subjects, brown hair falling like an avalanche down his shoulders, instead of the lank silver mane he had now.

I knew why Anna-Marie had said he got his drops from a prior awakening, because I didn't think it was the last one. Maybe the one before? I wasn't

73

sure exactly how long it had been since the last time the Glade opened. No wonder he was looking for an heir.

He stared down at us coldly for a minute or two, the silence seeming to crush down on us, before a voice like breaking rocks at the bottom of a steep cliff boomed out from that barrel chest. "Outsiders," he mused. "Young. Though aren't you always. I find myself... unimpressed. Still, you won't be the last. I assume my daughter has enlightened you on the situation?" That question was addressed to me, and I nodded, since I didn't want to run my mouth and screw us over.

"Good," rumbled the king. He picked at the sleeve of his well-tailored brown doublet. "Then you know you will choose one of my children to support. Traditionally, the child who finds the outsiders has first claim, but you may waive it should you wish for someone more..." His eyes raked over Anna-Marie. "Useful." His tone wasn't scornful really, just dismissive, but I felt Callie bristle as the blue-skinned princess wilted under his apathy. "Make your choice."

Callie did not, thankfully, say anything. I was pretty sure we'd die if we tried to fight our way out of here. The guards might not be higher Impact than us, but they all seemed to be far into, or even at the peak of F-rank. And suddenly... I just didn't care. I wasn't going to be disrespectful or actively hostile, but I just didn't have it in me to be afraid of this giant Ascendant bully.

I looked him dead in the eye without flinching and said, "We already have. We're with Anna-Marie." Even if we hadn't agreed to that already I'd have said it. I wouldn't give this dick the satisfaction. It was funny, because when I first came in, he'd intimidated me a bit, but that one action had shown me what he really was. Just a big fish in a small pond who thought he was important.

My tone wasn't derisive either, but it had enough edge to raise one of those thick woolly eyebrows. I could see him deciding if he should take offense, but he needed us and we were the first group of outsiders his kingdom had found, so he ended up deciding to be amused. His lips spread, exposing large blocky teeth that looked like they could grind diamonds. "Very well. I look forward to your performance. You have a spine, if nothing else."

He looked away from me then, over our shoulders and off into the distance, like we'd ceased to exist. I knew that was a dismissal, despite him not saying it, and smiled as we were ushered to our feet and out of the chamber, Anna-Marie trailing behind us, looking a bit shell-shocked.

She'd been expecting us to change our minds I think. So used to being written off by everyone that even when we told her she had our support she didn't really believe it would happen. Callie stepped up next to her, putting an arm on her hand. "Hey. Don't let him get to you. Our parents don't decide who we are. Even if they may decide who other people are sometimes. We're here to help you."

I nodded. "Damn straight. Speaking of which, I need to know a *lot* more about all this. I need to know how much Dew we get and where we get it from. Like is there some kind of flower or tree it collects on?" If there was, we might have an advantage, because my plant seeking Skill should be damned useful.

Callie turned and kicked me in the knee sharply, causing me to yelp and hop back. "We don't need to talk about that right now," she said firmly, glaring at me. "We can worry about those things tomorrow. Tonight you can just show us to our rooms and you and I can talk for a while. You seem like you could use a friend."

"And you can cuddle with Randall," Jessie chirped. "He gives the best hugs. Normal teddy bears have nothing on snuggling with a real-life chonky boy." The bear snorted loudly and she rolled her eyes. "No, I'm not calling you fat. You're proportionally chonky."

Anna-Marie laughed at their antics. Celine looked like she wanted to weigh in too, but I saw her pull back with a sigh. She and Benny would probably want to befriend the princess too, but she clearly didn't feel like part of the group still after her betrayal and subsequent atonement.

Valk was also seemingly feeling protective, having stepped in closer to the princess, looming slightly in a menacing way that wasn't aimed at her. Figuring those members of our group had it covered I didn't try to inter-ject. I wasn't the most comforting person to anyone except my close loved ones.

I was curious about one thing. Slipping back, I came to a stop next to Abel. "So…" I said slowly, making sure to use Stealth so we weren't overheard. "The king. He was pretty strong. Do you think you could have—"

"One punch," he said shortly. "He'd have crushed me with a single blow. I've seen F-rankers at the peak before, like Rime, but he… he reminded me of an E-ranker. A gulf you just can't cross." He grinned widely, showing all his teeth. "It was fantastic. I can't wait to get my Impact to the same level."

I shook my head. "I know she said the drops give diminishing returns, but I'm guessing he's had a lot of them to get to that level. Probably past the point where most people would have given up. I'd be shocked if we could make it to thirty-five Impact, and that guy seems to be at forty."

There wasn't much Dew in between awakenings, but the king would definitely get what there was to get. I wondered how many drops we would get. We'd have to share with Anna-Marie, so we'd need to be going all out to accrue the stuff too, since there were ten of us.

I was so lost in my own thoughts that we came to the rooms before I even noticed, having to pull myself up short to stop from running into Randall's giant furry ass.

"Well," said a much happier Anna-Marie, "these are your rooms. Three couples' rooms and four singles."

Jessie frowned at the door to hers, popping it open and then sighing with relief. "The hallways here are huge, but I was worried the rooms might not fit Randall. Looks fine though, even if the door is a bit of a squeeze." She looked at Abel. "Hey Apollyon, you mind helping me out here?"

Muttering about not being a bear delivery service, Abel slouched forward, ignoring his giggling girlfriend as he used his spatial lubrication to slip the bear through a door half his size. Once Randall was through I could see inside the room and noted that it was plenty big. This huge mountain castle seemed to have been made with a bigger is better attitude in mind.

With a thank you to the princess, Callie and I headed into our room, where we promptly collapsed into bed. I was unconscious before my head hit the pillow.

Chapter Fifteen

I WAS FEELING MUCH BETTER when I woke up. This bed wasn't nearly as comfortable as the one at the Inn, but it was still pretty nice. Sleeping in my armor wasn't ideal, but with my Vitality it wasn't exactly going to give me problems. I got up, stretched a bit, planning to change the clothes under my armor to something clean (because I didn't want to have to wash the coat and the leather armor every day) after a shower in the fairly huge connected bathroom.

There was probably something insulting about being relieved there was a shower here, but I honestly didn't care. I'd been terrified for a minute when I woke up that I'd need to have servants fill up a tub for me like some kind of ancient barbarian. Cleansing water should rain down from above like the tears of heaven, smoothing away the cares and worries of your life. Soaking in your own filth was disgusting, and I held no appreciation for baths.

Sadly, my daily communion with the gods of falling water was interrupted by a banging on the door. "Shane. We're busy today—you can't just sit in there for two hours like you usually do."

"I always get things done!" I yelled back. "I only shower on my downtime. Can't I have five minutes of peace?"

Callie groaned. "I have to shower too, and you're... Well, I don't know how much hot water there is, but you've been in there an hour. Get out so I can get ready." I did, grumbling the whole time about controlling girl-friends who don't appreciate the finer things in life.

She just rolled her eyes, shoving past me rudely, and I returned the gesture as I went to get dressed, first in new clean clothes and then in my armor and coat. My mask I waited on, because I preferred not to wear it when possible. It starts to fuck with your sense of self when you see a blank piece of wood every time you look in the mirror.

After ten minutes or so Callie slipped out, throwing on her own clothes. She had to wash hers daily since she couldn't really wear an outfit under it. Since we figured the Glade would lack accessible clothes washers, she'd picked up a box at the bazaar, some kind of water magic item she kept in her spatial ring that could clean everything in five minutes or so. Sadly it wasn't made for leather stuff like mine.

"Oh, don't pout," she chuckled as she looked at me. "You can take another one before bed tonight."

I shrugged. "Fair enough. I wasn't really that upset about it, it's just early and I felt like sulking a bit." I winked at her. "Gotta save the little fits of pique for alone time now that I'm the boss. Wouldn't do to have my people see me as undignified."

"Lucky me," she drawled sarcastically. Still, she strolled up and kissed me good morning. "Oh, by the way. Thank you, for everything with Anna-Marie. I know you didn't do it for me, but you made the right decision with no hesitation. It's really sweet." She blushed. "I know it's lame but she kind of reminds me of myself. I feel bad for her. Her dad is a controlling dick and she has no confidence."

I chuckled. "Not that I object to the gratitude, but she seemed like she needed help." I hesitated before saying gently, "Although if you insist on sympathizing with every person in the universe that has a shitty dad, we're going to get sucked into a lot of bullshit."

"I know." She winced. "I'm working on it. Being away from home helps—out on my own I have to think about it less. Plus the thought that I'll prob-ably be stronger than him next time I go home. I think in this case it worked out for us though. But hey, you're the one in charge now, so you can make sure I don't go overboard. It's a win-win."

My smile melted into a frown. "We're still partners you know. Paired duel-ing, and... you know, us." I reached out and pulled her against me. "You always listened to my ideas when you were in charge, and honestly I don't think I could do most of the things that need doing without you. Your understanding of politics and just people in general. I mean, Celine helps, but…"

"She does though, right?" she said emphatically, her voice tinged with shock. "Like, damn she's useful to have around. I was just doing Benny a favor, but she's helping a ton."

Our conversation was cut off sadly, as *another* knock came, this one from the large door to our room rather than the bathroom. I headed over to pull it open and found Anna-Marie waiting outside with a pair of guards. She smiled brightly at me. "Oh, Solomon. It's nice to see your face. I admit your mask can be somewhat unsettling. Knowing there's a person under it is a relief."

I cursed internally as I realized I wasn't wearing it, but honestly it wasn't like secret identities mattered. It had defensive properties, but I didn't really need them in my room. Still, I pulled it out of my ring and slipped it on, both saddened and secretly relieved to be wearing the damned thing.

"Sorry I can't stay like that. Safety thing," I said wryly. "But I'm glad to put you at ease. Anyway, what can we do for you? We just woke up so we haven't really had time to eat or anything yet."

Her face brightened even further. "Oh! That's why I'm here. I wanted to invite everyone to breakfast in one of the feast halls so we might discuss the awakening."

"That sounds lovely," Callie cheered as she shoved me out of the way. I rolled my eyes as she bulled past me to snag the princess's arm, noting that Valk was towering off to the side, the red bearded warrior having been the first person she picked up apparently. I raised an eyebrow at him, and he huffed and averted his eyes. Interesting.

It took us all of five minutes to get everyone else, though we had to stop for Abel first so we could get Randall out of Jessie's room. Apparently there was also a balcony off the room he could theoretically use, but the weight of a giant bear falling from several hundred feet up would leave a huge hole, even on the off chance that it didn't hurt Randall given the extra gravity here and the hardness of the stone below.

My State of Grace would actually be perfect for getting down from there, and I filed it away as an emergency exit if we needed one, though I hoped it didn't come up. When we all made it to the feast hall, we sat down and servants began to bring out heaping plates of food as Anna-Marie chattered animatedly, telling us all about the castle and the kingdom.

Once again I noted she spoke more about history and landmarks than current citizens, not that I blamed her there. She loved the kingdom, clearly, even if she could take or leave the people in it. It made me wonder exactly what kind of ruler she would be if we helped her get the crown. She seemed like a sweet person so far, and mixed in with her history lessons, she had some pretty novel political ideas (at least to me).

Finally, I decided to get us on track. "Anna-Marie, I'm really enjoying the stories and the information about the kingdom, but I think maybe we ought to talk about the actual awakening. How do we harvest the Dew, how much will we get, and how many chances? Not to cut you off, but we want to make sure to get as much as possible for both of us. Speaking of, what kind of distribution did you want?"

She winced. "Well, the standard is half, because of the resources needed to ferry the outsiders around and the guards we lend them." Her eyes went wide and she hurried to add. "We can talk it over though. I'm open to changing things. As for the rest…" She sighed. "I'd wanted to wait until after breakfast since it can be a bit involved." She took a dainty bite of her breakfast, some kind of filleted fish breakfast sandwich, chewing and thinking before finally swallowing to speak.

"The god Dew spawns from flowers. Specifically Lunar Cascade Lightblooms. They're extremely rare, and they die after being harvested." She closed her eyes, as if trying to remember a lot of information. "They tend to concentrate in high places, require dense humidity, and are obviously nurtured by moonlight. Outside of awakenings, moonlight is difficult to come by—the sky becomes dark and turbulent. We get the occasional streak of moonshine breaking through, but that rarely coincides with a patch of flowers, hence the rarity of the Dew in normal circumstances."

This was useful info, though not the kind we needed now, so I waited for her to continue. "The flowers are incredibly difficult to find, but we've noticed over the years that outsiders seem to be drawn to them unconsciously. We believe our attunement to the planet makes us too accustomed to the energy they use. Fantasy can draw one toward opportunities, but the flowers aren't opportunities for us. They're slightly unusual but they do pop up and then die with some frequency, even if they aren't saturated with moonlight at the time."

"That's pretty fascinating," Callie remarked. "I didn't know fate sense worked like that. I could see why you'd need us then. What are the flowers like exactly, and how much Dew do they produce?"

The princess winced. "Not much. Six drops per flower patch, usually, sometimes a bit more, sometimes less. The ones we find will also most likely be contested. Maybe by our own, maybe by the teams from neighboring kingdoms. They're most often found in the mountain ranges north of Ladrigan, which act as a sort of core for the ring of kingdoms." She pointed out a window at the end of the room. "Those mountains, actually. The castle was placed here as a defensive rampart against invasion, though the mountains are treacherous enough that few try."

That didn't sound ideal. "Define treacherous. Like... slippery and with poor visibility?" I wasn't sure how those things would dissuade an army of F-rankers, so I suspected it wasn't that.

"There are monsters that roam the mountains," she said apologetically. "Arctic werewolves, yetis, snow women, ice goblins, and dozens of other creatures at home in the frost. Some of them have harvested the flowers themselves and grown strong. There's even an ice wyvern nesting somewhere up there, though we aren't sure where."

"No wonder they want to send us," I said with a wince. "You mentioned resources earlier though. What kind of resources? Some kind of enchanted gear to make travel easier?"

She nodded in relief, clearly having expected me to flip the table and storm out when I learned we were being used as fodder. Not like I expected much better from someone like Crighton. "Among other things. Warming enchantments, certain antidotes to frost poisons common up there. The list is... extensive." She looked troubled. "But I have nothing to trade for the necessary resources. We'll be at a huge disadvantage."

Having slept and gotten back all my wishes (though I was pretty sure I'd forgotten to use one or two of them in the hubbub yesterday) I just grinned at her behind my mask. "Well, maybe I can help with that," I said mischievously. "Tell me, what do you know about the Wish Curse Palace?"

I wasn't going to tell her the whole story, but claiming to have access to wishes had worked before—no point not using that excuse again.

Chapter Sixteen

My favorite part of being the boss was delegating. I think Callie should have done that more, because I didn't see any reason to take all the small stuff on myself. For instance, resupply was not something I had any real desire to learn, so we left it to Celine and Benny. Sure, I had to sit in on it, but it was still a relief not to have to try to think of every little eventuality. I was just the purse strings here.

Which was how I found myself in negotiations with one of the other princes. Wulfric Deville was the third prince of Ladrigan, and one of the better-connected. His mother was the king's current wife, and a transplant from a kingdom on the other side of the ring called Eledar. She had a lot of political sway, and her son used it to great effect, being one of the favorites for the heir position.

Not that it mattered. He saw Anna-Marie as pretty much the opposite of competition, and the chance to get some wishes was too good to pass up. To his credit, he was fairly polite to her so far during this meeting, but it was clear he didn't think she was a threat. "Anna," he said with a grimace, "must you be so stubborn? You and your friends could trade these 'wishes' for money, power, influence. You don't need to get involved in this hunt. Even if no other outsiders are found in the kingdom, you could still back out. I would be willing to act as their patron—I can fulfill any commitments you made."

I bet he would. Luckily Anna-Marie wouldn't budge. Celine cleared her throat. "Your generous offer is noted, Prince Wulfric, but as of this time we are determined to continue. In this scenario it would be in both of our best interests for you to meet our needs. After all, such a connected person will obviously be able to recruit his own team of outsiders, and having us as allies would be advantageous in the field."

That was probably going to happen. The other royals had begun scouring the surrounding areas for teams, and I was sure one would pop up soon. There were a hundred teams of ten in this dungeon, and only ten kingdoms total in the ring from what I knew.

Seeing he had no chance of convincing us, he sighed. "Alright. I'm told you have six of these wishes in your possession. What exactly are you asking?" I'd decided to give my daily limit as a hard cap. I'd use one day's wishes here, but I could just pretend to not have any more and keep the others to myself for the moment. If I had to contradict myself later I'd just claim to have lied, which I hadn't actually done technically, except by omission, so if anyone with truth detection powers was around I could feasibly get away with both statements.

Anna-Marie had spoken with us at length about our needs here, so we'd made a pretty comprehensive list. "We want fifteen pounds of summerspark crystal, eight bottles of frost antidote, sixteen ice goblin teeth traps, eleven snowstep enchantments, ten stonestrider goats and a blizzard-bane ward," I said. We were going to need to negotiate, Anna-Marie had been clear that this was the absolute best possible haul we would get, but that it was nearly impossible for us to get it all in the quantities we wanted.

Wulfric hissed in dismay. "That's absurd! I don't even *have* fifteen pounds of summerspark crystal. And while I do have ten stonestrider goats, that's all I have. I'd be depriving my own forces of valuable mounts. Five pounds of crystal and three goats. We can discuss the rest as we go. But those two are easily worth a wish." He wasn't peak F-rank or anything, but I knew eight points wasn't a huge deal. Luckily wishes weren't limited to points, and while stats were all important, sometimes you needed a more subtle solution.

"Wishes aren't so casual a thing," I said gravely. "Haven't you ever had a Skill you couldn't find? A location you wanted to discover? Wanted to look different? Perhaps change the ability of someone you know? I can do all these things and more." My voice was low and soothing, trying to lull him into daydreaming of the possibilities. I saw his eyebrows crease in uncertainty.

He looked down at the list. "I… that is… ten pounds. And five goats. I really can't do any more than that. I'll be dangerously underprepared with just that, so you can take it or leave it."

I looked at Celine, and nodded subtly. "Then that is what we shall accept," she said with a smile. "Wonderful, two down and four to go. Now, we can assume the blizzardbane ward will be acceptable, we only want the one, but if the goats are going to be halved, the snowstep enchantments will be twice as necessary." Anna-Marie had been pretty sure we wouldn't be able to get the goats. The snowstep enchantment allowed you to walk on the top of a snow drift without sinking in or slipping.

Sadly, it was consumable, hence the numbers we asked for. But without the goats to navigate (stonestrider goats apparently had absurd balance and never slipped) some of us would need to walk, and we would need two of the enchantments at a time for Randall, since he'd be making the trip with Jessie on his back.

Wulfric sighed. "I can part with the ward. I'd prefer to downgrade it to a coldgap barricade, but if you're set on it, I can make do. The enchantments… I can do ten. That really is as far as I can go though. Fifteen traps are all I have for trade, and the antidote… I can part with that. I want you to be safe after all." He smiled warmly at Anna-Marie, who actually seemed a little touched.

I didn't know if they had a good relationship, but she clearly thought well enough of him to believe he had her best interests at heart. Celine, doing her job, retorted with a counteroffer, and they bickered for a while until they finally settled on ten traps and six antidotes in exchange for five more goats.

Once that was done, Wulfric looked nervously at me. "So… how does this work? I just say what I wish and you can make it happen? No matter what it is?"

"No," I laughed. "Even pre-made wishes like the ones I was given have limits. It takes stats to grant them, and I have a limit to what's loaded into these." I actually wasn't sure if it worked that way, since I couldn't make wishes like that until D-rank.

Which made me excited to think about. Wish scrolls were essentially currency, and unlike wishes themselves, there were no rules about their use or trade. Paying for things at D-rank would become much simpler, not to mention none of my wishes would ever go to waste again.

Sure, there were downsides. I wasn't positive stored wishes were limited by the creator's stats but it did seem likely. Even with that though, it would be damned useful to have the option.

Swallowing hard, Wulfric nodded. "Right. I wish for the Subtle Persuasion Skill. Beginner rank." He had been warned I couldn't do Intermediate Skills already, I guessed. Or he was just hoping to upgrade things his own way.

Wish detected. Grant wish?

I confirmed, and after a moment got the stat requirements which I met easily. I was an F-ranker now—I didn't need to worry about paying for Beginner rank Skills.

I felt that familiar charge on my skin as the electricity built, and I reached across the table to set it free. The prince stiffened, gritting his teeth as the sensation of my power poured through him, and when it faded he was panting and sweating.

He was also grinning. He'd clearly gotten what he wanted, not that I was surprised. Having the confirmation made him excited for the other wishes though. He'd paid the first with summerspark crystal, and we crossed it off the list.

We went down the list. Each new item paying for a wish, slowly stockpiling what we needed as the prince got more powerful. Or at least developed the potential to do so. He'd been wishing for Beginner Skills, which were a bit behind F-rank, but long term he was clearly making a good choice.

Finally we finished, and he wasn't the only one sweating and panting. I'd used up a lot of energy binging them all like that, but it was worth it. The prince rose on shaky legs, smiling wanly at me as he bid us goodbye, then staggered out of the room.

I looked at Anna-Marie. "So. How did we do? You know the value of this stuff better than we do. Did we get ripped off?"

Not that I expected her to say yes. But asking her to confirm it would make her feel valued, and would remind Celine of her role in things. Callie said little acknowledgements would help me with the group, letting everyone know I noticed how much they did.

Shaking her head, she shot me a grin. "We did excellently. Granted, it's hard for me to measure value for something as ephemeral as a wish, but we got what we needed."

"Preaching to the choir," I said emphatically. "Celine?"

The elven girl smiled at me subtly, as was her way. "I think we did well. In the future, it might behoove us to offer a cheaper wish as a demonstration and negotiate from there. The effect of seeing such an impressive ability clearly swayed him, but we'd already settled on a price."

That was a good point actually. It was also possible we might not even need to. The prince had gotten his wishes and that might get around. Then again it was also possible he would keep a lid on it. I probably would if I were him. Even without more wishes as a motivation, wanting new Skills to be a surprise was only natural. They'd make a bigger splash that way and be much more effective.

As we talked, servants tromped in and out carrying trunks and boxes. Some large, some small. None of them contained goats—I suspected those were outside. We stashed the materials in our spatial rings and once they had been packed up, I turned to Anna-Marie. "I think we're ready for a trial run. Is there a place nearby where we can enter the mountain range?"

She nodded with a worried smile. "Yes. As I mentioned, this castle was built on the edge of the ring. There's a back entrance that is fortified against assault. We have patrols running through the immediate area to prevent ambush attempts. We'd have to travel away from the castle to enter territory where we might find the flowers, but not too far."

"That's perfect!" I said excitedly. "We can make it a day trip. Since it'll be a short distance we can even push the goats a bit harder. That way we won't need to waste the enchantments early."

Her face lit up at my enthusiasm, and she started filling me in on helpful tips. I couldn't contain my grin. Adventures were almost as much fun as battles. I couldn't wait to look around and see more of this place.

I glanced over at Callie, whose eyes were burning with glee and intensity. I had a feeling my sensing Skills would be getting a workout, not just the plant one either. There was treasure up in those mountains, and I was damned sure we were going to find some of it.

Chapter Seventeen

IT HAD SOUNDED like an easy enough task in the abstract, but getting out of the castle and into the mountains at the core of the ring was much more time consuming than I had expected.

The guards at the rear exit weren't the issue, as much as one might assume. Mostly the problem I ran into was actually getting there.

The castle wasn't just a whole mountain hollowed out, it was a space-expanded mountain. Aside from that, it seemed almost specifically designed to be difficult to traverse, with a mazelike layout sectioned off in layers meaning we often had to descend into the depths of the mountain to cross into a different section, then climb almost to the peak to move onto the one after that.

Between the design principles at work, we needed to traverse miles and miles of complicated hallways and dead ends, and because of crowded design and the large number of people and buildings along the way, we couldn't exactly run it at top speed.

"The person who designed this place should be shot," I huffed as we descended for the eighth time, drawing closer to the back exit.

"Oh, he was," Anna-Marie said. We all looked at her quizzically and she blushed an odd shade of lilac. "Not for the design. It was unrelated. He tried to poison one of the princes at the time. Apparently the royal poison taster had killed his brother. He figured the taster would intercept the attempt and die. The taster was out sick that day. Food poisoning."

Benny burst out laughing. "Oh, that sucks. Hope the prince was okay."

The princess just shrugged. "Got a little sick. He was obviously much stronger than a random food taster. Being royalty comes with some benefits." It occurred to me that she was F-rank and around the same age as us.

I'd been wondering about all the smaller kingdoms but thinking about it, I understood. Sorting people into smaller areas made generating the needed renown easier, and the king and his family had effectively managed to funnel it towards themselves. Not just their own kingdom, either—they would be infamous in neighboring kingdoms, as would their best and brightest soldiers.

Considering how big the planet was (not to mention the size of the mountain) there was probably a lot of people in this kingdom. Hell, we'd passed tens of thousands of people in the last hour or two.

Finally, we reached the last segment of the mountain we needed to traverse. The entrance was at the bottom of the mountain, deep in the earth.

"Alright," Anna-Marie began, "this is the bulwark. The section directly abutting the exit out into the Hopecrash Mountains. The entire section of the mountain is designed to be a deathtrap for invaders, riddled with traps and choke points, and even supported by entirely separate magical supports so it can be collapsed in emergencies. The ramparts outside are effective, but knowing this is here has prevented most attempts to bypass them."

As we stepped from one segment of the mountain to the next through a door at the bottom, I could see what she meant. Gone were the massive expanded halls lined with shops and bars. Gone were the crowds of people. The hallways and staircases of the bulwark were tight corridors made of dark mountain stone, lined with enchantments and tight turns to cut line of sight.

Callie reached out, sliding her fingers into the shadows as she closed her eyes and whistled. "I can sense some of the traps where shadows have gathered inside, and I somehow doubt that's all of them. This hall *is* a deathtrap."

Anna-Marie looked smug. "Yes. It's one of the finest defensive construc-tions in the world." She pointed at the door we'd come through. "That's one of the most durable F-rank enchantments ever made in the kingdom, and it's tied into the structure of the whole segment. The supports for this area of the mountain are tied to the defenses. This entire section of the mountain would collapse on your head before you managed to break through it. Millions of tons of stone and traps dropped right on anyone who managed to survive the gauntlet of deadly traps and elite units stationed along the descent."

The layout was mind-blowing, and I couldn't help but be impressed. Based on the trip, the mountain was laid out in rings, with each segment being circular and surrounding the core cylinder where all the important people lived. The bulwark, though, didn't connect to the rest of the layout, being its own separate chunk of space designed to be collapsed at will. It was like an addition on a house, but bigger and way harder to survive.

It begged the question if the hollowed-out mountain had even had a section like that, or if some Ascendant had slapped it on later. It seemed rude to ask though so I kind of left it alone.

The trip up the bulwark showed us a lot of what she'd been talking about. Going from the bottom up meant we saw the defenses in reverse, getting to see the choke points and kill boxes from the defenders' sides. It gave us a firsthand view of exactly how fucked anyone trying to break in here was as we spotted various instances of cover and side chambers made for ranged attackers and spearmen.

The traps were, as Callie said, not all obvious, but even with my low level of trap understanding (I no longer had the Skill) I spotted about fifty hatches and holes for boiling oil and acid to pour out onto unsuspecting passersby.

Finally we reached the top of the bulwark, and after going through several very fortified checkpoints, we stepped out onto an absurdly narrow bridge overlooking a deep canyon between this mountain and the next.

The bridge was manned with multiple checkpoints, and based on the design of the mountain I was guessing it could be collapsed. "Isn't this all kind of overboard?" I couldn't help but ask. "Like it's impressive, but is it necessary?"

Anna-Marie nodded. "The castle is the only one of its kind. The rest of the kingdoms built their fortifications away from the mountains. We're uniquely protected because of it, but we're also uniquely vulnerable. The defenses prevent that vulnerability from being exploited. Ladrigan is not the most powerful kingdom in the ring, but we are the best protected. We've never been breached."

The truly scary part was that despite them not existing here, I was pretty sure this would kill an E-ranker. Perhaps even a peak E-ranker. This was my first time seeing large scale defenses enacted by an F-rank faction, and unique environment or not, this would be enough to hold back a real army.

I was so used to the idea of needing a powerful Ascendant to counter another that I'd never even considered something like this. As much as I'd like to say this was unique to the Glade because of the limitations, I knew there was nothing stopping a larger faction from doing this on a larger scale. I wondered if there were fortress worlds built with the cooperation of everyone on the planet, massive fortification of C-ranked defenses made to stop B-rankers or armies from other factions. The universe was much more dangerous than I'd imagined.

I felt Callie through the bond having the same realization, and gripped her hand tightly as we crossed the bridge. To an outsider we might seem nervous about falling, but I could feel her awe and intimidation as well as my own.

Besides, if we fell I'd be able to use State of Grace to save us. Though I wasn't sure what was at the bottom of the canyon—it seemed far too deep to be natural. "What exactly is down there?" I pointed off the bridge.

"That's the maw," Anna-Marie said solemnly. "It's a natural moat surrounding the Hopecrash Mountains. Spans the entire edge of the ring. Most of the kingdoms have natural bridges across. It's one of the reasons for the founding locations. Crossing any other way is nearly impossible. The gravity over the maw is massively amplified without the stone of the mountains around to nullify the effect."

I looked back. "I thought you said Ladrigan was the only kingdom with natural fortifications like this?"

"It is. But there are connecting paths in multiple places. Mountain passes and things like that. They just aren't fortified like the castle. Like I said, most kingdoms build further back. They have camps set up at the passes, but it's not nearly as effective. We're not completely cut off—there are normal mountains like spokes on a wheel along the ring, but they're just hard to navigate. We have to watch out for invasions from either side still."

The more I heard, the weirder this whole world seemed. I couldn't imagine this being natural—someone had to have designed it. But why and how? Was there someone with an earth manipulation Skill at B-rank that could make planets? Probably. There was probably a clan where you could have them customized. The unstable space could be done with abilities too, like Mad Madigan's mazes. But I bet it would take a whole bunch of powerful people working together to make a place like this.

Was it some sort of funnel for the moonlight to create the Dew? This kind of question was so far above my paygrade I might as well not be asking, but it was interesting to think about.

When we finally finished crossing the bridge, we met a relatively large force with Wulfric, waiting for us beside a series of incredibly weird animals. Goats, to be exact. Well, sort of. They had goat heads, but the bodies of hooded kangaroos kind of, with long bunched up hind legs and weirdly sharp claws on short arms that looked good for hooking into rocks.

There were ten of them, meaning these were our rides through the mountains. Wulfric gave us a nod as we approached. Unfortunately, we hadn't figured out a way to get Randall through the Bulwark. Large animals normally had to climb the outside of the mountain through specialized protected trails that we didn't have time for, so Jessie's best defense had needed to stay behind.

To compensate, all four wolves were with her, and they growled menacingly as we approached the goats. A gentle touch with glowing green fingers calmed them but their chests still rumbled with discontent. We thanked Wulfric and mounted up, Anna-Marie having her own goat already independent from our ten. Then we set off into the mountains.

The goats were able to traverse the snow easily, hooves gliding over the frozen drift without really sinking in. They leapt and bounded up onto outcroppings and rock faces, moving almost unimpeded in the dangerous terrain, and I saw immediately why Anna-Marie had been so insistent we get them. These were an invaluable survival tool.

Once we got a bit farther away, sure we weren't followed, we stopped, and my team turned to me expectantly. Closing my eyes with a grin, I reached into my Path of the Doom Sovereign and felt around until I discovered what I wanted.

With a click of intent, I triggered one of my new skills, letting Rhythm of the Wild roll out over the nearby mountain pass to delve deep into the snow and the cracks in the earth for any plants as I looked for the flowers we needed. I came up short after just a couple dozen feet. "Well, good news is I found something good. Bad news is... this is going to take a while."

I hadn't found the flowers I needed, but I'd found another rare plant. Still, hard to complain about good fortune. Best get harvesting.

Chapter Eighteen

THE MOUNTAINS WERE huge and gorgeous, and the goats were amazing, hopping us around like they were spring loaded, but I was much too distracted to enjoy it because of one factor. It was so fucking cold!

I felt my hands tingle as I dug in the snow, annoyingly high enough ranked to actually bother me. Much like the stone, the water from the sky came from sources on the planet, which meant it was F-rank like the rest of this place. How or why this presumably F-rank planet was more powerful spot-for-spot than Callus, which was pseudo D-rank, I had no idea, but I suspected it had to do with the nature of the restrictions.

Nothing here could surpass F-rank, but as the number of F-rankers on the planet rose, that renown had to go somewhere. Apparently it had been seeping into the planet, slowly raising the power. In that environment even more F-rankers broke through, and the cycle continued.

Was this a factor of being a dungeon? I'd been told dungeons were different than normal planets. Whatever the case, my hands were freezing even through my damned gloves, and I was going to start losing feeling if I didn't warm… I froze, cursing myself for being an idiot. I triggered Conse-cration of Flame on my gloves, sighing as the warmth soothed my aching hands. I grimaced as I accidentally burned a rare plant though, and sighed, letting the Skill drop. I couldn't afford to waste these things.

Blissroot was apparently an extremely powerful pain relief plant that sold for quite a bit in Ladrigan. Slipping it into my ring, I stood up and turned around to survey the area. "Okay, that's all of them nearby. There's a field of powerful plants in that direction." I pointed to my left tiredly. "But I need a minute to gather my strength."

Despite the relative lightness of the snow to my enhanced body, the conceptual weight of it seemed to tire me out, much the same way lifting my staff did over a long period of time.

There were murmurs of agreement from everyone else as they all slumped down onto the backs of their nearby goats. Callie inched closer on the back of her own mount, her tiny form adorably burrowing into the thick fur for relief from the cold. "You think we're close?" she asked hopefully, teeth chattering in the freezing wind. "Because I can't take much more of this. At this point I want to get in a fight just to warm up."

I laughed breathlessly. "I couldn't tell you. The skill I'm using isn't quite so exact. We've gotten a ton of materials though, which we should be able to sell for a pretty credit." I paused. "Actually… what currency does Ladrigan even use? I mean they have to use something, but considering chits are regulated by the merchants I don't see how they would be made or traded here."

Anna-Marie overheard the question, which wasn't surprising since I hadn't stealthed when asking it. She glanced over with an embarrassed smile. "Ah, right. I should've perhaps addressed that during my little history lesson. Ladrigan uses royals, a type of coin made from heartstone. It's a special mineral that can be used to strengthen earth-based materials. The coins are extremely low quality, so you need quite a few of them to have an effect, but they allow an increase in defensive potential for the homes and territory of those in the castle."

That was interesting. Was the stone actually being turned into something else? Or was heartstone just some kind of side effect of the Dew, a method of slowly and minutely increasing Impact in quantities too low to detect? Either way it was a reasonable currency for the absurdly defense-focused Ladrigan.

Benny seemed to have a different thought though. "Wouldn't you run out? If they're consumable I mean. It can't be easy to find more of the stuff, even if you're alloying it to make coins with a low percentage of the stone."

That was a good point, and I looked to Anna-Marie, who shrugged. "Heartstone recovers. Active versus inactive coins are tracked, and they're cycled out as they're used up, tossed in kingdom vaults to refresh their effects. It takes quite a while though, and the effects have diminishing returns, so most people stockpile them for a rainy day unless they need to reinforce a new territory or they have a surplus."

"Fascinating," murmured my best friend absently, his voice remote as he lost himself in a bit of an Inventors fugue. "I could see how that would be an invaluable resource. No wonder the mountain seems so solid. Even more than the normal rocks here. It must have been heavily reinforced over the centuries or even millennia." He shook his head, as if clearing away the cobwebs of Inventing. "Anyway, I take it we'll be able to pick up a pretty huge bundle of the things with all these fancy plants?"

She nodded with a bright smile. "Oh yes. Each of these is difficult to procure because of the environment. This would normally be the haul of herb gatherers working for a week at least. Granted, they have their own Skills for sensing plant life, but it doesn't have the same range or specificity I've seen from Mr. Solomon's Skill."

That was gratifying to hear, though I was guessing there were upsides to their abilities that mine didn't have. The specificity she spoke of was only the ability to detect rough value. Herb gatherers probably had the power to tell what exactly the plants they were picking up were.

Still, I had a good feeling about the flowers being close. I could sense the rarity of plants to an extent, and the patch I sensed now was definitely rare as hell. Now that we'd had time to rest up a bit, I stretched to loosen my muscles and adjusted my seat on my own goat. "Well," I said firmly, "that skill says we're coming up on something big, so keep an eye out. If it's the flowers, chances are good we might run into another group of outsiders."

We'd been traveling for hours, hopping from plant to plant and collecting them as best we could. Knowing our speed and the goats' agility, chances were good we were deep enough into the mountains to be in general territory. I led the group up onto a thick ridge of rocks, climbing the outcropping with speed so we could look out in the direction I'd detected the plants.

When we got to the top, I froze in awe. "Those... those would be the flowers I'm guessing?" I said quietly, feeling the urge to keep my voice low out of some kind of inherent unwillingness to break the tranquility and harmony of the scene before us.

The flowers were beautiful, of course. They looked like liquid silver hammered into the shape of petals, set on black glass stems with glowing golden pistils rising from among them. No snow or frost. A huge area of grass surrounded them in their little valley, shielded from the weather by stone outcroppings. That wasn't what rendered me so stunned though. No, what shocked me was the *moonlight*.

Vortexes of lunar majesty swirled above the flowers, forming a seething sea of rioting silver and rainbow sheened light. Inside the moonlight, I could see worlds and galaxies being born and dying, see my dreams coming true as I watched versions of me accomplish every goal, and others fail their life's missions and be left broken and bereft of joy.

This wasn't just magic, or renown. This was *impact*, the moonlight cascade tainted by the weight of raw creation and reflecting the possibilities of a million legends. Anna-Marie swallowed hard, before whispering, "the Lunar Nexus." She sounded shocked, almost disbelieving. "I... I'd heard the stories. But this one is stronger than most. Larger, more complex. It's awe inspiring. There must be a dozen drops of Dew down there to create a phenomenon this intense."

That was shit-ton based on what we'd been told. That was six drops for us and six for Anna-Marie. She was already moving forward, but my hand shot out to catch her arm. "Whoa there princess," I said firmly. "Take your eyes off the prize for a second and look around. We're not the only guests at this party."

Her eyes widened, snapping up and around to take in our surroundings, and she realized what I meant. "Three other groups," she said, voice hushed again, not that it would do any good at this point. I didn't recognize the others, but I could remember some faces from the markets back at the bazaar. These people were outsiders like us, at least some of them. It made sense since they'd been drawn here like I had, though I was guessing it had been a much less productive trip for them.

Since we'd been speaking unstealthed, they would know we were here, of course, but that wasn't my issue. "Why haven't they gone in?" I asked quietly, staring across the field of flowers at the competitors. I wished I'd known some of them. We could have maybe worked out an alliance, because I had the sinking suspicion we weren't going to be able to pick these particular flowers on a leisurely stroll.

Abel answered. "That whole field reeks of bloodlust. I'm more sensitive to that stuff than most. A lot of people have died in that little valley, and most of them went badly."

Jessie nodded. "The life energy down there is way too thick to just be flowers. I can't sense bloodlust or anything, but there's a creature in that field, and it's pretty big from what I can tell. I just don't know where it is. The energy is spread out in a weird way, like it's part of the earth somehow, but I know the difference between plant and animal life force. It's a... flavor thing. That's an animal."

I grimaced but gave them both nods of thanks. It was good information to have. It was also enough to go on for my Eye of Revelation to probably pick up some clues, so I triggered the skill, using my ability to see that which was hidden to reveal the truth of this place.

Unfortunately, when you open a hidden eye, sometimes a hidden eye opens back. As I stared down at the field, a pair of eyes opened in return near the base of the flower patch. Big ones. The ground rumbled, and I swallowed hard as the flowers began to move, not one at a time like they would in the wind, but all together, as the ground itself rose up into the air.

"I think," I said faintly, "I figured out why they didn't move in to take the flowers. And also why there's no snow around them."

Benny gave a strangled scoff. "No shit. Do you think it might have been because of *that?*" He jabbed a finger at the creature that had just finished rising from the dirt.

A massive stone stingray, its bottom covered with a hundred separate mouths full of jagged gnashing teeth, hovered above us, the flowers situated on its back as it loomed over the valley menacingly.

"Yup," I croaked. "That was going to be my first guess. Anyone have any idea what that is?" I asked desperately. When no answer was forthcoming, I sighed. "Yeah, I was kind of afraid of that."

Chapter Nineteen

THE MONSTROSITY FLOATING above us was one of the scariest things I'd ever seen. Even the Bone Wyvern, the previous holder of the title of 'creature most likely to make me piss my pants' didn't stack up to its sheer overwhelming horror. It wasn't the shape or the size, or even the pressure from the flowers—there was just something... awful about it. Each of its many mouths held *darkness* behind sawblade teeth. Not just normal darkness, either, but an empty, gaping abyss.

I found myself hypnotized almost, drawn into the depths of the yawning chasms littering the underside of the ray's stone underbelly. Then the thing *screamed,* and literal cones of sonic force exploded from its mouths, overlapping and combining into one blast that flew right at us.

Before it could hit, a massive avatar of Abel constructed of blue gel appeared above us, intercepting the attack and shielding us from harm even as it disintegrated. It snapped me from my stupor, and I spurred my goat back from the rocks, yelling for the others to do the same.

The mounts bounded off the outcropping and down into the snow, giving us a bit of cover as the ray let out an unearthly howl of rage. "Shit," I panted as we moved out of the strike zone. "How the hell do we get the flowers off... that?"

Benny looked at me in astonishment. "Seriously? That just happened and you're worried about *floral arrangements?*" He glanced at Jessie apologetically. "No offense, Jess."

She just snickered. "Some taken. But I get your point. Can't we find the Dew in other places? Is challenging... *that* worth the short-term advantage?" Her voice was gentle, but I could hear an undercurrent of stress and worry causing it to tremble.

"Yes," I said, "for a few reasons. First, we aren't getting out of here while that thing is after us. We'll need to put it down before we can run. Second of all, I have a plan, and third of all, if the other teams get their hands on the damned Dew, it'll make it that much harder for us to deal with them later. And if *we* get it, it'll make us that much safer going forward."

I saw them pause and think it over. Benny didn't look convinced. "I mean... I can't really poke any holes in your logic. But it *feels* like a really bad idea." His smart-ass tone was not appreciated, despite him having a small point, and I responded in kind.

"Let's not confine ourselves to things you think *feel like a good idea,*" I said acidly. "I doubt the ray is going to collapse in defeat from starting a band or convincing all its friends to wear those stupid orange shoes with the springs in them you talked me into buying when we were fourteen."

Benny's indignation was somewhat muted by the giggling of our nearby party members, but he still found it in himself to glare around at them until realizing no help was forthcoming. Then he crossed his arms and sulked, playing it up a little bit for attention.

Celine, who clearly knew my friend well at this point, just rolled her eyes and ignored him, turning to Anna-Marie. "You're our local guide, princess —do you have any ideas? Any rumors of a creature like this? A plan is wonderful, but it behooves us to gather as much information on our enemy as possible."

When she shook her head, I cracked my neck and hopped down from my goat. "Okay. My plan is pretty simple. I'm not sure how well this thing can hear or comprehend us, so out of caution, I'll put the first steps into motion and let you guys join in."

I turned to Abel with a grin. "Do me a favor and throw me at the stingray." I tried to project confidence in my plan with my tone, but everyone else whirled on me, Callie and Nat both yelping exclamations of surprise as Abel grabbed me in a giant hand and *hurled* me at it in less time than it took to blink. I'd already triggered State of Grace and quickly activated Ripple Running, transitioning into an aerial run to better guide my trajectory.

Of course, the ray turned slowly to face me, and I worried that this *might* have been poorly planned until a giant fist slammed into the thing, knocking it aside as Abel smashed it with Expert ranked Ragam. It squealed in pain and rage as it was knocked askew, and I stepped lightly three times, changing my direction to land on its back. State of Grace allowed me to stay on as I bolted toward the field of grass outside the flowers.

Dropping to a knee, I glared at the grass in front of me and triggered Pit of Despair. It was *hard*. I had to push against the resistance of the ray, but my soul was strong enough that the earth skill was able to create the silt pit. A ten-foot hole bored right through the stone creature, and I had to roll sideways to avoid its tail as it whipped up to smash me.

I bolted for the flowers, crashing into the field to collect them before any of the other teams got up here. Hitting the crazy warping mass of Impact infused moonlight was… weird. Like running through a hundred worlds in sequence, each step taking me somewhere else without moving me at all. But it didn't matter. I started snatching up flowers and stuffing them in my ring, not bothering to be careful.

Some of them seemed to have more pistils, and I made extra sure to get those, but I couldn't see the special ones that collected the Dew, so I had to hope I'd get lucky. Which I did. I was picking a specific flower without looking too hard, and there was a pulse of power. The moonlight cascade condensed into a cloud, the flower rapidly becoming more moisturized as it did so, until three drops of mercurial liquid moonshine gleamed on the petals.

I grinned as I put it away, diving for more, yanking them up to try to create the same effect. The ray shook, and I almost fell off, grabbing a few more flowers and managing to accumulate ten drops. There was still moonshine floating above a small portion of the field, but I sadly couldn't go for the whole enchilada because my Danger Sense twigged hard.

I threw myself sideways, Ripple Running helping me change direction twice to make sure I was clear, as a massive waterfall of cerulean gas slammed into the back of the ray, gouging a huge hole in it. I stared at the tall woman with canary yellow hair in shock as she snarled something at me, too far for me to hear in the ruckus.

She tried to tag me as I retreated, and for a second I worried she would, but Valk's blue gel appeared in front of me as a hand construct swatted aside the resulting frozen attack. I redirected my fall, landing on the rock outcropping with a grin and hopping on the back of my goat. "Let's ride!" I bellowed gleefully. "I got ten drops and they were *not* happy."

"You lunatic!" Callie screamed as we booked it in the other direction. "You could have been killed. What kind of plan was that? Tactics require fore-thought and consideration. Planning isn't just thinking 'I bet if I do some-thing stupid, this will happen.' That's just madness!"

I cackled with joy, adrenaline flooding through me as my heart pounded. That had been intense. Callie's words drew me up short, and I was derailed completely as Benny rode up to smack the back of my head as we escaped. "Hey! Stop gloating and listen, asshat. That was stupidly dangerous."

Sighing, I let my rush recede as I looked at things objectively. I *might* have rushed a bit. "Yeah," I said with a wince, "it might have been. I should probably have given you all the details before going. I just—" Danger Sense BLARED again. "Move!" I roared, urging my goat to hurl us side-ways. The others listened to me, avoiding the attack as a massive war axe made of crystallized sunshine smashed into the ground where we'd just been.

The snow hissed, steaming away as we turned to face the new enemy. A short black-haired man with wide shoulders and olive skin grinned at us, an axe just like the sunlight construct hefted up on his shoulder. His eyes burned with golden light, and I saw his feet scorching the grass under the recently melted snow as he walked.

"Hello there!" he called cheerfully. "I'm afraid I can't just let you walk away with those drops." He looked over his shoulder. "How's about you let me take them off your hands nice and easy, and I'll owe you a favor. Christina distracted that thing with her Azureblaze Fog, but it won't hold her team for long. I'd rather be gone before she gets here."

I pointed back the way we'd come. "Well, that thing still had flowers on it. Why not go grab some of those? What makes you think we're the easier option?"

He shrugged. "Christina and I had a run-in at the bazaar. She's a nasty piece of work. I'm Raul by the way, if it matters. I hope me taking those drops won't make things too tense. I don't enjoy sewing enmity." His smile was apologetic as his grip on the axe tightened, but he took a menacing step forward anyway.

"Wow," I said with an impressed tone. "That was the politest way anyone has ever tried to rob me." I glanced at Abel. "You think you can take him?" I could sense that Raul wasn't at the peak or even midway through F-rank, so there was a decent chance.

My mentor grinned, strolling forward to stand between us and the threatening axeman. "Never know until you try. I've been dying to test out my Expert level Ragam Mastery."

Raul glanced at him, eyes flicking away then jerking back as that tangible feeling of terror and violence that Abel projected when he was serious. "Shit. You're not the Adamant I heard about are you?" His eyes narrowed consideringly. "No, I don't feel perfection. More... pure violence. You don't walk the Path of the Adamant. You're on the Path of Blood. You must have spilled a *lot* of it to get that kind of aura."

He sounded worried. Which was a good sign for us, but despite that, he set his feet, clearly preparing to engage. I had to give him credit—I knew how terrifying Abel could be and facing him as an enemy had to be even worse.

My mentor didn't bother to wait. He blurred forward, body splitting as Cicada Stacking Step condensed multiple images of him. Unlike the last time, he was an Expert now. The images weren't brief flashes of combat capable constructs. They were real clones spreading out to surround the axeman before surging inward all at once to attack. I glanced up at the battle in the distance, seeing the ray snapping weakly at a massive snake made of Azure gas.

We didn't have time for this—if they ganged up on us, this would be bad... And that's when I remembered something important. We'd all come into this dungeon in teams of ten.

I activated Eye of Revelation and groaned. They weren't moving yet, which was why my Danger Sense was silent, but we were definitely surrounded. Joy.

Chapter Twenty

It was a testament to how distracted I was by the attackers that I didn't notice Jessie vanishing. Luckily, no amount of distraction was enough to make me miss the giant *bear* exploding from the snow at one of the hidden attackers. Apparently, Jessie had noticed them and used her Shape of the Wild Skill to attack the closest one head-on with all the animal fury of her big fuzzy companion. Or would that be animal furry?

Either way, the ambusher wasn't expecting that shit at all, nor was the one to his left expecting my girlfriend to step from the darkness cast by his shadow and jam a black bladed dagger into the base of his spine (enough to paralyze him but not beyond Jessie's ability to fix). Sadly, expecting it wasn't necessary when you were wearing armor, and the dagger skidded off the thin breastplate with a shower of sparks.

Callie's outline blurred as she activated her armor and then vanished in a blur of motion as her six clones took off in separate directions, her victim freezing with indecision. Meanwhile, my cousin had faded out of existence —I'd seen her flip her hood up and render herself invisible rather than just concealing her face. It was pretty cool.

My own staff came free with a swish, toxic flame crawling down it as I imbued it with my standard skill combo. I could feel the death energy humming inside, though it was nowhere near full. I had no interest in burning my strongest shot early, so I'd charge it up more before I dropped the hammer, so to speak.

Valk intercepted a trio of fighters alongside Perit, and seeing those two actually fight in conjunction was kind of terrifying. And finally, Celine and Benny were backing up Mel, the three of them fighting a pair of big fighters who looked like brothers, leaving me with two fighters of my own to handle.

The two I needed to fight were distracted, not having focused on me yet as they reacted to the mass attack. I triggered double trouble, bringing my Stygian branch up and around in a whirling smash aimed at the taller of the two's head.

Rather than block, which I could have phased through with my weapon, the tall man dropped boneless, the staff flying over his head as he hit his hands in pushup position, then kicked up his long legs in a whirling attack aimed at my neck.

With State of Grace still active, it was easy to slide aside, triggering Moonlit Night in the surrounding area. The fog filled the space around us, completely translucent to me, but more than enough to obstruct their view as I took them both in for weaknesses.

The tall one I'd attacked was a pale man with long crooked teeth and stringy hair. The other one, who was circling around us, was a dark-skinned girl with long wavy hair and big hazel eyes. She *also* had a really disturbing smile on her face, and her fingers appeared to be literal knives, at least at the moment.

She dove in for an attack, and I whirled my staff into position, grinning internally as her claws sparked off one of the metal endcaps and I felt the thrum of life force entering the storm of converted power inside the staff.

It was almost unnoticeable, but I'd realized over time that the staff had been slowly adapting to me as I used it. The weight had been lessening, my grip seeming surer, and the power seemed more in tune with me. It was a powerful and dangerous weapon, and I absolutely loved how it felt as I got more and more used to it. It still wasn't light, granted, but it almost felt like it was learning to suppress its Impact most of the time, only releasing it when in combat.

My pondering was interrupted by the big guy lashing out with a pair of whips made of blood which also seemed to be on fire. It flowed in crimson rivers from his open wrists. The scarlet flames pinged my Danger Sense hard, so I knew touching them would be a bad call.

Rather than dodge normally, I planted my staff and shoved off, using the combination of force and State of Grace to soar up into the air. They continued attacking the same spot, though once they didn't land a hit, they eased up. They'd probably seen the beginning of my dodge as I activated my concealment, and they'd inferred my destination from that.

I bounced off nothing, Ripple Running still active (though that was my last step with it) and landed softly on the grass behind them. Tall guy didn't notice, but claws girl whirled and lashed out at me with her knife fingers, creating literal tears in the air that rushed toward me, even temporarily clearing small lines in the fog. They sealed themselves right after, but the girl's grin told me she'd noticed it, too.

I spent the next five minutes dodging hails of air slashes as she did her best to tear enough holes in my fog to be able to spot me, which failed because any time she tried I just jumped away. I considered closing in, but I'd triggered my overlay and saw the ways my attacks would probably fail if I went in too soon. Instead I waited, letting her tire herself out and accidentally cut up her buddy at least once, much to my amusement.

He seemed much less amused, and after the third time he lashed out with one of his whips, and she yelped as it cut into her. Eyes wide with rage, she whirled on him and lunged, and I took the chance to put her down. I used Double Trouble, arriving in the air behind her back as she dove forward, parallel to the ground. I triggered Mercy Kill, Marked for Death, and Flurry of Blows, then slammed my Stygian Branch straight down into her spine, doing my best to avoid any vital organs.

I pinned her to the ground like a butterfly on a card. She screamed, and the other guy lashed out with the whips, only for me to use Double Trouble again and appear behind him. The whips didn't hit the girl, he had way too much control, and he yanked them back once they passed through the space I should have been in.

Backing off, I kept an eye on him as he crept closer to check on his fallen teammate. She was lying on the ground, eyes wide and pained, shuddering like she was cold as her lips basically turned blue.

It took me only a minute to realize exactly why. The staff drained life force on contact, and I'd driven it into her. It had been sucking up life energy until I vanished, and while she was clearly still alive, it had obviously not been a pleasant experience. I winced in sympathy, but the roaring of deathly power in my staff had grown louder by a substantial amount.

Apparently that was a faster way to absorb the stuff. I didn't bother to use the death burst on the tall guy. He was disturbed and alone, and it only took me a few minutes to smash his elbows and knees in one at a time with hit and run tactics.

Moonlit Night made stealth attacks more deadly, and the staff was heavy and brutally powerful. It was a deadly combination. Once my battle ended, I looked around to find the others mostly done. Abel was still going, but the rest of them had already subdued their own foes. Some of the enemy had clearly run off, which was amusing, but it also meant they could come back at any moment with backup.

I let Moonlit Night drop, striding out of the dispersing fog as I stowed my staff. Above us, palms and fists crashed against a giant axe phantom, and seemed to be getting the upper hand. Expert versus Intermediate was a big gap, even if I suspected Raul had higher stats. I looked around, finding Callie leaning against a tree, wincing and holding her side. I was next to her in an instant.

"Are you okay?" I asked in a panic. Her face was pale and bloodless and her eyes were a bit hazy. I planted a hand on her shoulder and triggered a scan heal and heal burst combo. She shuddered as the energy flowed into her, and I felt the break in her ribs through the scan as I watched it mend. I sighed in relief then looked around. "Where is Jessie? Why didn't she come fix you up? Is she still fighting?"

I couldn't see my friend for a second, but that was because I expected her to have turned back. It only took a quick look to notice she had *not* done that, and was currently mauling a tree viciously while ignoring everything else. I blinked at her savage attack on the local flora for a second before realizing what had happened.

Jessie had put down her two opponents and even managed to keep herself from killing them (though she hadn't been gentle judging by the blood-stains and the two trails leading off into the mountains). She did not, however, have full control. She was battering the tree to keep from attacking anything else.

After I made sure Callie was healing (it would take some time—my heal bursts were still G-rank) I strolled over to the massive ursine form of my friend. "Jessie," I said calmly. She glared at me, snarling madly before returning to her tree murder. I sighed, slipped out my staff, and infused it with a tranq blow before slamming it down on the base of her bear skull with everything I had.

She yelped, stumbling away. Instead of whirling and trying to kill me like I'd half expected though, she started shaking her head. One shake, then two, trying to clear out... something. Finally, she fell to her haunches and threw back her head for a roar that turned into a scream of pain as she changed back. "Fuck!" she yelled at the top of her lungs as she slumped back into the snow clutching her head. "Ow, ow, ow."

I winced. Bear or not, that wouldn't have been pleasant. "Sorry," I said sympathetically. "I thought it might help."

She shook her head roughly. "It did. That was... fine. Maybe next time just punch me. How did you know that would even work?"

I just shrugged. "You looked like you were going crazy—figured being calmed down might help. Sedative and all."

"Well it did, thanks." She groaned. "My head is killing me, but at least it's not full of bear rage. Seriously. Bears are *really* angry. Not like... some kind of blood rage. Just grumpy and pissed off almost all the time. And it's not very easy to ignore. Remind me to give Randall a hug for being such a good boy."

I laughed, helping her up and walking with her over to Callie. "Cal got messed up pretty bad. I did what I could but my heals are weak. Older stuff, you know. Can you look her over?"

She smiled and nodded before kneeling next to my girlfriend. Above us, the sunlight axe shattered under a barrage of punches.

I hoped she hurried up. We needed to go before the ray went down. I didn't want another fight so soon if we could help it.

Chapter Twenty-One

WE MANAGED to get away before the others showed up, thankfully.

I was exhausted. While my staff wasn't heavy all the time anymore, it did unleash its potential when I was in combat, which was a strain. I didn't *really* mind—it was a good ache, like the kind you get post workout.

I mostly hovered over Callie, or at least as close as I could on the goats. I'd gotten a sliver of the summerspark crystal we'd bargained off Wulfric for her, and despite her annoyance at being treated like glass, she enjoyed its effects. When triggered, it created a bubble of pleasantly warm air for ten feet or so around her (which definitely wasn't at all part of why I stuck so close).

I'd been scared out of my mind when I saw her hurt earlier. It wasn't a novel experience, but seeing her like that, slumped back against a tree, was a wakeup call. I was in charge now, and being the leader added a whole new dimension to battle. Responsibility.

It was easy to put aside my worries and trust whoever was in charge, to just focus on the battle. But when anything that happens is your fault... It's brutal. I felt terrible for putting pressure like this on Callie for months without knowing.

Sensing through the bond what I was thinking, she sidled closer, reaching out to grab my hand. She winced, ribs still tender despite Jessie's boost to the healing I'd given her.

She gave me a warm smile, and I felt the love and concern from the bond as she said gently, "If you don't stop blaming yourself for my actions, I'm going to push you down the mountain." I burst out in a surprised laugh, and she grinned at me mischievously. "There he is. I was going to ask if you'd seen my boyfriend. He's a pretty upbeat guy, and the brooding self-flagellating thing isn't nearly as hot as some people claim. I prefer his particular brand of optimism."

"I don't think you can call it optimism when someone just bulls into every-thing without thinking it through," I said wryly. "I'm just trying to be a more responsible leader now that I'm in charge."

She snorted at that. "Shane, baby, you just had Abel throw you at a giant monster without warning anyone. You're not trying to be a more respon-sible *anything.* You're being an overprotective worrywart. I got hurt and it scared you. And that's okay. Do you remember how terrified I was when you got injured in the necropolis? Because I sure as hell do. And when the bond fried in the tournament. I love you, and you love me, and being scared for each other makes sense."

I groaned in frustration. "It's more than that though. I'm in charge now. You getting hurt is my fault."

"Yup," she said mercilessly. I blinked and gave her a hurt look she didn't need to see because of the bond. "What? I'm supposed to argue? Not like you would listen if I told you it wasn't. So, assuming your completely absurd claim that my own actions are your responsibility is even technically true, you could theoretically claim that you screwed up by not making a plan for engaging the enemy."

That annoyed me. "I didn't even *attack* them. Jessie did. I had only just realiz—" I trailed off at her smug look. "You know you get like... ten percent less cute when you're a know-it-all."

Her smirk turned sarcastically sweet. "Honey, I can feel your emotions. We both know that isn't true." I flipped her off and she cracked up, cutting off the laugh almost immediately with a groan as she strained her broken ribs. The amusement snapped off on my end too, replaced with concern. I reached out for a scan heal to check on her, but she batted away the hand.

"I'm fine," she wheezed. "Just hurts a ton to laugh. The feeling of my bones grinding together is... unpleasant. Worth it though, since I got my guy out of his head." She reached out to squeeze the hand she'd just batted away and I felt a rush of warmth flood through me. I adored this girl, annoying sarcasm and all.

Once she straightened up again and the pain had faded, I glanced over to where Jessie was running with the wolves. "How long do you think the healing will take? Should we look into buying something to help? Jessie's heals are damned effective, but some medicine might compound things. There are probably high F-ranked Vitality medicines with thousands of points of effectiveness. Even with her absurdly overpowered Vitality, Jessie is still new to the rank."

She shook her head, and I noticed how ginger the motion was, like she was trying not to move her torso at all. "No, it's fine. I'll be good after a night's sleep. She wrapped them for me too—that first aid Skill came in handy. I'll be fine tomorrow. Between your heal to stabilize things and her treatment there should be no problems."

I exhaled in relief. "Okay. Sorry, I'm just..." I shook it off. "So, what did you think of... that?" I gestured back at the mess we'd left behind.

"I think it worked out extremely well for us." She grimaced. "Your plan wasn't... terrible. Just not very well thought out. My main issue was you not bothering to tell us before you did it. If you're in charge you need a better communication strategy than 'hold my beer.' If we need a shorthand or something we can develop one, but impatience isn't a reason to leave the team in the lurch like that."

Rather than reassure or placate her... I thought about it. She was right. I needed to do better. I'd gotten lucky this time, but the gods forbid something happen to one of my friends, I'd feel terrible either way, but knowing I'd made a mistake and caused it would be even worse.

I was pretty surprised when Nat rode up next to me, my cousin giving me a sympathetic smile. "It's a bit overwhelming huh?" I blinked at her, cocking my head so she'd know I was confused even through the mask. "Being out on your own. I've been out and about for ages, but when I first left my home planet I was definitely pretty confused. I had a hell of a lot less people counting on me too. It's okay to be a little overwhelmed."

Blowing out a breath, I shrugged. "I get that, but it's not okay to let that feeling force me into making stupid choices, which… I kind of just did. When Callie was running things, she always found time to include us and ask what we thought. I didn't even really consider that. I just got excited because being in charge meant I could do things my way without letting anyone stop me."

"Yeah," she said comfortingly, "you're a weird guy." At my noise of offense, she just grinned. "What, it's true. Wishing is a support power. Nine out of ten candidates are hands-off back-rank types. Even the ones who go the leadership route usually play armchair general at best. Running headlong into danger isn't exactly our style. The only person in the family I can think of who fights like that is the current Wishmaster, and he cheats."

He did. I tried to imagine what that would be like, supplementing a completely separate ability with my Wish power. Maybe specialize in a specific kind of wish to boost one stat above the others. It would limit my ability to grant wishes at the same level, but I could make up for that with combat efficiency, not to mention I could still grant wishes to lower-level clientele with Impact offsetting the cost.

It made me even more interested in our trip to the Ruined Soul Temple. Getting another ability would be… amazing. Who knew what I could become with something like that. But that was a tangent, and an obvious attempt to sabotage my own self-reflection, so I forced myself to refocus. "What do you suggest I do?"

"Think," Nat said simply. "We came out here to gather information. To see what it was like in the mountains. So use it. Figure out a strategy for moving and working out here safely. Then apply that strategy. You have information, resources, and time—those are all the things you need to lead properly. That and the ability to care about your team, and you definitely have that too. You'll do fine if you just sit down and put some thought into things."

She was right. I was making this much more complicated than it needed to be. I didn't need to come up with some brilliant scheme to justify being put in charge. I just needed to go slow and steady and keep my friends as safe as possible.

"You know," I said with a smirk, "for an ally of convenience, you're pretty supportive. If I didn't know any better, I'd say you're worried about your little cousin and trying to go out of your way to make him feel better."

Shrugging, she just gave an embarrassed laugh. "You're not wrong. You're a good kid, and you seem to care a lot. I'd started to internalize the family's cutthroat mentality a bit too much I think. It's nice to have a relative who actually gives a shit and doesn't want to use me as a human shield or a patsy."

I winced at the statement. That sounded like a nightmare. Even Dad's cold rational approach to parenting was at least slightly based on my personal wellbeing.

"How long ago did you awaken your ability?" I wasn't sure if the contract Dad had sent was something usual for the WCP, but I got the impression it wasn't. Some sort of method of waking my ability early, which outside wishes I'd never heard of anyone doing.

"A few years now. Maybe half a decade. I lose track. I was like you to start, until I got in touch with some of the other family members and learned how it all works." She shrugged. "The candidates tend to accumulate over time once the competition starts. It runs ten years, giving everyone time to gather forces, and then when the time is up, they call us together for the inheritance conflict. We have some time before that, thankfully, but you'll want to make damned sure to be ready. If someone can *be* ready for something like that."

She sounded tired and afraid, and I winced sympathetically. This whole thing was so... brutal. I didn't mind some hard fights, but doing this kind of thing to your own family, just because it had worked before... Sending kids away from their parents, away from their homes, to be raised by strangers and tested through combat...

It was all awful, and if I became the Wishmaster, I was going to put a stop to that.

In fact, while finding my mom was my primary goal, that was good motivation to aim for the top. To save my family, even from itself. To make sure no one lived the life I did, or Nat did.

I felt something inside me shift slightly as my purpose became even clearer. I found my way forward, and another thing to push toward. Granted, it was a longer-term goal, but I was going to work toward it either way. I'd find my mom, ask her why she left, and then I'd save my family from its own bad choices, whether it liked it or not.

Chapter Twenty-Two

"I still can't believe we got away with ten drops of Dew," I whooped as we approached the bridge back to Ladrigan. I glanced over at Anna-Marie. "So, what's the allocation deal for these drops, five you five us, and do we get paid for the ones we turn in? Because we paid for the materials and everything, so it would only be fair for us to be compensated."

The princess laughed. "Eager, aren't you? Yes, you'll be paid for the drops —we'll need to head into the central cylinder to get your coins." She seemed to be in the same kind of giddy mood as the rest of us. After an initial period of exhaustion and reflection, the extreme danger followed by the escape had been energizing, and I wasn't the only one grinning like a loon. We'd been in trouble like this before off on our own, but being here inside the dungeon with no supervision to bail us out made it more... visceral.

I felt like I was getting emotional whiplash, going from the joy of battle, to guilt, to the glee of escape. Everything just seemed... more. More vibrant, more exciting, more important. Taking a moment, I felt myself almost buzzing with energy, and glanced at the others. "Hey, do any of you feel... weird? Like in a good way?"

Callie nodded. "Yeah, I can feel it through the bond. It isn't affecting any of the rest of us, I don't think." She smirked at me. "It stopped your pouting, so I consider it a net gain."

I muttered a nonsensical comment about catching *her* in a net, but she graciously ignored it as I turned a questioning gaze on Anna-Marie. The Naiad princess looked lost for a second, then her eyes widened. "Oh! It was the lunar event. You passed through the cloud. Must have been dense enough to absorb into your skin. It can take time to hit you. I've heard rumors there are some vintages of wine infused with that effect—they're supposed to be lovely."

That sounded delicious, albeit even more expensive than the insane drink Abel had tried to con me into buying for us back in Doomtown.

Nat rode up next to me, leaning in to mutter, "You might want to be careful wandering around semi-intoxicated like that. Easy to make mistakes or deals you shouldn't."

When we reached the bridge, a pair of men in thick black suits of armor stopped us, crossing their spears to block the way. "Halt," they said, somehow not snickering at the cliche. "State your business."

Anna-Marie glared. "My business is none of yours. Unless bridge guards are suddenly of a standing with members of the royal family? Or do you suspect that the fact one of my brothers paid you to harass me will protect you from my father's vengeance should he hear of your disrespect to crown and country?"

They visibly flinched, stepping back quickly and lowering both their spears and heads. Hopping down, Anna-Marie handed the reins of her goat to the closest guard and gestured us to do the same. "I'll consider you stabling these for us as recompense for being so presumptuous. Should they not make it to their destination, I may forget to be magnanimous. I suspect this bridge would be as well served with your heads on those spears as warnings to incompetents such as yourselves."

Apologizing profusely, they grabbed the reins and took the goats, running off toward a well-hidden shack in the distance. She shook her head. "Idiots. Involving themselves in politics out of greed. My brothers don't care if a few guards get beheaded. Sadly for them, I won't be passively bullied anymore."

I raised a brow. "You'd really have them beheaded for getting in your way?"

She shook her head. "No. Not unless it was a repeated offense. But they don't need to know that. My father would kill them for it if he found out, though. Respect for the royal family is a paramount value in Ladrigan. To disrespect a royal is to disrespect the blood, which is disrespecting the king himself. Not that it stops us from harassing each other, but it means games like this need to be subtle."

Celine made an understanding sound from her place on the other side of Benny. "Ah. Being at the bottom of the barrel made you easy pickings before. Now that you have, or are at least going to have, access to the drops, you're in a position to actually enact punishment going forward and need to start acting the part."

Our guide nodded as she led us further down the bridge. "Indeed. It is important to know one's place. Premature retaliation would have signaled my readiness to enter the political arena, which I was very much not. With this kind of head start though, I'll be more than capable of holding my own, as well as passing some of the drops to important loved ones who support me like my mother."

I was about to ask if a point of Impact made that much of a difference, but considering a single point made you an Ascendant I was willing to believe it. Plus, if things went well this would just be the start. Before we went out looking for trouble, though, I was going to get us paid and look into any protection we could buy, beg, or hire.

When we reached the doors back into the bulwark, we received no further trouble, though the trip back down took much longer, as we had to carefully navigate the traps from the enemy side, making stops to give passwords, take back passages, or request admittance.

Finally, we got through the bulwark and back into the ringed part of the castle, which made things much easier. To my surprise, once we hit the rings, Anna-Marie brought us a different route, using a series of secret passages to bring us through without having to scale up and down. I couldn't help but ask. "Why didn't we take this route last time? Wouldn't that have been faster?"

She just chuckled. "Yes, but these passages only take you *to* the cylinder. They can be sealed in an emergency, and automatically shut down completely when the bulwark collapses, but since you can't use them to *leave* the cylinder, they can't be used to reach the bulwark."

I wondered why they would set it up like that, but figured it was probably some inane reason I wouldn't care about, so I refocused on our entry into 'the cylinder.' Stepping through the final passage, we entered a short hallway with guarded doors. I could see a ton of defenses here, just in case, but it was still nicer than most of what I'd seen. Anna-Marie waved off the guards, and they opened the doors for us, allowing us to enter... a whole new world.

The cylinder ran through the entire mountain, and as such was huge. Based on the dimensions I was betting it was spatially enlarged, because I could see miles and miles of space inside the thing that didn't match up with it being the smallest area in the mountain.

I had to try hard not to stare. I'd seen plenty of things as an Ascendant, and they all had their own special kind of impressiveness, but the huge underground city was a new kind of amazing. Above us floated a glowing blue orb, close enough to white not to tint the light, and large enough to cast the whole cavern in what seemed like natural moonlight.

Silver trees festooned the entire area, and I could see skyways crisscrossing the distance in seemingly impossible ways, somehow holding up islands of stone in the air without supports, though all small enough not to really impede the view given they were spread out and at different heights. There was dark grass beneath our feet as we walked in, and I saw foliage and shrubbery along the neat path leading toward the ground level city.

"This," she said proudly, "is the cylinder. Most of the important people in the kingdom live here. We even have weather systems set up to water the plants and filter the dirt. The cylinder's interior is fifty miles across, though I know it can be hard to judge scale from so far away. It's a bit of a hike to reach the city, which is much bigger than it looks. Shouldn't be too much trouble for an F-ranker though."

That was fair. At top speed I could run seventy-five hundred miles per hour at this point. Well, on a normal planet. This one was huge and had much heavier gravity so it was probably less. Still, even at a brisk walk it wouldn't be hard to get there relatively quickly.

I held up a hand, stopping everyone. "Wait," I said. "I'm interested in heading in there, but I don't want to go at a disadvantage. We have an arrangement for half the drops, and I'd like to distribute them now. Will we get much effect from the first one?"

She nodded. "You will. First drop will give you a point. You'll need three drops for a second, and it pretty much doubles from there." I was appalled at exactly how many drops of Moonglow Dew the king must have used. He'd gotten himself about eight points. Knowing how rare the stuff was outside awakenings… it was terrifying.

"Alright," I said firmly. "Then we distribute it now. I want us at our strongest when we go in. Which means our strongest get first dibs. Callie, me, Abel, Nat, and Valk." I gave Mel a shrug. "If I had a sixth it would go to you, but I think this maximizes our capabilities. With Nat and I both getting one it'll make our abilities more useful, and Callie's recon abilities will be key out here where we don't know anyone."

Mel chuckled softly. "I get it. Just like I'm sure Agria and Clockwork do. It's not a bad lineup. But I want first dibs on the next round."

"Deal," I said with a grin. Pulling the others off the path, we headed into the silver trees, finding a clearing before I reached into the ring and removed the drops. I left the flowers in, bringing the Dew out on its own, but to my relief, that was fine. It just floated above my palm like some kind of mercurial star.

The Dew itself was… confusing. Silver mercurial liquid, shifting constantly and reflecting scenes of infinite possibilities from within. I passed the first over to Nat, then Callie, then Abel, then Valk. I'd gone out of my way to make sure to give them some of the first drops, because I wanted the team more cohesive, and because coming here had been mainly their idea. I could tell they were happy to receive them, especially Nat who looked like she was having ten birthdays all at once.

When we all had ours, I took a deep breath, and the mask slid away from the bottom of my face like it would when I ate. I popped the thing into my mouth like some kind of liquid pill and swallowed hard as the explosion of indescribable sensation washed over my tongue and plummeted into my throat like a waterfall of living lightning.

As the power exploded behind my eyes, it occurred to me it might have been a better plan to go back to our rooms for this. Oh well, live and learn.

Chapter Twenty-Three

THE FEELING of having your impact rise naturally through rank up was odd and hard to describe. It was interesting, and even notable, but it wasn't exceptionally dramatic in the grand scheme of things. It was something people were designed to do, a natural part of our evolution, and you had the stat points to act as a foundation for the Impact. It was like building a tower. You had a level of stats, then Impact to act as support for the next section.

Having Impact added independent of that was much more intense. The lightning storm coursing down my throat spread like wildfire, singing through my veins and out into my muscles. My body felt like arid ground, hungrily consuming the energy as it spilled out, rolling through me and somehow filling every individual cell. I could feel the change to every single atom of my body, but not consecutively. All at once, like I was a million people at the same time, each completely perceiving a change to a single cell.

My cells were singing to each other, belting out operatic harmonies as they ascended to a greater state, to a higher plane of existence, and carried my million brains along with them. I couldn't tell if I was screaming, or crying, or if I'd never make a sound again. I was in unbearable agony and suffused with the most exquisite bliss I'd ever felt, both hollow and empty and so full I was about to explode.

And then it was over, and I was just me. Just standing around as a single person, heart pounding, body coated with sweat, muscles twitching as I fell against a tree, wheezing and panting.

"That," I gasped breathlessly, "was so fucking weird. Gods, is it like that every time? I… don't even know how to describe that. Did I hate it? Did I love it? My brain hurts."

Callie groaned from next to me. "Yeah, I was getting some of that through the bond. I think it was worse because we were sharing it. I was getting the highs as well as the lows simultaneously because we were alternating."

I paused, thinking it over. "That might have been happening to me too. It was so hard to tell, everything was confusing the shit out of me." I cocked my head at her. "You doing okay? I'm starting to settle down I think. Or maybe I'll never settle down again? I can't tell if I'm wired or exhausted."

She let out a bark of laughter. "I feel that." She looked at my cousin, Abel, and Valk. "How about you guys? You feeling alright?"

Abel shrugged. "That was weird, but I've had worse. I'll be fine in a minute, just need to get my head on straight."

Nat shuddered. "I'm less sanguine about the whole thing. I can't really say it was awful. But also I can. It was definitely the best worst experience of my life, as little sense as that probably makes."

Valk stood to his full height from where he'd been hunched against the dark bark of a silver tree. "I feel like a wrung-out toothpaste tube made of chewing gum stretched between the two ends of a sporting field," he croaked hoarsely.

"That!" Nat exclaimed. "That's exactly how it feels. Like… to a T." Weighing the words, I nodded, as did Callie. He was right. Like I was empty and stretched in a weird way that I couldn't exactly put my finger on.

Anna-Marie looked interested. "That's fascinating. I suspect I'll want to space out my consumption in that case. Who knows what multiple drops at once would do to a person. Do you feel well enough to continue?" The princess had been watching us like a hawk since I'd mentioned what I was going to do. Her eyes were wide and focused, desperately trying not to miss anything.

If I had to guess, the king wasn't the kind of guy to do something as risky as dropping Moonglow Dew in front of his kids, or pretty much anyone barring his most trusted guards. This was probably her first time seeing the process up close, and given how big a part of her life it was going to be, I was guessing she wanted to know as much about it as possible. She wanted every detail before her first drop, though I was skeptical we'd been helpful with our descriptions.

"Jessie," I said, "how about you hit us with a little pick-me-up?" My teammate had been a bit quiet since her time as a bear, but not upset exactly. She seemed pensive, and at the sound of her name her eyes jerked up to me. She shook off her thoughts and nodded.

"Sure. I can do that." She sounded as chipper as ever, so I wasn't too worried. I was sure she'd talk to us when she was feeling up to it. She stepped forward, her hand on me as she flooded me with green lifegiving energy. I felt my body fill with power and vitality, and it synergized well with the wired feeling the drop had left, leaving me bursting with energy.

She did Callie next, then Nat, then Abel, and Valk last. The big bearded man looked a bit more jittery than the rest of us, so I think she wanted to give him extra time to settle before she shoved a live wire into his brain, so to speak. Once that was done, she smiled widely at all of us, stepping back to lean against Lily, her wolf, as the other puppies surrounded her. Energizing all of us had taken it out of her, and I could see the sweat on her brow, but she'd be at the back with us all surrounding her so I wasn't worried.

I bounced in place a bit, letting the energy flow through me. I felt amazing. Not just vital, but... more. The recovery and the extra Impact really were a hell of a combination.

"I think we're good to go." I glanced down at Jin. "Take care of her, will you? You and the others." My wolf gave me a deadpan look and a sniff of disdain, as if telling me not to make stupid unnecessary comments. I got no respect.

The puppies circled up around Lily, making a triangle formation as Jessie rode on her wolf's back. Oddly, they seemed more... maybe not intelligent, but more aware. I suspected Jessie's rank up had allowed her power to boost them in a less restrictive way.

We headed back out to the path, following it along to the city. There was a huge black stone wall around the perimeter of the place that I hadn't been able to see from further away. There was an iron gate cutting the path off from entry, and two guards stood waiting there for us to approach.

To my surprise, Anna-Marie didn't just wave them aside, stepping up and pulling out a cerulean token carved from some kind of gemstone. "We seek entry into the Spiral Grove." I could literally hear the capital letters on those last two words. The guards took the token and there was a surge of energy that caused it to light up. A pattern shone on the dark wall, and the guards stared at the patterns for a minute before nodding and stepping back to allow us entry.

As we walked in, I couldn't help but comment on the token. "What is that? Some kind of light key or something?"

Anna-Marie smiled. "Royal seal. Every member of the bloodline gets them. They're made of a special type of living crystal that shifts randomly over time. The guards here and in the royal chambers have samples of the crystal that shifts in the same randomized pattern. Anyone outside the bloodline has to go through a careful vetting process when entering or leaving the Spiral Grove."

"That's awesome," I said appreciatively. "Probably the best security system I can imagine. I guess they check the patterns daily to make sure they know what each seal is supposed to look like?" She nodded in amusement and I put a pin in the idea for later. Might be a neat idea for my own faction later down the line.

"So, I take it this is the Spiral Grove?" I said, waving around at the massive city we'd only just entered. Buildings filled the area, some on the ground, some in trees with walkways between them. I could see some of the walk-ways leading up to the islands in the air I'd seen before, too thin to have been visible at a distance.

She grinned. "The heart of the capital. All our highest-ranking officers, nobles, and even foreign dignitaries hang their hats here." She closed her eyes and took a deep breath of the clean, fresh air. "One of my favorite places in the world."

I could see genuine fondness on her face as she opened her eyes again. It was strange to see the dichotomy of how much she cared about her country and how little she seemed to care about the people. The idea of Ladrigan (the places, the construction, the culture) seemed almost sacred to her. But the citizens were almost an afterthought, like they just got in the way of all the things she loved. Like they were just unpleasant additions to the kingdom itself.

As we strolled down the main street from the gates though, I couldn't say I didn't understand at least the first part. While the rest of the castle was utilitarian and brutal, the buildings down here were beautiful. Carved stone etched with bas relief scenes of ancient battles and heroic deeds, all set in the forest and inset with silver to give it depth and impact.

It was beautiful, and I couldn't help but notice that the Spiral Grove, hell the cylinder in general, was almost a mirror image of the rest of the castle. It was like they took all the beauty they were forced to forgo elsewhere and shoved it all in here so they could enjoy it in private. She walked us along the path, showing us buildings and sculptures and parks that were a feast for the eyes.

Finally we came to one large but fairly squat building with massive silver doors. Anna-Marie strode up to it and shoved the doors open, leading us into a huge marble foyer with a large desk on the opposite end. The desk had windows along it, and the whole thing was heavily reinforced. A bank.

Strolling up to the bank window she withdrew her seal and slipped it into a gap in the window. "I'd like to withdraw ten hundred-coin markers. Infused, not blank." She turned to me. "I'm offering two hundred heart-stone coins per drop, along with future considerations. The infused coins are worth more, obviously, and a thousand is plenty for the deal we've made so far."

I glanced to Celine, who nodded. She'd been looking into the economy here during her downtime, while we'd been working on trade deals and such. The banker nodded, passing over a dark wooden case. The princess opened the case to find a series of long thin tokens made of dark stone with red glowing cracks running through it. "Each of those can be traded for one hundred infused coins. Just bring them to the bank to trade them in, or spend them as is."

That worked for me. Carrying a thousand coins would be substantially more trouble, and since we'd probably be spending in bulk the markers would do for now, plus we could always swap if we needed to. Once I received the markers, she gave me a wide grin. "Now. You can hand over the drops and then I'll take you somewhere to eat before you start shopping for the longer trip."

I chuckled at the forwardness, but didn't disagree. That sounded like a plan.

Chapter Twenty-Four

I GROANED in enjoyment as the stroganoff hit my tongue. "This is amazing." We were at dinner with Anna-Marie, and Callie and I were sharing a local dish called Plazkish. Which was stroganoff. Like... almost exactly. It was also amazing, with fresh juicy mushrooms, smooth hand-made pasta, and a delicious creamy sauce so well-made it felt like the noodles were almost slithering down my throat without me needing to do anything. They weren't doing that, obviously, because that would be horri-fying, but they were so easy to eat they almost gave that impression.

Callie was just as enamored with the dish, and moaned her agreement as she slurped her own noodles, neither of us caring that the others were staring at us. Well, some of the others. Abel, Mel, Jessie, and Benny had all eaten with us before so they didn't much care.

Looking up at the horrified and fascinated face of the princess I swallowed and cleared my throat. "Sorry. I'm weirdly hungry after gaining that extra point of Impact. Did you say something?"

She giggled a bit at that, and Callie finished her own bite and washed it down with a sip of wine, looking embarrassed. "I said," repeated the princess, "that I was wondering exactly what you're looking for in terms of preparations for the next trip. We're going to be staying out much longer next time. Did you get a good grasp on what we'll need for a journey deeper into the core?"

I nodded thoughtfully. "We still have the herbs to sell, so that should get us a bit more money through sheer volume. What we can get depends on how much we earn, but I have a few things in mind. First is shelter. I'm hoping to pick up some portable housing. Maybe tents at worst, though I'm hoping for something a bit sturdier."

That got a beaming smile. "That sounds like a wonderful idea. I'll most likely acquire some lodgings of my own. Accompany me shopping and I'll make sure the owner knows you're good friends of mine and to treat you with respect."

Giving her a grateful nod, I smiled internally. I figured she'd do that. Part of the future considerations she mentioned. If possible, I wanted to find some kind of portable cabin or bunker, specifically one that had defensive enchantments on it. A portable and stable home base was invaluable, the latter having been made clear during the scavenger hunt.

Sadly, an invented building wasn't likely to be viable in this instance. Too likely to end up in enemy hands.

Nat took a sip of her chowder, nodding along. "My suggestion would also be to buy some sort of mapping item. Something to show us where we've been and where we're going." She raised an eyebrow at Anna-Marie. "Do you know if they have anything like that in town?"

"Of course!" the princess said brightly. "That's a wonderful idea. Returning home would be so much simpler with a nice map to rely on."

I agreed. "As well as having some sort of emergency defensive measure. Some kind of portable shield spell we can trigger. I'm curious, are there any E-rank items in here? I mean, I know people can bring them in. I... saw some people wielding them." I decided not to mention my own E-rank weapon. It seemed like information they didn't need, especially since it was suppressed most of the time. Maybe they'd noticed it in battle, but no reason to help them along.

Anna-Marie nodded gravely. "There are, but they're in the treasuries. E-ranked items are considered national treasures, and they can only be redeemed for extreme merit. Even that only happens at wartime usually. We have powerful spells made by those with higher than standard Impact though, and we usually call them half step E-rank. No one like my father, of course, but some powerful crafters can trade for or gather god Dew like the royals do."

"They don't just take it?" Callie asked in surprise. Which made sense given how closely they controlled the stuff.

"Well, sometimes," admitted the princess. "Not all of it though. It's a similar setup to yourselves. If they seized it all, the finders might hoard it and never let anyone know what they'd found. By rewarding them a share it makes them more likely to come forward. Usually not half, usually more along the lines of a third. But still, it's a tempting reward. Mixed with the fact that it's detectable when you use the Dew, it's common practice to come volunteer your supply."

Celine looked dubious. "Isn't that just forcing them though? Since you can tell when it's used, what possible way would there be of keeping it secret?"

"Defection," Anna-Marie said flatly. "Before it became common practice to share it, people who found a stock of god Dew would defect to other kingdoms. They would use it all up before arriving. Since the Dew can't be retrieved once used, the other kingdoms had the option of turning away a perfectly good Ascendant with higher-than-normal Impact, killing them out of spite, or letting them stay."

I nodded in understanding. "And since any powerful fighter for their side would be a benefit, they had no problems taking them in. I can see why you would do things the way you do. Anyway, I'd love to see some crafting from some of those half step E-rankers. A stronger defense can only be a benefit, and maybe we can find some other spells to suit us."

She gave a cheery nod. "Of course. Giancarlo Spirella was going to be my first stop in any case. He's the most well-respected crafter in Ladrigan. Some people claim he's already a Master." Which was interesting, because it meant Master Candidates existed here. Though I didn't know what you'd call one that had already reached mastery. Still, it was useful information, especially about a crafter.

Wolfing down my food, I got prepared to leave as the others finished, and once everyone was done I gestured for Anna-Marie to go ahead. "Lead the way to this Giancarlo guy." I paused. "Wait, can he buy the herbs?"

She nodded. "He buys basically everything. He's an enchanter but he does some work Inventing as well."

I shot Benny a look. My best friend looked intrigued. I knew he was always looking to make new gear.

Leading us out of the bistro, Anna-Marie walked us back onto the main thoroughfare. "Giancarlo's studio is in the oldest district in the city. He's got one of the treehouses, and there's no ground access." She led us to a seemingly innocuous if huge silver tree, knocking on the black bark in a specific spot and smiling widely as the trunk slid open to reveal a too-large shaft with a spiral staircase.

As we climbed, I was forced to marvel at how integrated the city was. So many different moving parts all working in harmony. This setup must have been incredibly difficult to put in place. Between the external defenses, the cylinder, the islands, the trees, and all the walkways, Ladrigan was a complicated ecosystem.

When we reached the top, we stepped out onto one of the walkways, which seemed to have much more room than one would expect based on the ground view. I wasn't sure if that space was more spatial manipulation or if it was just the angle and distance, but seeing the city from up here made it even more striking. Sparkling gems of light polka-dotted a sea of silver leaves, with buildings peeking from behind the cover.

She led us in a seemingly random direction as she smiled happily around us. "Most of the popular shops are up here. Ground level tends to be reserved for residential places. There are so many trees around that there's always room for another building in one if needed. Houses on the ground level get exceedingly difficult to acquire as you move inward. The central district of the Grove is the oldest, and where we're headed."

It was hard to keep track of things like directionality when surrounded by nearly identical foliage, but when she mentioned that I did kind of notice we were heading inward. It didn't take us long to reach the interior, and once we did the foliage started to thin, revealing more treehouses grouped close together and creating almost a second city above the tree line.

We stopped at an extremely intricate house made of white wood, seasoned with age but still extremely sturdy looking. The wood presented a strong contrast to the bark of the tree, though it blended well with the silver leaves. Anna-Marie strolled up to the front door and knocked politely, waiting for a minute before a polished older man in a crisp suit opened the door looking politely disinterested.

When he saw the princess, his expression got a lot more polite and a lot less disinterested. "Your grace," he said with a bow of his head. "An honor to see you. Please, come inside." He stepped back, gesturing us in, and Anna-Marie gave him a winning smile.

"Thank you, Humphrey," she said sunnily. "It's wonderful to be back, and I brought some new friends. I assume Gio is around?"

He nodded. "You've come at the perfect time. Miss Zelda was sick today, so Master Giancarlo arrived late. Lady Sandra was otherwise engaged, but she was able to relieve him just an hour ago."

Her sunny demeanor dimmed. "Oh. I do hope Zelda feels better." Glancing at us, she clarified. "Zelda is Giancarlo's daughter, she's twelve. His wife, Sandra, is a healer at the local hospital, so Zelda is in good hands. Zelda is a lovely young lady. Her curiosity and intelligence always brighten my visits."

Humphrey smiled softly. "Which is why you are his favorite customer. So often they simply ignore or dismiss her. You always make time to talk to Miss Zelda."

"Yes," rasped a high-pitched voice, clearly rough with disuse. "She does at that." We turned to see a tall, tan man with wild brown hair sticking out in all directions. He gave us a wild smile, eyes wider than a normal person's. "Anna dear. Lovely to get a visit from my most loyal customer. And you've brought friends. What can I help you with today?"

The sunshine was back on Anna-Marie's face. "Gio. It's good to see you. My friends and I are actually here for a few things. We have herbs to sell, and then we were hoping to look into defensive spells. Something powerful and portable."

It was impossible to miss that the man was radiating the same kind of Impact I'd sensed from the king. Perhaps not quite as much, but he was head and shoulders above all of us.

"Well then," he cackled excitedly. "I suppose I'll need to break out my best." He turned, gesturing us back through the door he'd come through. "Please, follow me. I'll take a look at what you have, and we can find the best fit for all of you for your magical needs."

Looking at Nat and Callie uncertainly, I shrugged. At least she hadn't brought us somewhere boring. I had a good feeling about finding what we needed.

Chapter Twenty-Five

THE ROOM GIANCARLO came out of was... weird. Which was to be expected, he was a powerful Enchanter and Inventor. But still, even expecting it, the massive variety of random objects in jars and bottles lining the walls was surprising. Boxes full of materials were stacked at the base of the shelves, with metals and wood stuffing them and carelessly written names scrawled on stickers slapped across their sides.

"Oh! You've cleaned recently!" Anna-Marie said in delight. We all turned to gape at her as we looked back around. The place was nominally organized I guessed, but it was packed so full of random nonsense that it wasn't possible to apply any adjective to the place except 'cluttered.' "We brought you quite a few interesting herbs and flowers—we'd love to hear what you have to offer. Solomon, if you could set them on the counter?"

She gestured to a flat countertop, probably the only non floor space clear enough to see more than a foot of. Shrugging, I waved a hand over the counter, swiping my spatial ring with a thumb to access it and dump all the herbs out onto the surface. I blinked as I did, not having quite realized how absurd the number of herbs we collected was. There was a huge variety of color, shape, texture, attribute, and any other measurable quality you could name.

Giancarlo had somehow appeared behind the counter, which was a neat trick since I hadn't seen him move. He nodded sagely, reaching behind the counter and pulling out a complicated set of goggles. They were made of pure gold and had about a dozen lenses made of what looked like ruby, sapphire, emerald, and other precious gems set along its side, each on levers that allowed him to swap them in and out, whether individually or stacked in groups.

He flipped through the settings, looking at the herbs through various lenses and combinations thereof, making humming noises and interested sounds as he picked up, fondled, licked, sniffed, and in one notable case, bit the herbs. Eventually he slipped the goggles off and looked up at us impassively. "A hundred coins for the lot. I have a marker on hand. Can't do any higher."

I saw Celine open her mouth, but Anna-Marie cut her off. "Of course Gio. I know you don't haggle, and that's a more than perfectly fair price. Thank you for your generosity." She didn't emphasize the words or say it with deep and meaningful tones. She didn't have to. It was clear she'd just saved us from possibly alienating the old man.

Nodding my head, I gestured that I accepted, and he swept them off the counter into a box, passing over one of the black stone markers with the red energy cracks. I smiled at him, not that he could see. "I'm looking for defensive enchantments. Something portable probably, and maybe some sort of portable shelter if you have anything like that. Let's start with defenses though—we can pick the shelter based on what those will cover."

He grinned at me. "Smart boy. Too many try to do it the other way. Picking your defenses to suit your home means you only get what works best with that home. If you do it the other way you can pay for the best. You might end up a bit less comfortable, but you'll also end up much less dead."

I laughed. "That's the idea anyway. Do you have any mobile defensive spells?"

He just scoffed and reached under the counter again, withdrawing a crystal orb made of what looked like a thousand chips of slightly different diamond, each with a unique rune on it. "This one is popular. Sovereign's Sanction. Creates a powerful defensive bubble. Useful but not mobile, and once deployed nothing enters or leaves until it runs out. Good for bunkering down to wait for backup."

I took it from him, weighing it in my hands. I was fascinated, but it wasn't what we were looking for exactly. "The mobility is a big thing for us. Unbreakable defense is great, but we don't really have backup, at least not reliably. You got anything that moves with you?"

Nodding, he pulled out a bracelet. "Abjuring Ring. When activated it creates a circle of protection around you that keeps out enemies. Moves with the wearer, and works well for setting up temporary camps. Sadly it only works on actual beings, not attacks, and it's not foolproof. Ranged assaults aren't covered and the strong-willed can force their way past it, though it takes active effort to maintain position, so they're weakened inside."

That one was more interesting. "I like it. Put that one aside for possible purchase. What's your most powerful defense? Not popular—you showed me that. What's the most unbreakable spell you have on hand?"

He sucked his teeth. "You don't mess around, do you boy?" Reaching down, he pulled out a box made of old worn wood. Reaching into his shirt he pulled out a key and put it into one of the locks on the box, pulling another from under the counter where it appeared to be literally chained down. He turned both and opened the box, revealing a large, glimmering ruby pendant the size of a baby's fist. It practically radiated malice and death.

"Blood War Pendant," he said solemnly. "Half step E-rank. It creates a field of blood shades, manifestations of those killed by the attackers, the defenders, anyone inside the circle. The shades reform endlessly, and are always at the rank they occupied when killed. Only way to stop it is to wait it out or break the pendant, and anyone who dies inside the circle becomes part of the spell. It's a bit situational, but it's damned powerful in the right hands. It costs four marks. Because I'd be a fool to sell it for less than four hundred infused heart coins."

I weighed the possibilities with the item. It wasn't perfect, if only because most of us were going to be spawning G-ranked blood shades. Still, there would be a decent amount of F-rankers from Abel I was pretty sure, not to mention any incoming attackers most likely. Even if not, an army of G-rankers that couldn't die would be useful.

Four marks was a decent chunk of our money, but I could see how that would help immensely. "How mobile is the pendant? I assume the circle of effect moves with us, otherwise why make it a pendant?"

He nodded solemnly. "It works for an hour a day, and it can move. It's shockingly effective, even for those who aren't too steeped in blood." He nodded to Abel. "I don't think that will be a problem for your group."

Setting a mark down on the counter, I flipped open the box and laid three next to it. "Apollyon, you'll wear this one." I gestured for him to take the pendant.

He raised an eyebrow at me. "Okay, I can guarantee I have nothing that goes with that."

Mel rolled her eyes. "I'll wear it." She pushed her hair back. "Between the link and our proximity, not to mention our long partnership meaning I'm almost as blood drenched as him, it should be fine, right?"

I shrugged. She wasn't wrong, plus now that I looked the Ruby pendant actually *did* go with her mask. "Fine whatever." I turned back to Giancarlo. "Any other impressive bits of enchanting?"

Staring at me for a minute, he sighed and pulled out another box, this one made of bone. Flipping it open, he handed me a finger bone suspended in amber. "Bone wall. Single use and not mobile, but a huge interlinked wall of F-rank bones is a hell of a defense to pop instantly."

Another ruby, this one brighter and mounted in a ring, came out of the space beneath the counter. "This one is a flame ward. Basically a mobile wall of fire. Not perfect since you can go over or under it, or even push through if you resist fire."

I mulled over the options. "Okay. If we did the Bone Wall, Flame Ward, and an Abjuring Ring, what would our best bet be for lodging, and can we get a deal for the lot?"

His eyes narrowed, but he didn't reject the request exactly, weighing his options. "Landrock Bunker would be the easiest to defend. Bit of setup time when you move it, since it reinforces itself with natural stone. Still, I could do... ten marks for the lot. Including the Blood War Pendant. Take it or leave it."

Three defensive items, the bunker and the Blood War Pendant, which was four on its own, seemed like a solid buy. Based on what Anna-Marie had said before I resolutely nodded, and he grinned. "Smart boy. And since I like you and you're bringing my Anna along, I'll even throw in one of these."

He tossed us the Sovereign's Sanction, his most popular defense. "Wow," I said in surprise. "Thank you. We appreciate that. What exactly are the specs on that, if it's alright to ask?"

He just chuckled. "Don't be daft boy. Never be afraid to ask what you're getting. Every one of those chips came from a different type of F-ranked diamond. The Sanction erects a spherical barrier with the durability of all one thousand combined."

I whistled at that. No wonder it was popular even though it didn't move. That was some serious defense, and if we had actual backup it would be amazing. Even without it though, I wasn't going to complain about free defense. If nothing else we could use it to recover energy during a huge fight.

Stowing it all in the spatial ring (except the Blood War Pendant and Flame Ward which we gave to Mel) I looked to the last item on the pile. The Landrock Bunker. "Any chance you could give us more info on how it works? Just so we can make sure to pick the best possible location when we use it."

Giancarlo chuckled. "Of course. It's not complex. Stab the rock focus of the bunker"—he pointed at the sharp spike of stone on the counter—"into the earth, and it begins to grow. It leeches the durability from the surrounding rock and when you pull out the spike it slowly drains out over time. My only advice is to find a place with lots of exposed stone. It will spread furthest that way."

That did seem easy. "How big is it on the outside? Most buildings this level are expanded inside."

"True," he said with a smile. "The bunker is a twenty-five-foot square. The defensive enchantments built in are uniform, but if you want to take best advantage of all of those defensive spells, I'd personally suggest somewhere with a backdrop. Against a cliff wall or some such location. It will enable you to make the most of the bone wall."

Slipping the last mark into my ring, I thanked him, packing up everything we bought. "One more thing," I said intently. "We were hoping to buy a map, something auto updating, and if you can give me some advice, what's the one thing you suggest any adventurer take on a long journey?"

He reached under the counter and pulled out two things. One of them was a rolled piece of paper, and the other was a canteen.

"Water," he answered. "Clean drinking water. You would think with the snow around it would be plentiful, but it isn't always. The canteen refills passively and will last centuries. I'll take ten coins for both. Consider it a discount for asking a wise question."

I passed him the last mark, and he returned me a bag with ninety infused heart coins. With that done, we headed out. We'd be staying at Anna-Marie's manor for the night. Tomorrow we'd set off again.

Chapter Twenty-Six

We slept at Anna-Marie's manor in Spiral Grove. We actually met her mother, Salara, a full Naiad who strongly resembled her daughter. Where Anna-Marie had a blue tinge that reminded me a bit of blue lips from cold or lack of air, her mother was a deeper cerulean, and all the more beautiful for it. Her features were aristocratic and incredibly delicate, like she'd been hand-sculpted by a master glass blower, but a single touch would shatter her.

Of course, that was ridiculous. She was a peak F-ranker, and a dangerous and powerful Ascendant. Anna-Marie had waxed on for ages over dinner about her mother's accomplishments in battle, and it was easy to see how proud the princess was of her mother.

"So," began Salara, "tell me about yourselves. My daughter so rarely brings home friends for dinner." Her wide smile managed to occlude the razor-sharp teeth her daughter inherited, seeming warm and supportive rather than intimidating or challenging.

She had the same shining blue eyes as Anna-Marie, those metallic blue orbs with no iris or pupil. Oddly, hers seemed more ethereal, less solidly colored. It was fascinating, and I had to tear my eyes away from them so I didn't get lost in their depths.

I left Celine to answer, and our diplomat fielded the question with aplomb. "We've been so grateful for her assistance since we arrived. Your lovely kingdom is so novel for us, it was lucky we met such a generous and knowledgeable guide."

I blinked at that. I couldn't imagine a less revealing answer. She'd essentially just said literally nothing at all except things Salara already knew.

The Naiad's blue lips quirked up in something more akin to a smirk than a smile. "You are just the cutest thing. But unlike my tree-dwelling cousins I'm not one for politicking. I tend to say what I mean, and if people have a problem with it, we... address the situation in an up-front and direct manner." She winked at Celine. "See, I can be diplomatic too."

Anna-Marie groaned, burying her face in her hands. "Mother. Can't you ever play nice?" Even when she was embarrassed, I could hear the note of pride in her voice. No wonder she detached herself from the locals so much. She was trying to emulate her mother, but the duties of her royal blood pushed her to at least consider the country itself important. "Please forgive her," she said apologetically. "My mother is known to be forward. It's one of the reasons my father was drawn to her."

She snorted. "I assure you Crighton was drawn to much less nebulous aspects of my person." Another wink. "But my forthright nature has kept him at least occasionally entertained as well. My personal power doesn't hurt. The two of us are a dangerous pair when operating in tandem."

I was surprised she didn't have any extra Impact herself, but it seemed rude to bring it up. Plus it wasn't my business who Anna-Marie gave her drops to, since I'd already been paid. Her statement made me curious though. "Are you? Anna-Marie mentioned her inborn gifts don't lie in that direction."

Salara nodded solemnly. "Quite right. My girl has an aptitude for the subtler arts of the waves. Healing is her strong suit, along with some fairly impressive alteration abilities. Naiads are expert shapeshifters, not just of ourselves, but of others as well. Anna-Marie inherited that talent and can make anyone look like almost anything."

That was... interesting. The princess shrugged. "It's not a useless talent, per se, but it's hardly necessary in my daily life. I can't even shift myself, only other people. My abilities with healing are more of a side effect. If I weren't royal, I could make quite a bit of money offering fleshshaping services, but such mundane activities are below my station, so I can't put my abilities to much use."

Her mother nodded. "She isn't wrong. It's frowned upon. I think it's a wonderful talent, and I'm proud to see her inherit it. Born a hybrid, she has access to a diminished version of all the Naiad standard abilities, but her first Skill was what determined her specific talents. It's sort of like our version of an ability."

All the racial traits I'd seen involved the transformation process via alchemy. I'd never dealt with anyone born with one aside from I guess Celine. "So… are you worried about her going out with us?" I asked impulsively. I was curious to see what a real mother would think about something like this.

"A bit," she said lazily, waving the question away. "Not too much though. Children need adventure to grow. Anna-Marie has been held back far too long by Crighton's silly rules. Take her out and get her into some trouble for me. She's plenty strong—she just needs a chance to figure that out for herself."

The princess blushed, and I smiled approvingly. That sounded like something I wish my mother thought about me. Salara was a lovely person so far. Callie clearly thought so too, because my girlfriend was quickly pulled into conversation about customized combat styles and how they fit into advancing Skills like her Balam Mastery.

Turning to Nat, I saw my cousin looking curiously at the blue-skinned older woman. Her expression was almost sad, and I recognized it easily. It was the same one I wore sometimes when I saw families together. I reached out to put a hand on her shoulder, squeezing lightly to reassure her. She chuckled a bit and nodded at me.

We finished up dinner and retired to our rooms to sleep, and the next morning I went to find Jessie before I did anything. Yesterday had been a long day and I'd used up my wishes trading, but today I had more, and I planned to stock back up on healing charges with the new power upgrade while I had the chance.

To make sure I didn't have some dud charges lying around, I used my last heal burst on Abel, who wasn't as worried about getting to sleep as the rest of us and decided to take a pass on rest tonight. Which officially meant no more heal bursts in reserve, and I could replace my whole stock from Jessie in one shot.

Naturally I could only hold ten of them, but I was able to backlog plenty as advance payment. Those kinds of things work better when I need them most, so setting up a bunch of advance charges would let me drop a lot of points on her. In fact, I decided to try pushing my four-point cap to five, given all the upgrades to my stats since I last tried.

Jessie, Callie, Celine, Benny, and I were all in my and Callie's room before bed. My blonde friend was fretting at not being able to go up and check in on Randall, but we'd decided bringing him down here wasn't worth the time, and had sent word to have him taken over the mountain through their animal paths so we could take him with us on our long trip, which mollified her a bit.

"I just worry about him," she said with a pout. "I don't like leaving him alone for so long. What if he gets sad or lonely?"

"Can't you feel that stuff with your bond?" Callie asked. "I don't know how your bond works versus ours, but I can always feel when Shane is upset. At least when we're close enough. Is your bond not active at this distance? I could understand why that might suck."

Jessie waved her hand in a fluttering gesture that could mean literally anything. "Sort of. It's complicated. I can feel him but not well. Our bond is pretty strong, and different from yours at least partly because of the stat impact. Like I've gotten twenty-five points of Might from Randall since my rank up." She glanced at me. "I'd like all Vitality from you by the way. Though I guess that needs formalizing. I wish for thirty points of Vitality in exchange for thirty heal bursts."

Wish detected. Grant wish?

I confirmed, and was greeted with the requirements as usual, which she did meet. Five points per wish was valid after all. It also confirmed that her heal bursts were far more valuable with all that Vitality behind them. I accepted and held out a hand as the electricity built. Jessie snagged it and the power leapt from me to her, funneling the points into my friend.

Because of the incredibly small percentage of both total stats and Vitality those thirty points represented, adjustment should be instantaneous and pretty much unnoticeable. Jessie sat through all six wishes before walking over and slumping onto the bed. Apparently the wishes still took it out of you even if the stats weren't enough to shake a person.

"You good?" I asked cautiously. Maybe I should have spaced them out, after all.

She groaned. "Yeah, just a little fried. Still, worked like a charm. Just eight points of Vitality shy of eight hundred. It's a far cry from my one hundred seventy-five Might. I'm definitely a specialist. Still, it works for me." She whistled. "Lily, sweetheart, carry mommy to her room, I'm too lazy to walk." The large wolf chuffed, once again seeming smarter than she had before. She walked over to the bed and Jessie slumped over the huge beast's back.

"I'm going to go get changed before breakfast, see you guys down there." She burrowed into the wolf's fur like Lily was a big snuggly stuffed dog, and I had to chuckle.

Callie looked amused. "That girl." She groaned. "We'd be lost without her for sure." I laughed at how accurate that was. Not just because of her amazing power, but also because Jessie kept us all sane. She was the heart of our group, the one who kept us happy and focused on the positive.

Looking at Celine and Benny, I decided to double check. "You both ready for this trip? We'll be gone for a long while. That summerspark crystal will help keep us warm, and we have defenses, but still, this is a bit more than a camping trip. We'll be out in the wilderness alone for weeks, possibly months."

Benny shrugged. "I'm already on a strange new world—why not take the whole novelty angle to extremes? Who needs a city—we'll have a house to sleep in, so it's all the same in the end." He looked at his girlfriend. "How about you, Cel, you feeling good about this?"

She gave him a soft smile, leaning up to kiss him on the cheek. "I feel blessed to be brought along and every day here is a gift."

Callie rolled her eyes. "Boo!" she jeered. "Political answer. We're friends, you don't need to be so formal. Complain a bit, say you're pissed the sheets won't be soft enough. You're making the rest of us look bad." She had a big smile on her face, and Celine looked amused and touched in equal measure. I thought it was sweet how Callie was trying to make Celine feel like part of the gang.

"Alright," I said with a laugh, "let's go down and get some breakfast before we leave." I gestured to my girlfriend. "You don't want to see this one when she's hungry."

I climbed out of the chair I was reclining in and headed for the door, eager to get some food and be on our way. The truth was, I was nervous about the trip, and the sooner it started the less time I'd have to worry.

Chapter Twenty-Seven

SETTING off on our second expedition was a bigger deal, and not just for us. Salara sent actual guards this time, a pair of peak F-rankers to watch over Anna-Marie.

The princess herself had already taken her Dew drops. She'd given one to Salara, but it seemed like she'd taken the other four drops herself, making it to thirty-four Impact total. She was now the most durable of all of us.

As we met Randall off the back of the mountain, I turned to Anna-Marie to ask her about what the deeper parts of the core were like. "What can we expect out there, going deeper?"

She bit her lip in thought. "Well, there are a few old fortresses and encampments out there that have been abandoned or reclaimed over the years. Every kingdom on the ring has some kind of operating base that's been lost. Some still have active defensive locations, though Ladrigan doesn't."

I made a contemplative noise. I could see how that would play out. People would try to take the fortresses to use as staging grounds for their operations. It would turn into a war for positioning. Since the flowers appeared randomly it could take time, which meant they needed a good place to deploy from.

It was a solid way to force competition, but there was definitely room for cooperation. I wished we knew where any of the people we'd met before were landing. Bethy would be a hell of a teammate to have right now. Hell, I was betting we could persuade Brightlaw to collaborate if we needed to. But I hadn't seen a single familiar face since we'd arrived.

We'd reached the other side of the bridge, mounted up on our goats, and headed out along the same path we'd taken before. Not because it would lead us anywhere important, but so we could fill in the map we'd picked up. It would only fill in as we traveled the route with it in our possession, though interestingly, it interfaced with my Song of the Wild skill to mark down herbs and plants, and I suspected the skill that found metals would work as well. We didn't have the time to make a survey sweep right now, but we'd definitely be coming back after we'd gotten entrenched and set up a command post in the central core.

"We need to be careful," Anna-Marie added. "The mountains make up the ring and the outer areas of the core, but most of it is a bit more... complex. If we keep traveling, we're going to hit the central area after we leave the mountains and that'll be much more complicated to navigate."

"What should we be expecting down there aside from the fortresses?" I asked. "Are there any locals living in the core area?"

She nodded. "No kingdoms, but there are wandering bands of nomads who have broken off from ring kingdoms to hole up there. It's extremely dangerous and there are thousands of terrifying monsters to contend with. There are also ruins of... older things. Wizard's towers, temples—the core is the oldest area on the planet and has resisted all attempts to properly settle it. We usually don't enter it outside awakenings."

"Well, guess we know where to head," I said with a grim smile. "That'll be where everything happens." It honestly sounded kind of amazing. "You said there are... Wizard's towers? What are those?"

She shrugged. "Places you learn magic. Books and crystals for Skills that can manipulate elements, transform things, and other similarly powerful tricks. Those who possess Wizard, Necromancer, and Cleric jobs can develop unique and interesting Skills, both from their inborn abilities and from training."

I blinked at her in shock. I hadn't really considered there might be *magic* Jobs. I knew Jobs would relegate an inborn ability to a Skill, and that those

143

could be taught and learned, but it never occurred to me that might mean there was an entire subset of people with Skills aimed in that direction. It sounded amazing, and I desperately wanted to mix them into my DS Mastery.

Callie was as excited as I was, and I had to smile at the thrum of excitement from her as she heard about the possibilities. The goats carried us forward at speed, and it didn't take us nearly as long to reach the area where the last patch of flowers had been without needing to stop constantly for plant- and flower-picking.

When we arrived at the spot we'd last seen the ray, I had to stop and stare. A massive sword of pure crystal pinned the flying ray's crumbling stone remnants to the ground where the dead animal had been clearly harvested for parts.

I whistled loudly at the sheer power behind the kill. "Guess they had backup. Or one of them got sick of holding back. I'd say we should avoid that group in the future."

"No shit," Benny said in a hushed tone. "I don't want that to happen to any of us."

Nat shook her head. "It won't. We'll be fine. Killing animals like that is one thing, but remember, this isn't a slaughter. We're in competition for resources, and it's more trouble than it's worth to kill off a bunch of juniors from a powerful faction. Don't fall into the trap of thinking all we have to do is kill everyone. It leaves you vulnerable."

Celine nodded. "She's right. This is not going to be a straightforward war or scavenger hunt. People will make alliances and connections. Not just with other factions but with local kingdoms. It's going to get complicated, and we'll still be in danger. The kingdoms won't be quite as circumspect, and more than a few of the factions involved might use them as an excuse or as cat's paws to take out competition without doing the deed themselves."

I turned to Callie. "Keep an ear out as we move—try to use your shadows to get as good of an idea of incoming threats as possible. When we find anyone in range who doesn't know we're there, I want you to spy on them for a while before we make contact. That work?"

She gave me an approving smile. "Sounds like a plan."

It warmed my heart hearing the pride in her voice and feeling it through the link. I grinned back even if she couldn't see it and led everyone to continue. We rode for another few hours, and I made sure to detect all the plants and metals even if we didn't stop. It was fun watching the map fill with treasure we could pick clean on the way back.

Slowly though, the snow began to thin, the crags became rockier, and the paths became steeper and oddly easier to traverse on the goats. They were all-terrain animals apparently, at least as far as mountains went. Eventually, we came over a rise and came to a stop, staring down off a massive cliff at what I could only describe as a lost jungle.

The core, because that was definitely what this was, extended out before us for further than the eye could see in every direction. It was filled with thick green foliage and massive trees. Intermittently I could see gaps where there had been buildings I was sure were the fortresses we'd heard about earlier. I could also see slight disturbances in the trees that I was almost positive were ruins.

"Okay," I said with a wide-eyed stare. "I don't know if we're going to be able to find any flowers. Is it really completely random?"

Anna-Marie chuckled. "Mostly. They tend to be at least near massive animals or important places. If we check near the ruins, we're likely to run into other teams and eventually some flowers. Of course, we need to be able to keep what we find, so our first job will be taking one of these fortresses and possibly finding allies to help hold it."

Benny looked at her in confusion. "Wait. Didn't we buy our own mini fortress for that?"

I shook my head, knowing the answer before she said it. "No way. That's for overnight trips, but if we try to hole up in there with a bunch of Dew we're going to fall under siege, and no way it holds up. All the defenses are designed to be temporary." I paused. "Maybe not the bone wall. We can probably use that on the main fortress."

Callie stepped forward. "We're pretty damned high, but I might be able to extend my range in a straight line if I push it. It'll put some strain on my soul, but that closest fortress is within reach if I do that, and I can get us some info on who and what is in there so we can take it."

"You sure?" I asked. "That kind of strain is dangerous, though I admit taking the closest fortress to the path toward Ladrigan will give us an advantage. If we manage to call reinforcements, it'll make things easier, not to mention we can hold the cliff so no one tries to sneak back along our path."

She waved me off. "I'll be fine. Just keep an eye on me while I'm distracted." She hopped off the goat, kneeling to stick her hand in the shadow of a rock. Her hand passed through the solid ground and into the darkness, like she was testing a bath with her fingers, and she closed her eyes to focus.

I hopped down after her, looming next to her with my staff in my hands. The necrotic energy thrumming in the wood was comforting as I waited for any sign of attack, though none came. Eventually, she opened her eyes. "Alright. The fortress closest to us is lightly defended by the kingdom of Kargath. Fifteen F-rankers, five locals on the higher end and ten outsiders. No one I'd heard of."

Looking around, I counted our own force. Pretty similar in size, honestly. Our ten-man group and then another five locals. Four guards and Anna-Marie herself.

I remembered what Zeke had said. This wasn't a fight—it was about resources. That didn't just mean we avoided lethal fights. It meant we had other methods of entering and taking them out.

"Callie," I said after a minute. "How long can you hold someone unaware with your shadows?"

She bit her lip. "Maybe a minute if I get them good. Depends. My Might isn't low but it's not high, especially compared to some others. If I wrap them up without any leverage, it'll make it much harder to break free. Why?"

I grinned at her and leaned in, pulling on her Stealth Skill as I told her the whole plan. My girlfriend gave me an evil grin. "That," she said with relish, "I think might work. You have eight of them right? Will that be enough?"

As I went over my resources I nodded purposefully. "I can make it work. Once we take out the strongest, we can switch tactics. Seven on fifteen should work out fine." We began to discuss details, the others looking on in confusion as I mentally rubbed my hands together. This was going to be a lot of fun.

Chapter Twenty-Eight

AFTER WE GOT everyone up to speed, we identified a way for everyone to get down to the ground with the goats (which could apparently walk nearly vertically when needed) and Randall. As per my brilliant plan, Callie and I decided to take the quick way down. To hit our targets at the right time (in the middle of the night), we waited up on the cliff while the others took the slower path.

"So," my girlfriend said after the team left, "you're taking to this planning thing well. This is a step up from having Abel throw you at a flying monster."

I gave an embarrassed chuckle. "Not my finest hour, but this should work out. With State of Grace I can float us down over to the fortress and you can bring us in through the shadows. You can transport me like that, right?"

She nodded. "I can. Our bond means you can use my Skills and can count as an extension of me if I push. Luckily my ability is still much less complicated than yours."

I sighed, wincing as I remembered trying to let Callie tap into my Wish power. It had been a painful and completely fruitless experience. "In any case, it'll take them a few hours to hit the ground, and by the time they do it'll be go time." I gestured to the cliff edge. "Care to sit and watch the sunset with me?"

Beaming, she dropped down to snuggle. "I'd love to. This is a beautiful view, don't you think?"

I smiled softly at her. "I'm becoming accustomed to being overwhelmed by the beauty I see every day." I made sure my tone and the bond left no doubt I was talking about her. I also took my mask off, because it seemed like it might kill the moment.

Her kiss was giddy with affection and contentment, and I reveled in how intense it could be feeling her emotions like that while she was feeling mine. The feedback loop of adoration and happiness was kind of intoxicating.

Leaning her head against my chest, she looked out over the core. "I love you," she said softly. "Not just for all this, but... This is amazing. I would have never imagined any of this before I met you."

I smiled, putting an arm around her. "It wouldn't mean half as much if you weren't here. Getting to travel the universe is pretty cool. Getting to do it with the woman I love is a dream."

"Speaking of dreams," she said wryly, "I felt a bit of a shift in the way you were feeling not long ago. You seem more purposeful, more driven. Kind of like you did when you decided to look for your mom. Make any big life decisions?"

It occurred to me that I hadn't mentioned that to her. I'd made the call in my head, but I'd never shared the realization that I wanted to save my family from themselves.

"I realized why I need to win this," I said quietly. "Up to now, this has been a game, or a means to an end. I decided to push on to help with my goals, but this is going to be more than that. I'm going to be the Wishmaster. I need to be. Because I realized the other day that the way I was raised, that Nat was raised... I *hate* it. I don't want any of my relatives to have to grow up like I did."

It felt stupid saying it out loud. I was so far from the Wishmaster title that it wasn't even funny, and who was I to gainsay the way my family had been doing things for centuries. But... I didn't care. It was my path, and I was going to walk it the way I wanted.

Callie must have been feeling what I was through the bond. She laced her fingers through mine and squeezed. "Hey," she said. "That's a really great goal. And I'm in."

I paused. "If I do become the Wishmaster, I wonder if there's an office you inherit. Like is there a Wish Mastress?"

She pinched the bridge of her nose with her free hand. "The female form of Master is Mistress. Mastress isn't a word. And if that was you proposing to me, I'm going to kick your ass. And also say no. Not because I don't love you, but just—"

"Too soon," I cut in. "*Way* too soon. Trust me, I'm not crazy—It was a joke. Not that I might not someday. I probably will. But I'll put a lot more thought into it."

Her smile was brilliant. "You'd better."

It was funny, the bond saved so many misunderstandings. She knew what I meant, what I felt, and I knew her. There was no offense taken. We loved each other, and we both knew it, and that was enough.

We stayed like that, holding each other and watching the sun set. Once it went down, we stared up at the colossal moon above us until finally there was a red flash of fire off to the side of the cliff.

The signal meant that they were in position.

I double-checked the map, which had filled in for everything we could see from up here, and once I confirmed they were in the right spot, I stood up, reaffixing my mask. "Alright love. You ready for this? The plan hinges on you being able to get us in and keep us stealthed."

She snorted, blowing a strand of hair from her eyes as she stood and fixed her costume, smoothing out wrinkles that admittedly wouldn't have stuck around anyway and brushing dirt off her coat where she'd been sitting on it. "Please. I was born ready."

I snickered and offered her my arm. "Shall we? Careful of that first step. It's a doozy."

Smirking, she took my arm as I activated State of Grace. We stepped off the cliff, drifting much slower than we should have, angling forward as we fell leisurely toward the distant fortress.

Shifting in the air, I aimed us nearby but not on the actual building. As we touched down, rather than hit the ground, we slipped through the shadows and into... nothing.

I'd never traveled through the shadows with Callie before, and the sensation was like nothing I'd ever felt. Cold and dark and empty in a way I'd never experienced, then within one heartbeat and the next, I felt warmth wash over me as I was shoved back into the real world again.

I shuddered a bit as we emerged. That had been unpleasant. I glanced at Callie, who shrugged apologetically. "It gets easier. The space between shadows is weird. Kind of a void. I've been in a few times, and my Shadow Manipulation Skills make it easier. We're under Stealth by the way."

I hadn't noticed, too distracted by the jarring sensation. After adjusting, I nodded. "Alright. Can you identify which of them are the locals? They'll be the strongest. We want to take the peak F-rankers out first."

She grinned. "I know which are which. I did a search through the shadows when we entered. I should be able to hold them for a minute or so especially with the extra Impact. Are you sure you can take them out? Your tranq attacks are all G-rank, aren't they?"

I hefted my staff. "Yup. But the Stygian Branch is E-ranked. That won't increase the effectiveness of the tranquilizer attacks enough to put them down easy, but if I use the poison as a carrier, the combination should be close to enough. I'll be using Afterburner at the same time, which works for ten attacks. If they're immobilized and I target their heads that should keep them under."

I'd have to be careful not to hit them too hard or I might kill them, but all the modifiers combined with my staff directly impacting the brain should do the job assuming they didn't struggle.

Triggering Afterburner and Touch of Tears, I decided to forgo Consecration of Flames, since that would be more geared toward damage. Overwhelming their regen would be great, but not if I was targeting the brain— I might accidentally kill them.

This was already risky, but as peak F-rankers, their Vitality should fix any incidental damage. I nodded to Callie, who had waited for me to process and get ready. She gestured for me to follow and led me toward the first target.

She'd found one of them asleep, letting us slip through the door easily under stealth. As we approached, she closed her eyes and gestured. The shadows around the bed snapped up into chains, encircling the local warrior up the length of his body. He sputtered awake, but pinned to the bed with an arm under his head and one between his legs, he was in a supremely awkward position. My measured smack landed squarely, and his eyes rolled up in his head as the compounding effects delivered the tranquilizer to his brain.

I nodded and we moved on. We took out the other four locals the same way, some of them standing guard and not expecting an attack from behind, some sleeping like the first. After we subdued each, we tied them up with a more durable rope that wouldn't dissolve, making sure they were bound in too tight and too awkward a position to escape.

Once that was done though, we ran into a small issue. I had three more tranquilizer blows in stock, and four more hits with Afterburner (the poison had taken one). We debated whether to try to take out the leader of the enemy team, but decided it was too risky.

Sneaking into the nearest rooms to the gates, we took out the three most likely to notice the gates opening. Stealth served us well, and we managed to remain completely undetected. Their sentries had been the locals we'd taken out, attention all focused outward.

I could see why Callie liked this kind of thing so much. This whole attack had gone off without a hitch. Granted, it had been pretty much an ideal situation, but it felt good to operate how my build was meant to, and better to do it alongside my girl.

Once we took down the last one, we made our way to the front gates and opened them. Sadly, our luck could only hold for so long. The gates made a huge racket as they opened, and I heard the shouts of alarm as the defenders realized their companions were gone. We'd hidden the subdued team members so they couldn't find and free them before this was over, so all they could do was attack.

A column of red ice smashed down from above, and I prepared to block, but it wasn't necessary. Our part was over, and a massive fist slammed against the descending column, stopping it cold before a huge cloud of flame consumed it entirely.

Abel and Mel stepped past us calmly as the enemy filed out, Randall looming behind them with Jessie on his back. Stepping in front of Callie, I used my last charge of Afterburner to trigger my Mountain Stance and prepared to tank anything that made it past my team.

I wasn't too worried though. This had been a perfectly executed raid, and now I'd leave the rest to the people best suited for the job. It was my first real time experiencing it, but damn, I loved it when a plan came together. I could get used to this whole leader thing.

Chapter Twenty-Nine

THE WEAKNESS HIT me after I finished with Afterburner, and I felt Jessie's hand on my shoulder almost instantly. Randall had continued into the fray, but our team's healer had stopped to check on us first. Callie was fine, if winded now that she'd had a chance to slow down. I was exhausted, though Mountain Stance was keeping me up. Jessie's life energy boost certainly helped, and I was able to keep my feet while I watched the others go at it.

The red ice had mostly shattered rather than melting properly, a shower of red smoking shards plummeting toward us, but Mel erected a shield to stop them. Despite being sturdy enough that the inner portions of the ice pillar hadn't melted, the ice wasn't fireproof. Abel rained down phantom punches at them from above while the remaining seven defenders grouped up, surprisingly in tune with each other.

The leader, a small, pale looking guy with dark circles around his eyes, had a hungry expression on his face as he inhaled, creating a dark vortex that ripped a chunk off one of Abel's fist manifestations. My teacher cursed as he pulled back, shaking his hand and flexing his fingers, clearly trying to get it to move properly.

"Shit," he cursed quietly. "That hurt."

I kept my defensive ability up as I walked forward. Mountain Stance required ground contact to function, and it usually worked better from a standstill, but I was familiar enough with altering skills that as long as I walked slow and took it one step at a time, I *could* move. It had the added benefit of being really intimidating, and as I thumped forward, I called for everyone to stop.

"Let's talk," I said loudly enough for the enemy to hear. "We're from the Starchaser Pavilion. We got you, this fight is pointless. Your local escorts were the only peak F-rankers you had, and we took them out, while ours are still very much active. Beginning F-rank to peak F-rank isn't a fight anyone could manage with these numbers."

The leader raised an eyebrow. "I assume you have some idea how this should go? Or are you just laying out our loss because you're a braggy asshole?"

I grinned at him. I liked this guy. "We want you to switch sides. You're one of the dungeon groups like we are, which means the kingdom you're working for is a temporary employer at best. We took out their representatives and now you're free agents. You work with us and we're willing to cut you in for part of our Dew haul. We have ways of making sure you don't switch sides again, of course, but nothing painful or problematic long-term."

I'd had the idea to offer them wishes and use their service as a cost. With them under a geas to temporarily work for us, we wouldn't need to worry about backstabbing, and we would have someone to man the fortress when we had to head out to search the core. I didn't want to be cooped up here all the time when there were wizard's towers to explore and other teams to meet. Plus when we were back in the fortress, they could do patrols to look for flowers so we had no down time.

The guy looked pensive. "Maybe. I'd need to hear about these 'ways.' You're right that we don't have any real loyalty to our current hosts. The prince of the kingdom who picked us up is an asshole and spends most of his time flirting with Tiffany." He pointed at a tall, slim girl with olive skin and purple hair, her eyes slitted like a cat's. She gave an embarrassed cough and waved at us.

I nodded. "We'll need to restrain you. Nothing personal, but we don't know any of you. Before we do though, I can bring out the restrained locals and the three members of your crew to show you that we haven't hurt them and can be trusted with members of your team at our mercy."

He didn't look happy, but I think he knew that even if he said no, we'd just kick their asses and restrain them anyway. I gestured for Valk to go and get the others and smiled when he glanced at Nat for approval. My cousin smirked at me but gave him the go ahead and he went to retrieve the unconscious bodies. He brought back seven of them, dumping them in front of me, and I froze. "Where's the last one?"

Valk raised a brow at me. "These were the only ones." I looked over the faces, realizing one of the locals had somehow slipped his restraints and escaped. I cursed, looking to the leader of the other team. "Okay, two questions, who is missing and what's your name? I can't keep referring to you as 'team leader' in my head."

He chuckled at that. "I'm Samuel. Samuel Stark." He looked over the bodies and winced. "Shit. Mazrik is gone. He was our scout, nominally, but more realistically he's a spy for Prince Bertrand. I imagine he went to go tell the prince about us losing the fortress. Guess side switching is our only option. I'd wake up my boys there if I were you, because you'll need us to defend this place. We're going to be ass-deep in Kargath soldiers in less than an hour."

Cursing, I focused my Eye of Revelation on him, looking for any signs of deception. I found none. Luckily, we had options. I called Nat over, explaining the plan to her.

She grinned. "Geasa are a traditional way of making deals with shaky allies. Your old man is famous for that, and I approve. I haven't used up my wishes for today. I usually keep them in reserve, so I can bind six of them, and either you or I can do the other four tomorrow."

"Alright," I said firmly. "Get the leader and five of the others that are still functional. The one with the red ice powers and Tiffany, since we know they're relevant, then pick three more."

She chuckled, nodding and heading off. I also glanced over to Callie, gesturing after her. Ostensibly it was to give her support, but letting my cousin make the contracts wasn't exactly risk free. Callie knew some tricks from working with me on the subject, and she'd make sure Nat didn't slip any extra instructions in while she was at it. Trust but verify and all that.

With that done, I looked for Abel, finding my mentor nearby talking to Anna-Marie. I strode over in time to hear him asking her about defenses, and I decided to jump in. "Hey," I said as I reached them, "we think

Kargath might hit us soon. This is a fortress, and it's literally designed to stop an army. Can you tell us anything about the defensive capabilities of this place? Any standard they might use?"

She shook her head. "I'm not even remotely up to date on this kind of thing." She looked at the five peak F-rank guards. "Do any of you know how these places are laid out? This is close enough that it might have been a Ladrigan fortress when it was built."

The closest, a small, severe woman with dark skin and tightly braided hair, shook her head. "No, your Highness. This would have been before our times. Perhaps if we had a map."

I saw the princess realize it at the same time I did and reached into my ring to pull out the map, passing it over. The guard looked over it. "I can work with this. I'll start setting up our defenses."

"Oh," I said in realization. "Here." I passed her the bone wall. "This is the only defensive artifact that will be overtly useful here I think. If you find any uses for the others let me know—Anna-Marie has a list of what we bought. Thank you for your help…" I trailed off, unaware of her name.

She smiled. "Amaya, sir. Captain of Lady Salara's house guard. She sent me to keep an eye on her little girl, so thank you for making that easier." She looked around at the fortress. "Oh, and sir?" I cocked my head so she'd know I was listening. "This wasn't a bad plan, but in the future, remember to leave room for improvisation. Abilities and Skills make any plan a tentative failure. It's a common first-time mistake." I guessed she'd seen the guilt already starting to gnaw at my gut for screwing this up.

I nodded as she hurried off. I felt a slap on my back and jumped. Abel was smiling at me. "She's right kid. I can see the hamster wheel in your brain turning, but don't second-guess yourself. This was solid—you can't account for bullshit powers. Like yours, actually. That damned escape skill of yours would have made this whole thing pointless. Nobody is perfect."

It only took a minute for the purple electricity of my cousin's wishes to settle and for everyone to gather up.

"Alright," I said as they all assembled, including the now healed and only slightly grumpy three captives we'd set loose. "Callie, I need you on over-watch. Hit the shadows and figure out where they're coming at us from and how many. Jessie, I want Randall at the gate. They'll try to breach through there most likely. It's easier to pop open than the walls."

She nodded. "I can have him pin it shut, but I don't think it'll be an issue. There's a giant-ass bone wall in front of it now." I looked over and sure enough, Amaya had used the bone wall before the front gate, covering our major weak point.

"Mel," I said, moving on. "Can you do a flame shield that covers this whole fortress?"

"I can," she said slowly. "It won't be particularly sturdy or dangerous, but I can whip up something thin."

"Perfect." I grinned, exhaling in relief. "I'll work with you on that. Abel, you're on Callie. Make sure nobody takes her out while she's giving us intel. Once they arrive, escort her to where Mel and I are working. Valk, you're on Jessie with Perit, Benny, Celine, and Nat. Help her defend the front, but more importantly make sure our healer isn't taken out. Benny, Celine, make sure you don't get bogged down—we might need you to move."

With a plan in place, we all scattered.

I was... terrified. My last plan had gone wrong, and now I was throwing them to the wolves, so to speak. I followed Mel to the center of the fortress, climbing up on the roof as she looked around.

"I assume you have a plan?"

I grinned, putting a hand on her shoulder, triggering, Consecration of Flames, Touch of Tears, Mercy Kill, a triple-stacked density shift, and with a massive wrench at the skills via my soul, Stone Limb and Mountain Stance. "Do it," I grunted. And she erected the shield.

I nearly blacked out from the pain as I forced the two skills to work in a way they were never intended to, but managed to hold on. As my head cleared, I saw a massive dome of green, acidic magma form over us, reinforced with as much defensive power as I could reasonably handle.

Mel looked around with a long whistle. "Okay, that's actually kind of impressive."

My only response was a low keening whine. My head was killing me.

Chapter Thirty

THE SHIELD WAS *MASSIVE*. It hadn't seemed that big earlier. The fortress wasn't huge, at least not on the outside. It was just a reasonably large building, and given the scale I could work on when needed, I hadn't been worried about pulling off the invocation.

In retrospect, that was pretty stupid.

I could *feel* every inch of it. The actual working was so absurdly difficult it almost broke me. One massive crushing blow to my soul that would have shattered it if it lasted any longer, followed by continued pressure that I could feel Callie helping me offload. I had to stay standing with my feet planted to maintain Mountain Stance, and I'm pretty sure that was all that prevented me from passing out from the pain.

On the upside, the damned thing was *strong*. Mel's Might was ridiculously high considering her flame abilities. Not to Jessie's level of specialization, but closer than most. Her flames were extremely hot even spread out. Infused with Consecration of Flame to enhance them, Touch of Tears to make them stronger, Mercy Kill to boost their power, and then with all that offense turned to defense by Stone Limb, they were formidable already.

Making that dangerously hot and sturdy magma three times denser with a triple-stacked density shift, followed by Mountain Stance to triple the defense of the whole thing... It wouldn't stop them completely, not given the stat disparity in some cases, but even peak F-rankers should need time to get through it.

A working this size would have been impossible before my rank-up. Having an orange soul was a qualitative difference from having a red one, and being fifteen percent of the way to the next level gave me that extra bit I needed.

Mel cocked her head at me. "I'm impressed. Somewhat horrified, but impressed. Having just cast that, I realize the strain you're currently under. I have no clue how you're conscious."

"Practice," I grunted. "I'm not Abel, but I put in the work when it comes to soul strength. I'm used to working through the pain." Every word felt like someone was driving glass into the back of my eyes, so clearly not *that* used to it, but I didn't say that. As the leader, I needed to do *something* to help with this battle.

I saw a slight flicker and Amaya landed on the roof next to us. "Sir, I take it this defensive dome is your doing?" Her voice was filled with respect. I was glad I had a mask on since my face was bright red and probably currently dripped blood from my eyes and nose.

Unable to nod, I gave a grunt of affirmation. "It is. Hope I didn't disrupt your plans for our defense."

"No sir," she said, shaking her head. "To be honest, this is ideal. We've identified and begun repairing the defensive enchantments on the fortress. They're of Ladrigani origin, if somewhat out of date, and one of my teammates is classically trained. Our kingdom has a standardized set of enchantment runes for ease of repair. It'll take some time, but if we can fix them, we should be able to hold this position until we can send for reinforcements from Lady Salara."

I hadn't realized we had that option, but I supposed taking this place was a coup for Ladrigan. If it could be held, that would be a major strategic advantage. Salara would be stupid to pass up the opportunity, and even if she didn't have the guards on hand, she could always hire more or borrow some from the king.

"How long is it going to take?" I asked through gritted teeth. I might be able to hold the shield as I was, but I was functionally useless in any other fashion right now. Callie would be distracted too, though not as much

159

considering she was only offloading about a quarter of the strain. She kept trying to take more, but only one of us needed to be paralyzed by pain, so I only gave her what I couldn't handle.

Amaya looked uncertain. "Anywhere from an hour to four," she replied apologetically. "The enchantments are carved into the bedrock, but they're old and very damaged. Some of the runes need to be recast to get them running again. Luckily we're on top of a natural wellspring of energy, so we don't need to worry about a battery. In fact, the one working part of the enchantments is the power siphon runes. They've been soaking up energy for decades."

"I'll hold as long as I can," I said. "Work with Callie. Try to get your people into the best possible defensive position. Hell, try to get *my* people in the best possible defensive position. I gave them all orders, but I'm not a tactician. You have way more experience with this kind of thing, so command is yours."

Her posture straightened and her fist went up to her heart. "Thank you, sir. I won't let you down." Then she turned and stepped off the roof in a few quick paces.

Mel chuckled. "Good call there—always defer to the expert. Want me to follow her? I'm on the fence about whether or not you need protection."

"Go," I said firmly. "I'll be fine. Let the others know Amaya is in charge. Should have asked her what to do to start with. Didn't consider requesting the help since she's not one of my people. I won't make that mistake again."

She gave an approving nod and hopped off the roof, vanishing into the darkness. To my surprise, she was replaced shortly after by Benny and Celine. He grinned at me as he appeared. "New boss lady thought you might need a bodyguard, and apparently we're less useful out there than watching your sorry ass take a standing nap."

"I'd flip you off," I grunted, "if I could raise my arms." My head was swimming, but it was also helping to talk to Benny. Gave me something to focus on.

The help became much more pronounced when he put a hand on my shoulder and a wave of cooling, soothing relief rolled over me. Not enough to completely counter the pain, but enough to offset it quite a bit. My head cleared enough that I considered the remaining agony something like an ice cream headache instead of paralyzing waves of searing torment.

True to my word, I raised my middle finger at my best friend, who laughed. "Thanks," I said, voice hoarse. "That belt is awesome. You have anything in your new bag of tricks that might help? I never got the chance to ask about any of the upgrades, assuming you got them done."

"I did. Two of them. I got rid of the rope and the long-range attack attraction device in my left forearm. I managed to rig up a few things that would be useful, but the two I liked best were a G-ranked artifact that allows momentary intangibility, and an F-ranked defensive artifact that creates a small energy barrier of variable shape. Both useful, especially combined with my other tricks."

I whistled. "Not bad. Especially the shield. I assume the density shifting works on that?" I admit I was a bit excited about trading for some charges. Benny's new tricks suited me well. The intangibility would complement my combat style perfectly.

He grinned, raising his left forearm and manifesting a plane of energy in front of it that he shaped into a hand holding up a middle finger. Then he concentrated and the yellow energy became brighter and more opaque. I took that to be a yes.

Celine scoffed. "Honestly, can the two of you behave? If Callie found out I let you get each other killed because you were too busy making crude gestures and flinging veiled insults, she'd never forgive me."

"Veiled?" I said in a wounded voice. "Our insults aren't veiled. We're very up front about mocking each other. Aren't we fuckface?"

Benny burst out laughing, but quieted immediately when his girlfriend glared at him. What a pushover.

I felt a small burst of irritation from the bond, and remembered *my* girlfriend was currently inhabiting the shadows in the surrounding area to do recon, so I cleared my throat and stopped messing around. Which was totally different. For some reason.

"Anyway," I said with a nervous laugh, "I should feel if they breach the shield, but keep your eyes peeled for anyone who has an ability that can bypass it. That's the trick we used on them, so no chance we don't see it exploited. I'm sure the enchantments on this place have a failsafe, or if not our allies will add one. But until they're up, we're vulnerable."

The two of them nodded, taking up position on either side of me, Benny keeping his hand on my shoulder. It helped for a bit, but within five minutes I felt something smash into the dome, and my knees buckled. The only active connection I had was Mountain Stance, but that was keeping me on my feet, so them slamming into it like that threw me.

Benny and Celine caught me under the arms. "Whoa there," he said, voice light and unconcerned enough that I might have believed he wasn't worried if not for the death grip on my arm. "Don't trip."

My whole body shuddered as the enemy assaulted the dome again. And again. My brain was whiting out from the pain, but with the spiritual calming effect I was able to hold on. I became lost, set adrift on a sea of blazing white agony. I felt like fireworks were going off behind my eyes now, melting and cauterizing the shards of glass and their wounds. But I stuck with it.

Days. Months. Years. I lost all sense of time and meaning. Nothing but pain existed. Every second felt like it would be the end of me, like it would be too much, but I always managed to push just a bit longer. I started screaming at some point, I don't know when. But I realized I was doing it when my voice gave out and I couldn't anymore.

And finally... it stopped. The connection snapped, the dome came down, and I slumped bonelessly to the ground, heaving and choking out gasps of pain. I would have cried, I think, if I'd had any strength for tears. Instead I just lay there. After a few minutes my eyes started working again, and I groaned and sat up. Benny and Celine were posted up around me protectively.

I heard explosions in the distance, saw flame and fist and red ice raining from the sky. They'd gotten in. I turned to Benny, who gave me a fake grin that didn't reach his horrified and concerned eyes. I coughed, clearing my throat and taking out a bottle of water before managing to croak out. "How long?"

"An hour," he said shakily. "Give or take. They almost have the defenses up —Amaya was here a few minutes ago. They weren't as damaged as they'd feared. Are you... Are you okay, man? That was horrible."

I thumped back onto the roof and let my eyes drift shut. I was too injured to help with the fight. My part in this was over. I just hoped I'd done enough. "I will be, Benny. I will be."

The pain had been awful, but it was nothing compared to the pride I felt. Maybe I really could do this leader thing, even when my plans didn't go the way I'd hoped.

Chapter Thirty-One

"Ow," I said weakly. "Remind me never to do that again."

My head felt like jelly. I thought it had been a few more minutes since the shield fell, but I couldn't really keep track of time. Benny still had a hand on my shoulder, and now that I wasn't holding up the shield, the Spiritual Calming was helping a lot more, actually repairing the strain instead of offsetting it.

"Oh, trust me," said a furious voice, "I will." I froze, eyes snapping open as I looked up at the viciously glaring form of my girlfriend.

"Hey, honey," I said nervously. "I just got done helping with the defenses safely from behind a pair of guards. You know, all safe-like."

"Really?" she hissed. "Because it *felt* like you just got finished nearly collapsing your soul in an attempt to bear the brunt of a massive soul weight. One I had to help you with just to keep you alive, and one so crushing you very nearly destroyed your entire being."

I could have ignored the anger. But the quaver of fear in her voice broke my heart. "I…" I searched for words. "I screwed up, both here and on the plan. I figured helping defend the place could make it right. I didn't realize how much it would take to do it until I'd already started, and my options were take the pain or drop the shield and let you all get hurt. I'm sorry. I should have thought about how you would feel."

"You should," she hissed angrily, "have worried about your own damned *life*, Shane. Being stupid and reckless with your body is one thing—Jessie can heal that most of the time. Being stupid and reckless with your *soul* is something else." Her eyes started to swim, tears rolling down her cheeks, and I flinched. Callie crying was the most heartbreaking thing I'd ever seen. She never cried, especially not out in the open. I felt like someone was tearing my heart out.

She felt it too, because her face crumpled as she slumped down where I was lying and started straight up bawling. "I could *feel* it," she sobbed. *"Feel* your pain and fear. The whole time. The other times you were in trouble, the bond fried. This was... it was awful Shane. It felt like you were dying. Like I was dying. Please don't ever do that to me again. Don't *ever* scare me like that."

I put my arms around her, feeling like I couldn't have fucked this up any worse if I'd been trying. Tonight had been a rollercoaster. Infiltration had gone well, then I fucked up and didn't account for one of the locals slipping away. Then the shield had been helpful, but I terrorized my girlfriend by accident. I wasn't even sure what to feel anymore. Was I supposed to be happy about my victories? Guilty? I was mostly the latter honestly.

Looking around, I heard nothing, seeing the explosions and manifestations had stopped. "Did they get the defenses running again?" I asked the night at large, not willing to pull away from my crying girlfriend to check personally when she was this upset.

Callie, as a rule, was not a weepy or easily shaken person. I had seen her cry, usually about personal emotional topics we discussed in private. This was a whole different thing. I was worried I'd subjected her to something horrible. The pain had been brain melting for me, but arguably worse for her, because she was feeling how I reacted to it, on top of being in agony herself from her portion of the weight.

"Yeah, they got it done," said the surprisingly gentle voice of Abel. "The princess is consulting with her guards about possible reinforcements, and your cousin is keeping the new hires at bay while you two get your heads in order. Figured you might need a minute. That sounded like a bad one, kid. I've been through some shit, but hearing you scream like that was... unsettling."

I winced. If *Abel* had been worried, I must have sounded horrible. "Yeah... it's been universally agreed I kind of fucked up there. I think I miscalculated the strain because of the weakening from Afterburner." I hadn't expected it to be quite that awful. I'd reverted to reacting instead of acting. Which was fine, you couldn't always have the initiative, but I hadn't thought it through. I'd reacted on instinct, and mine weren't great yet.

"How are the defenses holding up?" I asked after a few minutes, when Callie and I both calmed down enough to sit up. Benny had stepped back, and my head was... not great, but working at least.

"Not bad," Abel said casually. "There's an exclusion field apparently. First thing that happened was every member of the enemy force was covered with hives. Helped most of them were poisoned already. That damned shield did a number on everyone who tried to get through. Even after it came down, they were all in serious pain. Not bad kid."

Callie's leg lashed out, slamming into his shin hard enough to make him wince. *"Do not,"* she snarled, "encourage him. There were other options. We could have all curled up in the bubble shield or something. We bought defenses for a reason."

I held up my hands in surrender. "Whoa. You're right, just breathe, love. I was hoping to save those for when we were out in the wilderness finding ruins. I realize that lagging on my decisions for some undetermined future moment isn't exactly a brilliant call. I'll do better next time."

She grabbed my coat, wiping her eyes with it and glaring as if daring me to complain, then stood up and hauled me to my feet. Then she took a long, soothing breath, and nodded. "Alright. I'm good. We can go meet up with the others. And..." She looked at our teacher. "Thanks Abel. I appreciate you covering for us."

He just shrugged, obviously not interested in talking about it. As we climbed to our feet (me shakily), I looked at Callie. "How did recon go? How many were there, and were you able to pick them up in time?"

She nodded, surreptitiously slipping close enough to tuck herself under my arm. She made it look affectionate, but I could tell she was trying to help keep me from wobbling. I hoped she could feel the gratitude and affection through the bond. "It was easy enough," she said simply. "There were about thirty of them. Thankfully most of them were either peak G-rank or early F-rank, so holding them back wasn't too much trouble."

That sounded like a sanitized version of events, but since they hadn't mentioned any casualties, I wasn't complaining.

Abel cut in. "Once the exclusion field got them out a shield went up. Some huge barrier that can somehow tell who is and isn't a Ladrigan loyalist. The enchantments here are peak F-rank, maybe even half step E-rank, as they call it. We were damned lucky to get them back up."

"This is true," said the pleased voice of Anna-Marie as she approached with Amaya. "That shield was brilliantly done, Solomon. We couldn't have held this place without you. It's so old I'd never heard that it used to be one of ours. Lucky we discovered it."

"How did they lose it if the enchantments are so strong?" I asked cautiously. I didn't want to find out the hard way there was some kind of secret back door that was going to screw us.

Amaya grimaced. "Probably the same way any of us lose them. They drowned it in bodies. The core isn't a great place for long term occupation. The awakening is ironically the best time, because the saturation of forces means all the old garrisons are being retaken. Committing too many men to a single assault is pointless when you're just taking one of a thousand fortresses. We got in early, and your plan let us take advantage of a gap in their awareness. I doubt it will be so easy going forward."

Anna-Marie nodded. "And despite the personalized enchantment style of the various kingdoms, my enchanters say if they get enough time to dig in, the enemy *can* activate the defenses on outside fortresses. Takes serious reworking, and it's usually fixable easily enough if you can get back in. That was what the damage to this one was—alterations by the enemy who took it last, whenever that was."

I guessed that completely reenchanting a whole fortress would be pointless if you could just make a new one, so I could see why they just kept jail-breaking them. Looking at Amaya, I cocked my head. "Does that mean we have actual reinforcements coming to help us hold this? Being so close to Ladrigan makes this a strategic win, right?"

She grinned, the first real smile I'd seen from the taciturn warrior. "That it is. We've already contacted Lady Salara to send more forces our way. She's speaking with the king now. We'll most likely see the army arriving soon. I take it you'll be heading out once they arrive?"

"Yes," I answered. "We definitely will. The longer we wait the more behind we fall. We got a bit of a head start finding the flowers so early, but we don't want to rest on our laurels."

Callie cleared her throat menacingly and I chuckled a bit. "Though of course we'll be staying here tonight no matter what. It's dark and going out on our own at night without scouting would be a stupid choice. Plus, we should talk to our new employees." And wait until tomorrow so I could finish binding the rest of them. I wasn't trusting the last four to abide by the contract just because of their buddies.

Anna-Marie beamed at me. "Well, you're certainly safe here. You can have your pick of the rooms. We'll keep them clear for you when you're gone as well, so you can come back for a rest at any point. I take it you'll be searching for ruins?"

"Yeah. Wizard's towers, temples, that kind of thing," I said excitedly. "We can search them for interesting artifacts or books between finding new patches of flowers."

Even Callie, as bad a mood as she was in, looked thrilled at the idea of exploring ancient ruins for treasure. I should start carrying treasure chests in my spatial ring to pass her when she got mad at me.

Still supporting me, she grabbed hold of my arm and smiled at the princess. "Those rooms sound lovely if you could lead us to them. We're all tired and we could do with a nap."

Anna-Marie nodded to Amaya. "Captain. If you could take them to their rooms? I know it's a bit below your pay grade, but the others are clearing out the rest of the fortress to make sure there are no traps or anything. The cleared hallways have been marked so finding a room should be simple enough."

Amaya nodded solemnly. "It would be my honor, Highness." She turned to us. "Please, follow me." She turned and strode off, and I shrugged my free arm and followed her, the rest of our party trailing after. The wolves encircled us as Randall tromped behind, and I saw Abel next to the bear, ready to help him through any too-small doorways.

It didn't end up being necessary—the halls and doorways were huge, made for armies and not people, so he got through fine. When we reached a cleared hallway Amaya gestured us in, and all of us picked out rooms to rest in.

I limped over to the bed and lay down, Callie climbing in to curl up against me. I expected more yelling, but she just held me as I let myself finally drift off to sleep. It had been a long day.

Chapter Thirty-Two

I woke up with a headache. Go figure. It wasn't a bad one, just a light throb of pain. A bit of spiritual calming should get me up to speed.

One of the first things I did was snag a mirror from my spatial ring. I'd picked the piece of equipment up in the bazaar to monitor and check the progress of my soul. Pressing my thumb to the base of the mirror's setting, there was a hum as the reflective surface turned orange. Specifically orange bleeding slowly to yellow.

I had to do some calculations, but I was able to clarify that I'd officially reached nineteen percent of the way to yellow. I whistled. That was the result of tons of training and long weeks of practice, but last night still must have been quite a bump. I was almost a fifth of the way to the next level of soul strength. I knew it would get exponentially more difficult as I went, but it was still nice to know that my pain had been worth something.

"Oooh, testing the soul mirror?" Callie said sleepily from her place next to me. Sitting up, she smiled softly at me, and I was just blown away by everything about her all over again. Her black hair cascaded around her delicate face like a waterfall of the shadows she communed with, and her blue eyes were always just a bit brighter first thing in the morning. Like they were saving up the radiance for when she opened them and had to vent all that sparkle immediately.

Grinning, I held it up. "Sure am. Want to give it a try?" She didn't train her soul as much as I did, but she *did* train it—or she'd started to, anyway.

She groaned. "Can't we just relax for now? I just want to cuddle and sleep in." She buried her face in my shoulder sulkily, and I chuckled, running my hand through her hair. Somehow it never got tangled in the morning, always managing to be more 'windswept' than messy. Styled by pillow, I called it, though she insisted on brushing it out every morning anyway. I told her I liked it the way it was, but I was informed I knew nothing of hair care and that I should keep my bad opinions to myself.

"Relax?" I said in surprise. "What is this… relax? It sounds delicious." She giggled and elbowed me in the side, and I retaliated by tousling her hair. She tried for mine, but being so much bigger I was able to keep away, and she was forced to pounce on me. I squawked and pulled back, and we both fell off the bed in a tangle of sheets as she ruthlessly messed up my sandy hair.

"Victory!" she crowed, throwing her hands in the air like she'd just won a tournament. I just slumped back on the floor, laughing softly and staring up at how the light framed her sheet wrapped form. "Now all your treasure belongs to me. I've defeated you and lay claim to all you have."

I snorted. "I wonder what that's like." I grabbed her and tossed her onto the bed. We were near the same level, and she was much smaller than I was, so it didn't take much effort. Standing up, I stretched, raising an eyebrow reproachfully as I caught her propped up on her elbow leering at me. "I'm not a piece of meat you know."

She winked at me. "Dragon steak baby. Only the finest." Her lips quirked up as she stifled her grin.

I just rolled my eyes again and headed to shower. "How did you make that sound like a compliment?" I turned on the water and raised my voice a bit. "So, what do you think we should do once we head out on our own?"

Her voice carried over the water from the room easily, given our Perception stats. I probably hadn't even needed to raise mine, but it let her know who I was talking to. "Don't be obtuse. You know you want to raid a wizard's tower. You were straight up drooling over the idea of spellbooks." She made an incredulous sound. "Still can't believe people used to write skills *down*. That's just crazy. Wonder how long it takes to learn them that way."

"Ask Abel," I called back. "He did that with Ragam, remember? Probably takes a while. Upside is there's no limit to how many people can read a book. Crystals are limited use."

I forced myself to shower relatively quickly, much to my horror. We had things to do today. I was almost surprised they even had showers here (the whole rustic kingdom thing seemed like more of a bath environment) but even if they used a more old-timey aesthetic, the people who founded this place were still Ascendants, and showers had existed for a long time.

Stepping out to slip into my armor I groaned with relief. It felt good to be back in my second skin. You'd think the armor would get uncomfortable or claustrophobic, but it just made me feel safe. It was comfortable, durable, and had saved my life plenty of times.

When I stepped into the room, I saw Callie waiting in bed still, watching me with a dopey smile that made my heart pound a bit. "I'm gonna go search for breakfast. I know how you get when I don't feed you. I'll talk to the others about where we should head and catch you up when you're done."

She stuck out her tongue at me and I laughed, turning and heading out as she went to take her own shower. Stepping outside, I walked over to knock on Benny's door.

"Ugh!" came an annoyed grunt from inside. I laughed and knocked again. I heard feet slapping against the stone floor as he stomped over and threw the door open with a glare. "What do you want?"

"Come on nerd, we're getting breakfast." I turned my attention to a rumpled pile of blankets. "Hey Celine, you hungry?" A slim hand emerged from the blankets, flipped me the finger, and then retreated. I burst out laughing. "You are a terrible influence, Benny. What happened to our proper self-contained noble? You're turning her into just as much of a hooligan as you."

Benny grinned. "She's been trying to teach me manners, so it's only fair I teach her to have more fun. Besides, you deserve rude gestures on principle. Who wakes someone up at... Noon? Shit. We must have been wiped from last night."

I blew out a breath, nodding solemnly. "It was pretty rough. But we're past it, and once we're out and mobile we're less likely to undergo a siege. We should be on the offensive, looking around for ruins to explore. When we find somewhere good, we can use my skill to detect the flowers."

He grumbled. "Fine, I'll come eat." He looked over his shoulder, calling, "Cel, get up sweetheart, we need to go get some food before we go, it's noon." She groaned loudly, and he laughed and turned to me. "Go look for some food, we'll meet you there."

I turned to look for the others and almost jumped out of my skin to find Abel, Mel, Jessie, and Randall behind me. I also spotted Callie grinning at me from one side. Apparently she'd rushed her shower so she could sneak up on me. Damned stealth skill.

I raised an eyebrow at her. "How did you even get them all out here that fast? No way you hit all their rooms."

Rolling her eyes, she held up her hand, the one opposite her spatial ring. "Group text, genius." I cursed. She must have messaged them as soon as I was out the door. I laughed it off and we waited, discussing possible food we might try to throw together if they didn't have a premade breakfast.

Finally, Benny and Celine came out, Benny looking much less sleepy and Celine somehow managing to look both furious and blank faced. We all set off after stopping to get Nat, Perit, and Valk and headed into the fort proper, looking for some of the guards. Once we found one, they directed us to where Anna-Marie was currently eating lunch (we'd missed breakfast).

"Princess," I said with a grin. "Mind if we join you?" The bottom of my mask was receded so I could eat, so my smile was fully visible.

Anna-Marie beamed at me from her place next to Amaya. "Solomon! I was beginning to think you'd sleep the day away. Come in, please, have a seat." She gestured and a bunch of formally dressed people appeared to slide chairs up to the table. "My mother sent reinforcements, and we've gotten the entire fortress de-trapped and ready for habitation. My father was over the moon that we've reclaimed this location. He sends his thanks."

I kind of doubted that. The king wasn't the type to say thank you from what I'd seen. "We were thinking about heading out today—have you seen the other team?" My cousin had contracted the leader and a bunch of the others. The last four I needed to do, or have Nat use today's wishes, but as shitty as it felt, I wanted the insurance of having a bunch of them bound to me directly.

I didn't think Nat would hurt us, but better safe than sorry. It made me all the angrier at my family, to raise us in such a way that I had to fear betrayal from my only nearby family member just because we were related.

Anna-Marie nodded. "We've got guards on their rooms. Your cousin told us that they were safe to leave alone, but we prefer to trust but verify."

I shrugged. Her suspecting them wasn't a bad decision. I probably wouldn't take them with us either. Sending them off on their own might be a bit risky, but not as much as sleeping next to them would be. We'd stop in and talk to them before leaving. "How about scouting? We were hoping for a basic layout of the area outside the map. Or folklore? Any stories about this place any of your guards know that might point us to some ruins or something?"

"Any notable location nearby is bound to be empty," she said dismissively. "At least ones we have an exact location for. The core itself has thousands of legends about random palaces, temples, and ruins—you're free to go over any of our books. As for scouts, yes, we sent some out to look around for any ruins. As expected, they didn't find anything nearby or it would have been picked clean."

I nodded with a sigh. That made sense. We needed some way to find ruins or a wizard's tower or something. Worst was that a lot of them might be underground. Anna-Marie had mentioned subterranean buildings were big here in the core, given how chaotic the surface was most of the time.

Getting into a reinforced structure like that would be a nightmare. Especially since a lot of them were *literally* reinforced, surrounded by metal structures to prevent...

I paused. Metal. Large deposits of underground metal.

I turned to Callie, a grin splitting my face. "I think I know how we can find a place to start looking." It was time to get some use from the other new skill I'd made. Song of the Soil was about to get its trial run.

Chapter Thirty-Three

I STOPPED in to talk to the other team. Their leader, Kagan, was polite enough, even if he clearly wasn't a fan. I spent four wishes on them, binding them to us. Sadly since the geas was the payment, I didn't get anything for those wishes, and I only had two left for the day, but I felt better knowing they were locked-in on our side. Once that was done Nat and I told them to go look around for any fields of flowers and report back with whatever they found.

We promised them half, which was enough that I suspected they wouldn't try too hard to shake the geas, and since they were the ones looking anyway it wasn't like we lost anything. Paying people with their own stuff was kind of a win-win from my point of view.

Once that was done, the whole group headed out into the woods. We didn't use the goats, obviously, though the summerspark crystal and other snow counters weren't going to be completely useless. Anna-Marie informed us that several of the ruins we'd run across would have other biomes inside. Entire worlds could fit into some of them, so it was best to be prepared.

Standing outside the fortress I took a long, deep breath as I called out for Song of the Soil. My voice rose into a tempo of cascading vibration. The music was a medium, the resonance of my voice acting as a translator between my mind and the earth around me. Singing came from the mind, and vibrations bridged the gap between that and the ground.

The skill formerly known as Earthseeking would help me find minerals and metals, both of which would be large portions of any underground structures. I felt my consciousness spill out into the dirt, rolling through the earth like otters gamboling in a river. It was a weird sensation, my Perception sort of... dispersing.

I'd describe it as something like I imagine echolocation would be, except I wasn't using hearing to receive the feedback. I could feel every worm, every beetle, every rock for *miles*. It was overwhelming and jarring, and I was pretty sure I could literally taste mud. I grimaced, forcing myself to concentrate. Song of the Soil was information overload, but after a few minutes of the song I was able to make some sense of things.

I started to walk. Not in a specific direction or toward anything. My eyes were closed, but I could feel the earth and had no problem avoiding obstacles. Trees and plants had their roots in the dirt, rocks were buried below the ground, I started to speed up, breaking into a jog and then a run.

Making sure not to flat out sprint and leave my friends behind, I raced through the jungle vaulting large boulders and bushes without ever opening my eyes. It was... glorious. I was lost in the song, one with nature. Each step made me feel freer, and I poured that into my music which made me more in tune with the world around me.

After an uncertain amount of time, I felt something interesting. A spire of stone rising up into the air and plunging down into the ground. I turned and bolted for it. I heard yelps of surprise from behind me as I changed direction.

I reached a clearing where the spire stood and stopped, letting my song come to an end as I breathed heavily, my lungs pumping like bellows and burning from exertion. That had been harder than it should have been. I leaned against a tree, panting as I tried to regain my balance and rest up a bit.

Breaking branches heralded the approach of the others. "Damn," Abel said as he jogged up. He wasn't winded, but he sounded annoyed. "A bit of warning next time? Running in the woods is irritating, all sorts of stuff in the way." He looked around, spotting the spire in the middle of the massive clearing. Above the earth it wasn't exactly towering. Maybe two or three hundred feet. The trees nearby were about that big and easily obscured it.

Beneath the dirt it was much larger. This spire was just the tip of the iceberg. "How far away are we from the fortress?" I asked with a frown. I... had no clue where we were.

I heard a giggle behind me and turned to find Callie smirking at me. "You're the one carrying the self-updating magic map."

Blinking, I froze for a second. "Oh. Shit I forgot about the map. Sorry my brain is kind of fritzing. Plus I still taste dirt, which is objectively not pleasant." Reaching into my spatial ring I slipped out the map to glance over it. I wanted to know where we were in case we had to make a quick exit later.

We were... far. I must have been in that trance a while. We looked to be hundreds of miles into the core, so we'd probably been going for an hour or two. It still blew my mind the scale of distance Ascendants dealt with. When you could run more than a thousand miles per hour your definition of 'far' had some marked differences. Of course, the core and this entire planet in general were huge, as evidenced by the gravity here, so it kind of evened out.

"Anyone have any idea what that is?" Benny asked, pointing at the spire. "Like, I know it's a building... kind of. But there were a bunch of options for what we'd find. Is this a temple, ruins, a wizard's tower? Also, what are we dealing with if it *is* a temple? Like... there are only six gods right?"

"Now," Nat interjected. "There are only six gods *now.* There have been others. Not many, but they've existed. It's kind of a mystery what happens to them. General consensus is that gods usually go somewhere after ascending, though that's not universally agreed upon. Different religions have different opinions on where that might be."

"So there might be temples to vanished gods here?" I asked with concern. I'd dealt with the worshippers of gods a few times. The Red Revenant Church, the Black Sorrow Cult. Devotees of gods could do strange things. They sometimes had access to imitations of their patron's powers. "Will they have any vestiges of those deities in them?"

She looked troubled. "Maybe? Not many gods still means hundreds over many thousands of years. Some predate the current six, some were contemporaries. Some people think the vanished gods were killed by the six. Whatever the case there might be remnants of their strength. You've

176

seen power from gods manifested by worshippers without their intervention. Black Sorrow does it all the time. I can't promise we won't see something like that."

Left unsaid was that if we were going to run into that, it would be somewhere like this. Somewhere mainly beyond the control of the six and their organizations. As much as this little dungeon run felt like a carefully curated field trip, this was a good reminder that this place was ultimately wild. Just because the other humans we were meeting up with probably wouldn't try to kill us didn't mean nothing would.

I was suddenly feeling a lot less sanguine about this raid. "We need someone familiar with local lore," I said firmly. "Because Benny is right. Running headfirst into a building without knowing what it is would be stupid any time. If it's a wizard's tower we need to know so we can keep an eye out for... magic... traps... or whatever. I don't know shit about wizard protections. If it's a temple we might want to just avoid going in."

Callie nodded. "You're not wrong. I take it we do our flower search first? Then make our way into the spire if we decide to do that?"

That sounded good to me. I closed my eyes and triggered Rhythm of the Wild. It was much less primal than Song of the Soil. Something about the musical aspect made the earth skill hit harder. Rhythm of the Wild was much more functional for quick and easy use.

I pulled out the map again and pored over it. I saw dozens of tiny spots of plant life, lots of them seemingly useful or valuable. Even if the flowers didn't grow, it was clear proximity to places like this made for a nice bump in plant rarity. To my disappointment, we didn't find a field of Lunar Cascade Lightblooms. It made sense—we'd gotten lucky before.

I put the map up. "Alright, call Anna-Marie. Have her gather her people and ask around about some of this. Take pictures of the spire, get close if you have to. I want to know exactly what we're walking into." Scan rings, aside from usually being connected to an overarching network, had walkie talkie functionality through a special short range (relatively speaking) signal that allowed them to communicate even without a network.

While Anna-Marie hadn't had one when we arrived, I'd had Callie pass her one before we left just in case. With a nod, my girlfriend peeled off with Jessie and Randall to approach the spire. I turned to my cousin. "Nat, can you take Perit and Valk to scout a perimeter? I'd have asked Callie, but she can use her shadow perception to get an idea of what's inside without actually going in. Might help with the identification."

She nodded. "Yeah, we can set up a cordon. Don't want to get snuck up on." She gestured for her guards to follow, vanishing into the trees at the edge of the clearing.

Celine also went off into the trees, doing some kind of wood elf mojo I didn't ask about because she already had a job, and Benny went with her, leaving just me, Abel, and Mel.

"So…" I said slowly, "what do you guys think about all this?"

Mel shrugged. "We don't have much of a background with this nonsense. We're city dwellers. We can fight, but this adventure shit isn't our speed." She jerked a thumb at Abel. "This one will be happy if you find him something to punch. Personally, I'm intrigued. But then, that's not what you're asking, is it?"

I shrugged. "Maybe not. I admit I'm curious how you think I'm doing. As a leader I mean." They'd both led their own factions, or at least Mel had. Abel… I wasn't sure he knew or cared much about leadership. He was kind of a loner, just often one with company. It was an odd thing to think about, but it was the only way I could really describe him.

"Want to know a secret, kid?" she asked warmly. "No one is a good leader. You make decisions. Sometimes they work out and sometimes they don't, but it rarely has shit to do with you. A leader is just a fancy name for a person who has to deal with all the bullshit. Deal as best you can and move on. Unless people start dying, you did your job. Sometimes even then."

That was a sobering thought, but… she wasn't wrong. That didn't mean I'd stop trying to be better, but maybe it meant I didn't have to take fuck-ups quite so personally.

I gave her a nod of thanks and turned back to the spire to watch my girlfriend and teammate send back their report. All I could do was my best.

Chapter Thirty-Four

CALLIE CAME BACK about twenty minutes later, having photographed all the symbols carved into the spire and several that had been sealed inside in the dark. "Well, we figured out what this place is," she said cheerfully. She held up a screen on her hand, showing an image of Anna-Marie, who waved happily.

"Hello, Solomon," she chirped. "You all made excellent time finding a place. I've had several of the older guards reassigned to a library Amaya had shipped down. They've been combing through all the legends and old forgotten stories we have, both native and from nearby countries. Based on the script, that spire is from the Binvari Empire. It's an extinct civilization that eventually ended up becoming the Banwar kingdom. They kept the language alive orally."

I made an intrigued noise. "Does the script tell you exactly what this is?"

"The spire is the ruins of a mining outpost. Most of the mine was underground. As for what's in there... who knows. It's possible it was cleaned out and abandoned. It's possible they all died out without moving any of the ore or got half of it and then left the rest."

"Good to know. I'll talk it over with the others and we can all decide if we think it's worth the risk. Do you know what they were mining?"

She smirked. "Of course. The only thing near Ladrigan worth mining: heartstone. There was a massive vein of the stone branching off the mountains. Most of it might be gone, but if there's anything down there, it will be *very* valuable."

I said goodbye and nodded to Callie, who cut the call. "Okay. So... what do you think? As the only person here who's gotten a look inside, and our resident trap master, you've got the best idea of whether this will be literal suicide or not."

Biting her lip, Callie glanced back at the spire. "I'm not sure," she said haltingly. "It's not suicide, I can say that for certain, but... I don't know if it's worth it. Can your ore detection power be used more... specifically?"

"Nope," I said with a sigh. "It picks up big-ass rocks and metal. It doesn't pick up big-ass rocks *full* of metal. It doesn't do anything that in-depth. It's only part of an Intermediate Skill."

She grunted, seeming annoyed but still obviously understanding. Skills could be pushed, but only so far. Sometimes you just needed a different Skill.

"I think we should go in," she said finally. "That much heartstone, even if they only left a fraction of it, could fund our operations out here indefinitely. With that much cash, we could afford to not only kit ourselves out even better, we could literally just hire an army most likely." Considering it sounded like Salara had done that with part of the reinforcements, we could go through her at the very least.

"Alright," I said, because really, I agreed with her. This was a possible treasure trove. But we needed to be careful. "We go slow," I warned, "and you and I will be up front looking for traps. With the bond I can use your Trap Mastery a bit for a second opinion." It wasn't that I didn't trust Callie, I was more worried about her getting excited and impatient.

She felt the concern, and rather than getting offended she just sighed. Callie had her faults, but she cared about the team. She wouldn't put anyone in danger because of her loot madness. Not if she actually stopped to think about it.

She gave a short nod. "Yeah. I can do that. Anna-Marie said that places like this, aside from more specific stories that make them more dangerous and powerful, also benefit from the overarching legends of the core. People know that ruins out here are all dangerous and filled with monsters, so..."

"So they are." I sighed. "Sometimes it's really inconvenient living in a world where concentrated belief can alter reality."

She chuckled as we rounded everyone up and told them what was happening. Benny looked excited. "Fantastic. Even if the heartstone is gone, mining operations strip out tons of small pockets of different materials. There might be some even rarer metals or stones they didn't need or recognize stuffed into a corner."

I blinked but then remembered that Benny's dad was a big shot in the mining community back on Callus, and my best friend had experience with this kind of thing. "Alright man, you're up here with us. Try to identify anything important, though stay back to avoid traps." He grinned and took up a position behind us, while Mel and Abel stepped to either side.

We approached the spire, finding a door at the base. As a precaution I triggered Eye of Revelation. It would be supplementary to the Trap Mastery and help me discover any issues. It also made things easier to spot. Less knowledge based when things lit up.

Stepping down into the long stone tunnel, I noticed all the carvings around us light up. It wasn't a lot of light, sort of a dim ominous glow, but there were so many of the things that it created a sort of ever-present luminescence throughout the tunnel. The place was, as usual, bigger on the inside, and we had no trouble getting in, even Randall.

Speaking of Jessie's big bear, as soon as he crossed the threshold a rumbling growl bounced off the walls, and Jessie tensed up. "Something is nearby," she said in a low voice. "We need to be super careful here, guys."

I nodded. "Probably past the traps, but we'll keep an eye out." Callie and I stepped forward, scanning the ground and walls of the tunnel. I noticed as I searched that some of the symbols glowed just a bit extra under my Eye of Revelation. I tapped Callie on the shoulder. "You seeing this?"

"Yeah," she hissed. "There are... a lot of traps here. Not all of the symbols, obviously, but there's a bunch. I can see a path through but it's going to be really tight. I'm not sure some of us can even make it. No way Randall can squeeze through there."

Grinning, I pulled her back. "I have an idea." I dragged her and the others fully out of the tunnel, then triggered one of my shadow clone charges. The clone saluted me and then bolted past me into the tunnel. I pulled back far enough to avoid any splashback and then waited as the clone ran headfirst through every single trap.

There was a dull thump of displaced air and then I felt a burst of pressure and heat as a massive jet of flames burst from the tunnel. We were off at an angle so we weren't in any danger, but it was still shocking. I walked back to the hallway, looking in and whistling. "Damn. It only tripped like six of them before it died."

I triggered another two charges, then retreated again, dispatching the clones one after another, making sure they sprinted full speed to set off as many traps as possible. Considering how much Might I had, that was fast, even with the enhanced gravity. The second clone tripped a dozen of them. The third managed to get about forty, because he tried jumping off the walls to hit different spots.

Finally the explosions settled. Callie and I approached the tunnel, eyes peeled through the smoke and debris. It was chipped and cracked, several hundred symbols were dimmed or completely extinguished, and there were rocks and dust everywhere, but still, from what I could tell there was a path now.

The clones hadn't hit every single trap, but they'd gotten all the ones on the floors along a specific route. "Alright, looks like we should be good to go." I looked to Nat. "I figure Mel, Abel, Perit, and Valk should be the ones up front now that we've cleared things out. That work for you?"

My cousin grinned. "I have guards for a reason. If I wanted to directly endanger myself I'd be more like you." She gestured them ahead. "You heard the man, you two. He's in charge. If you get blown up or crushed by a giant rock it's all his fault and has nothing to do with little old me."

At my glare, she shot me a mischievous smirk. "What? Being in charge means you get all the blame. Everyone knows you're supposed to blame the boss." I just rolled my eyes as the four of them got in formation at the front like we had, Randall taking up a space behind them in the center of the tunnel to block off anyone getting past. Jessie waited behind him, and the rest of us brought up the rear.

"Am I the only one thinking about the fact that there are primed traps in here?" said Benny. "Because that either means they cleaned it out already and set the traps behind them, or they tried to use this place as a fallback post. Whatever happened to the Binvari Empire anyway? Did Anna-Marie happen to mention that?"

The sounds of our footsteps echoed down the hallways as we headed further in. I forced myself to speak as low as possible, because the echo made even whispers sound like an avalanche. "No. But she didn't really have to. This place is a hotbed of conflict. Chances are good the Binvari got wiped out by some other faction in the core. Maybe one of the nomadic groups that lived here, or maybe an early equivalent of another kingdom. If they were still around someone would have noticed or mentioned them."

He nodded grudgingly, and we continued down the tunnel, my Eye of Revelation sweeping the walls and floors for more traps. There weren't any. Like at all. Which seemed weird until the tunnel let out into a new chamber and symbols hidden in the engravings on the walls lit up brightly. I hadn't had time to notice them before they triggered, since they were on the wall above our entrance. There was a grinding sound and four stone walls smashed down, sealing us inside the stone chamber.

I heard scraping and chittering, and I looked around through my Eye of Revelation to see from where. I froze in trepidation as I finally caught the glow. They'd been hiding outside the room and had entered in, but the weird... humanoid spider centaurs with green chitin and praying mantis heads and claws were quick to spread themselves out around us, surrounding our group.

Letting out a whistle, Abel looked around impressed. "Damn. I mean, they're entry level F-rank, but the sheer number of them is impressive."

Deciding to at least try to negotiate, I stepped forward. "Excuse me," I called. "I don't suppose any of you are willing to talk? You all seem like reasonable... bug creatures." My Danger Sense triggered (apparently it didn't count them as threats until they decided to actually attack) and I sidestepped some kind of chitin spine fired from a hole at the end of the claws of one the smaller ones in my field of view.

The spike slammed into the stone, gouging in deep, and I sighed. "Yeah, I guess that would have been too much to ask. Mel, no big blasts of flame, this is a sealed room and you'll cook us. Abel, don't collapse the walls or ceiling by accident. Cal... go nuts and don't get hurt. Valk, use your gel to protect Celine and Nat. Everyone else do your normal thing, and don't get in each other's ways."

I triggered State of Grace. Guess it was time to fight.

Chapter Thirty-Five

I'D SEEN a lot of weird creatures, but these... Whatever the hell they were, they were near the top of the list for horrifying imagery. My staff was out and spinning before a barrage of those chitin spikes rained down on me as I sailed backwards, triggering my usual combination of Touch of Tears and Consecration of Flame. The others had scattered when we started, and I saw Mel whirling a tightly contained helix of golden flames. Her rank up had given her some serious boosts to control it seemed, because the fire was so dense it looked almost solid.

A flick of her wrists had the helix whipping up and around, disconnecting at certain points and reshaping as she spun it, incinerating the spikes before they even got close. Callie had vanished and was emerging from the wall a hundred feet up even now, driving a pair of shadow spikes into the head of one of the monsters before vanishing back into the dark. Abel was leaning on his ability to slam blows into the monsters in tight quarters without using his manifestations.

I was forced to abandon my surveillance as I finally came down from my backward leap, feet hitting the ground and back hitting the wall just like I'd aimed for. Triggering Mountain Stance, I used the complete lack of room behind me to funnel the monsters my way as my staff swept out, crushing heads and knocking aside slashes. Poison fire licked from the wounds as the creatures fell back, some roaring in pain and some just straight up dead.

The storm of energy inside my staff grew with each hit, and I felt several more spikes smash into my armored body, bouncing off as my triple-strength defense prevented them from harming me and my armor held off the piercing damage. I kept wanting to use some of my skills, but it was hard to know when I should. My tricks were mostly made for damaging single large enemies.

Using Pit of Despair on either side, I at least tried to funnel them in a bit tighter. The pits of frictionless dust created a single alley of usable stone between them that led the enemy towards me.

I heard a colossal roar that shook the ground and saw a wave of the things thrown free from around Randall, who was tearing through them like paper. There were so many. I had no clue how they procreated, but however it was, they did it *a lot*. Hundreds of the monsters poured out of the tunnels above us.

I snarled in annoyance. "Alright, everyone group up," I bellowed. "I have a plan!"

Bulling through the enemies, I headed for where I'd left Valk protecting my cousin and Celine. Benny had stuck with his girlfriend and was putting all his unique tricks to good use, but when we all got close together again I made a gesture to Abel, who bumped his fist with Valk, then cupped a hand and created a massive blue simulacrum as a shield.

"Alright. I assume we don't have long." I nodded to Abel, who winced and returned the gesture, one of his hands clenching to buy us time. "Mel, can you create a massive firebomb on a time delay? Pack a ton of flame into a sphere or something and launch it up into the air?"

The masked woman shrugged. "Don't see why not. Worst case I just set it up to blow when it hits the ceiling. Why? I thought you said no big fire blasts because it would cook us all?"

I reached into my bag and pulled out a sparkling sphere made of chips of diamond. "From what Giancarlo said it'll keep us totally protected while it's up. You can't attack through it, but if you send up the attack we can raise it pretty fast. Granted, we can't take it down, and we'll need to wait an hour for it to expire. I figure that works anyway because it'll give the room time to cool down."

She chuckled. "Yeah, that'll work." Glancing over at Abel, she said, "Give me a few minutes, hon. I know that has to be painful." He grunted as she cupped her own hands, beginning to condense golden flames into a baseball-sized orb of fire. I felt no heat coming off the thing, but it was getting brighter as time went on, the flames becoming denser and more powerful. It was shocking to me that she'd managed to control the heat so well we couldn't even feel it.

"You ready for this?" she asked me as she focused on the orb. I grunted in acknowledgement, and she let out a long breath and closed her eyes as she concentrated. After a few moments, she opened them again, shouting, "Now!"

Abel and Valk released their powers, and Mel hurled the fire sphere up. I spat the activation word Giancarlo had given me for the defensive bubble, and a massive white shield wrapped protectively around the group, reaching about ten feet in every direction.

There was a slight shift in the light, and then the bubble was completely drowned in golden radiance as Mel's flame attack burst, completely coating the room in a powerful flame. I heard hundreds of high-pitched shrieks as the creatures were all incinerated by the wave of fire, and I whistled as I watched Mel's handiwork.

"Damn," I said in amazement. "You weren't messing around." Granted, I imagined having slightly more Impact than the bug things had helped. All her attacks would be just slightly higher level. Still, that kind of power and volume was nuts, and I made a mental note to trade Mel for some flame attacks at some point. Maybe I could help funnel some of her stats into Might. Even as a fire user she couldn't have gotten the kind of focused distribution Jessie had.

She shrugged. As the flames faded, it was shocking to see what became of the room. Melted rock, heat warped air, blackened walls—the whole place was a burnt-out graveyard. To my amazement though, the melted rock appeared to be pouring out of the way of the four exits to this place, opening it back up to the rest of the tunnels and letting the heat disperse, albeit slowly.

We sat down to wait, and I passed around some jerky I'd picked up at the bazaar. I wasn't sure what animal it was from, but they had free samples and it was really good. Sort of a naturally spicy red meat, kind of like dehydrated sausage.

Callie busted out some nice smoked cheese she had on her, and Nat ponied up some wine, and we all spent the next hour having a mini picnic and chatting over how we were enjoying the dungeon.

Finally, the sphere of energy flickered a bit (an automatic warning built into it) and then five minutes later went out, leaving us in a slightly warm but completely survivable room.

"Well, I have to imagine that killed most if not all of them," I said grimly. "But Callie, why don't you do a shadow check just in case."

She nodded but grinned at me before dropping into the darkness. "Don't forget the loot."

I groaned as she vanished, but triggered my Eye of Revelation, looking around for anything legitimately useful. To my surprise, there was actually a lot. The mantis blades had been actual metal, and as such hadn't been vaporized in the fire. Picking one up I tapped it a few times. "Hey Benny," I called. "Come give me a second opinion on this stuff?"

He walked over. "Looks like some kind of silver. Probably F-rank based on the fact that it survived that attack. My Inventing Skill is decent, but I don't have the same absurd foundation at this point that I started with. The further I go on my own, the less that initial knowledge matters. I'd ask a local."

Which was fair. I spun up my scan ring, a screen appearing with Anna-Marie's face in it. "Solomon," she said with a smile. "I didn't expect to hear from you so soon. Everything alright?"

I showed her the room, briefly describing the creatures. She passed it on to her research team, who were able to find the monsters fairly quickly given their unique appearance. After a few minutes, she came back, around the same time as Callie appeared from the shadows. "Apparently the creatures you encountered are called the Rakshari. Some kind of hybrid guard beast of the Binvari empire."

"Makes sense," I said with a grimace. "Nothing that ugly could be naturally occurring. How are they not dead though? Like... what do they eat? Aside from handsome Wishmaster candidates."

The princess snorted. "Personally, I find your resting expression a bit wooden." Callie snickered behind me at the comment. "But they seem to eat metal. That's where the blades come from. They consume raw ore and their bodies process it." I held up the scythe, and she asked me to do a few tests before her eyes widened. "Starbreak Silver. There must have been a small pocket of it near the main vein."

I raised an eyebrow. "What exactly is it? It sounds… dramatic."

"It's poetic," she said excitedly. "Starbreak Silver doesn't break stars. It fractures *moonlight*. It's a rare metal that can be made into special mirrors that refract and condense the light of our moon. They can be used to accelerate the condensation of the god Dew. Granted, you still need the flowers for it to work, but they can speed the process immensely."

I started immediately picking the things up and shoving them into my spatial ring. She just laughed. "Don't get too excited. I would imagine there are plenty of other metals mixed in among the Rakshari remains. Star-break Silver is rare. Still, it will sell for quite the price back in the city."

Thanking her, I continued picking up the metal blades after hanging up. Of course, Callie was grabbing them even faster, using shadow tendrils to snatch them up en masse. Once we finished collecting them all, we reoriented and headed further into the tunnels.

The Rakshari were apparently pretty vehement about territory, because it turned out we had killed them all. Callie found no living being in the rest of the mines. When we reached the lower levels where the vaults were, we confirmed that they had in fact emptied out the heartstone. There were, however, several caches of secondary metals left behind, including a small stack of partially eaten Starbreak Silver.

We packed it all up, and after we finished up, we headed for the surface, happy with our haul and looking to head back to make camp for a while before going out to look for more ruins. As we emerged from the tunnel though, we froze. Or at least, I froze. I could almost feel Abel and Mel shifting into position behind me, in case we needed to fight.

Staring down at me from the clearing ahead was a large blonde man with a square jaw, seated on a massive steed made of coagulated starlight, a V of similarly seated riders arrayed behind him. His piercing, slate gray eyes were focused on me intently.

"Well," said Gabriel Brightlaw. "I see another team has beaten us to this particular bounty." He gave me a cold smile. "Perhaps we can have a discussion about what you found down there."

Chapter Thirty-Six

I DIDN'T FLINCH. Brightlaw was scary. I could feel a pressure off him that reminded me of the bloodlust that came off Abel when he was angry, but it was... cleaner. Like I was standing in front of a force of nature. Smelling the storm on the air before it hit. That didn't mean I was going to let him screw me over.

"Why exactly would we do that? That's a pretty confrontational attitude. Can't we all just get along?" My voice was slightly mocking, but not enough to start a fight. I knew we couldn't win a fight with this guy, and I didn't want one anyway.

The horseman to the left of him, a tall, athletic, pale guy with floppy dark hair, snorted. "You think anyone wants to get along with the WCP? You're parasites. Leeches sucking the blood from the entire universe. You don't care who you do business with as long as you get paid."

"Wow," I drawled sarcastically. "You sure know me pretty well. You're telling me shit about myself even I wasn't aware of. It's amazing. Got any more insight for me? Maybe you can tell me what I'll have for lunch? Or what kind of socks I should pick up next time I go shopping. Knowing a guy with all the answers seems convenient."

"Riley," Brightlaw said flatly. The dark-haired guy fell silent, but kept up his glare. "As distasteful as his attitude is, I can't say I disagree with my friend. The Wish Curse Palace might not be a plague on the order of the

Black Sorrow Cult, but you're still intergalactic spies and assassins. I can't see much issue with relieving you of your ill-gotten gains."

Nat snorted. "What a surprise, the Red Revenant Church has a high opinion of itself that justifies robbing us blind. Must be nice to always have the moral high ground."

Before he could respond, I held up a hand. "Stop," I said firmly. "This is… Well, to say a misunderstanding might be inaccurate, but it's certainly not what you think. I'd been hoping to run into you, actually. My mother is a member of your faction, and I was hoping you might be able to give me more information about her."

Brightlaw raised a single dark eyebrow. "Truly? I'm afraid you've got the wrong idea. I'm not involved in personnel. I'm unlikely to have any knowledge of your average church member."

It was Benny's turn to snort. "Well good thing his mom is a Saintess. I guess you guys call her the Star Queen?"

The ice blue eyes that had been pinned on me snapped to Benny. "That is a very stupid and dangerous claim to make. Her Excellency is the daughter of his Holiness, the Radiant Pope. Her name, even her title, is not something shady individuals like yourselves have the right to invoke."

"Don't know what to tell you," I said, doing my best to take his attention off my best friend. "My mom's name is Sasha and she's an A-ranker. We were told the Star Queen was the only Saintess the Church had who fit the bill. Regardless of what you might think about it, barring some gross miscommunication, she *is* my mother, and I'd very much like to know where she is."

"If," he said, "and that's a big if, I had any idea where I might find someone of the Star Queen's level, I would never tell a person I've never met from a faction that brings the universe nothing but pain and destruction. You're lucky this isn't a more confrontational situation, or I'd end you just for making that claim."

I shrugged. "I'm not taking it back. It's true. What are you gonna do about it? Fight me?" I really hoped he wasn't going to fight me. There was absolutely no chance I could win—hell, Abel probably couldn't win.

He shook his head. "If I fight you, I'll have to win. You might die, and while I find your organization distasteful, I'm not so foolish as to end the life of a Wish Curse Palace representative. No. You have a choice. We can attack as a group, wage war upon your friends here, or I can select one of my number for you to battle. Think of it as a punishment. If you win, I'll allow you to move along unimpeded. If you lose... I'll take what you retrieved personally if necessary."

I felt that same pressure again, but stronger. I didn't mind though. He wasn't engaging me directly, and I had a vague idea why. I'd done a bit of looking into Adamant cultivators before entering the Glade. While being undefeated was an impressive feat, there were obviously limits. No D-ranker was going to beat a B-ranker, regardless of their path or momentum.

People like Brightlaw often traveled with powerful protectors who could intercept threats that far outstripped their level before they had a chance to lose. Unfortunately for him, the dungeon capped out at F-rank. His protector almost definitely couldn't come in, same with my own guardian. Which meant he had to be selective about who he fought.

"Fine," I said. "Pick your champion, and I'll fight them myself. But I don't go in for gambles where only one side wins. If I beat your champion, I want whatever answers you can give about my mother. I know you don't have a location for her, but I want any information you deem... acceptable to part with."

He hesitated, which was good, because it meant he was considering consequences. People don't hesitate when making false promises—there aren't stakes so nothing is holding them back. Finally, he nodded. "Only information I feel doesn't breach the security of the Church. But fine. I can give you a few odd facts. *If* you manage to win."

Gesturing to one side, he called, "Archimedes—I'll leave this one to you, my friend."

An olive-skinned man rode forward out of the formation and hopped down. His hair was shaved on both sides of his head and long on the top, pulled into a ponytail. His dark eyes bored into me as he walked forward, withdrawing a pair of hand axes covered with runes. They were clearly enchanted and were both F-rank weapons.

I slipped my staff from where I had it secured under my coat and spun it casually a few times. "So, what are the rules here?" I said calmly. "I'm assuming this isn't a death match. We going off the first one down?"

Archimedes gave me a grim smile. "Down is fine. This shouldn't take long." He twirled the axes, eyes burning with malice. He felt... strong. Higher end of F-rank. His stats were way higher than mine, except for the lack of the extra point of Impact I had. I triggered my usual poison fire, sort of wishing I'd just kept the weapon burning after the fight earlier.

He raised a brow as he saw the weapon start to glow but shrugged it off. "So... you ready?" I nodded. "Then watch out—"

I vanished. Double Trouble. Afterburner. Mercy Kill. Moonlit Night, triple-stacked density-shifted attack, Flurry of Blows, Marked for Death. And I topped it all off with the release of all the death energy stored in my staff as I brought it crashing down on his collarbone from behind.

There was no big fight, no struggle. I couldn't beat him in a drawn-out battle. So I cheated. Afterburner applied to every single one of those subsequent boosters with the stacking combination was an overwhelming burst of power he had no chance of standing up to.

Double Trouble left behind a duplicate and Moonlit Night shrouded me the next second. He was bracing for an attack from the front and the Stealth kept him from perceiving it before I landed my hit, not to mention my E-ranked weapon and my own enhanced Impact.

The blow slammed into his shoulder and collarbone and I felt it crack, Marked for Death bypassing his armor. To my shock, it didn't crush him entirely, but it drove him to a knee with a roar of pain, and he dropped one of the axes. I let Moonlit Night vanish, keeping the extra Afterburner charges in reserve as I stared down Brightlaw, who I was pretty sure would have managed to either tank or deflect that.

"We good?" I asked dryly. I tried not to let on how tired that made me, or the slight headache developing from all those stacking attacks. The fact was, that was *not* repeatable. I'd saved a bunch of death energy since I'd gotten my staff, and that had been the basis of most of the damage.

I'd taken advantage of the extra point of Impact and my powerful weapon to sucker punch him, but even that wouldn't have worked outside this exact scenario. I might have been able to kill him in a one-on-one with that shot if I aimed for his head, but he had teammates and I wasn't trying to kill anybody, so my only chance for winning this little contest had been a one-and-done blow with everything I had.

Brightlaw appeared pensive. "That was... an impressive blow. I felt a hint of a Path in that attack, though not one I recognize."

Path of the Doom Sovereign. I wondered if it was just using the Skill that did it, or if it was because I'd been utilizing my Fatewalker build to its full potential. How did one walk a path? Something told me the answer was different for everyone.

"You aren't pissed about the sneak attack?" I'd honestly been unsure if he would even accept the sucker punch. It had been a bit shady for the way I'd seen the Church doing things. Well, I hadn't seen much from real Church cultivators. Mostly fakes and distant relations. Still, it didn't hurt to make sure there were no hard feelings over how things went down.

He just snorted. "Don't be absurd. The match had started. Once it begins, attacking is simply the best course of action." He paused. "Well, for this opponent. I'd have been more difficult to ambush in such a way." Looking at his absurdly long lance and the shining charger he sat on, I could believe that. Marked for Death made a shot unblockable against anyone close to my level, but it still had to land on the target. It could be parried or deflected.

I offered a hand to Archimedes. "I can heal that up for you. It's going to take a long while to heal on its own." The death energy mixed with the poison was a nasty combo. Even after the poison skill ended, it would take time to mend. Especially given my E-ranked weapon. He grunted, nodding tightly, and I put a hand on his other shoulder, using one of my new improved heal bursts. It didn't close visibly quickly, of course, but that should speed up the repair.

Brightlaw nodded approvingly. "Alright, well, I did give my word. A bit of information sharing won't hurt." Looking back at his riders, he called out. "Disembark. Set up a table for us to sit at while we talk to our new... friends." He sounded a bit unsure of that last word, but I figured this could have gone a lot worse.

They dismounted, setting up a table, and we all sat down. I admit, my heart was pounding in excitement. My mom. I was going to learn more about the woman I could so faintly remember. I was going to learn more about myself.

Chapter Thirty-Seven

THE TABLE WAS SURPRISINGLY LIVELY. Everyone seemed energized and excited, except Archimedes, who was groaning as his buddies smacked him on the back and laughed at his misfortune. He didn't seem upset about it though, either with me or them, just taking the ribbing good-naturedly.

Brightlaw looked over his team and snorted, shaking his head in amusement. "Incorrigible, the lot of them. Sorry for the wait, I wanted to get everyone settled before sharing what I know. Mind you, that isn't much, but a deal is a deal. Before I begin though, I have to ask... Are you really the grandson of the Radiant Pope?"

"That's what they tell me," I said with a chuckle. "I'd love to hear about him too. I hear he's a terrifying guy, but then, any S-ranker has to be, right?"

He hesitated. "He is... driven." He sounded hesitant to speak. "His Holiness is a powerful and complex man. His youngest daughter was the only one of his children to become a Saint, though he has one son who is at the peak of Arch-Paladin, the church's B-rank combat Job. It's the combat equivalent to an Arch-Bishop. Regardless, the Radiant Pope was a household name long before the Saintess was born, and was, in fact, the youngest Pope in church history."

I nodded. "I heard someone mention he killed one of Black Sorrow's daughters personally. That's got to be a big deal."

"The Saintess of the Drowning Shade." He nodded. "She was, by all accounts, a complete monster. We've all seen the kind. Spoiled little brats with powerful parents who think they're the gods' gift to the universe. The problem was that Drowning Shade was *right*. She was a natural genius with her mother's ability, Enshrining Darkness. You've seen tame versions of it, learned as a Skill, I'm sure."

"That... weird conceptual rotting dark?" I said cautiously. "Because yeah, I've seen a few people use that. A Skill huh? That makes sense. Sounds like she must have been a nightmare. How did he beat her? And what power does he even have, like what's his main Skill, since he's obviously using the Job system?"

Brightlaw shrugged. "No one knows. No one has ever seen it and lived. He arranged a meeting with her on one of the Church's A-ranked planets. The challenge was very public, and she accepted without hesitation. Rumor says she brought her three strongest guards along, against their bargain, but none of them were ever heard from again. There is no planet there anymore."

I blanched. An A-rank planet. Even if he was at A-rank at the time, that was just... monstrous. How many people had died there? Cultists or not, the thought of inflicting that level of slaughter was just nauseating to me. Luckily my mask hid my expression.

"Yeah... complex. I see what you mean." I wasn't sure I wanted to hear any more stories about my grandfather. "What about his son, the Arch-Paladin you mentioned?"

"Samuel," he said with reverence. "The Shining Hand. One of the strongest of the combat order. At A-rank, Sainthood is achieved, and the clergy and combat orders merge in preparation for the ascent to the Papacy. Some say Samuel reached the limit of B-rank some time ago and holds himself back so he might continue to serve."

I nodded. "Sounds like a scary guy. Tell me about my mother. You have to know something about her, right?"

"Some," he admitted. "I know some of the stories. The Fist of the Radiant Pope isn't exactly a common sight in the Holy Dominion. She often travels, and even when she returns to the central system, a place I'm rarely able to go, she keeps to herself. I know she's powerful. I know she has two abilities, and..." He paused. "I can't say everything. Some of this is faction secrets."

I opened my mouth to protest but he held up a hand. "I know. I under-stand your frustration, and I do not seek to abandon my honor. I must simply decide what I may share." He paused, thinking it over. "Her loca-tion is not closely guarded, given her power. I don't know where she is, but I know where she will be after this. The trial at the Ruined Soul Temple. She'll be there accompanying some of our most talented."

I let out a breath. That was more than I'd expected. I'd have loved to hear stories about her, but it was clear there was something he couldn't reveal. Knowing where she was going was a big deal. I gave a shallow nod. "Thank you. I realize you could have just fed me some nonsense. That's more than I've ever had. I'd like to work together at some point, if you're open to it. Maybe if you see you can trust us, sharing more would be acceptable."

He gave a slow hum of consideration. "Perhaps. I will consider it. We did find a building some distance from here we were... hesitant to approach. It bears the stink of the fallen gods. Perhaps we might journey inside togeth-er." His blue eyes pinned me, looking for any sign of cowardice and weakness.

Grinning, I nodded. "I'm definitely interested. You'll need to tell us more about it, and I might run it by some of my local lore experts to see what they know. We found out the hard way that forewarned is forearmed. You guys have a hookup for local information?"

"No," he said with a shake of his head. "The kingdom we find ourselves allied with is... distasteful. They simply throw us at problems, hoping we'll either come back with the Dew they require or not at all, so they might steal it from our corpses. We've not found any of the Lunar Cascade Light-blooms. I suspect we're being steered toward the most dangerous areas possible to clear the way, while the local forces do all the real searching."

That sounded stupid as hell, given what I knew about how the flowers reacted to us. We were their best bet for finding them. Whoever was running his allied kingdom was too greedy to be sensible. I took a bite of the pastries that Brightlaw had laid out when his people set up the table. Cherry, and delicious. "Are you willing to switch to a different kingdom? Ladrigan is trying to scoop up as many of us as possible, and they're actu-ally being smart about it."

He grimaced. "The Banwar Kingdom has several dangerous generals that have been augmented with Dew over a long period of time. I believe I could defeat one in a direct fight, but sadly, I don't think I'd get the option. If we try to renege on our arrangement, chances are good they'll send someone after us. Not that I'm not willing to do it anyway, but I plan to wait until more kingdoms get involved and things are more hectic."

"Fair enough. Do you have any pictures or anything from the ruins you mentioned?" Probably more accurately a temple, given what he said about fallen gods.

He shook his head. "No. We didn't think to photograph the site. We can lead you to it if you wish to attempt your own research." He seemed pretty interested in how we would do that, and I didn't mind showing him. I'd be avoiding the Banwar Kingdom like the plague.

"Sounds good, we can go whenever you're ready." I heard a loud groan from Benny's direction as he heard me. He and Celine were chatting amiably with some of Brightlaw's team. Callie heard me too and turned to give me a nod as she started getting everyone ready to depart.

Brightlaw (who insisted I call him Gabriel) had them pack up the table and led us off into the jungle. My Danger Sense remained pretty damned silent given where we were, so I had no issue following him. Plus I got a good feeling about the guy. He was scary as shit, but he was also a man of his word.

It didn't take long to reach the overgrown building, a massive stone mono-lith of a place covered in moss and vines. It was so densely coated I thought it was a hill until we got closer. I turned to Mel. "Can you clear some of that greenery out without covering up the stone with soot?"

Abel waved the question away. "Soot can be blown away with force. Just burn it clean. Worst case somebody can water blast it. I'm sure someone here has an ability that can manage."

At my nod, Mel just shrugged. "One flashfire pressure wash coming up." She snapped her fingers, sparking a small blazing light, then tossed it at the building. She didn't put too much power into it, since we were trying to clean off the stone without damaging it. The moss and vines were G-rank, so lowballing the power was more than feasible.

The structure went up in a sea of golden flames, and to my surprise, it burned absurdly hot for just a second and then went out like a candle. Mel had excellent control. Abel stepped up and swung his hands, manifesting a pair of giant images that clapped together in a short, sharp explosion of force and pressure. I felt wind buffet me as the soot was blasted off the building by the sheer force of the vibrations.

"Cal? That good for you guys?" I asked my girlfriend, who had already spun up her scan ring to contact Anna-Marie.

The blue-skinned princess nodded with a wide smile, returning my nod of greeting. "I think that's plenty. Make sure to send over some more pictures for us up close, but that exposed enough of the building to work with. Not just symbols—architecture can be a big clue to what we're dealing with. The researchers tell me that building methods, materials, and things like that vary as time passes, when certain types of materials have more renown at certain times you can see wide shifts in style and construction."

After hanging up to take the pictures and send them over, it didn't take long for them to go over the new information and get back to us. Those Anna-Marie had hired or cobbled together were excellent researchers, and she must have dropped a pretty penny on books too. It was shocking what you could do with enough resources. Salara was clearly bankrolling her daughter generously.

Gabriel looked impressed too as the return call came up and Anna-Marie gave us a worried look. "We found something. You're at some kind of… sub-temple? But also probably a tomb. There's no concrete information about when the place was built, though based on the materials used we can tell it's *old*. A few of the symbols were translatable, though more because they seem to be proto-versions of symbols we've seen in ancient dialects."

"Sub-temple?" I asked cautiously. "So this isn't a temple to one of the fallen gods?"

She shook her head. "We don't think so. The symbols we managed to translate meant guardian, servant, disciple, and trove. That kind of thing. At least, that was the meaning more recent symbol variants had. We think this person was some kind of priest. A direct disciple of one of the fallen gods you mentioned. We also suspect they were buried with quite a bit of wealth. We don't know anything else."

I nodded. "Thanks. We appreciate that." I looked over at Callie. "I have a weird feeling that this place is important, but I don't want to just jump in and get us all killed. Can you check it out?" I knew she'd want to go in when she heard trove, but I was determined to play this safe.

She nodded. "I'll be careful." Then she melded with the shadows and was gone.

Chapter Thirty-Eight

WHEN CALLIE RETURNED, she looked... concerned. "There's something down there. I felt it in the shadows with me, roaming the halls or protecting the tomb, not that I could actually see it. Are you sure you want to do this? We can just go—there's no reason to go down there."

"Because I think we have to." I looked at Brightlaw. "You're feeling it too, aren't you? That's why you brought us here. Your fate sense is picking up something weird."

He nodded. "This place is somehow related to the nature of this dungeon. The way this entire construct works is too... deliberate. Too structured. It's been active for millennia, and should be safe enough, but something about it is just..."

"Off," I finished. "Agreed. I think this opening of the Glade is different. I don't know how. Or maybe it's not, and there was something weird going on here the whole time. Regardless, something down there is involved. I can just... feel it. We could turn around and leave it alone, but I feel like I would regret it."

I'd wondered before about the reasons for the Glade being like it was, but I'd just shrugged it off as Ascendant weirdness. This place, though, this was related. My fate sense had never been this overt before, but I knew what I was feeling. I was being actively pushed toward something important. I wasn't entirely sure this wasn't a side effect of my Path either. The Fatewalker build was partly rooted in divination—maybe there was some synergy with my fate sense?

Callie smiled and took my hand. "Hey. You don't need to explain it to me. You were willing to charge in headfirst when you thought it was loot because you knew I'd want to do it. If you think this is necessary, I trust you. Just… we should be careful. There *is* something in that place, even if I couldn't see it."

While I wished Brightlaw's team could do some recon on their own, I knew they would have done so earlier if they had the skills for it. It would be up to us.

"I'll send in a clone," I said cautiously. "Just because we're going in doesn't mean we can't be smart about it." Circling around to the front of the squat, imposing stone building, I approached the front, triggering a charge of my stored shadow clones. I only had three of them left.

A dark version of me warped into existence nearby, nodded, then headed inside. Closing my eyes, I focused on the connection and shifted it slightly with my soul. It took some effort, but with the progress I'd made after that shield incident, it wasn't too tough. I was able to force my vision to connect to the clone, looking through its eyes.

It was… weird. Not just seeing through another set of eyes, but the way I saw. Shadows can't exactly see in the dark because they don't see how we do at all. Vision is just the eyes picking up light, and shadows don't do light. The washed-out shades of gray the clone had instead were, at the very least, completely functional in pitch black.

Until the clone got ripped apart violently by what appeared to be some kind of huge angry cat beast made of pure darkness.

My eyes snapped open as I felt the connection snap. I winced. That was much more intense when I was leaning on the connection so heavily. "Well," I said hoarsely, "I know what was in the shadows with you."

Spinning up my scan ring, I called Anna-Marie. I wanted every bit of information possible before we went in. She answered quickly enough, raising an eyebrow. "Solomon, calling again so soon? What can I help you with?"

"Cats made of sentient dark," I said bluntly. "There appear to be a bunch down there, ever heard of them before?"

She frowned and turned to the side. "Amaya, doesn't that sound familiar? Not from the books, but something I heard as a little girl." Her brow furrowed. "I don't... Where have I heard that before? It's on the tip of my tongue."

"Suvaya," Amaya said quietly. "You're thinking of the Night Pride."

Anna-Marie's eyes went wide. "Oh!" She sounded disturbed. "I suppose I am. I almost forgot about those stories. So few people worship the Moon Lady anymore. You think the tomb belongs to one of *her* priests?" I could hear a tension in her voice I'd never heard before.

"The Moon Lady?" I prompted. Sounded like one of the vanished gods. "Is she important here?"

"She created this place," Anna-Marie explained. "At least, that's the story. The moonlight, the Lightblooms—these are all hers. But her priesthood has been extinct for longer than anyone can remember. You only hear about her from old family lines that passed down the teachings orally. Giancarlo's family were worshippers, that's how I remembered about the cats."

Well that was certainly a hell of a coincidence. Thanks, fate sense. "Tell me about the Night Pride."

"At first one darkness, then apart. The Night Pride comes to take your heart," she recited mechanically, in the style of a children's rhyme or parable. "They're big cats that don't exist until they do. They're completely silent and very fast."

"Charming," I drawled. "Any special methods of defeating them? I assume something with light might help?" Or maybe not, since my poor clone got ambushed in pitch black. The entrance descended down sharply and the light vanished pretty fast. A sharp flight of steps and then *bam* pitch black.

"The Night Pride doesn't fear the light," she said. "They are, however, somewhat special. Though they are ambush predators, they attack in such a way as to be seen at the last second. If you don't see them, they're just regular darkness. It's why their eyes glow."

I hadn't known they did, but that wasn't important. What *was* important was that I had an idea. "Awesome. Thanks Anna-Marie. Also, when we get back, I want to talk more with you about this Moon Lady."

I didn't think whatever was going on was a right now problem, but it might be soon. It occurred to me that this temple suddenly showing up now of all times probably wasn't a good thing. We said our goodbyes and then the entire group assembled in front of the entrance. We filled Gabriel's group in on what was going on. He just nodded, not asking any questions. My team didn't seem quite so confident.

"Evil shadow panthers that only exist at the last possible second when you see them… Anyone else not liking this?" Benny asked hesitantly.

"We'll be fine, especially with both our teams going in. And put your hand down Abel." I glared at my mentor, who snickered lightly until his girlfriend elbowed him in the ribs. I thought I heard Mel chortle a bit as she did, but it was impossible to tell under the mask. "Anyway, I have a plan to get us through. The Night Pride can only attack after we see them, right? So what if we don't see them?"

"You want to walk in blind?" Benny asked incredulously. "Because I'll be honest, that doesn't seem like the best idea."

I shook my head. "No. Not blind. I'll be able to see, but the rest of you will be following by touch, and they won't be able to see us either." I took a moment to explain Moonlit Night to Gabriel's group.

When no one argued, I shrugged and closed my eyes. "Alright all, everyone put a hand on someone's shoulder." I felt a hand on each of mine and triggered Moonlit Night.

A cloud of dense mist enveloped everyone, and I opened my eyes to a world bathed in light that only I could see. Striding forward, I focused on the skill, shifting it slightly to make sure the mist followed me, keeping us at the center instead of letting me remain mobile in the cloud.

"Remember before when you said we would *not* be blind?" Nat complained as we walked forward. I heard a yelp and a curse as someone tripped and fell into someone else, and my cousin groaned. "Ow, damn it Valk. Watch where you're going." I heard a muttered apology, and I had to tamp down on my laugh.

"Just be careful," I said in amusement. "On the upside, this will keep us under stealth, so we don't have to worry about talking. Not that you knew that a second ago. Also, I can *see* you sticking your tongue out at me Natalie. *You're* blind—I can see perfectly."

She froze, then shrugged, looking away innocently. I just rolled my eyes at her antics. It felt kind of nice to banter with family.

Our team and Gabriel's adapted to moving blindly pretty quickly. The hardest part was keeping Randall covered. His massive form was a pain to deal with, not that Jessie would let me get away with criticizing her teddy bear.

As we traveled, I felt something subtly shift the fog in a few places. It was hard to pick up, but Stealth is a form of Perception, and the movements of what could only be the Night Pride were barely detectable.

Callie gave directions as we walked. She hadn't really been able to search thoroughly, but the layout of the tomb wasn't complicated. A dozen hallways surrounded a central room, which was where we were headed.

We walked for about twenty minutes, my head starting to swim from stretching Moonlit Night so long and pushing it to follow us. When we finally reached the door, I pushed it open and led them all inside, slamming it shut.

After checking with Callie, I let Moonlit Night drop, and I collapsed to my knees, holding my head. My Stealth had covered twenty people, and I'd held it for almost half an hour. Still, the soul strain was already receding, and Benny put a hand on my shoulder to help.

"So, there are no Night Pride in here?" I asked as I stood up, breathing through the pain. Looking around, I noticed something weird. "Wait—I think I see why. There's no dark in here, or light. The whole room is like… red?" It was weird to look at. A sort of bloody twilight that dyed the room visible shades with no visible light source. Like using red night vision.

Callie squirmed. "I don't like this. There's no shadows here. This is… gross." She glanced around before starling. "Oh!" She pointed off to one side. "A coffin. Is that ruby? F-ranked Ruby too."

Gabriel followed my girlfriend's gaze. "It is. And I'm surely not the only one who feels what's inside."

I looked at the coffin, the stone exuding a bloody radiance that blurred the static red like a flare, almost painful to look at, and swallowed. Whoever was entombed was F-rank like we were, though they had more Impact.

I triggered my Eye of Revelation, looking for traps, and blinked as the red was forcefully suppressed. The coffin was the sole source of light now, also red, but less pervasive. More like a red light than red night vision.

I stared at the thing, until it began to twitch. Both teams tensed, everyone's gazes focused on the coffin. My eyes widened as the lid started to push open, slowly rising as a desiccated hand emerged, forcing the ruby covering aside as the corpse inside sat up. Its socketless mummified face turned to look at us, and its dry, cracked lips peeled back from yellowed and rotten teeth.

"Oh good," the obviously ancient undead rasped. "Visitors."

Callie stared at it for a minute, and I expected her to mention us being too hasty coming in here, but after a second I realized she was just drooling over that giant gemstone coffin and rolled my eyes.

"Howdy," I said with a wave. "Nice to meet you. Think you could answer some questions?" Because sadly, from what my fate sense was telling me, this guy was the reason we were here.

Chapter Thirty-Nine

THE BEING that climbed from the coffin was... wrong. Not a lich—I'd seen one of those before. This thing was corrupted on a fundamental level, to the point where even its Impact felt like a distortion. And it had Impact—a lot of it. Maybe not as much as Crighton, but way more than any of us.

"Sacrifices," it cooed. "Always so curious." The voice held a hint of mockery, and I could tell why. I hadn't seen many situations where the word sacrifice was a good thing.

I shrugged. I was kind of hoping this guy predated the concept of mono-loguing and wouldn't be too careful about what he spilled. "If you're planning to kill us anyway, might as well answer the questions. If we're dead, we can hardly spread it around."

My tone was light, but I felt a growing sense of dread. All this Moon Lady stuff was bothering me. The things I'd noticed about the dungeon and how deliberate it seemed. Something here was off, and I had the sneaking suspicion it would kill us if we didn't find out what it was. This dungeon wasn't what everyone thought it was, and with my luck I was pretty sure I'd gotten sucked into the endgame of whatever was happening.

"Foolishness does not become wisdom in death." It clucked. "But very well. Amusement, then. If only for a short while. Ask your questions, sacrifice. Though know too that your suffering will not be abated. Merely postponed."

I grimaced. At least this thing really loved to talk. "What are you exactly? And are you a servant of Suvaya? I—"

The undead stomped once, the floor cracking as we as stumbled to get our bearings. "Heretics!" it howled. "Speak not the Lady's name! Find Her magnificence squirming twixt your unworthy lips again and I'll rip them from your faces to sew myself a coat!" We all stared for a minute, and it stared back before hissing, seeming to calm down for a bit. "Very well. I am undead. As for my specific provenance, that is irrelevant. Simply know I was a great power who allowed myself to be diminished in service to my Lady."

I didn't even realize that was possible. I mean, I did, but you could only do that if you didn't have too many stats. Unless… I considered what Zeke had said, about being able to diminish Impact safely if you hadn't exceeded the stat threshold. You could have stats taken too. So maybe… "Did she strip all your stats away? Before… diminishing you?" What would that even be like? Valk said even losing a few was horrible.

The undead cackled. "A necessary toll. Millions of points of me, ripped away, dripping my soul out. Once they were gone, I was primed to be the fuel for her ruse. Not alone, no, there are others. Other servants. We give the weight of our existence to fatten Her prey. She waits for the harvest, to recoup from them all we have given and more. Enough to make us all as She is. A new pantheon of gods!"

"The flowers?" I said, appalled. "She's squeezing out your Impact through the moon and allowing people to absorb it through the Dew. How is that going to give you more Impact? Hell, why would she even *need* to do that? She's hurt too, isn't she? Did she get injured by the other gods?"

"Jealousy!" it wailed, the sardonic sadism fading into literal lunacy. "Despicable pretenders, envious of her majesty. They'll pay! They've fallen into the trap already. So many of their children and descendants have supped of our strength. It seeps into them, becoming part of them, infecting. When She reclaims it, the interest will kill them all! They'll suffer the fate they visited on Her. Emptiness, nothingness, condemned to exist as a wisp of a thing, if they continue to exist at all!"

So… this whole fucking place was a trap. Some old god who had been killed by the six wanted to return to life and she was going to kill a shitload of Ascendents to do it. Which was a huge problem because *we* had used that fucking Dew. I saw the others shifting uncomfortably. They understood what he was saying too, and they weren't any happier about that shit than I was.

"Alright, I've heard enough. Abel, Gabe?"

The undead cocked its head in confusion... right before a massive fist train-wrecked him into a stone wall hard enough to leave a psycho-shaped hole. The sound of hooves followed and a lance slammed into the spot his head should have been.

Sadly, 'diminished' or not, the undead was a fucking monster. The lance bit into the stone deeply, but Gabriel had to release it and hurl himself sideways to avoid a vicious claw of sickly green flame aimed at his throat. The big warrior rolled seamlessly to his feet as the charger he'd been astride dissolved into silvery starlight, and the lance returned to his hand with a snap of his fingers.

Peak F-rank stats then. His Impact wouldn't be enough to hold any more. Being able to strip him away layer by layer was crazy, but it didn't change the rules. What he'd said about the others, though, was deeply ominous. How many more of these crippled old monsters were in sub-temples like this around the core, tombs that were resurfacing now, presumably because it was almost time for the 'harvest'?

Now it seemed less crazy we'd stumbled on this place, or that Gabriel had at least. I was betting more than a few people might have walked into similar tombs. I hoped it wasn't anyone we knew because if our teams hadn't come here together, I didn't like our chances, and neither of us were pushovers. And even together, we might still die. Speaking of which.

I withdrew my staff from under my coat and started stacking attacks. I needed to wait for a proper chance to strike, but as soon as I got one I'd do everything I could to help. I cursed the fact that I'd used Afterburner earlier. The skill didn't last forever, so even though I hadn't finished all ten attacks I'd dismissed it. At least I'd already recovered from the weakness it induced.

Touch of Tears, Consecration of Flame, Mercy Kill, Marked for Death, triple-strength density-shifted attack—I stacked the blow high. My E-ranked staff should easily bypass the Impact difference. I assumed that was what was making Gabriel and Abel's attacks so inefficient.

209

They were… scary. Abel was up close, spinning around the undead like a top. He kept getting hit with vicious attacks, only for his form to melt away, revealed as a double. He was even doing damage, not much, but some. Cicada Stacking Steps was making each blow multiple times stronger than expected.

Gabriel had dropped the lance and drawn a short sword, stalking forward to engage the monster alongside my teacher. He swung the blade in short, sharp chops, mixing in stomping kicks and backhand blows with holy light, and he was somehow everywhere Abel wasn't. The two of them seemed to meld together perfectly at first glance, but on closer inspection I realized what it really was.

Abel was attacking all out, and Gabriel was slotting himself into his onslaught flawlessly. Every move was perfect, the exact angle, the exact speed, the exact power needed to keep the pressure off my mentor. It looked like they were playing music almost, except in reality, Abel was just the rumble of thunder, and Gabriel was composing an entire symphony set to the crashing booms.

The others were trying to limit the damage from ranged attacks. Randall had taken up a spot in front of them as a shield, Callie had a massive shadow barrier up, and Valk had crafted a layer of his blue gel-like defense in front of it to protect them further and to stop Mel's flames from adversely affecting the shadows.

It was shocking to see how much damage the undead's green flames were inflicting. At short range they were dodgeable, but the further they went the more the attacks expanded. By the time some of the blows reached our people, they were huge. Several of Gabriel's riders had taken up places in front of the shield and were softening up the attacks with counter abilities and their own blows. The holy energy they commanded was less effective against the green flames than I would have hoped, but everything helped.

I flicked on my overlay, focusing hard on the fight with the undead, as well as using Eye of Revelation to notice any traps as I waited for a weakness to exploit. I saw nothing. But I didn't give up, even if my head was killing me holding onto all my skills. I gritted my teeth and waited.

Finally, Gabriel managed to land an admittedly shallow cut on the thing's leg. It flinched as Abel slammed a blow into its nose, and I triggered Double Trouble. My staff whistled through the air as it smashed into the back of the undead's skull, carrying literally every ounce of force I could muster as I smashed my strongest blow into it.

E-rank staff plus plenty of other bonuses made the swing an absolute nightmare. If it had connected properly it would have been a crippling blow, or at least a severely debilitating one. Sadly, it was neither. I hadn't used Moonlit Night, which not only robbed me of a stealth attack bonus but also meant the monster heard the blow coming. It managed to impose its arm between the attack and its head before it landed.

There was a thunderous crack as the arm shattered, and the monster howled and leapt back, clutching the glowing, burning limb. My mentor didn't let the attack go to waste, blurring forward and driving a brutal fist into the injured limb before hauling back to attack the monster's face and head.

As it spun to keep up, Abel whirled alongside it, keeping in its blind spot and leading it away from looking at Gabriel, who had once again mounted up on his silvery charger. The blue-eyed man had his gaze focused hard on the undead and began to murmur something that I couldn't make out (maybe it was under stealth?). The lance he'd been using started to glow a brilliant gold.

With an earth-shattering bellow, the Adamant cultivator *charged*, every bit of his aura and intent behind the attack. I saw why he'd chosen the combat style he had because his whole attack strategy was *momentum*—crashing toward the enemy with all the power of an unstoppable object.

Abel, who was on the other side, saw the attack coming and smoothly flowed out of the way. The monster, still disoriented from the all-but-destroyed arm, took a second to realize he was gone, and actually tried to catch its breath, so to speak. That was the last decision it ever made. I felt Gabriel's attack in my bones as the floor rumbled with a shout of, "Rubrum Gloria!"

The tip of the lance smashed into the side of the monster's head like a freight train, driving the head of the thing to the side with a blazing flash of golden light. The lance point went into the undead's ear, lifting it off its feet and driving it forward with the charge... until it hit the wall. Then the charge kept going. And the undead's head did not.

Gabriel's charge stopped pretty much at the wall. His lance had been driven halfway into the stone, and the expanding length had exploded the head of the monster as it pushed in further. The big man was panting, looking drained, but I could see why he was an Adamant cultivator. Even without a weakness to holy energy, I couldn't have tanked that blow.

I nodded to the others, wincing at my own exhaustion, and gestured for Jessie to top us up. "We have some serious shit to talk about."

Chapter Forty

WE DEPARTED the tomb and gathered outside to discuss our next steps. Despite everything, Callie was pretty chipper since we'd kept the ruby coffin (apparently the Church crew didn't want something so… corrupt).

"Alright," I said as we all sat down. "Lot to unpack there, but before we start, do any of the rest of you feel… different?" It was hard to put into words.

The surrounding Ascendants looked confused except for Callie, Abel, Nat, and Valk. I recognized a pattern in the ones who raised their hands. Five of us—the exact five who had taken the Dew.

Callie nodded. "So only those of us with enhanced Impact. There has to be a reason for that. Do you think it has to do with the whole… Impact theft thing they were talking about? Like that our Impact came from them?"

"Shit," I said emphatically. "It probably does. He mentioned a harvest. I don't know how all this fancy higher-level shit works, but if she's using Impact she gives to harvest the full power of whoever incorporates it, why not just… keep it all? She'd have been done millennia ago right? Tons of people have been through here. She has to have a reason for making her 'pantheon' right?"

My girlfriend's eyes went wide, because as usual she followed my train of thought best. "You think she needs them? Like they act as some sort of conduit for the Impact to return once it's gone out? That would make sense. If that's the case then the Impact we got must have come from dead-head in there. Which makes sense, since this is relatively close to Ladrigan and the mountains where we harvested our Dew."

I nodded. "Maybe. Could be a whole other reason, but if that's the case does that mean we're safe from being sucked up like juice boxes? Or just safe-*er*. Because who knows if that Impact all came from one person. Maybe it was a mixture."

Nat cut in. "Agreed. We need to get in touch with the others and tell them what's going on. Not just for protection or to save them, but because we need to call a conclave to figure out what to do. If these assholes are waking up after who knows how long, chances are solid this shit is coming to a head. This 'harvest' is about to go down, and it's going to tear a hole through the five factions and the WCP when it does."

"Really?" I asked. "Given how rarely this place opens, how many people who have used the Dew are still alive?"

"High rankers live for thousands of years. They were the ones who knew about the Glade and sent us in. If they all go down at once, it'll be anarchy, not to mention that's potentially thousands of Impact, which *is* enough to make several hostile gods. I'd rather not be standing in their nursery when they're born."

"Point taken," I said, grimacing. "I'm guessing even if we weren't on the hook for this because of using the Dew, we couldn't just dip out?"

Nat shook her head. "Nope. We're here until the dungeon space starts to destabilize. Those marked by recent use of the slides are ejected, so we can't go back the way we came. It's why they said this could take months."

"It's true," Gabriel confirmed solemnly. "As for the conclave, that's a good idea. At the very least we have a place to start now. Perhaps if we kill all of these conduits, we can slow or stop this 'Moon Lady.' I have several friends among the other factions. Do you have anyone you can contact?"

"Bethy," I said without thinking, then winced and changed the form of address. "That is... Bethany Lark. The Vampire's daughter. She's friendly enough and will probably be willing to listen." Speaking of listening, I was guessing the mask didn't let Zeke listen in unless I was in active danger, or he'd have tried to contact us by now. We really were on our own down here.

Callie looked worriedly off into the distance. "That undead was scary. If any of the others run into one like him and they're a little light on muscle, they won't stand a chance. We need to get in touch with everyone fast." Her face lit up. "Wait! You have two more wishes left today. I wish for a message to go out to all the outsiders in the dungeon immediately to warn them." She fished into a pocket, withdrawing a small bag of coins. "I'll pay up front."

I caught it without looking as the familiar words scrolled across my vision.

Wish detected. Grant wish?

I accepted without bothering to check the stat requirements. It was a message wish—it shouldn't be too crazy. There was a flash and a small scroll appeared in my hand. I passed it to Callie. "Write your message and burn it. It'll carry over to everyone who came in with us."

It was a smart play, and I was glad she'd thought of it. Taking the scroll, she started to write, pressing the unfurled paper against the stone side of the temple. I turned to Gabriel. "Should we pick a time and place for the conclave now? Might be best to do it while we have a way to reach everyone."

"Agreed," he said. "I suppose sooner is infinitely better. Perhaps tomorrow? We should give people time to arrive. Speed is not something Ascendants lack, but the core is very large. For the location... Perhaps here, so we can show them the truth of our words in person."

I shook my head. "Too close to Ladrigan, and I don't trust them all. Plus finding it would be a nightmare. I think we should meet *there*." I pointed up at a mountain on the very edge of the skyline, one shaped like a closed fist. "That should be visible from plenty far away."

"I've heard stories about that place," Callie said gravely. "Fist Mountain. An ancient forbidden place where everyone fears to tread."

"Really?" I said, raising an eyebrow.

She grinned at me. "No, but it kind of seems like every place we go here ends up being like that right? I give it even odds." She winked at me, clearly trying to lighten the mood.

It worked. I burst out laughing, and Gabriel and his people looked at us like we were insane. I just shrugged. "Sorry, just sometimes things can be ridiculous. Laughing at the absurdity is a good way to keep things in perspective. Plus Callie always knows how to make me laugh."

She gave a satisfied smirk as she continued writing before passing the scroll to me. "What do you think?"

I skimmed it, and it looked solid. Information about the trap and about the time of the meeting, which I approved of, and generally just everything I needed them to know.

I handed it back to her, and she handed it to Mel. "Got a light?"

The red-masked woman rolled her eyes, grumbling about never having heard *that* one before, but sparked a flame and burned the scroll.

The paper went up nearly instantly, being consumed by the same purple fire I saw roll across my vision every time someone made a wish. Once it was done, Callie turned to me and grinned. "Also, I wish we had a compass that would lead us to Bethany. I'll pay that one off with one shadow jump."

Wish detected. Grant wish?

I excitedly confirmed, flashing past the requirements without caring. I was really interested in trying out the shadow movement aspect of her abilities. While our bond let us share some easily accessed tricks, stuff like her shadow jumping and my wishing wasn't so easily copied.

It also took me a second to realize she made the wish in Stealth and no one else had heard exactly what she said. They were pretty shocked when the compass manifested. The scroll was interesting, an item being a more convenient way of sending out the message. Turning to Gabriel, I pointed up at the mountain. "So we'll meet you up there tomorrow? We need to go pick up a friend on the way and we want everyone to have time to make it."

He nodded. "Some won't, most likely, but we're in a bit of a hurry. Waiting around doesn't seem like a wise choice. The question is, what to do if we find more of the Lightblooms. Should we avoid using them? *Can* we avoid using them if we hope to get out of this?"

That was a solid point. I grimaced. "Keep any Dew you find on you. We can discuss it at the conclave as a group. I can see both sides of that argument, and I feel like putting it to something like a vote is our best bet. Assuming we can even get everyone to play nice."

"Please," Callie snorted. "Gabriel and Bethany both having our backs will be a powerful motivator. Everyone has heard about the Adamant, and nobody wants to piss off a Vampire." Which was true. I knew I certainly didn't. Bethy was... mercurial, in a way that made her scarier than someone who actively wanted to just kill you in some ways. Though she seemed to be mostly under control.

The Adamant cultivator nodded. "We'll see you there. I'll try to contact any groups we see on the way. I hope most of the important teams are close enough to make it on time. We should be able to muster at least ten teams of the hundred that came."

We waved off our new friends and wished them luck. Once that was done, we set off in the direction the compass pointed. There was no indicator of distance or anything, but given how fast we could move I doubted it'd be necessary.

As we walked, I thought over everything we'd learned. My mom's upcoming location, the fact that this was a trap, and the possibility that we might die. Not to mention all the people in the dungeon that would die, people like Anna-Marie and anyone else who got access to the drops.

Just another reason we had to try to stop things. Self-interest aside, there were so many natives that could and probably would die during the harvest. Not all of them were awesome people, but some of them seemed pretty cool.

I felt a hand slide into mine and looked over to see Callie smiling at me comfortingly. She squeezed my fingers and I squeezed back, the weight lifting just a little bit. This might be a mess, but it was one I didn't have to tackle alone. We'd be okay—we just needed to take things one step at a time.

Chapter Forty-One

"IT'S SUPER DARK HERE," I said uneasily as we wandered deeper into the jungle that was the core. "Like, obviously I'm fine with the dark—we've been in worse—but this feels... thicker. Like why isn't my perception piercing this?" The trees had started to shift as we walked further in, from jungle palms and... other jungle trees to more forest-like pines and oaks and stuff.

As that had happened, the light coming through the trees above us got thinner and weaker, and the dark began to condense in a weird way. Callie looked particularly unhappy, and I realized a lot of the worry I felt was coming through the bond. "I feel like I'm swimming in mud," she muttered. "The darkness here is gross." She held up a hand, and I saw the dark above it writhe slightly as she tried to condense a shadow snowflake, but it dissolved before completion.

I triggered my Eye of Revelation, through which I saw... trees. Right. Middle of a forest. "What's the compass say?" I asked Callie to distract her. As an Abyssal Infiltrator Callie didn't just use shadows, she *was* shadows, at least in some ways. And being cut off from such an integral part of her legend was seriously disquieting for her.

She just pointed deeper into the woods. "That way. You think this darkness is something she did? It is kind of... Vampirey."

She had a point, but I just shrugged. "Could be— Wait, what was that?" Something had flashed past. Something *fast.* I froze. Wait, could this be more Night Pride? There was a rustle behind me, and I spun around, seeing another flash of movement out of the corner of my eye. Benny laughed uneasily. "Anyone else feeling like we're in the last twenty minutes of a bad horror movie when the characters get killed off?"

Abel snorted. "Please. No one as cool as me gets killed in horror movies." He paused. "Though, you would probably be the first one down. Quirky comic relief. They always die first." His vicious grin was all teeth as he aimed at my best friend, who looked even more disturbed.

Benny made an uneasy noise and Celine cleared her throat. "Mr. Castleton, please do not *terrorize* my boyfriend. It's petty."

"She's right," I said solemnly. "That's my job. Get your own verbal punching bag."

I seamlessly dodged a random rock Benny snatched up and threw at me, but I grinned. The exchange had deflated the tension, at least for a minute.

We all lapsed into silence. Abel, however, seemed... ill-at-ease after the exchange. "I don't pick on easy targets," he said finally, "and the kid isn't one to shake in his boots."

I'd thought Benny was hamming it up, but thinking it over, maybe he'd been truly spooked. The thought was disturbing.

Callie narrowed her eyes. "It's the dark. It's... doing something. Something bad. I can feel it scratching at the back of my head like nails on a chalkboard. Scritch. Scritch. Scritch." She twitched with each word, and I felt her uneasiness grow as the dark seemed to condense even more.

I cursed. "Shit. This is some kind of fear feedback loop. It makes us freaked out, which makes it darker and less passable." I saw another flash of movement and whirled, missing the source completely. Then my Danger Sense went off hard and I hurled myself to the side. Looking back, I saw a massive black cat congeal from the dark right where I'd been. But it vanished a second later.

Shooting to my feet, I scowled and triggered my Moonlit Night, concealing us all in fog. It *was* the Night Pride. Why were they outside? Had another of the conduits gotten out? Using Eye of Revelation, I approached my team, grabbing them and linking arms as we went. "Alright guys, cool it. We're safe in the fog."

"Oh yeah," Benny said lightly. "Because nothing terrible ever happened to anyone in impassable fog." At the pointed silence he just shrugged. "What? I'm not freaking out because of the dark anymore, but walking around in nothingness is unsettling."

Jessie nodded. "I hate to agree with him, but he's right. This is almost as creepy. What happened?"

"What do you mean you hate to agree with me?" Benny said indignantly. "Fuck you. I'm right about a ton of stuff. See if I let you date my sister now."

"Alright children, enough," I said with an eye roll. "Don't make me send you to your rooms without dinner. I got attacked by what I *think* was a Night Pride. What is the singular for the Night Pride? Is it just Night Pride? Because that might get confusing, but are they just called cats individually or…"

"Honey," interjected Callie, "I love the curiosity, but cat-killing idioms aside, I don't think now is the time. You saved our asses with the fog, but we can't just stay in here." She held up a hand. "For one, the stealth is fucking with the compass. Thing is just spinning in circles now."

I cursed. "Do you remember the direction it was in before? Maybe we can move in fits and starts. Walk a while in that direction then stop and drop the fog for a second?"

She nodded, pointing into the fog. I could see easily since it was my fog and the dark underneath couldn't occlude my Eye of Revelation, so I started leading us that way. Once we'd walked a few miles I stopped and looked around. "Alright," I said slowly. "Dropping the fog. Everyone be careful." Letting the skill fade, I held up the compass… which stopped spinning and then started to shift quickly but steadily to my front.

I felt my Danger Sense, but before the cat that materialized out of the dark could hit me, a gleeful voice squealed, "Kitty!" And a fucking *blur* of blue satin and black hair smashed into the thing mid-lunge and carried it clear out of sight. I looked down and almost burst out laughing as I saw the compass needle had followed the blur right past me.

Sighing, I climbed to my feet, calling to the others. "I found Bethy!" I listened to the thrashing and slamming through the trees until our Vampire friend came jauntily skipping back into the small clearing we'd stopped in, dragging a particularly large and scary looking panther made of solid darkness by the tail. Which was bullshit—that wasn't even supposed to be possible.

"Hey guys," Bethy practically sang. "Did you see my new kitty? Thanks for distracting him. He ran away after I killed that gross zombie guy." She pouted. "The others all got away, but this one was too slow. I couldn't pin him down until now, though." She paused. "I think I'll call him Donuts."

My eyes widened. "Zom— Wait, Bethy, did you go into an old temple?" She was a *lot* scarier than I had expected. Holy shit. The other conduit had taken me, Abel, and Gabriel together to put down. Had she killed one all by herself? That was crazy.

She nodded. "I liked the ambiance. Daddy says crypts and temples are good thinking places. He calls it the 'majesty of the profane' but only when he's around other people and is trying to sound pretentious. I think he does it half the time to see if anyone has the guts to laugh at him about it. Nobody ever does though. I got your message by the way. Super cool delivery method. But I'd already killed that old corpse by the time it showed up."

That was probably more than I should safely know about the trolling habits of the strongest S-ranker in the world. But it was nice to know the message delivery worked properly. Not that I'd doubted my power, but I wasn't sure how immediate the delivery might be. Or how overtly noticeable. For all I knew the thing might have dropped a scroll into their pockets or something.

I stared at the manifested shadow cat that didn't seem to be following the rules of its own existence and pointed at it tentatively. "I... I think it might be suffocating."

She looked back at the cat casually before releasing its tail. "Donuts, go to your place." The desperate and terrified shadow panther dove for Bethy's shadow, immersing itself in the darkness behind her which looked... deeper than it should. Apparently Vampires *could* mess with darkness.

Acting like she hadn't just completely subverted most of the rules we were given about the Night Pride, Bethy gave us a wide, toothy smile. "So you guys came to pick-me-up? That's super sweet. I was totally going to head to the mountain myself soon. I gotta find my besties though." She giggled in embarrassment. "I *might* have ditched them when I was chasing Donuts, but I'm sure they'll catch up, yeah?"

I somehow doubted Aida and Tracey were so sanguine about being left behind. "Sure, we can wait. Sorry we can't help you find them or anything, but the compass only works on you." Callie held up the device. It was pointing right at Bethy still, which was interesting. I supposed the wish hadn't been that specific, and going with an item meant the effect wouldn't fade, at least not soon.

"Whoa!" Bethy said, eyes going wide. "That's badass. You have a compass that always finds me? That sounds so useful. I bet Aida would totally buy that off you."

Pausing, I considered that. It was Callie's compass, she'd wished for it, but the fact that it still existed was pretty useless to us now. "We can talk about that later." I turned to Callie. "Since apparently Bethy chased away the Night Pride." And let them *loose*. "Can you check the shadows near us to make sure we're clear of any more unwanted visitors besides"—I paused, grimacing as I forced myself to say the ridiculous name—"Donuts?"

Even in a situation like this, it was hard not to smile at the absurdity, and Callie had to fight down a giggle as she nodded, which might have been Bethany's entire point to picking it. My girlfriend closed her eyes, knelt down, and slid her fingers into the shadows at her feet, just enough to barely breach the surface.

I wasn't sure if there was a connection between how deep she went into the shadows and her range, but I didn't think so. More likely she was dipping a toe to be safe in case she needed to pull out in a hurry. The Night Pride were dark creatures, so it was probably a smart move.

Bethy just giggled. "Let me know if there are any more. I want to get Donuts a friend." I could swear I heard a whimper from her shadow as she said that, but I chalked it up to my imagination.

Callie's eyes snapped open. "Nope. Whatever weird corrupted darkness they were using is gone—they really did run. I did, however, find the rest of Bethy's team. Aida and Tracey are ahead of them, charging off after you." She pointed. "They're in that direction."

Shrugging, I looked at the Vampire. "Want to go pick them up before we leave?" She seemed comfortable out here. Somehow she'd avoided having her blue velvet dress and long fingerless gloves ruined during the scuffle, and none of the plant life seemed to dare to get near her.

Nodding happily, she turned in the direction Callie had pointed and raced off. I sighed, looking at my girlfriend with grim amusement. She just shrugged, holding up the still active compass, and we all trekked after her.

Chapter Forty-Two

FIST MOUNTAIN WAS *HUGE*. There was some spatial bullshit going on with it, because once we got close it seemed to multiply in size. Climbing it was a trial since its surface was nearly smooth and the rock was fucking F-rank stone. Chipping through it took effort and energy. Making handholds up the side would have taken weeks.

"This mountain is much bigger than it looked from that temple," I complained as I hauled myself further up the rock face. "Like... unnecessarily big. Also nearly completely vertical up the sides. What is this even for? Like nothing could possibly live up here unless it flies. Are there, like, dragons?"

Callie snickered from her place hanging off my back. "Less talking, more climbing. Also, this is a plateau, not a mountain—it's flat on top."

I glared over my shoulder. "First off, that's just being pedantic. Second of all, why am I climbing with you on my back? You have a higher Might than I do—I should be riding on *your* back." I paused and leapt for a crevice about a thousand feet up that I could barely see because of Eye of Revelation. I missed, and pushed off the air with Ripple Running to course correct, snagging it and holding on while the others used the ropes to climb up to my last handhold.

In truth, I knew why I was climbing. State of Grace made any screwups irrelevant (important given the enhanced gravity and the absurd altitude) and Ripple Running let me catch myself if I missed.

Callie poked me in the ribs. "Don't you know you aren't supposed to comment on a lady's weight?""

Even as an F-ranker Callie wasn't that heavy, given I was the same rank and twice her size, but I still groaned and wobbled back and forth dramatically. "Can't. Breathe. Darkness. Closing in." Then I paused. "Speaking of darkness, why don't you just port us up there?"

She giggled at my dramatics, but when I asked the question, she looked genuinely ashamed. "It's too far. I think you're right about the spatial bullshit. It's hundreds of miles up this thing. If it helps, once we hit the curve of the fingers on the fist shape, this becomes a normal mountain climbing trip."

I boggled. Hundreds of miles. That was... insane. "Did you ask Anna-Marie about this mountain? If it's warping space this badly there's no way it's normal."

She shrugged. "She didn't know anything. Probably predates the books she's using. This rock is... harder than the stuff the castle is made of. It's got to be old as shit. It might be half-step E-rank. I think the gravity is even worse here too."

Nodding, I huffed out a laugh. "I didn't want to say anything, but yeah. This is winding me more than expected. Of course, the extra cargo isn't helping!" I bellowed pointedly down to the literal twenty people, four wolves, and giant bear hanging from the ropes tied around my back and shoulders.

"Shut up, you wuss!" Benny yelled back, trying not to cackle in glee. "What's that giant lumbering ass of yours for if not to be a beast of burden? We don't pay you to think. Mush!"

"I will *drop* you!" I yelled back, but he completely ignored me, giggling up a storm as I glared down at him. "I hate this place," I grumbled. "I can't wait till this bullshit is over and I can go meet my mom." I grinned through the mask at Callie. "I wonder if she's going to be as welcoming as your mom was. The thought of you two teaming up against me kind of fills me with dread. Like... in a good way."

"Ah yes," Callie said sagely. "Because mother-in-laws always get along with the wife." Her mouth snapped shut, and I felt mortification through the bond as I let out a gleeful cackle of my own. "Shut up!" she yelped before I could respond. "It's a turn of phrase. Don't say a word."

"Yes, dear," I drawled, grunting as she elbowed me in the ribs again. Worth it.

Identifying a new spot, I jumped again. Another one or two thousand feet, but unfortunately, this time it was mostly horizontal.

"About your mom," Callie said softly. "Just... don't have too many expectations? It's great that you might find her again, but she *did* leave. Even if your dad made her, that's not... great."

I sighed. "Yeah. I feel you. I'm trying to keep things low key. Hope for the best, expect the worst, and never be disappointed. I won't get ahead of myself." Some people might have taken it personally, might have assumed she was being negative, but I could feel the love and concern wrapping around me through the bond. Callie was terrified my mom would let me down, be just another bad parent to complete my set. She didn't want that. She wanted me to have a mom like hers.

"Are we there yet?" bellowed a bored voice from below us.

I rolled my eyes. "Bethy, don't make me turn this spelunking expedition around. We will *tell* you when we get there."

"But I'm *bored,*" she wailed. "And Donuts is hungry! He says the razor taloned eagles that nest on this mountain taste terrible!"

I froze, looking down at her. *"What razor taloned eagles?"*

Even from dozens of feet up, I could see the look of confusion on her face as she pointed. "Those razor taloned eagles."

I turned to look over my shoulder, past Callie, as a *massive* bird whose talons appeared to be literal steel razors silently swept down on us. I tensed and readied myself to attack, but I stopped as a massive hand materialized and slapped the bird out of the air. It fell about a hundred feet and then caught itself, eyeing us angrily as it circled away, staying within range but steering clear.

I looked down to see Abel shaking out his hand. "How many more times

226

can you do that?" I called down to him. I wasn't sure how much good it had done, but it seemed to have at least deterred the beast.

"A bunch!" he yelled back. "But it's not really going to hurt them. Airborne enemies are more vulnerable to a stable attack like that, but it's more jarring than damaging. We need to hurry up—once more show up we're screwed."

Glancing to Callie, I made a sound of consideration. "So… how durable is this rope do you think? Like, could I swing it around without it breaking? Because I feel like a bear on a rope is a good counter to eagles." It was an F-rank rope, but there were a lot of F-ranked people on it, and it could get cut or something by the talons.

A chorus of voices echoed up from below as every member of my team started screaming at me *not* to use them as a bludgeon to attack flying apex predators. Wimps.

"Shane," Callie began slowly, "that's a *really* bad idea. We're dozens of miles off the ground next to a gravity-warping super mountain. If the rope gets cut, they'd all fall to their deaths."

Sighing, I nodded. "I know. I just figured I'd bring it up. How often do you have a giant bear on a rope? My question is, why haven't we seen more of the eagles? You think they might be nocturnal? Because if so, Abel is right —we need to hurry up. I don't want to get swarmed in the dark."

"Maybe." She grimaced. "How long do you think it'll take if you push? To get us up to the fist's curvature?"

"I could… probably manage it in an hour if I'm willing to fry myself," I said hesitantly. "If I spam Ripple Running, I could just jump us right up the side one step at a time. My head will be mush by the time we hit the top, though—I'd be useless for hours."

I really *didn't* want to do that. The extra gravity meant the jumps would be even less effective, and it seemed to be increasing the higher we went. That last jump hadn't been quite a thousand feet, even horizontally.

"Could you do a pair of shadow wings, Cal? Combined with State of Grace they should increase hang time and the distance I can go in a single bound."

"Of course," she said with a slow nod. Closing her eyes, a pair of massive shadowy bat wings unfolded from behind her, and she clung to me. "If you start getting too out of it, tell me. We can look for another handhold and give you a rest. It's more important that you're okay than that we get to the top fast. We can always fight off some birds."

I nodded, swallowing hard. "Alright," I called down to the others. "We're taking the express elevator here, folks, so hold on!" I waited until I got agreements from all of them, then pushed off backwards to get some room. There were screams at the abrupt motion, but with the wings and warning, nothing too bad.

I still had a few steps left of Ripple Running. I planted my feet on the air, bent my knees, and pushed off *hard*. Two hundred fifty Might goes a long way, even with enhanced gravity and tons of animals and humans hanging off you. I felt the rope jerk as the pressure shot us upward, aided by State of Grace. When I felt myself begin to fall, I stepped again, another powerful shove with my legs. Then a third. I mapped the distances in my head, and I could feel myself going just a bit less far with each jump.

After four jumps I ran out of Ripple Running and triggered the skill again, bouncing once more off the air to carry us up. I felt my legs begin to burn a bit, but I wasn't worried. I triggered a heal burst, flooding my body with energy, and it easily countered the strain. I jumped again and again.

This was going to take a long time, I could tell, but that wasn't a problem. It would be ages before using Ripple Running would start to affect my soul. It was just a normal skill, after all. I felt Callie clinging to my back, wings folded, spreading them at the apex of each jump to slow us down.

I hoped there was a decent amount of hiking to do once we hit the curvature—a basic hike would let me recover after the ordeal of pulling everyone up. This conclave was going to be a big deal, and I wanted to be at my best. Wouldn't do for everyone to know how out of my depth I was here.

Chapter Forty-Three

To my surprise, I wasn't fried by the time we reached the top. I was sore and my head was ringing a bit, but I was more than functional. That whole mess with the shield had really worked out my soul, and I was starting to see real gains from the constant grinding.

Once we hit the curvature, we had to pull everyone up, and I smirked a bit as I saw them all glaring in annoyance. Benny flipped me off when he finished untying himself. "That rock is *hard*. We smacked into the damn mountainside like six times on the way up. You couldn't have been a bit more careful?"

"Considering I made like a thousand plus jumps?" I shrugged. "I feel like I did a damned good job." I slumped down with a groan, breathing hard. It was an interesting sensation. Unless Impact was involved my physical prowess had mostly been more than enough to handle anything I got into up to now. Not that I hadn't been overpowered on several occasions, but just wearing myself out through constant physical effort was something I attributed to the old me.

Benny rolled his eyes. "Whatever." Looking up the mountain, he winced. "So, this curvature thing isn't going to be a small trip huh?"

I sighed. "Probably not nearly as far as the trip up here, but given the sharp incline and the ice, not to mention whatever else is probably up here, we'd best take it slow. It's coming up on nightfall, and I think going through frozen steep mountain terrain in the dark is a stupid plan. Luckily, we brought a ton of useful materials for exactly this environment."

I snapped my fingers and a glowing orange stone appeared in my hand. Tossing it to Benny, he gave a pleasant groan when he caught it. "That feels amazing, like taking a dip in a hot tub. What is this?"

"Summerspark crystal," I said as I withdrew another and passed it to Callie. "We traded for it with Anna-Marie's brother. It'll be used up after a few hours, but while it's active it cocoons your body in warm air. You can use a larger amount to cover an expanded area, creating sort of an exclusion zone for cold. I'm going to set one up for the bunker. The conclave is tomorrow and showing up early won't have much point. Might as well rest up."

He nodded. "Seems like a good plan. I know I could use a break—slamming into rock walls and being dragged through the air for hours isn't much fun."

"Next time *you* can jump on air for hours to drag literal tons of F-ranked beings up the side of a gravity-altering space-warping super mountain," I said sweetly. Then I paused. "Oh wait, no you can't, so shut up." Callie snorted at that, but when Benny and I turned to look she was gazing back at me innocently.

I heard a squeal of glee and Bethany basically appeared out of nowhere, scaring us all shitless. "That was *so much fun!*" she cheered. "Can we do that again?" Clearly, she hadn't had a problem with hitting the side of the mountain. Somehow that didn't surprise me.

"I think we'll have the next conclave somewhere a bit less... hostile," I said with amusement. "In the meantime, we're going to bunker down for the night, literally. You guys have your own accommodations or do we need to share?"

She waved me off casually. "Oh no. Daddy makes me travel with lodgings. My Bone Burrow is pretty comfy. What about you? What did you guys bring to camp in?" Her cheerful demeanor made it clear she considered this a fun little outing, despite the circumstances. I also realized she wasn't holding a summerspark crystal and yet she was clearly fine in the cold. Vampire stuff probably.

Reaching into my spatial ring, I pulled out the spike of stone that was our enchanted bunker. "Picked this up in town," I said, brandishing it proudly.

I really hoped it could actually penetrate the mountainside or we'd be screwed.

She looked it over with interest. "Wow, lots of really tiny runes on that, it must be super enchanted. This your first time using it? I bet it looks pretty cool when it makes your bunker for you. I can't wait to watch!" Her eyes were blazing with crimson glee as she stared at the device. It was honestly kind of terrifying.

Not that she was wrong. It did sound like it would be pretty interesting to watch. "Alright," I said with a laugh. "Let's get a bit further up the slope, maybe find a patch of more level ground or at least something away from the edge."

Callie nodded, pointing off to the left and ahead. "I scouted as best I could. I think there's a flat spot over there we can use. Hard to get a read with all this snow. The shadows aren't exactly numerous up here—it's stupidly bright."

I paused. She was right. We were high up in the air, and night had fallen. The oversized moon above the dungeon had turned this snowy mountain slope into a field of blinding white light with barely any shadows to be found aside from a few random spikes of rock jutting up.

That was... unsettling. Seeing the moon so bright and close made me nervous, given what we'd learned about Suvaya. What exactly was this mountain? I shook that thought off. I was being paranoid. Not everything was some huge conspiracy. Probably.

Following Callie's advice, we did find some flat ground, a small indent in the steep rock. I stepped inside, looking around with Eye of Revelation to make sure we were safe. Then, kneeling down, I cleared some snow and slammed the rock spike into the mountain as hard as I could.

It sunk in about an inch. I growled in annoyance, cracked my neck, took a firmer grip, and triggered Mercy Kill as I brought it back down. Heavy Hands was passive and with Mercy Kill boosting the attack and all my power behind it, I got the damned spike halfway into the cold rock.

Once it dug in, I pulled my hands back, watching as a series of runes so small they were almost unreadable lit the entire spike with yellow-orange light. The light traveled down the spike then back up a few times before it finally expanded out into the small cracks in the rock around it.

The cracks widened, pushing themselves open as the ground under us shook slightly. As I watched, the stone began to spike up around us, the spears joining into joints and lines as they began to outline a rather decently sized building. I stepped back, watching in awe as the bunker constructed itself out of the mountain itself.

Once the rumbling stopped, I stepped inside and walked to the center of the floor where the spike still sat, yanking it out and looking it over. The thing looked... drained. I knew it wasn't single-use, but it would take a while for it to recharge off the ambient energy. I stowed it away and walked to the door.

The stone had formed a barrier on a sort of interlocking rock hinge that could be pushed open easily. Pushing it open, I stepped out of the spacious bunker and looked around, spotting my friends a bit away.

Benny whistled as he approached. "Well that's a neat little trick. Is it like a temporary template made of the natural rock? You removed the original spike, right?" His inner Inventor seemed to be at the forefront, and I passed him the spike.

He looked over it. Benny wasn't an Enchanter, but runes played a part in enchanted items of all kinds and he could understand their basic meanings. Studying the tiny script, he hummed in interest.

I admit I was curious myself. I knew what it did, but not much else. "How does it work?"

He handed it back. "It's basically a rechargeable enchanting template. It makes the bunker and enchants the thing as it does. The bunker's enchantments fade over the next twenty-four hours as the spike recharges. The structure'll be gone by the time we can make a new one. You can leave the spike in place if you want to make a more long-term shelter, but it won't charge while it's embedded."

Nodding, I reached into my ring, withdrawing more of the summerspark crystal. "Alright, help me set up an exclusion zone around this place. Rock doesn't exactly retain heat, especially not up here. I don't want to sleep freezing my ass off."

Benny snickered. Then he, Callie, Bethy, and the Vampire's two thralls all took crystals and laid them out in the formation I gave them. The Landrock Bunker itself was, as we'd been told, a twenty-five-foot square. At least on the outside. It was bigger internally, which could have been a feature of the enchantments Benny mentioned or could have been because of the nature of the mountain. Giancarlo had said it drained power from the nearby rock when creating itself, and I wasn't sure exactly what that would do in a place like this.

Once we set up the exclusion zone for the cold, I turned to the others. "So, everyone can pick wherever they want to sleep inside. I have sleeping bags in my spatial ring if any of you don't. Bethy's people will crash in her Bone Burrow."

Ten people inside of a relatively spacious bunker wasn't too tight a squeeze, especially since several of us would be sharing sleeping bags. The interior, based on the quick look I'd had, was probably about a hundred feet in each direction. Stepping inside, I was relieved to see there was plenty of room. Well... for humans. Randall slept outside, playing guard bear and enjoying the warmth since he couldn't fit comfortably into the bunker.

After we confirmed everything with Bethy and agreed on a time to wake up, we all piled into the bunker, setting up our sleeping bags inside. In fact, the place was so big we were able to set up whole tents for a bit of privacy. Once we got settled, we all gathered around the spot the spike had been stuck in and I set up a small magic stove I'd picked up at the bazaar.

I cooked everyone a nice meal of grilled cheese, and we washed it down with some canned tomato soup. It was delicious, of course, and everyone seemed to be in a good mood by the time we finished.

Once we were done, I paused a second before speaking to everyone. "Guys, this conclave tomorrow—it's going to be tense. No one will be happy finding out we're all sacrifices. Hell, some of them might not believe us. Be on your guard, okay? I don't want to lose anyone."

Abel nodded solemnly. "People do stupid things when they're scared. Don't worry, kid. I'll keep an eye on everyone best I can. That Brightlaw guy seems like the type to back us up if we need it, too. Between me, him, and Bethany—and our teams—I doubt anyone will pull anything."

I chuckled, remembering how we'd put down that undead in the temple. Abel wasn't wrong. As a combination, our groups were pretty damned scary. I wasn't going to take anyone's safety for granted, but at least I felt a bit more secure.

With all that out of the way Callie and I retired to our tent to sleep. We had a big day tomorrow.

Chapter Forty-Four

AFTER A NICE REST, we packed up and headed to the site of the conclave. We hadn't specified where it would be, but the most reasonable place to meet was the flat area on top of the mountain, so we kept going up, enjoying the brisk mountain air and *not* getting frostbite thanks to the summerspark crystals. I could see why Anna-Marie negotiated so hard for them—they were life savers.

We hadn't set any specific time for the meeting, though I'd been planning for somewhere around sunset. When we arrived at the mountaintop, we had plenty of time left before that. Even the several hours of hiking the mountain only put us at midafternoon when we arrived.

We were greeted by a small gathering of people, all sitting in what appeared to be furniture they brought themselves. It was a motley assortment, some of whom I recognized from descriptions, some of them completely new. One of them, a girl with absurdly long golden hair, was sitting on a canopy bed, reading a book while several other girls held up and brushed her voluminous locks. Another of them was a dark-skinned girl with purple hair and eyes, sitting at an easel and painting the faded form of the still huge moon in the daytime sky.

"Okay," I said slowly. "Guess some of them beat us here. I wonder how many teams will show up?" Of the hundred teams that had entered the Glade, ten were in the general vicinity. Between the two groups here,

Bethany's team, us, and Gabriel's, that was a full half of the nearby forces. Fifty people all told. Of those other teams, I knew the identity of two of them—my distant relative Alistair and the team with the twins, Flicker and Blink. That left three more mystery attendees and their own teams.

Speaking of Gabriel—looking off to one side I noticed the man sitting on a padded red couch with Archimedes and a dark-haired woman with what appeared to be a frequently broken nose. I'd never seen that before on an Ascendant, but I supposed it must have healed slightly wrong. She had delicate features, but her shoulders and arms were thick in a way I'd seen in boxers. The gloves she wore had no fingers, but they were plated at the knuckles.

Heading over, I nodded to the big Crusader. "Gabriel. I see you made it pretty quickly. You bring one of those others with you?"

Sipping gingerly at a teacup that looked way out of place in his big gauntleted hands, the blonde man nodded. "I did. My friend Valsa is at the easel over there. She's an Imperial noble. The one with long hair is from the Faerieland. Her name is Annalise, and I believe she's some kind of fae." His eyes flicked behind me. "I see you found the Vampire."

Bethy cleared her throat. "That's *Doctor* Vampire. I didn't spend five years in Vampire medical school for nothing." He just stared at her, face stony, and she rolled her eyes. "Ouch, tough crowd. Shame, you're kind of cute. I always like the driven, warrior of faith types."

He cracked a small smile. "Get thee behind me, Vampire."

She just winked and said, "That *is* where I prefer to bite from." Flouncing over to sit on the opposite end of the couch, she gave an expansive yawn, showing off her fangs. "So, when are we starting the meeting? Do I have time for a nap... or maybe a quick bite?" She grinned at Gabriel, but the Adamant cultivator didn't rise to the bait, ignoring the Vampire and drawing a pout from the charismatic girl.

"Well, Alistair isn't here yet," I said, searching around. "At the very least having another candidate in this would be useful. I'd also prefer to confirm he hasn't been torn into tiny pieces by some millennia-old corpse."

Nat nodded. "I'm betting his people are probably pretty scary. Most candidates have an impressive retinue. Not all of them, of course, but a few people with serious power." She gestured to her own minions. "Perit and

Valk are mine. I find keeping it to two makes the process faster, though as you know people vary in that respect."

Bethy, who had given up on teasing Gabriel when the situation got serious, frowned thoughtfully. "I don't mind a bit of a wait, given the severity of the situation, but we'll have to start eventually. Not everyone will necessarily show up, and some of them may have died." Seeing her switch back to her serious mode was a bit jarring.

Aida and Tracey were standing behind the couch, remaining almost perfectly still as they stood guard, and their presence gave her a sort of gravitas, like some ancient queen. It was kind of weird to see funny, silly, admittedly scary Bethany look so poised. Her comment made me think of something else, though.

"You said you killed the conduit you ran into, right?"

She grimaced. "Yes, though not without some difficulty. The one I met wasn't particularly well-protected against enthrallment. I hypnotized him like I tried to do to you. He stood there monologuing as we surrounded him and impaled him with a variety of dangerous high-ranking instruments, most of them coated with poison." I shuddered a bit. That was... terrifying. Being unaware as ten people ran you through all at once. She gave me a toothy grin, her voice slipping back into her usual friendly chirp. "It's so much easier to take down the baddies when they sit still and let you work, huh?"

Aida cleared her throat. "That said, most of the weapons we used on him were single use. Bloodbound stakes that Lord Lark provided us. He tends to be... sensitive to the threat of undead. Many of them hold grudges against him for his purge of vampiric cultivators. The stakes are single-use consumables designed to inflict a great deal of damage on undead. We have more, but not many."

Bethy's eyes snapped up to Aida, and the woman flinched slightly under the ruby glare before the Vampire sighed dramatically. "I suppose that would have come out regardless. But watch what you share, Aida—that information was not yours to disseminate." Her tone wasn't formal this time. It was cold.

Lowering her head, Aida curtsied to the girl. "Apologies, mistress." Weirdly, her voice wasn't shaking or frightened, it sounded more... ashamed. Bethy's face softened and she offered her thrall a soft smile, which seemed to placate her. I got the impression the relationship there was much more nuanced than it had seemed. The thralls weren't her keepers, not really—she just liked people to think they were.

It occurred to me that ditzy Bethy was as much of a mask as Vampire Bethany, maybe more. Whatever her real personality, the girl was clearly more dangerous and focused than she liked to appear. I saw Gabriel studying her too, clearly taking in the same things I was, maybe learning even more.

"If possible," I said, waiting so I didn't interrupt and give up possible information, "I'd love to get my hands on one or two of those stakes. If not, I get it. If your dad made them, even if they're restricted to your own rank, they must be special."

She bit her lip. "I can't... those aren't mine, exactly. They're emergency measures to keep me safe. Using so many of them was problematic. I'm not saying no, but it would need to be something we negotiate. I'll reserve judgement until we see who comes."

Speaking of who was coming, I noticed a form resolving itself off in the distance, a familiar figure with red hair and a beard. Craygen. The big man spotted Abel and grinned, waving over at us, and Cady joined him as he made his way over, leaving their team with Chad.

"Apollyon, my friend," he boomed as he came in close, holding out a hand to grab Abel's and pull him in for a slap on the back. "We got your team leader's message. We appreciated the warning. We had located one of those damned temples not long before and we'd already entered. Thanks to you, we dodged the inevitable dust-up with a super zombie. We owe you one."

I realized Callie had been in charge when we met them, but I didn't see a reason to correct them. We were partners, if they wanted to treat her as the leader that was fine. I nodded to him. "We appreciate you making it here. Must have been a hell of a run."

He guffawed loudly. "That it was. The climb was even more irritating. Luckily one of ours had a set of enchanted spelunking gear that made things much easier."

I grimaced. I should invest in something like that. It would have been so much less tiring than the way we actually got up here.

"We're still waiting on the others," I told him. "I want to explain the details as few times as possible, so we can just tell all the groups as they show up."

"We saw one of them on the way up. Recognized one of them from the party. Raul. Short guy. Dark hair, carries a big axe. They should be here soon." He pointed off into the distance, and I looked out to see a series of figures. The one in the lead wore a dark cloak, and Raul and another smaller figure were trailing him in a way that seemed familiar. They followed him like Perit and Valk did. Alistair most likely. They didn't approach us, instead walking over to speak to Annalise where she sat reading on her canopy bed.

Three teams were left, one of whom was probably associated with Christina, the blue-fog-wielding psycho I'd been warned not to take lightly. Meeting her again might be tense, but we'd get through it. This was bigger than a bit of petty squabbling, and hell, we might have been doing her a favor by seizing the Dew.

Speaking of... "Any of you guys find any more drops?" I asked of the collective allies I found myself amongst. "Because we didn't run into any."

They all shrugged, except Gabriel, who nodded. "I came across a field of Lightblooms. We collected the Dew and are keeping it in reserve until we all discuss the circumstances. It might be worth using it, trap or not, assuming we can find out the details of this little plot. I had some ideas about that, by the way, once everyone arrives." He looked at me and Nat, and I understood where he was going with that.

Wishes. Wishes weren't great with uncovering secrets (hidden information had a weight to it that drove up the price) but there were ways around that. I was sure between the three candidates here that we could get *some* inkling of what Suvaya was going to do and when, especially since we already knew a fair bit of the plan. Or at least suspected.

With that in mind, I reached into my spatial ring, pulled out a chair (albeit a much less comfortable one than most of the others), and sat down. Now all we had to do was wait.

Chapter Forty-Five

WE WAITED for a few more hours, and two of the remaining three teams showed up. One was the team with Christina in it. She glared hatefully at us, but didn't attack, staying behind her apparent boss, a weaselly dark-haired guy with a pencil mustache that Gabriel sneered at.

"Bad blood there?" I asked casually as we watched the other team approach the cloaked man who I suspected was Alistair. My relative reached out a hand and greeted the mustache guy.

Gabriel, literally the most controlled person I'd met up to this point, *spat* on the ground to one side. "Templeton."

Bethy hissed. *"That's* Templeton? As in *Simon* Templeton? The youngest current descendant of The Whispered Lie?" Her eyes narrowed. "I'd heard he was going to enter, but I didn't think he would make it in. His powers aren't suited for a tournament setting."

The Crusader sneered. "Templeton doesn't do his own dirty work. He probably had a dozen participants lined up waiting to pass him the entry slots."

"Okay," I said cheerily, "How about we pretend not everyone is part of your super special young masters and mistresses club and that I don't know who any of these people are. And then we can *stop* pretending because

239

that's the exact case here, and you can just tell me what the hell you're talking about."

Bethy giggled at that. "I knew there was a reason I liked you, Sol. Sorry. I'll explain." She gestured us closer, triggering a Stealth Skill so her voice wouldn't carry. I'd been developing a feel for that kind of thing. "The Whispered Lie is… Well, he's a monster. A mind mage who brainwashed his entire planet into being loyal servants. Templeton is a descendant, and he inherited the Lie's powers, but they aren't a clan. The Lie only has one son, and he only has one son, Templeton."

"What kind of mind mage?" I asked uneasily. Magic, I knew, was just Skills that were distilled from unusual abilities and taught. Mind magic would be the same, but mind control seriously skeeved me out. I didn't like the idea of telepaths or mind readers.

Gabriel interjected, "The Whispered Lie's power is complex. When he speaks, his words are… weighted. If he says something untrue and you believe it, he can then say something true and make you believe it's false. The more he talks the more the truth starts to bend. He can convince you of anything, and he uses his ability to deadly effect. Templeton does the same. It doesn't sound like mind control, but that's what it is when used the right way."

"Do we need to worry about him?" I asked. "And what about the other group, anyone know them?"

Craygen, who was in our little group and could therefore hear us, nodded. "Dralka. He's Imperial. Nothing special or weird, just a scary ass fighter with a ridiculously powerful sword ability. Master Candidate. Dralka isn't one to mess with. We're still missing one though."

I shrugged. "We'll need to ask around about them. But this is the end of the waiting period—we need to get this party started." Bethy nodded, letting the Stealth Skill drop, and I walked towards the center of the flat space we were occupying so everyone could see me. "Excuse me," I called, "we're about ready to start. Anyone seen the last crew?"

Valsa, the girl at the easel, shook her head, her purple hair bouncing. "Ferak was the last but… he was closer than I was last I talked to him. He wouldn't have missed this either, not with your warning. I suspect he's dead. We can check after the conclave, but I move we begin proceedings."

"Seconded," intoned Dralka, a huge bear of a man with thick black hair and bushy eyebrows. Apparently we were being super formal about this. Good to know.

"The motion carries," I said smoothly. "We'll begin immediately. Allow me to introduce myself before we begin. My name is Shane Wyndham from the Wish Curse Palace." I decided to use my real name because if I didn't, no one would listen to me, and it wasn't like these people had any context for it anyway, so my identity wasn't a huge deal.

Alistair stepped up, pushing back the cloak to reveal a fine-boned, gaunt man with green eyes much like my own. I could see echoes of my dad's features around the eyes, but it was faint. Apparently we'd inherited some stuff from the Wishmaster in terms of looks, since this guy was supposed to be from a whole other branch. "Greetings," he said in a quiet voice. "I am Alistair Wyndham. My branch elder is Darius." He looked at me expectantly.

"Mine is Malachai," I said. "My grandfather." I was assuming branch elder referred to the S-ranker who was allowed to found a branch and start a family. Alistair's eyes narrowed a bit, but he was interrupted as Nat stepped forward. She nodded and I pointed to her. "My cousin Natalie, same branch."

Alistair looked floored. "You're in an alliance? Well... that speaks well of you. It's uncommon someone so low in rank manages to make an ally in the family. You mentioned a threat, but weren't too specific, just that there was a problem with the Dew and powerful enemies. I mostly came because the Crusader and the Vampire were involved, but I'd be willing to hear your story."

Nodding, I looked around to make sure the others were listening, then began to fill them in. The temple, the fight, the information we'd gotten from the others, and all the suppositions we'd made based on the evidence we had. It didn't take too long to tell it, but I was still glad I waited and told them all at the same time.

The biggest reason for that was that with my Eye of Revelation active I was able to observe everyone's reactions. There were several interesting things I noted during my recitation. Templeton, for instance, didn't look worried or afraid. He seemed to momentarily light up, then his gaze shot over to Gabriel. I was assuming Templeton was thinking that he might have the means to get rid of the Crusader.

Annalise looked tense and worried, and I was pretty sure she knew the team that had gone missing and agreed with Valsa about their probable death. Alistair looked wary, though even my skill didn't give me any clues as to why that might be.

Chad was the one who reacted first after I finished speaking. "Well... shit," he said succinctly. "Show of hands, how many of you have ingested some of the Dew?"

I put my hand up and so did more than half of the assembled ninety people. I sighed. "Well, seems like most if not all of our teams are stuck here. Anyone in contact with any of the others? Seems like the Starlight Slides might have dropped us off at least somewhat in the proximity of our closest neighbors, considering we all seem to know each other. I can only assume the other teams are further away since they didn't respond to the message. Any of us have means of contacting them?"

A few people nodded.

"Alright. After the conclave, I suggest any of us who can contact the other teams. There are a thousand of us out here and that's a solid force to bring to bear. They've already gotten the same message you did, so they know the basics."

Annalise nodded, before interjecting, "I'd like to stay here. We can use this place as a sort of home base. Some of the more distant teams may have only come into sight range of the mountain recently, or might not have done so at all. If they make their way here, I can relay what we've learned."

"Speaking of which," Templeton drawled, "I believe we have quite an advantage here. Three Wishmaster Candidates in one place. The right questions in the right places would give us information that might not be the most complete, but eighteen points of correlation is enough to find the shape of the issue, as it were."

His voice was... oily. I disliked him almost immediately, and his power made trusting anything he said suspect and incredibly uncomfortable. But he'd basically repeated what we'd already considered doing, and he had a point. Gabriel spoke up. "True. But I think I speak for all of us when I say *you* shall not be the one asking such questions."

Templeton shrugged. "So suspicious. I'm naturally the best fit for such a thing—my skill at sussing out information is legendary."

It was... nerve-wracking, listening to the man talk. I kept trying to figure out if he was lying or telling the truth. If I believed a lie, he'd be able to make me disbelieve a truth later. While that seemed innocuous, being able to tell someone something you *know* they won't believe is as good as being able to tell them something you know they'll take as fact.

Annalise cleared her throat. "We of the fae are known for our gift for such matters. I take it no one has a problem with *me* being the one to try to suss out the direction of this vanished goddess's plans?"

Most of the rest of us breathed a sigh of relief, shaking our heads. Alistair smiled at her. "Personally, I have no issue with Simon being the one to attempt to wrangle us some answers, but I'm always happy to work with the fae. Such fascinating people your lot are." Annalise raised an eyebrow, clearly unimpressed with the obvious flirting, and Alistair turned his attention to us. "How many wishes do the two of you have remaining?"

"Six," I said directly. "I haven't used mine yet today. Nat?" My cousin indicated she was full up too. "How about you?"

He nodded. "Eighteen in truth then, Templeton is right. Even with our... limitations, we can get some decent information. Not to mention we already have a decent idea of the shape of things. Whoever makes the wishes can simply confirm things we believe and then go from there. Yes or no questions are easier than just asking for information, not to mention we have so many chances."

Sighing, I agreed, and we all gathered around Annalise's canopy bed. Her maids had started plaiting her hair into a ridiculously complicated braid that somehow shortened it by about twenty feet. Sitting up, she poked her bare feet out, and one of her maids slipped a pair of dainty slippers on her feet as two others helped her down from her perch.

She gave us all a calculating look, then pulled out a small journal and a pen. "If we're to do this properly, we must learn as much as we can and extrapolate as much as possible from what we know. Please repeat everything the undead said. You as well, Vampire. Then we will compare notes and decide what facts we can take as indisputable. When we verify those, we can then begin to deduce."

I blinked, because that sounded pretty damned effective. Bethy shrugged at me from nearby when I looked at her, and then she began to tell her story. I had a feeling this would be a long day.

Chapter Forty-Six

I GROANED, slumping back onto the couch that Annalise's maids had brought out after the third hour of our little powwow. Alistair was lounging not far away, and Nat was on the other side of the couch next to Bethy. All three of them looked as annoyed and drained as I probably did. Not physically exhausted, obviously, but mentally drained from literal *hours* of constant annoying back and forth.

We'd told our stories. Then we'd told them again. Then we'd told them in reverse order. Then we'd told them with our eyes closed (apparently to check for any scents we might have overlooked, though why that would be important I had zero clue). Annalise just sat there, constantly scribbling in her stupid little book, making us repeat things as she compared facts from both recitations.

Once that was done, she started asking us questions. Nonsense stuff mostly, asking us how we felt about individual word choices, what the undead's voice had sounded like at any given time, and a host of other weird things that didn't seem to mean anything. After an hour—*an hour*—of questions, she finally made her first wish, asking for confirmation of a yes or no question.

Which she wrote down. In her book. I hated that book. But that question seemed to act as a new lens through which to view every detail she'd dragged out of us, and she forced us to reexamine every comment, interaction, and minute pause before asking the next. That one didn't take an hour, only about forty minutes. Then we did it again. And again. *Eighteen times.* I got a solid deal on the wishes though, getting a geas for help with a future contract negotiation each time.

Finally, Annalise snapped her book shut. The second half of our little session hadn't just been us. She'd called Anna-Marie and grilled her on the legends she'd heard of Suvaya. Had her gather all her researchers and anyone she knew nearby that might have any understanding of the situation. Once all that was done, she'd altered the questions somewhat, though kept them to yes or no.

It *did* really bring down the cost of the wishes when she did that. Considering how absurdly expensive it had been the other times I'd tried fishing for secrets, it was a relief.

"So," I said with an exasperated huff. After closing the book, Annalise had closed her own eyes and just kind of... sat there. No one else was nearby, the others had gotten bored and wandered off ages ago, some to go talk or drink or play games, others to explore the mountain, though my own crew stayed within sight.

Annalise opened her eyes. "Ah. Yes. Apologies, merely... sorting information." She had to have some kind of investigative or information gathering Skill. Maybe some kind of nobility thing.

Finally, she exhaled. Which I noticed easily, thanks to the twenty-four points of Perception I'd gotten from her for the wishes she'd made. At least there was one upside to this nonsense. "So... what did you figure out?" I asked. "Aside from the obvious stuff we already knew."

Shrugging, she tossed her thickly-braided hair. "It was mostly confirmation of what we knew, as well as context for why this is all happening. You aren't stupid—your suppositions were accurate for the most part, though somewhat incomplete. You lacked some background information."

I'd gathered some of that listening to her questions. "You know why she picked now to act?"

"Oh, that one isn't a mystery." She laughed. "Bad luck. Her net has been cast far and wide, but part of the issue is that in order to utilize her 'conduits' as you call them, they had to be willing. She had to make them promises, and her promise to make them gods delayed things quite a bit."

I paused. "So she was really going to follow through on that?" She hadn't asked for that confirmation, so I wasn't sure where she got that bit of info.

"It's the only thing that makes sense," Annelise said firmly. "Suvaya was a goddess, which means a full thousand Impact. That's the threshold for godhood. Among other things. Regardless, she had thirty-three high priests bound to her, all of them powerful and high ranking Ascendants. B through S-rank. When the six destroyed her, part of her consciousness landed here, but it was too damaged to reconstitute."

"So she decided to farm Impact," I said impatiently. "Yeah, we gathered that. That was one of your questions, if all thirty-three survived to become conduits."

She nodded. "They didn't apparently, though we don't know how many did. That's where the local legends come in. Suvaya isn't just the moon goddess, she's the *moon* as far as these people are concerned. The story about her seventeen stars is obviously a reference to the priests. Well, fifteen now."

"You said she needed to honor her promise. Does that mean she needed eighteen thousand Impact worth of Ascendants? Because… that's a *lot*. Especially considering how many people never make it into the triple digits. Sure, the people who come here tend to be elites who usually make it higher, but still. And what happens if someone dies early? Does she still get their power?"

Annalise shrugged. "I have no idea. I'd assume so, otherwise this would have taken much longer. Honestly the fact that she managed to make this place is absurd. She must have used the stripped stats from her priests to fuel its creation. No other way some damaged soul shard could manage it."

"I'm guessing she couldn't strip them past F-rank," I said with a grimace. "Otherwise, why limit the dungeon like that? My question is how the hell do the six not *know*. They've been sending us here for millennia."

Nat answered that one. "There's no end of weird shit out there, cuz. Since they were never able to actually come here themselves, it's no wonder they didn't notice. It's not like they have anything to compare it to. No reason to jump to the conclusion that one of the vanished gods was somehow still around."

Put that way, I could kind of understand. The Universe was huge and weird. Belief warped whole worlds in unexplainable ways and constantly shifted what could be considered fact. The six, being at the top of that pyramid, probably saw crazy and unbelievable things daily. I just wished this particular issue hadn't been the thing that slipped their notice, considering it might kill me and everyone I cared about.

Moving on, Annalise continued detailing her findings. "In any case. She's recently come close to stockpiling the needed Impact. Something about the process requires her to imbue it all at once, probably the limits on the dungeon itself. The actual ritual for her to reform and for all the priests to Ascend will take place relatively soon, though I wasn't able to confirm a specific date. We didn't have enough questions for me to even try."

I nodded. Aside from being a secret and therefore expensive as hell, something open-ended like a date would basically require process of elimination.

"Okay. Do we know where exactly the ritual will happen?" I asked hopefully. She'd clearly gleaned a lot more from the stories and questions than I had. No wonder she'd been writing so much. It was a fascinating look at the potential uses of my power when combined with the right inputs, and I'd seen Callie watching us intently, clearly trying to learn something.

She looked at me archly. "You didn't figure it out?" I felt my stomach sink. I knew what she was going to say. I didn't even need to think about it after hearing her tone. The world sucked and fate sense tended to push us in the most interesting possible direction.

"This…" I grimaced before continuing. "This isn't a mountain, is it?" Which would explain the gravity and spatial warping. Because of *course* the hand of a vanished god was just sticking out of the ground in the middle of this dungeon.

Her answering smile wasn't really happy so much as cynically amused. "No. No it is not."

"Should we leave?" I asked tensely, ready to book it off the edge and State of Grace my people to the ground if need be. I wasn't taking any chances with the safety of my friends. I cursed my damned fate sense for being so annoyingly inconsistent. Pushing me to the temple to figure out the problem then up here to, what, die?

"Unnecessary," she said with a wave. "She can't interact at the moment or we'd already be dead. She's in stasis after using most of her energy to create this place. The sleep of the moon, as the locals call it. This isn't her *actual* hand, obviously. Just the spiritual representation of the fragment of her manifesting when she created this place. She's a goddess, but they don't randomly grow to thousands of miles tall."

Which meant it might be a decent idea to keep a presence here, especially since more of the teams might be coming to help. Leaving them to wander around up here and possibly die couldn't be a smart call. "You're the one who should stay here when we leave, are you okay with that? And speaking of leaving, does this mean we have an actual plan that can help us stop this?"

Annalise nodded. "Yes to both. You were on the right track. Seventeen priests. Seventeen conduits. If we kill them, it disconnects the threads she's woven through all the possible Impact she could harvest. Granted, some of the dead ones might have been harvested early, but she'll need Impact to make herself a new body and reform, not to mention repair the damage from the severed connections. If we disconnect all the conduits before she manifests, she SHOULD come into being as an F-ranker."

"Okay, that shouldn't be too bad," I said with a relieved sigh. "We *did* kill that undead with just two teams. We can take the others. Especially with so much help."

"If only it were that easy," she replied wearily. "I told you the priests vary in strength. They're all severely weakened and damaged, but some of them had a higher starting point. None of them will be able to breach the E-rank, but some of them will be literal former S-rankers. Even damaged and stripped of much of their strength... I shudder to think what they might be capable of."

I shuddered too. That sounded terrifying. Abel made it clear to me what advanced Skills and techniques could do at the same level. "So... what do we do? Can we even kill them? It sounds like we'd be fighting a Master Candidate on steroids. Are their souls still higher level?"

She nodded. "Much. It's the only way to explain the possibility of Ascension. Still, even with absurd Skills and soul power, stats are the building blocks of abilities. Without the stats to back it up they won't be able to throw around high-rank power, just use what they have *really* well. If we attack as a group and plan things well, we can manage. Also, the more of them we kill the more strain is placed on the others."

"So we off them in reverse order," I mused. "Take the weakest and make sure the big dogs are under more pressure when we come for them. Can you identify which priests are which?" I wasn't sure how she'd be able to, but hey, didn't hurt to ask.

"Some of them," she said, to my surprise. "The three I suspect are S-rankers were mentioned more than the others. At the very least we ought to save them for last. But even then, there's going to be quite a bit of power disparity. We need more of the teams on this. Luckily, while I didn't identify when the ritual would be, I did identify when it will *not* occur. As in, it will not be taking place in the next month."

My shoulders relaxed. That helped a ton actually. "Alright," I said. "So, the plan is to find and recruit more of the teams. Once we have enough forces, we move in and wipe out all seventeen of the conduits within the next month. Then we jump Suvaya a thousand to one and crush her with numbers so we can get the hell off this hellhole." I paused. "Plus... maybe get some more those drops after she's dead if we can."

From the grim smiles of the others, I suspected I wasn't the only one thinking about the fight that was going to be, but we had time for that later. For now... I guessed we needed to get ready to kill a god.

Chapter Forty-Seven

AFTER WE DIVINED what Suvaya was doing and decided on gathering support, we pooled our information on the local geography to determine what teams most likely ended up where. By mapping out where we'd all been when we got on the Starlight Slides and where we'd ended up, we were able to create a vague formula that predicted the way the distance changed from one side of the slides to the other.

Using that data, and the knowledge we all had about where the other teams were in the bazaar, we estimated where certain teams may have come out. I personally had assumed it was random, but once he got the idea in his head Benny had insisted on at least checking to see if there was a pattern, and it had paid off huge. His investment in Focus up to this point was definitely paying dividends.

"With this information we should be able to match people up with a list of teams to contact," Benny said, scrawling some more numbers on the page of the notebook he had borrowed. "Our list of known teams and their locations isn't huge, granted, and nowhere near complete, but the more teams we bring in, the more information we can get. Especially if the searchers note down the location their quarries landed so I can refine my formula."

"Ah," Templeton said greasily. "So this little exercise won't be accurate?"

Benny sneered at him. In the time we'd all been working on mapping this out, pretty much everyone had grown to dislike Templeton. We also did our best to let him speak as infrequently as possible. "It *will* be accurate, just not to a fine degree. With so few use cases I was only able to calculate rough areas. The more data points we get the more exact I can get it. At the very least it'll give us a direction and an approximate distance. Which is more than we had before."

Gabriel nodded, cutting into the discussion. "Clockwork is right. We have, what, two teams listed for each of us? When we bring them back, we'll have another eighteen teams and can gather data from them. Then we have twenty-seven teams to send out to find the rest. It's the fastest and most accurate way to gather everyone quickly."

"Agreed," Valsa sneered. "So shut the hell up, Templeton. Nobody needs to hear from you anyway." While the rest of us disliked him, it seemed like Valsa held a special grudge. I didn't much care as long as she helped keep him quiet.

I looked down at our own list. We'd been given the names of two team leaders, one of whom was selected because he was someone Nat knew personally. My cousin had traveled extensively and had run into quite a few famous people of our own generation, so it wasn't a shock she might know one of the team leaders.

"I think we're ignoring a major issue," Chad said grimly. "Designated meeting place or not, can we really ask Annalise to stay up here? It can't possibly be safe. I suggest we change the meeting place to somewhere else."

Nat snorted. "And how would we do that exactly? Alistair, Solomon, and I are completely tapped for wishes for the day. That means we have no way of reaching them until tomorrow, and chances are someone will make it here by then. Hell, how do we know the other teams aren't all already on their way? What if we miss them and they show up here? We'd be wasting our time showing up at their landing spot."

"I don't think so," I said. "Anyone close enough to see the mountain would be close enough to have gotten here by now. You know how fast we are, especially anyone at the peak of F-rank. I think our best bet is assuming all the attendees who are coming are already here. I see Chad's point— Annalise, you sure you don't want out?"

The fae shook her head. "It would be a meaningless gesture. If we don't prevent this ritual from taking place, we're all going to die regardless. Being here doesn't put me in any more danger than being elsewhere. If nothing else, I suspect the manifestation will shatter this planet. You *are* familiar with what happens when someone ranks up on a planet too weak to withstand the process?"

My eyes widened. "Shit. This place is peak of F. Forget the injunction against E-rankers, if she Ascends here it'll push the Glade into ranking up early. It'll collapse itself."

The others looked worried. "Well," Abel said grimly, "at least we have a strong source of motivation. Self-interest will be important even for those that haven't used the drops."

I paled as another possibility crossed my mind. "If Suvaya comes back at the peak of F-rank, she could attempt to break through to E-rank anyway. Wouldn't that cause the same problem? We'll need to put her down immediately. Moreover, once she hits E-rank she could use the stockpiled stats to rank herself up again pretty quick, couldn't she? Could she shoot herself back up to S-rank?"

"Doubtful," Annalise said. "I'm sure you know how painful it is to grow your stats too quickly. But you're right that she'll probably commence her Ascension rapidly. We will need to stop her as soon as she restores herself. We were expecting that fight in any case, though."

I turned to Alistair. "I think you should stay. Giving Annalise access to wishes while we're gone will give her a way to narrow down the exact timing of the ritual, something we're going to need. She can also help Clockwork refine his formula... which is why I think he should *also* stay. Along with Celine, Perit, and Mel." Half of our team, but it would give him enough backup for me to be comfortable without leaving my own portion of the team vulnerable.

Benny, obviously, did not look happy, but I think he realized my end game here. This was important and we needed to find these people as quickly as possible. With access to wishes and someone with as keen a deductive mind as Annalise, he could basically make us a map to each team. It would massively save us all time. He'd already demonstrated how helpful he could be, and this would make his Focus even more useful.

He stared at me inscrutably for a minute before sighing. "Agreed. I'll stay and work. My suggestion is to keep in regular contact. Scan rings are good, but in person check-ins would be safer. Assuming we're writing off the possibility of Suvaya waking up and punching us all into orbit. I think we should dispatch the teams in a staggered rotation to pick up singular targets. Means the mountain won't be running on a skeleton crew for longer than necessary, and we'll have teams in and out."

I knew he wasn't worried about the priests—given what we knew about them they were all currently in their tombs. Annalise theorized that they needed to stay put to act as foci for the Lightblooms. No, he was worried that some of the other teams might decide they wanted to run the search, or that we were wrong, or any number of things. He was right—keeping the barebones crew we had set up here all the time would present a tempting target.

"Sounds good," I said nonchalantly. "Gabriel, Bethy—what do you guys think? If we stagger it, we can make sure one of us is here at all times." While I wasn't a powerhouse, Callie and I together were pretty scary, and throw in Abel and you had a nightmarish level of variety in a combat scenario. Plus with Nat we had two candidates, which was its own form of disincentive. The other two were straight up monsters. If we staggered it so one of our three teams was here, people would be way less likely to start shit.

Gabriel nodded slowly. "I'll move out first. I'm the fastest given my team is mounted. We'll head out today, and tomorrow you can leave on your own search. We can relieve the Vampire when we return, then she can head out, and you can relieve us." Lending his support (and theoretically Bethy's) to the plan made it much more likely not to kick up a fuss.

While being a candidate might make me someone worth listening to normally, there were three of us here. I wasn't the oldest, the strongest, or the most educated. I was making plans because of momentum, but I *did* have the biggest voting bloc in terms of raw power, and making the calls as a group would help add legitimacy to the proceedings. Especially once more teams showed up, because the power structure was bound to become more complicated as we went. Ascendants loved complicated.

After we hammered out the details as best we could, Gabriel took his team and left. How they got fucking *horses* up and down the mountain I neither knew nor wanted to guess at, but apparently they'd done so, or left someone down to guard them. I knew Gabriel's charger was a construct, but the others had been riding real animals. I didn't see them up here, granted, but it was a big mountain. They might be over a ridge or something.

Once he was gone, I turned to Nat. "Alright. We have a day to prep before we leave. Getting down won't be a problem, I can float us, but I still want to know more about this Renaldi person we're looking for. You said you knew him from your travels, right?"

She nodded. "Miles Renaldi. Absorber. He can take on the attributes of materials he touches for a time. He uses it pretty well—I'm not shocked he won a tournament. I ran into him on a little planet called Revarge about five years ago. Granted him a few wishes. Some Skills he made good use of. He paid, of course, but he considered it a bit of a favor so he told me he owed me one."

I exhaled a breath I hadn't realized I'd been holding. "So he'll listen to you if you tell him what's up?" That was a relief. I was pretty sure we were going to have trouble convincing some of them. The more we had on side when we approached the easier it would be. I wasn't going to turn down any advantage in this mess. "You know anything about his team?" Most of our information was incomplete. We knew most of the relevant team leaders, but no one had bothered to keep dossiers.

"I remember his girlfriend Sierra," she said with a shrug. "Earth manipulator. Other than that, not especially. He's a pretty relaxed guy. As long as we don't try to sneak up on him, we should be fine."

"Alright," I said with a sigh. "I'm going to set up the bunker over there." I pointed off into the distance. "Then we can all crash. If we're going to ride all out tomorrow, we want to be as well-rested as we can be. After hours of that deduction shit I could use a nap, and I wasn't even deducing."

She chuckled and I slipped the rock spike out of my ring. Tired or not, no way was I going to sleep without solid walls around me. Not in mixed company, and not here. I couldn't get off this mountain fast enough.

Chapter Forty-Eight

GETTING BACK to the ground the next day was actually really fun. State of Grace lasted five minutes, though stretching it out over five people (and a bear) was tough. Still, Callie helped me offset some of the strain through the bond, and we all plummeted through the air in a big spread-out circle, whooping in enjoyment with the wind in our faces. We touched down in the forest near the base of the mountain.

Callie, Abel, Valk, Nat, Jessie, Randall and me. We'd brought along our healer just in case, but the rest of the group was picked specifically because I thought they could handle themselves (or in Nat's case because she knew the guy we were looking for). I wasn't entirely thrilled leaving my best friend behind, but it helped that either Bethy or Gabriel would be there to help at all times.

"Wow," Callie said as we all caught our breaths. "That was bracing. We should definitely try the sky diving thing again sometime."

I snickered. "I'm betting we're going to do it another five times at least here. I'm more worried about getting back up. The way down is quick and painless. But, I could do without an agonizing trip to the top of the damned mountain."

She gave me an angelic smile. "That's weird. It seemed pretty comfy to me." I noticed Nat glare at her and stifled a snicker of my own. Callie had been hanging off my back, so she hadn't gotten slammed into the mountainside a few dozen times on a rope.

"What's our heading?" Nat asked. "You had Benny add it to that magic map, right?" We'd used the map to establish a baseline for the calculations Benny had been doing, and it had auto updated as it was supposed to do. The far reaches of it weren't really filled in, but we did have a basic idea of the scale we were working with and a direction to go. I slipped the map out, unrolling it to check our current location.

"Looks like we're heading northwest, at least based on where Renaldi probably landed. Templeton saw him around the time he hit his own slide. Benny's calculations say he probably landed about five hundred miles that way." I pointed. "It looks like more west than north though—we've already traveled a decent distance into the interior."

We'd considered bringing the wolves with us, using them as transportation, but given they were only G-rank it seemed like kind of a risk. Jessie had been working with them using her new and improved lifeweaver ability to try to get them stronger, but she couldn't just poof them to F-rank. Her ability was more about healing than enhancement, so the speed of improvement wasn't enough for our purposes.

Sadly, that left us all running the distance. Not that it was tough (we all had enough Might to make good time), but running in the woods, even with Perception to notice obstacles, Focus to process them, and Might to avoid them, was annoying as hell. It was anything but a straight line, and the trees grew thicker the further in we got.

We kept up our pace for a few hours before we drew to a stop in the approximate area that had been marked out. "Alright," I said as I looked around. "Keep your eyes peeled for any sign of passage. Benny didn't have the data to give us a solid location, so we're going to need to search nearby manually." I had my Eye of Revelation up, using it to search for any signs anyone had been here.

"What are the chances we actually find them here?" Nat asked skeptically. "I mean, no way they just sat around for days doing nothing. If they didn't get picked up by a kingdom like we did, they might have just gone out searching for Lightblooms."

"Assuming they know what those even are," I said. "That's actually the best case for us. Tracking them out of the core and into a kingdom would be nightmarish. Luckily, I don't think it's likely. They may have met up with someone, but it doesn't make sense to drag them out of the core just to meet up with some politicians and send them back in. More likely a kingdom sent out a mobile force with enough power to strong-arm them— either that or they really are free agents."

Nat nodded. "I could see that. I take it you're planning to look around for a while and then wish for some kind of tracking device if you can't find them?"

"Pretty much," I said distractedly. "But between my Perception and my Eye of Revelation I suspect I'll be able to find *some* trace of their passing. The approximate area Benny gave us wasn't small, but it's not more than a few miles wide. I wouldn't want to waste the wishes."

With that in mind, we spread out to look for clues. My Eye was damned useful for work like this, but it didn't turn out to be necessary. Within an hour I got a scan ring call from Callie with directions to where she was. When I arrived, I found her standing in front of a pretty large stone tower. It wasn't big enough to poke out of the towering trees, but it was sizable.

"So," she said in amusement, "what are the chances that they *didn't* go into the spooky magic tower?"

I snorted. "I don't know. If we'd landed near one of these and didn't have any idea what was going on, what do you think we would have done?"

"Yeah, I think they're inside too." She chuckled. "Think this one of those wizard's towers?" she asked, eyes scanning the length of the building. I could see runes carved into the stone, but they looked much less... ancient than stuff on the temples.

"Probably," I said with a shrug. "My issue isn't whether they went in, it's whether they're still there. Even if they did go inside, they could have cleaned the place out and bailed by now. Hard to say since we've never actually gone into one of these things. I think our best bet is to use a wish from Nat to get one of those compasses. It'll tell us not only if they're in there, but *where* in there they are once we enter."

I'd been hoping to keep our wishes in case of an emergency, but I wasn't too broken up about using one or two if I had to. Callie seemed to be on the same page, or so I felt over the bond. She didn't have time to respond because Nat showed up the very next moment. I did love Perception sometimes, letting me pick up things like shoes on leaves when I was listening for them.

Focus normally precluded that kind of incidental spillover from stats, but given where we were I was keeping my ears peeled as well as my eyes. Turning to see my cousin, I waved her over even as Randall and Jessie emerged from the woods, with Abel showing up about a minute later. "Hey, we think they might have gone into the tower but aren't sure they're still there even if they did." Slipping out a bag of chits, I tossed it to her. "I wish for a method of tracking Miles Renaldi. Preferably an active one like a compass."

She weighed the bag with her hand then nodded. I watched the gathering electricity flow over her skin and blaze in her eyes, the distinctive purple lightning that only we could use or see. It gathered in a blinding flash in the hand opposite the bag, and when it faded, a small golden compass was sitting in her empty palm. She tossed it over to me and I caught it easily.

Holding it up, I got a direction. It was pointed at the tower, but that could have been a coincidence, so I did a single lap of the outside of the building, and sure enough the compass continued to point right at the place. "Looks like we found them. Plus, we get to explore this place. I can't wait to see if there are any spellbooks!" I paused. "We're sure all the conduits are in *temples*, right?"

Callie shrugged. "Based on what you and Annalise puzzled out I'd wager the places were built as some sort of amplifier or focus. Or at least used to map out the ritual. This place doesn't look as old either. Probably just some random wizard's evil lair."

I shrugged. "Works for me. Give me a minute to call this in to Anna-Marie just in case she has information about this place." I retreated off to one side to spin up my scan ring, and the princess answered promptly.

"Solomon?" she said worriedly. "I haven't heard from any of you in a while. No one's hurt, are they?"

"Nothing is wrong," I assured her. "We ran into what we think is one of those wizard's towers, but we wanted to run the details by you in case it was something else."

She looked relieved. "Of course. I'm happy to help. Show me the location?" I held up my ring, showing the screen towards the building as I walked another slow circuit around it, letting her take in all the stones and the runes and all that. She consulted with her team of experts and their books, and within probably twenty minutes was back with an answer.

It was a wizard's tower, though not one that she'd heard of. We weren't lucky enough to learn the wizard's name or favorite breakfast food or anything that would help us traverse it safely. I thanked her and hung up, and then we all gathered at the entrance. The door inside was big, with a crossbar holding it shut. It was large enough for Randall to enter easily, which was nice, but I wasn't sure I liked that the wizard needed a door that size.

After Callie did her trap seeking thing and I gave the place a once-over with Eye of Revelation, we pushed the bar off the door (how it had gotten back on if Renaldi's team was still inside was another question I didn't want the answer to) and then made our way inside... and froze.

The other side of the door was dirt. Like actual earth you'd find outside. We stepped onto a huge chunk of rock and the door slammed behind us, a thump answering the question I hadn't wanted answered. I wasn't worried, we could break the door—it wasn't enchanted that I could see, and it was only F-rank wood.

That wasn't the part that stunned us though. Past the rock we were on there was just... empty sky. Purple and orange and yellow clouds, like a permanent sunset, with a few black ones sparking with white-blue lightning. The lightning struck out at the staircases that ran between our rock and other similar rocks with doors on them, grounding harmlessly about twenty feet out from the steps.

"Okay," Callie said in a hushed tone, "I have to admit, this is pretty cool."

I nodded along as we stared out into the endless expanse. Wizard's tower indeed. I just hoped it wasn't as dangerous as it was fascinating. Sadly, my luck never seemed to work that way.

Chapter Forty-Nine

I ADMIT to a bit of vertigo. Even standing on solid ground, the churning, lightning-riven sky around us was... disorienting. For once I didn't have some glib remark about our surroundings. I was just too blown away. "Stick close," I said to the rest of my group.

Luckily, the stairs were big enough for even Randall, so we didn't need to leave the biggest member of our party behind. Approaching the steps at the end of the rock we were on, I noticed something else unusual. The stairs were spiraled. They looked like a DNA helix. It was hard to see from a distance because of the strange warping effect around them (which was what had caught the lightning) but up close it was painfully clear.

The first section, at least, was oriented right, so stepping onto the thing wasn't an issue. Once we mounted the stairs the space started to sort of list to one side, and after a few steps it became clear *we* were spiraling along with the staircase. It was a weird sensation. It also didn't make a ton of sense. "Why the hell would they waste power doing this?"

Nat shrugged as we continued our climb. "It might be an incidental result of the way they altered space here. Sloppy spatial warping can have odd effects. Or it could be insurance to prevent people from breaking the shields around the staircases. If they're tied to the effect, then smashing them could drop us into oblivion. Hard to say really—there are just too many possible answers."

I rolled my eyes. "There are shorter ways to say that you don't know." She glared at me and I shrugged. "What? It's true."

"Never admit ignorance, cousin mine," she said loftily. "We live in a world where perception is reality. If you act like you always have the answers, that's how people will perceive you. Instead of saying you don't know, give educated guesses and state them with conviction."

"That explains so much about you," I said dryly. "But I'll take it under advisement." We chattered on about mostly nothing as we walked, following the compass as best we could. Unfortunately it pointed us straight at our target, but apparently didn't account for elevation... or depths, as the case may be. Since none of us felt like jumping into an endless void of lightning and clouds we did our best to follow it while sticking to the steps.

It didn't help that at the top of some of the steps were doors that appeared to lead nowhere but in fact came out on other landings with more steps. Not every landing had a door (some were connected to each other by stairs), but it seemed to be mostly random and it made trying to track anything in the whole mess impossible.

Which was why when we reached the top (bottom?) of the stairs where the first door was, I wasn't surprised to find the compass pointing out into the nothingness to the left of us. Panning up, I could vaguely see a rock island in the clouds high above us, not that it did us any good.

Deciding it didn't really matter since we only had one exit available, I pushed open the door (a surprisingly large one that Randall was able to squeeze through at an angle given how tall it was) then stepped inside. The other side of the door didn't drop us over the side of the stone and into a bottomless plummet like it should have. Instead it brought us to an entirely new place.

Past the frame we stepped onto a polished floor made of multicolored tiles. The tiles appeared to be made of gemstones fit together intricately to create squares of color that blended into a beautiful mosaic. Some squares were one solid block of gems, some were a variety, and the effect reminded me of nothing so much as puzzle pieces. I could see that they were F-ranked gems too, but when I tried to touch them, my hand stopped above the floor like it was hitting an invisible pane of glass.

Callie was almost drooling. "Those are *all* gems with naturally occurring runes in them. Whoever made this was... rich. Also a genius. I don't know

261

if you could call this a formation, because it was crafted, but it's not quite an enchantment either. No chance we can take any though. I'm pretty sure this is a force field, and based on what Nat said about breaking those in here it's not worth the risk."

I nodded. "I think it's some kind of node eye. I'm betting there are more rooms like this, probably at strategic points up and down the tower. This whole thing is a massive three-dimensional construct." At their looks I shrugged. "I still know the odd bit about Enchanting, even if I can't really do it anymore. This is… impressive. The question is which way do we go?"

Gesturing up from the floor, I waved at the four closed doors identical to the ones we just came through. The walls between them were black stone, smooth and unblemished, and all the light in here came from the floor, as the ceiling seemed to be a mass of writhing black clouds, though thankfully not ones discharging the blue-white lightning.

The mosaic itself was no help. It depicted a beautiful woman in a green dress dancing across a rainbow, followed unknowingly by shadowy demonic forms. Callie gestured for me to hand her the compass, which I did, and she held it up. "Well… compass says that way, but since we know that it doesn't take into account elevation and this place has literally turned us upside down a few times… I'm not sure how much it'll help."

"Better than nothing." I shrugged and headed for the door on the western side of the room. Pushing it open, we emerged onto another staircase. I sighed and then got climbing, following it up to another landing with another door. Inside *this* door wasn't just a room with more doors. It was something infinitely more interesting: a library.

The mosaic here was different, a picture of a female knight locked in combat with a massive grey skinned-demon. I noticed her hair was the same strawberry blonde as the woman in the dress, but she looked older, and she had a scar marring one cheek. I made a note of the images, which seemed to be different points in the life of one person. Turning away from that though, I took in the walls filled with rows and rows of books.

Grinning, I made to step forward and then stopped. The others kept moving and I held up a hand to stop them. "Hold up. This is too easy." Flipping on my Eye of Revelation I scoured the place for any clues or traps. I frowned as I settled on the glowing forms of mops and brooms leaning against the tables in front of the shelves. Reaching into my ring, I pulled out a random rock I had lying around from somewhere (it was hard not to be a pack rat when you had spatial storage) and tossed it.

One of the mops leapt up, spinning around in midair. Every tendril of its head lashed out like a whip, cracking the air as they reduced the rock to dust particles under a flurry of blows.

"Well... I think we can confirm that Renaldi's team didn't end up here," I said glibly. "Either the mop trap would be gone or there would be a body... Unless... do you think the mop trap cleans up after itself?" I mulled it over. "Nah, better to assume we just took a different door. The compass points to where they are, not where they were. So these traps should be bypassable." I hummed in consideration. "Abel, can you grab a book from here with your ability?"

He shrugged. "Maybe." Reaching out, he warped the air, creating a trail of lubricated space. It took him a minute to do since he was trying not to trigger the traps, but finally he reached the shelf. Space warped his arm, letting him grab a random book. It was still weird watching him work, and the mental glitch of the space just... coiling as he pulled it back made me pause for a second before he handed it to me.

"Cyringian Table Manners, fiftieth edition, third appendix," I stated glumly. Flipping it open to make sure it was what it looked like, I sighed. "Okay, so not all of these are winners. Fork ordering, dish size... guest execution methods? That's a world of no." I snapped the book shut and dropped it where I stood. There had been pictures. "Let's try another one, shall we?"

My teacher chuckled, reaching out again and coming back with another book. This one was bound in blue leather. "Tributaries of Power: Sources of the Water Tribes." I flipped it open. This one seemed much more academic, and *didn't* have pictures of people being murdered. "This is functionally useless to us," I finally declared, "but it might be a nice present for Anna-Marie." I stowed it away. "Again."

We spent the next two hours slowly clearing books off shelves. Encyclopedias, history texts, instruction manuals, geography books, local fairy tales, books on boatbuilding, books on boat *destroying*, books on building boats to *counter* the books on boat destroying (this wizard had been *very* fond of boats), books on music, art, culture, cooking (which I kept), shoemaking, and a number of other things.

We found exactly two spellbooks, one for a Skill called Cumulo Nimbus, which let you summon lightning clouds, and one called Fire Whip, which did exactly what the name suggested. Two out of roughly four hundred books on the one wall we'd already gotten through.

"Enough!" my tired-looking mentor snapped, fed up. "We have stuff to do. We can hit the other walls when we come back through, *after* we find Renaldi's team." I noticed he was out of breath and sweating, and was grateful my mask covered my smirk. He was right, though. Besides, I was pretty sure the spell books had been left here by accident—this was most likely just a normal library.

"Fair enough," I said, and pulled out the compass, holding it up to figure out where it was pointed. "Everyone, get ready to go—we're headed north." That got groans from various members of our party still combing through the piles of books we'd grabbed (none of them were spells but there was some interesting topics; Jessie found one on local flowers). Everyone stashed the books they wanted or that seemed useful in their rings, tossed anything that seemed weird or murdery with the table manners book, and we moved on.

There were doors in each of the walls of books, so we headed through the one the compass pointed through, following the stairs up to another stone island with a massive door. When we went through this one, though, we were pleasantly surprised to find the exact group of people we were looking for, at least based on the descriptions.

The leader, a tall bronze-skinned man with blue eyes and wavy black hair, looked up from where he was sitting in the middle of the empty room. "No wait, don't, it's a—" His warning was cut off as the door slammed shut behind us and the wood of the barrier melted into a solid sheet of stone matching the archway around it. Renaldi sighed miserably. "Trap. Oh well —welcome to the first day of the rest of your lives, I suppose."

Looking around, I realized there was no other way out. Well shit.

Chapter Fifty

SEEING the defeated forms of the other team slumped in the center of the room, I sighed and pinched the bridge of my nose. Not defeated in the literal, 'beat 'em up' sense, but just mentally run down. "Miles Renaldi and company?" I said with a wince. "I take it you *did* get our message?" It would be nice to know that the wish had gotten past the defenses here, because it meant we had at least one way out.

The leader chuckled. "Oh, we got it. Not that it meant much in here. We've been stuck here since the day we landed. Lucky we stocked up on food and other necessities." He gave my cousin a cheerful wave. "Nice to see you, Natalie. Shame about the circumstances."

Nodding to my friends, I walked about halfway to where Miles' group was seated and sat down. "You've been here since the first day?" I tried hard not to think about how shitty that must have been.

He nodded. "Not that we can tell you how long that is. The first day we kept track of the time but..." He shrugged. "It was making it worse, you know? So we stopped checking. The rest of our time has been spent trying to get the hell out of this place. The doors sealed behind us like they did with you. My girlfriend, Sierra, is an Enchanter, and she's been working on trying to decipher the enchantments on the floor to create an opening, but it's slow going."

The red-haired girl with blue eyes sitting next to him nodded. She'd had them closed when we entered, seemingly meditating, but I was guessing she was leaning into Focus, and had probably long since memorized the floor runes. "The enchantments in this place are complicated. They aren't just linear two-dimensional constructs."

"I noticed," I said. "They're part of a three-dimensional structure. Not just the enchantments we see, but a larger construct based on where in the sky the islands are hanging. I'm guessing you have to take all that into account with any changes you make?"

She sighed. "It's worse than that. Every rune is part of the whole, but they're also tied into vertically aligned enchantments strung along the length of the tower." She pointed at a square of sapphire. "This isn't just part of the enchantments next to it, it's *also* part of an enchantment tied into the corresponding tile in the floor above us, and one to the side, and they're all interlocked like that. I don't know who made this place, but they were a *genius.*"

"Well, we can help you look for a way out," I said with a reassuring smile. "And if not... we have other means of departure we can all use." Hell, with Nat here even I had a way out. But that was ignoring the obvious. We might be stuck, sure, but if wishes could get us out, they could get us *unstuck.* We could just wish for the doors to open back up or something.

Frowning, she shook her head. "I'm not sure what means you're talking about, but most of the options I can think of would trigger the tower's defenses. There actually is a way to open the doors, but my issue is that it's tied to some sort of super monster construct waiting to attack us if I do. It's peak F-rank, and I don't think we can take it."

Ah, so she'd been looking for a back door before triggering the defenses and killing them all. That was definitely a problem, but since this place was only at base Impact value it was less of an issue than one might expect.

"We might be able to help," I said slowly. "First, how do you know it's peak F-rank?"

"There's a script," she said, pointing to a segment of flooring. When I looked blankly at it she sighed. "Right, none of you can see the spell constructs stringing these places together. The monster is a gargoyle. Peak F-rank and it comes out of the doorways."

I wished we had Benny with us. His Focus specialization would have been useful here. I sighed and considered our options. "If I tell you we can take it and get you out of here, would you believe me?"

"Well," Miles said with amusement, "you have a bear the size of a bus behind you, and I already know Valk is pretty capable, so yeah, probably. That's not even getting into the fact that most of you seem to have more Impact than we do. I'm guessing you used some of the Moonglow Dew? Speaking of, what was up with the message? You didn't exactly tell us much."

I told him how we'd been taken in by Ladrigan and how we'd run into Gabriel, and described helping them out with the temple and finding out about Suvaya. I filled them in on everything we knew, and by the time I was done, Miles was wincing in sympathy. "So," I said finally, "we have people to find, and we have to get back on a timetable. You up for finishing this?"

He just laughed. "You know what? Fuck it. Why not. We've been stuck here for days. You sure you can take out the guardian? It might be safer to leave using a wish."

Grinning, I hopped up and walked over to the doorway. "Sierra, what sets off the gargoyle protocol, just the back door you found? Or is there some secondary trigger we need to watch out for?" I suspected there was one, and I was pretty sure I knew what it was, since it was the first thing any rational person would try.

"The doors," she said succinctly. "If you try to break open the doors."

"Just the doors?" I asked intently. "Or the doors *and* the frames?" The doors were malleable and designed to change, that's how they melded into the frames, but the frames themselves were most likely the source of that particular enchantment.

She studied the ground in front of her. "Just the door. The frame has fail-safes, but it's not actually protected in and of itself."

Grinning, I pulled out my staff and triggered Touch of Tears and Consecration of Flame. As the green cracks rolled over the shaft, I reached out and touched it to the archway. The green flame spread, and I continued to move around, using State of Grace and Ripple Running to reach higher up until I'd covered every inch of the doorway in acidic poison.

"Alright," I said quickly, "this is going to do enough damage to eventually trigger the defenses. Randall, get up front. Abel, it's going to be moving slow because of the erosion. Jessie, post up next to him and make sure he's topped up so he can throw hands. Valk, prepare to support Abel. Callie, I want you to string this thing up as best you can with shadows. Avoid the green spots—it'll have places that aren't covered." I didn't include Nat since she wasn't really a combatant. As for myself, I'd help out where needed.

Miles chuckled. "Well, you don't mess around, do you?" Snapping his fingers, I saw a dully glowing splinter of orange metal appear in his grip. He tossed the tiny sample back like a pill. I watched the skin of his body change color, and I knew he was using his ability.

Sierra withdrew a series of tiles, tossing them up in the air. They glowed with runes, hanging unassisted as she reached up and started rearranging them. The other eight members of their team stood up. One, a big green-haired man with a thick beard, stood behind a short woman with crimson skin and horns. A devil, most likely, though I'd never seen one before.

Once we were ready, I nodded to Abel, who sent a quick jab at the door, raising an echoing boom as it made contact. The attack didn't do much to the door itself, but as soon as it landed the frame began to shift as a massive pair of hands emerged from the stone.

The huge form of the gargoyle resolved itself slowly, and Callie started stringing every spare inch of it that wasn't glowing and acidic with containment constructs. Her shadows didn't have the Might needed to hold up against a peak F-rank monster, not with the difference in power and specialization, but they *did* have an extra point of Impact, which was enough to offset a solid amount of the gap.

The gargoyle finished emerging and roared in pain as it tried to break free of Callie's containment. Before it could, Randall slammed a paw into the side of the monster's head. The massive bear was even more gargantuan on his back legs. The gargoyle reared back, and another of Abel's fists (this one condensed from about a dozen punches stacked on top of each other and reinforced by Valk's blue gel) smashed into its head.

Spinning my staff, I stacked up a Mercy Kill and a triple-stacked density shift, and I stepped off the air, sailing up to get a better vantage point from which to attack the gargoyle. Once I got high enough, I bounced off the air again and sent myself hammering down, my E-ranked staff leading as I brought it smashing down into the head of the creature.

The stone split under the weight and power of my staff, which, while not a perfect equalizer, was a material much harder than the material that comprised the monster. There was a loud crack as the staff split the stone. Even as it landed, I saw giant hand constructs grip the horns and *pull.*

The crack widened and I jumped free, leaving Randall to crush his paw down on the damaged head, pulverizing it into chunks of pottery. The gargoyle fell over, dead, or at least as close as an inanimate object could get. The door behind it was revealed to have reverted to the normal wood, easily opened now, and I grinned. My team was getting the hang of punching up.

Of course, the distance between us and peak F-rank was still pretty huge. The extra Impact helped a bit, but we were going to need to start padding our points to close the gap soon. We only had a month until we had to fight a literal goddess, and I didn't want to rely any more on petty tricks than I had to.

That was why I wanted to continue climbing this tower. I wanted more spellbooks, and to find out who made this place. More than that, I wanted to find out more about the woman in the mosaics. After all, those black forms chasing her reminded me an awful lot of the Night Pride.

Chapter Fifty-One

"So, how long do we have in here before we need to head back?" Renaldi asked as we walked up another set of twisting stairs. We'd been through several more rooms, one of which was another gargoyle trap. "And what are we looking for here exactly? Aside from the spellbooks I mean."

I shrugged. "Couldn't tell you. I saw something on one of the murals that makes me think this place might have some relation to Suvaya. Whoever built it might have left behind some books or something that will help us identify the conduits. Knowing where each one is and what they can do would be a pretty big help. If not, then yeah, spellbooks are the main goal here. We still have a few hours before we need to head back."

Probably more than that, but I was accounting for the annoying trip back *up* the damned mountain, which took much longer than the trip down. Maybe one of these books would have a teleport spell in it.

He seemed unruffled. "How about the tower? Any idea how much further we have to go?"

Sierra, who was talking to Abel about sausage recipes of all things, looked up. "Oh, I can answer that. I don't have a map or anything but based on the construct layout used for"—she waved a hand—"this, we have maybe one or two more floors."

I sighed with relief. "Well, I just hope the library at the top is of more use. The one we found on the lower floor was just a dumping ground for books. Some interesting stuff in there, granted, but only two spellbooks. If we're lucky the rest of them will be up top." I still wasn't sure what type of magic the tower's master had done, since the two books we found had been based in different things.

When we reached the next room, we found another four-way intersection, and Sierra called us to a halt. She'd told us at the last one that the spiraling staircases served another interesting purpose aside from shielding. They also made it functionally impossible to tell if you were walking up or down. These four-way rooms were another sort of trap we'd bypassed with the compass.

Since Renaldi's team was with us, there was no way to know exactly which door to take, but Sierra was able to use the spell construct's orientation in regards to the tower to determine which spellwork was leading upwards instead of down. That let us at least keep moving in the same direction.

As she did her thing, I glanced over the floor. The mosaic here was different, in that the woman's strawberry blonde hair had faded to white. Her face was only lightly lined with age, which made sense since she was an Ascendant. In this mural, she sat in a chair, looking out a window at a darkened sky with a huge moon in it. Seventeen lines traveled from the ground to the moon, and I became even more convinced this place held some information about Suvaya.

We climbed another staircase, and when we reached the second to last room, it became clear that this was where we'd been meant to end up. Sierra turned around, double checking her work. "That four-way intersection is where all the other paths lead. Any way you climb the tower you end up here eventually." She pointed at the door on the far end of the room. "That'll be the way to the peak."

As the last of us stepped into the room, the doors slammed shut. I was half expecting another gargoyle trap, but instead the mural on the floor began to glow. No, not mural, murals. In fact, Surrounding the big final mural on the ground were smaller versions of *all* the other murals, seemingly in order. Laid out like this and interspersed with other murals from rooms we'd presumably skipped or bypassed, they told a complete story.

"She wasn't native," I said in realization. "She entered by accident. Not during an awakening, but just... slipped through the distortions by mistake.

271

She was F-rank, so she didn't die, but she was talented. She spent her life learning about this place. How it worked. Why it was the way it was. She found the temples, figured out what was coming, but she couldn't do anything to stop it."

As we watched, the murals began to move, one at a time, acting out the stages of her life, showing us what she'd been through. She'd made a home here. Made friends, found family. Tried to help the people here as best she could while she lived. She traveled for a while fighting monsters, hence the knight. But she'd lived too long. The awakening came, the outsiders descended.

"They killed her," Jessie whispered. "The worshippers in the local kingdoms convinced them she was evil. They sent people like us to kill her off, and they did."

"That's why I didn't contact the locals about the ritual," I said bitterly. "Aside from the insanity that is local factional politics, we don't know how many Suvaya loyalists are still here. They've dug in deep from what we were told. If they find out we're trying to ruin the ritual…"

Callie pointed at the second to last mural. The woman, looking sad and resigned, putting a map in a small chest and locking it. She handed the key to what looked like a younger version of herself who inserted it into her own heart. Some kind of golem or something. As the motions reached the final mural, the center of the circle lit up. A picture of the woman in the dress.

Gingerly, she stepped forward out of the image, walking into three-dimensional space, the world warping as she appeared standing upright, looking at us peacefully.

The golem was… a work of art. She looked like a real person, but somehow even more lifelike. Skin made of literal ivory, hair carved into curling waves from flickering rubies, eyes with irises of actual sapphires. She felt… strong. Like Crighton felt strong. Impact. Forty points at least. I didn't think we would be able to beat her if we fought.

Smiling warmly, she nodded to us. "Well done," she said cheerfully. "You found the combination. I do so appreciate the release—I was getting quite bored."

"Combination?" I said in confusion. "We just read the story. Exactly as it was laid out. I don't see how that could be considered a combination.

Haven't any other people managed to get this far?" I wasn't really in a position to argue, but that seemed a bit too easy.

She shook her head, the stone she was made from moving like flesh and hair without any stiffness. It was disconcerting to watch. "Not at all. Firstly, this tower was sealed with the death of its owner. The harvest approaches, and it shows itself once more. Secondly, the combination was for someone to learn the *whole* story. An understanding of the ritual was key to that puzzle, as was the perspective of an outsider. Had you lacked those components... this conversation would have gone much differently."

Which implied the tower had read our minds or something. I'd normally be creeped out, but I had other things to worry about. "Alright. So... can you help us? We need to find and eliminate the conduits before Suvaya manifests or a lot of people are going to die. Can you tell us where they are?"

"I can," she said calmly. "But before I do so, I must test your mettle. The key contains a map and a ritual diagram that the tower master compiled over her long life. To earn it, I must taste defeat."

I grimaced. Because of course she must. "We're expected to beat you? Because with your Impact I'm pretty sure you could crush us. You've got to be at the peak of F-rank stat-wise, and given you're an animated pile of rocks I'm guessing you're pretty Might focused."

She shook her head. "As I said, only a taste is required. A single blow to prove your competence. You must be strong enough to weather what's to come. To defeat the strongest of the conduits, this level of strength is the minimum. Should you fail the test... a quick death here would be much more merciful than the fate you may suffer when the harvest comes."

"I have one question," Callie interjected. "How did you make sure this place would be found? Just leaving it to sit and wait would have been way too big a leap of faith, even considering fate sense."

The golem chuckled. "The tower master mapped the starlight slides during the last awakening. She arranged for the tower to relocate when next the moon was revealed. Now, which of you will be attempting the challenge? Only one may attack."

I looked at Abel, who nodded, stepping forward. I laid a hand on his shoulder. Mercy Kill, Afterburner, and with a very large amount of effort, I even channeled Marked for Death through him, targeting the golem. I swayed on my feet a bit as I stepped back, but I could see the power thrumming through him. "If we pass, you give us the key and escort us to the chest?" I asked intently.

"Not only that," the golem said. "I will aid you in your quest." That was… useful. If this worked.

"Alright." I nodded. "Abel, hit her with everything you've got. No holding back." He grinned at me, cracking his neck as he stepped back. I saw him take up a stance, fist cocked back and readying for the blow. Afterburner gave ten hits of amplified power, and with his stacking ability he'd be able to layer those. To my shock though, I saw his hands start to glow as they transformed into golden flame.

It occurred to me the only time I'd seen Abel cut loose was in the tournament. Without the single fighter rules, he had another source of power. His bond with Mel. It had to be at least as strong as the one I had with Callie —he was the one who taught it to us.

Space warped, and he stepped back, leaving behind a flaming image of his body. Then another step, and another. When he finished, there were nine figures in varying positions in a line behind where he'd been. Like looking at a stop motion instruction for a wind up and a punch. Abel, standing at the back of the line now, took a deep breath, and then flickered forward through the lubricated space.

As he took each position he overlapped and stacked the flaming versions of himself, all of them heavily condensed from powerful flame but not harming him at all. It was like watching someone perform a martial arts kata on fast forward, and when he reached the end he let out a roar of challenge and *swung* with every single bit of force he had in him.

A crystallized image of living flame condensed from his Expert level Ragam Skill appeared in front of the golem and brutally smashed a fist into the figure. On impact, the construct exploded in a massive firestorm of force and fire, swallowing the thing whole.

As the flame faded, I saw the golem standing there, mostly unharmed. Mostly. From its nose dripped a single bead of melted ruby, like a drop of blood. Looking down at the floor I saw a small scuff in front of one of the dainty diamond heels. The golem nodded, smiling slightly as she wiped her nose. "Well done. You pass. Barely." Turning her back on us, she waved a hand and the door behind her opened on its own. "Now come—claim your prize."

Chapter Fifty-Two

YVETTE (as she informed us she was called) had been here for a *long* time, but had spent most of it in stasis. She seemed excited to meet new people and filled us in on lots of trivia about the tower and its functions. Once we reached the top floor, she made a beeline for the center of the room where a pedestal sat empty in the middle of another room filled with bookshelves. Pressing several symbols on the black and gold surface, she opened a compartment in the top and gingerly removed the chest inside, setting it atop the pedestal once it closed.

After she removed it, she pressed a hand against her chest and the ivory skin became... like a gel? Her hand passed through and emerged with a black and gold key set with an unsettlingly glowing ruby. She inserted the key into the lock without fanfare and twisted, the lid springing open to reveal a rolled-up piece of parchment.

"So, this is a map?" I said cautiously. "Or a ritual diagram?" She hadn't been super specific about that, though I couldn't tell if that was by design or if she just wasn't used to explaining herself to others. I got the impression she didn't have the chance to chat often.

"Both," she said as she withdrew it and handed it to me. I unrolled it, placing it down on a nearby table half covered with books (which I would definitely be examining soon). Looking over the parchment, I could see what she meant, and I sighed in relief. It would make finding the locations of the other conduits a non-issue. I frowned in confusion. "Wait, what are these lines?"

She cocked her head. "The conveyances. They channel power along the lines of the ritual. During the awakenings they reach through the distortions to allow transport."

"Wait… those are the Starlight Slides?" I hadn't considered they were part of the ritual, but it made some sense. This whole place was a trap from the start, including the distortions. Of course the entrances were part of it.

Yvette seemed impatient. "Obviously. The conveyances will be the mechanism of the ascensions, as well as the harvest. They'll connect the conduits to the moon herself. As you can see, the conduits must ascend in a certain order for maximum effects. Once they've all ascended, the conveyances will attach to the primary temple, and the moon's light will descend in full."

"Primary temple?" I asked. I'd forgotten the temples were called sub-temples; I supposed a primary made sense. "Is that on the mountain? We know that's some kind of remnant of her divine body."

She pointed to a symbol in between the other seventeen. "The primary temple accepts the lunar blessing and focuses it through the lens of the gathered power. It's redirected to the mountain. The moon is the mind, the temple is the spirit, and the mountain is the body. This is an important factor in stopping the goddess. Should she attain her fully functional form, even hobbled as she might be by rank, you will all die."

That… pretty much blew up our whole plan. "That doesn't really work for us. The plan was to kill all of her conduits and then gank her physical form when it limps in through the ritual, underpowered from the lack of energy. We thought she would be weak. The conduits are."

"The conduits," she sneered, "are remnant ghosts possessing their own rotting corpses. They are pathetic demi-souls hollowed out by the ritual. They can barely string together coherent thoughts, much less wield their Skills with precision and finesse. The goddess is the mind behind the ritual. She sleeps, her dreaming weaving the webs you see before you. When she wakes, she will wake whole, if diminished in scope."

"Fuck!" I snapped, turning to kick a chair. We'd had a plan! We'd had hope, had a real shot at this. "So what? You brought us up here to tell us we're screwed and there's nothing we can do about it?"

277

Shaking her head, she pointed to the temples. "No. I said when she wakes. The ritual is in its infancy. If you can disconnect the conduits in a specific order, or close to it, given your mention of killing them, you can force her to manifest as a spirit alone at the central temple. Without her flesh to act as a material, her created form will be much weaker, and she will lose access to many of her abilities."

Oh. I let my shoulders slump, allowing the anger and frustration to drain out of me. "I'm... sorry," I said woodenly. "This has just been a lot. We came here expecting to run around literally flower-picking, with the occasional quick fight among our peers. In no universe could I have imagined we'd be fighting a vanished god. I didn't even know those were a thing until I got here."

She just smiled reassuringly. "I understand. Now, the disposal of the conduits must be done in as exacting a manner as possible. The deaths of the already vanquished can be accounted for in the sequence, but it would be best to minimize the deaths until preparations can be made."

Callie spoke up. "I'll call back to base and let them know to spread the word. Those mapped lines—the places they lead wouldn't happen to be the landing points, would they? Because we could use those."

Yvette nodded and my girlfriend grinned, snapping a picture of the parchment. "Benny is going to be so pissed he did all that work for nothing. I can't wait to see his face." At my cocked head she just shrugged. "What? You're a bad influence on me. I was an angel before I met you."

"You're mispronouncing the word asshole," Nat drawled with a smirk. At Callie's scandalized look she just winked. "Seemed mean to let you pick on poor Benny when he isn't here. Someone had to fire back."

My girlfriend's face broke into a wide grin. "I knew I liked you for a reason."

"Nope," I interjected. "I do not prefer this. You"—I pointed at my cousin —"are enough of a pain in my ass without conspiring with her. Please bond with someone else. Jessie is available. She's excellent company, or perhaps I can interest you in an elf best friend? Maybe you'd like to make the switch to being a battle maniac for some strange reason, and then Abel might be less annoying to you than he is to the rest of us."

My mentor's middle finger was casual, so I knew he didn't take it personally. Nat just grinned smugly and I rolled my eyes, turning back to the map and the construct holding it. "Please give me more terrible news. I'd like to be distracted right now."

Yvette's ruby lips (not symbolism, actual rubies) twitched up in a smile. "Well, the ritual will take place relatively soon, so you'll need to begin your purge as quickly as possible. The order is also not based on power, so you will be unable to save the most dangerous for last."

I sighed. "The first time in my life someone gives me what I ask for and it's this. Is this why other people always say 'be careful what you wish for?' because I've never understood that phrase."

"Of course you haven't honey," Callie said sweetly. "But at least you're pretty."

I shot a flat stare at Nat. "Look what you've done. Now she'll be making wise cracks for hours." Letting out a breath, it was hard not to smile a bit at the sensation of camaraderie. Banter was excellent stress relief. Not as excellent as punching things, but close. I loved Callie for being there for me, especially given where we were standing and how much she must be salivating over the bookshelves behind us.

I turned to Yvette. "Since we got the map, does that mean the rest of these books are for us too?"

"Indeed," she said solemnly. "The world's largest trove of cartography books is now at your disposal. The years of study needed to accrue the knowledge to make this map are all contained within their pages. They used to be spellbooks, but the tower master stripped the ink to write more map making notes."

I blinked at her solemn expression. "That's... are you fucking with me right now?"

Her small smile came back. "It seemed to be entertaining. I wished to attempt such witticisms. I find them to be very amusing." She looked at Callie. "Did I do that properly?"

My girlfriend was nearly doubled over with laughter. "Yes," she gasped out. "You did great." At my glare she snorted, trying to control her laughter. "Sorry sweetie," she choked out. "It's just... your face. You looked so horrified. Plus the books are fine so there's no need to be all grumpy." Her laughter stopped. "The books... are fine right? They're all spellbooks?"

Yvette shook her head. "Not all, but several. They are, of course, yours to do with as you will. I do hope they will be helpful to you in your pursuit of our shared goal." She gestured expansively to the shelves.

I was pretty sure Callie's eyes would have turned into credit signs if it were physically possible. Smiling at her enthusiasm, I decided to follow her lead, spreading out along with the others to pore over the variety of books packed onto the shelves. Callie, being the responsible partner she was, forced herself to make that call back to base to let everyone know what was going on, but as soon as she was finished she dove into helping us sort through the books.

Granted, it wasn't exactly a quick process. Much like the downstairs library, the majority of the books weren't spellbooks. I'd expected this top floor to be packed with them, but apparently I'd underestimated the value of the texts. We did find many more than the previous floor, and the non spell texts were still useful, and much more locally focused than the ones downstairs.

I was sure that Anna-Marie and her people would find this particular library endlessly useful, even more so than the last. As for the spellbooks we did find, they ran the gamut. Some fire, some ice, some more esoteric spells like line-of-sight teleportation.

Most of them I passed on (despite my desire for new abilities) because I already had powers that could mimic their effects. My friends all found some interesting tomes to check out, but I was kind of disappointed with the options available, at least for myself. My mostly meta focused skillset wasn't exactly easy to complement. I was planning to look over them more carefully once the others had all chosen.

Finally, we finished stripping the place for books and it was time to head back. We had to make our way to the mountain and scale the damned thing in time to relieve Gabriel and his team. Bethy should have already switched places with the other group, and I didn't want to leave them stuck there too long, not to mention the new map and how useful it would be for our current project.

I felt much more confident than I had after the conclave. Between the map and Yvette we were in a much better position. Anyone tough enough to take a punch like that from Abel and barely get a nosebleed would be a welcome addition to the team. At this rate, we might make it out of this after all.

Chapter Fifty-Three

GETTING BACK up the mountaintop was surprisingly easier than expected. For me. Yvette made the climb, hauling us all up. She was literally ten times stronger than the rest of us, so it wasn't a tough trip, and she managed it smoothly and in like a fourth of the time I had, even with my little jump cheat.

Which meant we still had plenty of time to make it to the camp by nightfall even after getting up there. It made the whole thing about a thousand times easier and more convenient. When we arrived, I wasn't shocked to see Gabriel around, having relieved Bethany and sent her off to find the next team.

"Hello the camp," I said with a wave as I approached. I caught sight of Benny and Celine over by Annalise's canopy bed, and my best friend turned and saw me.

"You son of a bitch!" Benny yelled, more in irritation than anger. "I pulled a fucking all-nighter managing those calculations and trying to put together a proper map and you just *find* one!" From Celine's groan I was guessing this particular complaint wasn't a new one.

I smirked. "You realize if we hadn't found the map, we were all going to die probably?" I inquired politely, which I absolutely knew would drive him up the wall. Much like myself, the thing Benny hated most was being spoken to calmly when he was pissed off.

"I *know* that!" he hissed angrily. "You ass. But *now* I have to completely rearrange our search parties and factor in the order we need to kill these things in, whatever that is. I've been recalculating based on the drop-off locations we got, so the teams should be easier to locate, but I think you'll need to make some more of those compasses. I have Gabriel standing by for a rework, apparently his second target point was slightly off." Celine snorted, and Benny turned to glower at her. "Was *slightly* off, within an acceptable margin of error."

Annalise, who had been watching smugly as he spoke, added, "A hundred-mile margin of error." Her voice was saccharine.

"This is a big planet!" Benny scowled. "There's a lot of *stuff* here. And this stupid mountain doesn't follow the laws of physics, even the nonsensical version that *we* live by. I was basing my calculation partially off distance traveled on the way here. It was a perfectly reasonable thing to do."

Laughing, I turned to Yvette. "Can you help him with this please? Maybe consult with him for the calculations to decide the order we need to kill the conduits?" She gave me a solemn nod, and I rolled my eyes as I turned to head away from them, saying to Callie, "I forgot how whiny he gets when he's wrong about something."

"I heard that!" Benny shouted from behind me.

I just gave him the finger over my shoulder. "You were meant to!" Callie snorted and shook her head as I faced her. "Anyway, did you find anything good among the spellbooks? Any interesting shadow spells?"

She shook her head. "Too niche. I've been working on something though." She withdrew a pair of daggers I hadn't seen before. "You remember my bike?"

"The one I refused to get on for fear of a sudden fiery death? The one that looked like you'd crashed it a dozen times by the time I saw it?" I said flatly. "No, no memory at all."

She rolled her eyes with a huff of annoyance. Everyone in our team had agreed not to let Callie drive. It wasn't exactly that she was bad at it—she had amazing reflexes like any Ascendant. It was more that her definition of acceptable risk when driving pretty much anything was abnormal.

"Anyway," she crowed, "the reason I asked is because if you remember, I had it made from special materials like my coat is, so I could imbue it over time with darkness. Made it pliable to my power without it being part of me." She held up the daggers. "These are not made of special material, other than being F-rank. Seems like a side effect of the power change is that I can still do it. Eventually. It's taking a really long time."

I held out my hand, and she passed one to me. I weighed the thing in my hand. "Nice. That's huge, Cal. You have a dagger teacher you can work with?"

She nodded. "Gabriel's crew is here for a while longer, and one of the guys he works with uses daggers. One of the girls uses a staff, too. I figure the two of us could ask a favor, maybe get a little training if you're up for it. Your staff is damned useful, but you don't really know how to use it except for spinning it around and smacking things with it."

"I'd argue there's no other valuable use for a big stick," I said solemnly, "but a bit of hands-on training can't hurt. I assume you don't want to just ask on your own?"

To my surprise, her face pinched. "I want to get back into the habit of training together. We haven't been fighting like we used to since I got my power. I know the whole spy mistress thing is damned useful, but I don't want to lose our combat style. I have a lot of fun fighting with you."

I didn't know what to say for a second, then I nodded. "Yeah, I have fun fighting with you too." I reached down and took her hands. "Look, we're still getting our balance, okay? First you were way stronger than me, now that I've caught up you had this big power change. It'll take some time, but we're just finding our way on the battlefield again. We've got this, right?"

Her grimace smoothed out. "Yeah. We got this." She let out a deep breath. "We got it. So all we have to do is train together a bit more."

"Nope," I said bluntly. At her look I just shrugged. "What? We can't just punch stuff together and magically make things better. But I think we've already been doing other stuff. I think a lot of the problem is that you're having trouble finding your place in the group since giving me the reins. Or am I wrong?"

"Not... wrong," she hedged. "I mean, sure, I can do the whole intelligence gathering thing, but it's not really the same."

I nodded. "I know. But that's not all you do. You're my partner. You've been letting me take the lead to find my way, to... middling success. But you're still involved. We're still doing this together. It's not like you aren't up front when I do things wrong. And I'm glad. I need someone to yell at me when I do something stupid. It's going to happen sometimes."

"Sometimes?" she said skeptically, though I could tell she was fighting down a smile.

I rolled my eyes. "This? This is why we can't have nice things. I was *trying* to have a moment here. You couldn't let me be romantic for a minute?"

She smiled sweetly and took my face in her hands. "You're always romantic, sweetie. It's one of the things I love about you. Another is that you care enough to check in with me about my own insecure bullshit. Everything you're saying is true, and I know we're in this together. I'm feeling a bit aimless after transitioning between jobs. That's not about us, and I know the difference."

Blowing out a breath, I nodded. "Well... that's good at least. I guess that means I can't help with the whole aimlessness thing, huh?"

"You?" she said incredulously. "You literally just figured out what you wanted to do with your life like two weeks ago. That's not a dig, it's just my point. Sometimes it takes a while. Most of my life has been about sticking it to my dad, and now he's just some random asshole on a backwater planet. I'm adjusting to the change in scale before I set my sights on something new."

Which was fair. It wasn't like I could take shots at her for not having a life goal, especially not given what I'd been doing up to now. "Alright, well I still think training together is a good plan, and I'm glad you brought it up. Any time I get to spend with you pretty much guarantees a good day."

She rolled her eyes, but she was smirking. "I still don't know how you say gooey romantic shit like that and make it sound reasonable." Letting her hands drop from my face she grabbed one of mine and started dragging me toward Gabriel's group. "Come on you sap, let's go get started letting someone beat you violently about the head and shoulders with a big stick."

"Joy," I deadpanned. "Exactly what I always wanted."

We headed over to where Gabriel was, and the big blonde man nodded somberly as we approached. "So, you heard we've been temporarily benched, I take it?"

"Yup," I said succinctly as I dropped into a seat nearby (they'd set out a whole living room set for some reason and one chair was free). Callie plopped down in my lap since it was the only empty seat. "I take it you heard about the ritual and the fact that we were probably going to die following the original plan?"

He nodded. "I did. I'd say it was lucky Renaldi's team found the tower, but between fate sense and intentional placement, it doesn't seem like there was much luck involved. Still, it's certainly not a bad thing to have more information. We found another of the teams, and Bethany was sent out for one. The other seven search parties had varying levels of success. Four of them came back with their quarries, and the other three reported no results. Either those teams are dead or they were too far away to find."

"Fifteen total then," I said with a sigh. "And four potentially dead. Not ideal, but it could be worse. With the new map we should be able to dispatch another wave of search parties, but I have a feeling you, Bethany, and I will probably end up on a different sort of detail. In light of that, I was hoping I might ask a favor. Callie mentioned one of your guys is a dagger expert, and one of your team members uses a staff?"

He nodded. "Archimedes actually uses daggers most of the time. And yes, Willow is proficient in staff techniques. I take it you were hoping for some training while we wait?"

"If you're open to it," I said with a shrug. "I can pay for it with wishes. Callie is my girlfriend and making her safer is in my best interest since we fight together. And I could really use a better handle on my own combat style. The meta mechanics I have down, but some more advanced techniques would certainly help." I actually had plans to eventually create my own staff art based on the techniques I already had from DS Mastery, but walk before you run, right?

"I believe that could be arranged," he said after a moment. "We'll be working together on this in any case, and your gesture helping us with the temple turned out to be even more fortuitous than expected. You may have saved our lives by joining us, and I won't forget it."

I didn't mention the information he might be holding onto about my mom. Whatever it was, I didn't think now was the time.

Standing up, he gestured us over to where some of the team members not seated with him were talking. "How about we get started right away?"

Chapter Fifty-Four

WILLOW, the knight that was going to teach me (that wasn't her Job I don't think, but all of Gabriel's people wore armor and rode horses) was a tiny redhead, nearly as short as Callie, with bright green eyes and a friendly, heart-shaped face. She had a smattering of freckles and a friendly smile that made you want to like her, and generally gave off the impression of a cheerful, kind person. At first.

As soon as she drew her staff, she basically turned into a drill sergeant. Which wasn't to say that she was rude or angry. No, it was worse than that. The smile never faded, the friendly chirp never left her voice, and she never stopped being upbeat, even as she beat me to within an inch of my life.

"Nope, sorry. Elbow in," she chirped as her staff flicked out and slammed into my funny bone. My armor was supposed to prevent blunt damage. How was she even doing this? That stick wasn't E-ranked. I let out a low groan but adjusted my posture accordingly. "There you go," she cheered happily. "Now you're getting it!" I wasn't. As was evidenced by her next strike to correct my footwork... by slamming her gods damned stick into my ankle.

"Why are you doing this?" I whimpered. She was a demon. She was worse than Abel. I hadn't even thought that was possible, but at least he mocked openly. Her damned perky smile was mocking me, I could *feel* it, but she acted like she was just a genuinely nice person so I couldn't even be properly mad about it.

She giggled. "I'm just teaching, silly. You're doing so much better! Just keep trying." I hoped she was mocking me, to be honest, because if whoever trained her had conditioned her like this to the point she actually thought it was okay, I'd have to feel bad for her.

"You're a monster," I wheezed. And she just giggled again like I was making a joke, which I absolutely wasn't. Even a little bit.

I had to admit, despite the pain and annoyance, this was a fairly effective way to adjust my technique. Willow had demonstrated a series of katas upon our first meeting, and was now having me go through them from memory one by one. My Focus made that a completely viable approach, but seeing someone do something once isn't enough to perfectly replicate it, even if you can remember what they did. She seemed to have an uncanny ability to perceive the exact muscles I was using even through my coat and armor and was making minute adjustments to each kata until I performed them perfectly.

"You've got that one down," said the evil creature that wouldn't stop beating me in a deceptively cheerful tone. "Now I want you to try the next one. Raven in the Trees, please."

I nodded, clearing my mind so I could remember her exact movements when she'd demonstrated. My staff lashed out at ankle height, and I flowed back around in a reversal, spinning the shaft around my body and then striking at head level. Another smack to my elbow drew another yelp from me, and Willow chuckled.

"You could pretend you aren't enjoying this so much," I said, rubbing my elbow.

She shook her head. "Don't be silly. You're doing really well." Her excessive cheerfulness faded a bit, replaced with soft reassurance. I wished I could just hate her properly, but she was so *nice*. "I know this is tough, but you need to learn these forms properly. People like to say practice makes perfect, but only perfect practice makes perfect. These techniques can save your life, but they need to be learned properly."

"I know," I said with a sigh. "And unnecessary abuse aside, I do appreciate the help. I can see how these would be useful. What exactly is your style called?"

"Valtek," she said with a warm smile. "It's a fairly common staff form back on my home planet, but things don't work worse because people know about them. It's been refined over generations and is an excellent foundation for crafting your own techniques once you've mastered it. Now, try that one again, and adjust the elbow as you spin."

Ascendant martial arts, even ones without crazy built in abilities, tended to the dramatic. It was in our nature to seek attention. This particular movement was useful in more than just an offensive sense, though. The spinning was meant to be used as a deflection. I tried to incorporate that understanding into it and saw her nod approvingly as she smacked the back of my knee and dropped me on my ass.

"That was much better, though not good enough. I see you're starting to understand some of the nuances of the staff though. It's a uniquely powerful weapon, not for its weight or damage dealing capabilities, but for its versatility. People will tell you power is the most important factor of a weapon, but they're wrong. The spear can do many things the staff can, but I consider it an inferior weapon. Do you know why?"

I paused. I didn't—I couldn't think of a reason putting a blade on my staff would be bad. I'd even considered getting a spear at one point, but I'd decided the learning curve was too steep and that I wanted to take advantage of my existing abilities and skills. "Nope, can't think of a reason."

Willow didn't seem surprised, but she gave me a minute to sit down as she talked, so I listened. "Leverage." She whirled her stick in a circle. "With properly applied leverage you can shift a planet with merely human strength. Every force has to deal with leverage, and the staff is one big lever. To alter trajectories, to shift incoming force vectors, that's the true art of the staff. Offense and defense at the same time."

I climbed to my feet, thinking that over. "I guess that's true," I mused. "If you look at everything as force to be leveraged, that does kind of change your application. But at least some solid attacks need to be landed, right?" I tended to rely on single blows to win fights.

Her stick blurred out and landed on my knee with a slam and I hissed in pain, hopping on one leg. "Of course," she chirped. "You just have to know how to leverage your own power. You'll get it eventually. Now, I want you to try Raven in the Trees again, and I'm going to attack while you do it."

It wasn't hard to recognize that she'd been holding her attacks until after each attempt. Now she wanted to demonstrate what I could do once I learned them properly. I attempted the kata, moving exactly as she'd coached me. She stepped over the low blow, then attacked with a sharp thrust. I was already twisting, the staff close to my body, and I was delighted to see the stick swept into my spin as my staff knocked her wrist.

The attack was redirected and the weapon was seamlessly plucked from her grasp to fly a few feet away into the snow. She stepped back, withdrawing her hand without any obvious pain, and clapped excitedly. "That was fantastic! Did you feel what I meant when I corrected you?"

I nodded. "Yeah, it was all leverage. Caught your staff against my body and then used myself as a fulcrum. The blow to your wrist made you let go and the staff came free."

"Yup," she said as she walked over to the staff, kicking it up off the ground with some kind of small foot movement and catching it midair. "Try that one another few times just to make sure you've got it, then we'll switch to Stalking Tiger. Remember the most important thing here is that you get the katas perfect. Once you've got them mastered, you can repeat them on your own time. Our time here isn't endless, so I want to make sure you're properly prepared to practice on your own."

I gave a sheepish laugh. "Yeah, I do appreciate the help. I feel like you're being a bit harsher than needed, but I do appreciate the time and guidance." Speaking of which, I turned around to where Callie was standing in front of Archimedes. "How's it going over there, honey?"

Archimedes was *not* just constantly attacking her, part of why I was annoyed. He'd taken the inverse tactic. He was having her attack and putting himself in a position where only a proper strike would land. Daggers weren't nearly as evenly disposed to attack or defense as the staff. They heavily favored attacking, which meant training Callie on defensive moves was pointless.

She'd been working with him as long as I'd been working with Willow, and she was soaked in sweat and panting as she stopped to call back. "Not bad. I'm landing more hits now. Archie says I've got a knack for this kind of thing."

The other man nodded casually. "It's true. She's naturally gifted at knifework. I suspect her rock-solid foundation in—what did you call it? Balam?

—is helping. She's incorporating circular motions into her attacks as best as possible while following the forms I gave her."

Sadly, my own mastery of Balam wasn't anywhere near that point. Skills acquired through Wishing might need more work at Intermediate, but Benny had shown how valuable the earliest versions could be. Foundation was exactly right, and having learned mine through actual practice instead of having it dumped into my head meant mine was shakier. It also wasn't as compatible with the style Willow wanted to teach.

I'd learned a few katas for Balam too, or forms as they were called, but they didn't really translate to armed combat well. Callie's weapon of choice worked on similar mechanics and at a similar range to hand-to-hand. "Alright. Back to work. You'll be sparring in an hour or two," Willow said with a smile. "Got to make sure you're up to fighting different kinds of opponents."

I sighed and got back in position, moving through the Raven in the Trees kata again. I managed to get it perfect two out of three times, and she let me move on after that. I could already see how this could all be applied to my combat style and abilities. I'd be able to make my own staff moves to complement my Path soon enough.

Paths were something I hadn't really been able to understand well. It seemed like they were based on following an ideology of sorts. How that tied into your legend I wasn't sure, but I was positive they had something to do with it. I knew people like Abel and Gabriel had Paths and getting one early was a big advantage for some reason. I'd seen that I could exert more power when I was following my Path. Maybe my hypothetical staff art could be the way I merged my Path and combat style, once I figured out what it even was.

I was jarred from my thoughts by a strike to the side of my knee and winced. Right, I was training still. Had to get my head back in the game. If I wanted to make my own martial art, I'd have to learn one to base it on, and this was the best opportunity for that.

I sank back into my stance. One step at a time.

Chapter Fifty-Five

WE ENDED up finishing our training (at least enough of it to get a Minor Skill) within a few hours. Since it was already dark, we decided to camp for the night, and Bethany actually got back a bit earlier with the team she'd been sent to fetch. We all ate together at base camp before settling in, though the literal dozens of people meant we were mostly interacting in cliques. I sat with my own team, as well as Bethany, her thralls, Gabriel, Willow, Archimedes, and the wolves.

Bethany was extremely excited to spend time with the puppies, and particularly liked Jin, whom she showered with love and affection. She was occasionally interrupted by 'Donuts' (the Night Pride) who in proper cat fashion displayed his extreme aggravation with being ignored by acting like he was too good for scritches. The shadow cat repeatedly swatted at Jin from relatively far away, but my G-rank puppy ignored him, intent on snuggling with the petite Vampire while lolling his tongue smugly.

"So, you've got an idea where to send us now?" I asked Benny as we chowed down on a surprisingly flavorful stew. One of Gabriel's people had made it, and it was exceptionally well done. Stew is tough because... well, most stew is tough. Literally. It's easy to boil the tenderness out of the meat and end up eating shoe leather. This was pretty well handled, though—I wondered how they'd done it.

"Yeah," he said as he ate. Celine looked annoyed at his bad table manners, but I was guessing she recognized his good work enough that she decided not to yell at him. That or she was going to do it later. "Yvette was a huge help, and so was Sierra. We went over the matrices of the ritual and calculated exactly what feedback pattern will default the ritual to the central temple."

He pulled out a rolled-up map, not the same one, but something he drew by hand, and flicked it out to unroll on the ground so we could all see it. He used one hand so he could keep eating, and I made a note to force him to have seconds. He was clearly starving.

I looked down at the map and then scowled at him. "Seriously?" I pointed at the circled temple. "How far away is that? I don't want to walk that far. At least it's only a former B-ranker like the last one. I'm dreading having to fight any of the former A- or S-rankers. Do we know anything about this one?"

Benny snorted. "Not much, but as for the distance, I had some ideas there. Keep in mind how high up we are. I think with State of Grace as a factor you could probably glide there. Have Callie set up some kind of hang glider. Can't take Jessie though—Randall would be a bad fit for that kind of thing, plus I don't think bears like to fly."

I turned to Callie. "Can you do that? Because we're really high up. That might actually be viable."

"What do you mean, *actually*, you dick," my best friend complained. "I just spent the better part of a day rehashing math formulas to help point you at a target." He clicked his tongue in disgust. "Actually. I'll actually kick you in the throat while you're sleeping."

He wouldn't. After a particularly vicious prank war as children, we'd declared sleeping time sacred and made a pact not to mess with the other when they were unconscious. Waking up with half your head and both your eyebrows shaved has a way of motivating you to sue for peace, much less what I'd done to him in retaliation.

Callie rolled her eyes at us. "What is it about your bickering that seems to deflate your brains? Yes, I can make a glider, especially now. And yeah, I would avoid hanging a bear from it. What's the team composition for this going to be? I know I have to go because I'm the ride, and I assume Shane will be with me."

Bethy's hand shot into the air as she bounced excitedly like we were in a classroom. "Ooh! ooh! Me! Pick me!" We looked at her and she shrugged. "There's a bunch of us here now, so I don't think we need anyone to watch them. Plus we'll need all the power we can get. Me and crusader cutie over there should be part of the elimination team."

Gabriel rolled his eyes, but I swear I saw his lips twitch a bit. Bethy was a hard person to dislike, apparently even if you were part of a religious organization that considered her an abomination. The big man cleared his throat. "I'd definitely like to come along. We can leave some of my people here to keep the peace. Willow is more than capable of taking care of anyone that becomes a problem."

My body was wracked by shudders as I remembered the stick-wielding demoness and her big bright smile. "Agreed. So me, Mel, Abel, Callie, Bethy, Gabriel? Five-person team worked okay last time, and six should be fine, but are we sure we don't want to do a full complement of ten? We ARE going after an ancient undead powerhouse. The extra combatants can't hurt."

Yvette chuckled. She'd been so quiet I hadn't even noticed her. "You forgot me. With the seven of us we should be more than sufficient. I don't claim it to be a simple task, but it shouldn't be impossible."

Right, the forty Impact golem made of literal rocks. I wasn't sure if that would affect the hang glider, but I was pretty positive my State of Grace could offset her weight with enough effort.

"So we go tomorrow then?" I asked after a moment of thought. "I'd rather not take to the skies out there without being able to see."

Everyone agreed, and we got back to the business of dinner, digging into our stew as we told stories about our adventures. Bethy was particularly verbose, though Aida consistently cut in to correct her outlandish claims, not seeming to notice that her corrections were only slightly less outlandish. By the time we headed to bed we'd all spent a nice evening laughing and enjoying ourselves, and I felt pretty refreshed.

This whole dungeon run had been much more stressful and dangerous than expected, and as I drove my rock spike into the mountain and our bunker constructed itself, I was forced to admit that the downtime tonight had been much needed. Not just for me, but I could see Callie holding herself a bit less tensely, seeming a bit less primed to snap. It was a good reminder that being leader didn't just mean telling my people when to fight, it also meant telling them when not to. Given my own problems with that concept, it was something I'd definitely need to work on.

"So, am I the only one excited to see Bethany fight?" Callie said as we lay down in our tent inside the bunker. "Because she scares the shit out of me, and the closest we've come is seeing her little rumble with you, where I'm pretty sure she held back a lot."

I snickered. "You're just interested in how she tamed that shadow cat. You want one of those, don't you?"

"Obviously." She snorted. "I have power over shadows. I *should* be able to do the same thing, but I have no clue how the hell she managed it."

I just shrugged. "Vampires. Anyway, we can ask her on the way, it'll be a much shorter trip there with the hang glider. You're going to be key to this mission. I'm sure she'd be willing to talk about it and maybe help you pull off something similar."

"I'd be much more reassured by that if I was at all sure she *knew* how she'd done it," Callie complained. "But I guess you're right."

"I'm always right," I said solemnly. "I thought I was wrong once, but I was mistaken. Now go to sleep—we have a long trip in the morning."

She giggled a bit before snuggling up to me and closing her eyes. I let myself drift off peacefully, always happiest when we were together.

In the morning, Callie got up first, squirming free of my arms and waking me up as she rushed to get into costume and get ready to go.

Laughing, I put on my armor and we headed out into the bunker. I'd already pulled the rock spike, so we left the bunker to come apart on its own time as we headed outside. Bethany was already out there, a small decorative umbrella held up to give herself a bit of extra shade. Her skin wasn't burned by the sun or anything, but clearly she wasn't a fan.

Gabriel was sitting at a fire, cooking a skillet full of bacon. When they saw us he waved us over. The cold mountain air nipped at our skin, but I had to admit, something about sleeping in a tent and waking up to cold and the smell of bacon reminded me so much of camping trips with Benny's dad as a kid. There was just something so peaceful about it.

As we approached, I couldn't bring myself to talk. Something about the morning chill and the fact that everyone was still asleep except us just made the silence feel heavier, harder to break. It wasn't anything oppressive though, just the odd feeling that I was waiting for my ability to talk to wake up with the rest of me. I breathed out, letting a cloud of mist fog the air as I sat down.

Gabriel passed me a plate with some bacon, and for a while, the scraping of silverware on dishes was the only sound aside from the crackle of the fire. Even Bethany was quiet.

The silence broke as Mel and Abel showed up and my mentor flopped down onto a chair he brought out. "Man that smells good," he groaned. "Remind me why I'm awake this early?"

"Because shut up," Mel said shortly. She didn't have her mask on, which felt weird to see. She withdrew a thermos from her ring and poured out a cup of black liquid, sniffing it serenely before taking a long pull. Coffee, based on the smell. Abel grinned at her, holding out his own cup, and she grudgingly poured a small measure into his mug. He looked at it forlornly before shrugging and downing it in a single toss.

We all ate in silence, enjoying the morning, and even Callie seemed almost at peace, though she had a measure of nervous tension that told me she was anxious to get going.

Once we finished and found Yvette, we set out at a brisk walk toward the edge nearest to the temple we were aiming for. I wasn't convinced we could glide the whole way, even from a place this high up, but even if we couldn't we'd cut down the trip by a substantial margin.

Reaching the edge, Callie got to work putting together her construct. She'd consulted Benny a bit the night before on construction, and my best friend had given some notes on what pitfalls to avoid and how to make the whole thing a smoother and more relaxing experience. She created a giant hang glider with a platform at the base we could all stand on.

We all got on and I triggered State of Grace. We pushed forward, the tiny wheels on the corners rolling us down the steep incline towards the edge of the mountain. Then, with a stomach dropping yank, we hit the air, and we were flying.

Chapter Fifty-Six

SINCE MY ABILITY AWAKENED, I'd done plenty of amazing things. Seen places I couldn't imagine, done things I'd never dreamed of. I'd fought fucking undead dragons, stolen from evil necromantic castles, stood on the blade of a sword the size of a skyscraper, and dozens of other unbelievable things. Despite all that though, there'd always been a sense of... unreality, of being on the other side of the looking glass.

Flying was beyond all of that. I don't know what it was about this type of flight that seemed so much more amazing than taking shuttles, but as we sailed over hundreds of miles of jungle, I knew this was an experience I'd never forget.

Maybe it was the fact that I'd helped to do this, that Callie and I had made this possible together, just us. It was just... transcendent. I knew it wasn't just me, either. I could feel Callie through the bond, her amazement, her joy. She was experiencing every bit of this that I was, and as she took my hand and squeezed it, I couldn't help the smile that plastered itself across my face.

"Damn," Abel said in awe. "Now that ain't something you see every day." We could see the jungle far off into the distance, and behind us we could see the mountains that made up the closer side of the ring. I saw buildings out there, closer to the ground. Towers, temples, fortresses. All spread out among the trees and cleared of brush and debris in a way that made it obvious that they were long since claimed by forces unknown.

Bethany whistled. "This is so beautiful," she said in a surprisingly somber voice. "Thank you for letting me see this. I've never witnessed anything quite like it. It's not just the sight—it's the fact that I know this place is unspoiled by those above us. F-rankers and the only people who can get in here. This view is just... just for us."

I nodded. "That's it. That's what I couldn't put my finger on. We own the sky. Sure there are birds up here, but they're obviously leaving us alone. This is... the view from the top. At least temporarily." The beauty was remarkable, but there was more to this feeling, under all that.

The knowledge that we were literally on top of the world right now was a heady sensation. This was a preview of what it would be like, I thought, to be an S-ranker, or even a god. Even if we lost the extra Impact and never gained anything else from this trip, this moment was enough. This made everything worth it.

It was more than just feeling like a big shot. We were feeling it together. I wondered how many Ascendants lost their perspective climbing up this high in the outside world. How many abandoned their loved ones for these heights, never remembering the whole point of wanting to get here.

This was nothing less than a reminder to stick together, to keep climbing as a group. To help each other, so someday, we could stand above everything together like this and *really* know we'd made it. The feel of the wind, the sound of the rushing air, the green blanket of beautiful trees stretched out below us—I memorized it all so the next time I felt unsure of my path, I could remember.

I saw Callie's eyes tear up, though she subtly wiped it away. She'd needed this perspective just like I had. She'd been feeling small and lost since we'd left Callus, but it was impossible to look down from here and feel like anything less than a giant.

The world flew by for hours. Our starting point was so damned high (and the spatial distortion had kind of launched us as we got clear) that we glided for most of the day, gradually drifting down and frequently slowed by State of Grace. Its increased hangtime was a massive boost to the already lengthy trip, though I had to use it sparingly when we started to hit a downdraft, at least after the first active use.

Finally, after most of the day had passed, we came down. I used State of Grace to land us so we could avoid any bumpy contact when we touched down. We aimed for a clearing relatively nearby, and the landing was smooth. Hopping down, I offered Callie a hand and helped her to the ground as everyone disembarked. Taking out the magic map we'd bought, I checked our current location against the temple's position.

"Alright," I said as I eyeballed it. "Three quarters of the way there. It's about…" I checked my scan ring. "Three P.M. I'd say if we rush, we could arrive by nightfall, but I think that would be stupid. I think we should keep a steady pace and then camp a few dozen miles out. Let the night pass before we plan our attack. I don't know if these undead are stronger at night but… Well, they do worship a moon goddess."

Everyone paused. "Yeah," Abel chimed in, "I actually hadn't considered that, but it seems like a stupid risk to take when we can just avoid it." At the shocked looks he got he shrugged. "What? I like a good fight, I'm not suicidal. The less godly bullshit we deal with the better."

I chuckled at that, nodding along. "Alright, let's head out then." Using the map to orient, we headed for the temple as best we could. We made good time, of course, given our stats, and weirdly, we didn't run into anything that might slow us down. No monsters, no animals, nothing—they seemed to be avoiding us.

Triggering my Eye of Revelation, I pushed my soul to try to pick up what might be causing it, and concluded that they could sense that we were traveling with a bigger predator. Bethany was so fucking scary everything was avoiding us out of sheer terror at her presence.

That kind of aura reminded me of Abel, specifically the presence of danger he exuded when pissed off. With Bethy it seemed to be completely unintentional, just a natural side effect of her being an apex predator.

Once the sun started going down we all slowed to make camp. Yvette filled us in a bit on how the temples worked as we made dinner.

I wished we'd brought one of the compasses, but the search parties had needed them more. My wishes for yesterday had gone toward making sure they all had a method of finding their targets, and the twenty-five points of Might I'd gotten off it had been useful, but the assumption that having a stationary map would render the compass unnecessary might have been a bit hasty. At the very least I still had today's wishes, since I'd used the other ones last night.

"The conduit we're approaching is Jainus," the golem said as we sat down. "The tower master did extensive research on all of the conduits. Jainus has a summoning ability. He creates dogs made of storm elements. Water, wind, lightning, and sometimes combinations of the three."

I grimaced. Summoners were annoying to deal with. On the upside it meant the actual undead should be easier to deal with. Heavy fantasy stacking would mean less physical power to offset, especially with Yvette here to help.

The ability to tank higher Impact attacks would be crucial for us going into this, and someone who could take Abel's strongest attack to the face and barely budge certainly had that ability.

After she went over everything she knew about Jainus, we set up the bunker and Callie used up all my wishes for today. She traded me another six shadow jumps for thirty Might just to be prepared, and I didn't complain given how useful that would be for me.

In the morning, we woke up to get ready, everyone enjoying the fresh scent of grass and trees as we made breakfast. After, we headed for the temple with the sun overhead. Despite the sun being out, the moon was still huge and menacing in the blue sky, but was muted by daylight, which for some reason made me less worried about whatever tricks Suvaya might pull.

Of course, that was nonsensical, because she was a literal god and being in the daylight probably wouldn't stop her if she roused and decided to interfere, but comfort didn't have to be logical.

The last leg of our trip to the temple was peaceful, more of a morning nature hike than anything, and once we got there, we had Callie do her intel gathering thing while the rest of us warmed up just in case. Going into battle with something like a conduit while stiff and tired would probably be the last mistake any of us would make.

Bethy, alone amongst those of us who were human (Yvette was unfazed as always), seemed to be mostly relaxed and excited. She used her captive cat as a spy to scope out the inside of the building in ways Callie might not be able to pick up. After a few minutes she skipped over to us. "Donuts says there are other kitties inside." Her gleeful enthusiasm sent a shiver through the rest of us.

Callie, who had just returned, nodded in confirmation. "I caught the edges of the Night Pride too. Couldn't get any actual information on them. Like I said before they're a weird kind of unnatural darkness. We should be able to use the same trick as last time. As long as we don't— Where is Bethany?"

We all looked around to find that the Vampire girl had vanished. Callie knelt down and her fingers dipped into the shadows. "Shit, I think she... Yep. She went in by herself. She seems to be... I think she's chasing them." She turned to look at the temple, only to see the Vampire emerge dragging a now corporeal shadow cat a bit smaller than Donuts by the tail as she shouted after a series of fleeing shadows.

"No!" she shouted petulantly. "Come back! I just want to love you!" We all stared in disbelief as she stomped back over to us, still dragging her newest captive. She yanked it forward in front of her, where the cat lay down motionlessly, its eyes locked on the small form of our team member. "This is Poptarts," she said in annoyance. "He's the only one I could catch."

Abel raised a hand slowly. "I'd like it known that, though this isn't something I'd normally admit to, you scare the shit out of me."

Bethany's smile was way too full of teeth to be comfortable to look at. "Well aren't you sweet?" Her smile flattened into a pout. "Anyway, there aren't any more kitties in there. *Donuts*"—she said the name spitefully— "tried to warn them I was coming. He's such a naughty kitty. He's going to stay in time out for a while. I guess Poptarts will get all the cuddles."

The huge terrifying shadow beast flinched when she said the name. I noticed her shadow was actually touching it, though not at an angle it should be. I guessed that was how it was manifesting. Deciding it was better for my sanity not to think too much about how Bethany did anything, I decided to refocus the group.

"Well," I said jauntily. "That happened. Somehow. Anyway, I think we're about ready to head in." Hopefully fighting the conduit was as easy as getting rid of his guards.

Chapter Fifty-Seven

THE FIGHT STARTED FAST because the undead here wasn't nearly as talky. He just went straight to trying to kill us when we entered the chamber, having already long since left his coffin. Yvette was a big help. She was not, however, nearly as useful as we'd hoped. Specifically, she could stall the undead easily enough, but as a summoner, he had a bunch of storm hounds to harass us with, which made it harder for us to focus on him like we needed to do to take him down.

"How are cloud dogs a thing?" I snapped as I used the overlay to predict an attack and avoid it. Callie had a pair of shadow blades in hand she was tearing into our enemy with, but it wasn't really working. You can't stab clouds. Though apparently they *can* bite you. I had a wrenched shoulder to prove it. "Clouds are water vapor! Also that doesn't even look like a cloud. More like smoke."

Callie hissed, dancing back as her blades were consumed in sparks. "Smoke isn't full of lightning." She paused. "Most of the time. Someone probably has a lightning smoke power somewhere I guess."

"Probably," I agreed as I stepped off the air to avoid the jaws of the smoke dog. My staff lashed out and passed right through the damned thing. Despite the lack of contact, the monster whined and jerked back, clearly hurt by the high-Impact weapon even if not severely.

It took a minute for me to realize what had happened—the life draining feature of my Stygian Branch. I looked around to check on the others. Abel was fighting a pair of the hounds, one made of water and one made of pure lightning. Gabriel was fighting one that seemed to be lightning and water, and Bethy…

My eyes landed on the Vampire and I flinched. Bethy was attacking the undead with a pair of stakes that I suspected were the special ones she got from her father. More than that though, she was… different. Gone were the smiles and the bubbly cheer. Bethany Lark wasn't a ditzy friendly airhead. She was a monster.

Her jaw was unhinged slightly, extending her face in an elongated silent scream, her eyes blazed with hellish light, and her teeth were bared in a rictus of anger. Her nails had lengthened into claws, chalk-white skin paling even further, but despite all that, the most disturbing thing was the way she *moved*.

Ascendants have an inherent advantage in our movements. We have stats that make it easy to move fast, to calculate what we need to do beforehand, to pick up on minute changes in environment. Despite that though, the way we move (even if at a higher scale) is still *human*, at least all the Ascendants I'd ever seen.

Bethany didn't move like a human. She didn't even move like an animal. She moved like *death*. Not like a predator, but like *the* predator, like the force that comes for us all in the end. A sort of slithering, jerking, clipping movement that allowed her to cover ground in odd fits and starts that almost looked like stop motion. She would vanish and reappear, not just because of her speed, but because of a strange mental effect she didn't even seem to control.

The undead roared as he tried to get past Yvette to attack the Vampire, who had just tried to stake him and left a long shallow gash on his body. The golem stopped him in his tracks, but he flicked a hand and another pair of hounds manifested, one of whirling sleet and the other of pure cycling wind. They dove forward to attack, and Bethy vanished like she had in her fight with me—into a cloud of bats.

It became clear as she reformed that she had *not* been taking that fight seriously. As she manifested, her mouth closed, and her eyes still blazed like the embers of hell. Reaching up with a claw, she slit an arm open, dripping her blood onto the stakes, which began to sizzle and pop.

Another blurring jerking blink and she was on the monster again from behind, trying to jam a stake through his eye. Jainus snarled and leapt back, the wrinkled undead clearly genuinely worried about the monstrous girl.

I expected she had some multipliers on her stats like the wendigo had, but more than that, something about her blood struck me as profoundly wrong. It looked unnatural. Too red, like melted rubies, and the thought of touching it made me sick. I was pretty sure Jainus felt the same. I didn't get to watch more because the smoke dog recovered and attacked again, and Callie had to tackle me out of the way so I didn't get disemboweled.

"Watch it!" she snapped. I nodded, hopping back to my feet. "You okay? It's not like you to get so distracted."

Telling her I got distracted by cringing in terror from an apex predator in a frilly goth ball gown seemed like it might be embarrassing, so I just shook my head. "I'm good, but we need to figure out how to kill these minions. This guy is managing to hold off Bethy and Yvette both. Apparently the last one she fought wasn't putting his back into it."

She snorted. "I feel so honored that he thinks we're worth it. Any ideas on how to do that? Because I don't have any conceptual death abilities."

I paused. "I'll have to check a few things, but I can think of a few ways we might be able to do it. Don't suppose you can capture one with shadows? Actually…" I turned my head. "Hey, Bethy! Let us borrow your cats!" I shouted at the Vampire.

She turned her blazing eyes on me, inspecting me for a second like I was a bug on a card. I could tell she took a second to process who and what I was… other than food. I felt my skin prickle as my whole body shuddered, but it passed quick. Between one breath and the next, something shifted in her face, and she gave me her usual big toothy grin, somehow less threatening despite the fangs still being there. "Okay!" she chirped, then flicked a finger.

A pair of cats made of pitch black shadows barreled from beneath her feet, one of them hitting our smoke dog while the other one attacked the wind dog that had come at her to keep her off the conduit.

I saw a burst of flame as Mel attacked the sleet hound from the side, a blast of flame consuming the animal as it dissolved into a puddle. The Night

Pride seemed to be more than capable of damaging the summons, which was good, because it opened me up to try some of my ideas.

Glancing at the smoke dog, I used Marked for Death, then triggered Double Trouble, appearing behind it, swinging my staff down hard. The glowing green of poison fire didn't seem to do much, but when I triggered just a bit of the death energy inside, the staff made solid contact with the beast. I wasn't sure if it was the sure hit of Marked for Death or the death energy itself, but one of them made hitting the incorporeal monster completely possible.

Grinning, I turned to look for my next target... and my world went white. One of the summons, a lightning dog, had snuck up behind me and as I turned it went for my throat. As the teeth sank in, I triggered a heal burst, but unfortunately for me, that didn't really matter.

The monster, rather than tear out my throat, melted into me, slipping under my armor as the lightning funneled through my entire body. The charge raced down my limbs and through my chest, carried along my blood and muscle as it searched for an escape from the armor holding it in.

I dropped, screaming, as I felt my flesh cook only to be repaired by my supercharged Vitality and Jessie's stored heal. I dug my fingers into the stone floor under me as I heard Callie shout my name in panic as she raced to my side.

Despite that, she came to a stop standing over me, her face panicked as she tried to figure out what to do or how to help me.

Gritting my teeth, I stood. I triggered Double Trouble again, appearing behind a water dog that Mel had been dealing with, and I shoved my arm into it. The dog howled as the water picked up the charge, dispersing it to manageable levels even as it boiled the water, and the construct collapsed at the same time I did as the lightning grounded out.

I was breathing heavily as I lay there on the ground, smoking and smelling of charred meat as the heal burst continued trying to repair the damage.

"Shane?" I heard from what seemed like far away. "Are you with me?" Callie. I nodded jerkily, body still sore and burned.

"M'fine," I mumbled, trying to sit up. I triggered another heal burst and grimaced as my head focused. "Get me one of those stakes," I said through what felt like a mouth full of cotton.

She didn't look convinced, but seeing the room even now being stuffed with more storm hounds she nodded, sending a shadow clone off towards Bethy. While we waited, she tried to give me a once-over. "You doing okay? Where does it hurt?" I could see how scared she was, so I tried to be reassuring.

"It's not as bad as it could be. The pain is only everywhere." Judging by her worried expression my joke had fallen on deaf ears. I was confident that was just a side effect of the fear—I was definitely as funny as I thought I was.

The clone came back, and Callie held out a hand. The shadow construct slapped the stake down into her hand and she held it out to me. "What are you going to do with it?"

I plucked it from her fingers, pushing to my feet as I tried to force my body to move properly, not that I managed to do so. Even with the healing, my muscles were sore and damaged. Bruising, tearing, and plenty of other unpleasant things caused by rapid contraction from electrical damage.

"What are you doing?" she snapped. "You're not okay yet, give it at least a few minutes with the healing. You can't go into battle like that."

Cracking my neck, I rolled my shoulders painfully. "I know. But I've got the best shot at making this stick." I glanced at the undead, choosing not to think about how much this was going to suck. I needed a boost. Afterburner, Marked for Death, Mercy Kill, triple-stack density shift, Flurry of Blows, Double Trouble. I vanished, leaving behind an illusion and knowing Callie was going to be pissed about me leaving mid-conversation.

I was in too much pain to argue or slow down though. Afterburner filled me with energy and power, but it was going to end soon. Appearing behind the conduit, I shoved the stake forward. Flurry of blows made it faster, the other abilities made it stronger, and the ten percent boost to armor penetration from Heavy Hands combined with the Marked for Death defense bypass allowed me to slam the thing home right in his heart. Perfect to soften him up for the finisher from our resident cavalry.

Of course, I burned an Afterburner charge on five of those abilities and on the actual attack so that was half of my juice. As I felt the stake sink in and activate, I used Double Trouble again, slumping against the wall to catch my breath and using another three heal bursts to burn all the rest of my charges, flooding my body with super-empowered healing as I watched the stunned conduit stare in horror at Gabriel's incoming charge. I needed a break.

Chapter Fifty-Eight

GABRIEL'S LANCE punched right through the weakened conduit, carrying him off into the distance and pinning him on the wall. As soon as he was still, Mel unleashed a torrent of golden fire at the thing, and the combination of all the attacks finally did it in. The stake had been amplified, and given its usefulness against undead and Bethy's blood on it which seemed to synergize, it had weakened the bastard quite a bit.

The other hounds collapsed into their respective elements, leaving our group alone in the tomb. Callie stepped up next to me. She looked relieved more than upset. "You okay?" she asked tentatively. "Everything still hurt?"

"Only when I breathe," I grunted out with a chuckle. "I'm getting better though. I burned three Afterburner slots on heal bursts at the end there. Plus I already had two active. It's helping a lot." The heal bursts weren't instant heal abilities. Jessie's power was strong and useful, but it took time. With so many active though, it was doing a damned good job of repairing the damage, and the energy was combating the weakness from using Afterburner, so I felt... shaky, but alright.

"That was the right call," she admitted unhappily. "I was panicking. That lightning bypassed your armor and I felt the pain. I could literally smell you cooking. We needed to drop the conduit, and it worked out." She paused. "I've got to get better with my daggers. We were supposed to be a team out there, but we got split up and I wasn't able to support you when you got jumped from behind."

I could feel the guilt through the bond. She hadn't been watching my back. I didn't blame her for being distracted in that shitshow, but I knew saying so wouldn't do any good, so I just put my arms around her and pulled her close. Honestly I'd been freaked out myself. Sometimes you just needed a hug from someone who loved you. It certainly helped me focus enough to clear my head.

Half expecting Benny to be there to tease me about being too affectionate, it was almost a surprise when I let Callie go without anyone noticing. Part of me was a little bit sad not to have the chance to rankle my buddy a bit, and when she felt that through the bond, Callie snorted and rolled her eyes. "We should check in with the others, make sure they're all right."

"Good point," I said as I looked around, trying to find where all our team members were. Mel and Abel were over by the corpse and Bethy was nearby. I headed over to check on the Vampire, who looked winded and shaken now that she'd returned to a more normal state. "Hey there, how are you feeling?"

She gave us a brittle smile. "I'm fine. Sorry. I don't like going all vampy like that. It does weird stuff to my head. Makes people look like food." Her smile faltered, her eyes growing melancholic. "It makes me sad to see the world like that. People don't matter, they're just bags of blood. Some of my siblings are like that all the time, but I don't do it unless I have to."

It occurred to me that the rapid shifting between scary bloodthirsty and ditzy airhead might not be entirely a factor of blending in. Some of her mood changes were probably part of her nature. Hell, given how recursion worked, it was possible the cheerful flighty version of her was a purposeful impression she tried to give to offset the other side of herself.

"So you can turn that on and off? Or is it more like a dimmer switch?" I realized if I looked close there was always some element of unrealness to the way Bethy moved. I think that was part of what threw me about her at our first meeting—my subconscious picking up a predator. It was just a shadow though, nothing genuinely frightening.

"Daddy calls it the rising blood," she said miserably. "I can push it down, but it's always there. Vampires are legendary predators. In a literal sense. Not just as in we feed and are legends, but we feed *on* legends. It's how we drain away stats. The process of preparing ourselves to ingest that sort of thing changes our souls, makes them… different. It's hard to explain. It doesn't help that Daddy likes to be all vague and poetic about it."

"Is that just you though?" I asked cautiously. "I met a Wendigo once, and it was… very distinct from a person. Fae are like that too. Any racial trait alters what humans are at their core, it's how we get new races. Those can be passed on to children too, so it's a fundamental change. But part of what makes being an Ascendant so amazing is that *we* can change. That's what you're doing right? Trying to change your nature in a foundational way through recursion?"

She nodded. "I want to do it this way. I might be able to mess around with synergizing Skills to fix my nature, but that could go wrong as easy as right, and then I'm stuck that way until D-rank. Working with recursion and trying to stack my stats in a specific direction is a subtler but more stable way to change." She chuckled ruefully. "I even considered asking you for a wish, but what would I wish for, to be a friendlier Vampire?"

I shrugged. "I don't know if that would work, but if you want help, we can try. Doesn't have to be one big wish. There are subtler ways to change. I bet Nat would be happy to help you too. I take it your dad knows about what you're trying to do and doesn't mind?" I'd rather not piss off the strongest S-ranker in the universe if at all possible. I'd help her either way, but if he didn't care I could be more overt about it.

Honestly, in some ways this could be a trial run for my intentions to change my own family once I was in charge. Helping someone become something different. If I could help Bethy in her quest to change her nature, I'd be a lot more confident about overhauling the system of a massive deity-level clan.

Callie nodded from next to me. "Shane can't really coach you on wishes, but I'm sure I could help. We'll need to do some research on Vampirism and what elements of it interact with your personality. Do you think you could get us some books? I have to imagine your family has a decent selection."

Bethy shrugged casually. "Oh sure, Aida is a huge nerd about stuff like that. She's always reading, so I bet she has some books that could help. You really think we can figure out how to change me? How do you think we should do it? I've been working on recursion for a while, and it really helps most of the time, but it's not really a change exactly."

"Yeah, I think we'll need to be more direct," Callie said cheerfully. "Synergizing with racial traits is a bit tricky, but with the right Skill and proper research it should be safe enough if we take it step by step. If nothing else, we can use wishes to map out your potential options to make sure you pick something viable. I don't know much about racial traits though, so I'm not sure if you'll need a catalyst when changing yours."

Despite the uncertainty, I could see genuine joy on the face of the Vampire girl. I could tell this was something she'd been worried about for a long time. Some of the things she'd said implied her siblings didn't think anything of their bloodthirsty nature, so she probably didn't get a lot of sympathy for her point of view.

Leaving them to chat, I headed over to check on Gabriel, and with him, the corpse of the undead he'd killed. "Damn," I said as I approached. "I'm impressed. That lance is pretty scary. What's it made of?" I hadn't paid much attention to his lance, not with his crazy starlight charger ability, but it was clearly extremely powerful, and looking close I could tell it was E-ranked like my staff.

"Sunfury Platinum," he said with a chuckle. He was cleaning the weapon carefully with a well-worn but soft looking rag. "It's highly compatible with my combat style and with my charger. The weapon, the ability, and my path form a harmonious system that allows me to put forth my most powerful strength with every charge. In some ways, the lance is the ultimate expression of the Adamant. No retreat, no hesitation, only forward momentum. Unstoppable."

I nodded thoughtfully. "I could see that, yeah." That actually made me curious about something. "Can you tell me more about Paths? You mentioned them, and I know Abel is on one. I have a Path, but I don't really know how it works or how to improve it."

He sighed. "Sadly, I can't tell you much. Not because I'm being secretive, but because Paths are deeply personal and unique things. Even people on the same Path can manifest it differently and access it in different ways. I can tell you that a Path is something every Ascendant needs to gain eventually, but that getting one early isn't necessarily a benefit. If your Path isn't suitable for you, it's often better to try to find another one, or just to wait."

"What is a Path? Something to do with recursion?" The vague commentary wasn't as helpful as I'd hoped. I needed a straight answer, but it didn't seem like he could give me one.

Gabriel paused for a moment. "In some ways. Paths can provide some protection from recursion if used properly. If you think of your legend as a mountain you build with stats, a Path is literally the road you travel to reach the top. Lower down the mountain it isn't important, you can just walk anywhere, but as it becomes steeper and you climb higher, you need to follow a trail."

"So how do I access it? I've felt some small aspect of it in battle before, but I don't use it like you or Abel do." It sounded like this was something I wanted to gain a better understanding of. Something that could make me stronger and help me stand out from other people the same level as me. "And is a Path a Skill? An ability?"

"It can be either. Both. Neither," he said with a shrug. "It's complicated. The most reasonable way I can describe it is probably that a Path is the way you navigate your own legend. Recursion and renown may draw the map, but a Path is how you walk it. What form that takes varies from person to person."

I nodded slowly, thinking over what he'd said and the experience I had before. Fatewalker. My Path of the Doom Sovereign was paved with my Fatewalker class in the game. Following that particular track seemed to be a way to progress down my Path. Or resonate with it? Whatever the case, it gave me an idea how to move forward.

"I'll keep all that in mind. Now, why don't we go and check in with Yvette?" I suggested, gesturing to the construct who was currently investigating the ruby coffin. "She might have an idea for what we should do next. Or if we need to do anything. Worst case we can just move on to the next target." I wasn't sure how to reroute the ritual, but Yvette would know if there was anything we needed to do.

Gabriel finished cleaning his weapon and stowed it away, standing with a nod, and we both headed over to talk to the closest thing to an expert on this ritual that we had.

Chapter Fifty-Nine

"ALRIGHT," I said as we made it over to where Yvette was poring over the coffin. "How do we do this? I'm not really sure I understand how rerouting the ritual works. Do we just kill the conduits? Because that seems... too easy. Not that I'm complaining. But it doesn't really fit with how complicated this whole thing is."

"It doesn't," agreed Yvette, "because it's not that easy. Basically, the ritual is laid out in a specific way. As each of the conduits gets activated, it creates a channel that links every single one of the people who have taken part in the ritual. Killing the conduits severs the connections between them and the people who partook of the Lightblooms, but it doesn't remove the conduits from the actual ritual."

"So how does killing them in order change that?" I asked in confusion.

"It doesn't," Yvette repeated. "What it *can* do, if properly calculated, is reroute the energy transfer. There are redundancies built into the ritual to prevent things like what we're doing from stopping the harvest, but those same redundancies can be used against the goddess. She made backups within backups, and one of those backups is a contingency for what happens if the mountain gets destroyed before her ascension."

Callie, who had wandered over with Bethany, nodded as she stepped up next to me. "Ah, so we're going to trick the system into tripping that contingency so it defaults her manifestation point back to the central temple?"

The construct nodded. "Precisely. But to do that, we have to make some alterations to this chamber, and to the ritual itself. Minor alterations, because anything major might trigger a failsafe and kill all of us and everything within a hundred miles." We all froze, staring at her, and she blinked. "Did I not mention that could happen?"

"Must've slipped your mind," I said dryly. "What do we do?"

"Exactly what I tell you to," Yvette said flatly. "The changes need to be made in stages along the path we've calculated. They'll cause small alterations that will cascade further and further as each of the temples is accessed. Of course, this is assuming that the goddess banked the spare stats and Impact from the Ascendants who have already died in case of catastrophic failure, but that seems to be a safe assumption."

With the explanation out of the way, she started dispersing us to various parts of the temple. Looking close we could see small, easily overlooked grooves and carvings on the dark stone. Once she set up the ruby coffin back in its spot, she had us drag the remains of the undead conduit over and dump them inside. Once the coffin was resealed, it started to glow, and Yvette shifted it in a circle.

Like a deadbolt clicking into place, the coffin lit up the symbols on the floor, flooding the room with light. I could see why we needed to do this after we killed them. It looked like the coffin was using the remnant energies of the former conduit to temporarily activate the temple. We could make the changes now, but my understanding of Enchanting told me it wouldn't last long. In the other two temples we couldn't do the same because the energy had probably faded from the corpses already.

"Alright," Yvette began, "we don't have long to do this. Shane, go and stand over there." She gestured me to a spot about fifty feet from the coffin, adjusting her directions a few times until I was standing exactly where she wanted me. "Now. This is going to be complicated. I want you to put a foot on the L-shaped symbol to your right, and the other on the one shaped like a bull's horns."

I did. "Alright, I've got it. Not sure what you want me to do here though. I don't have an Enchanting Skill." I'd merged it into my DS Mastery during my prep for reaching F-rank.

"You won't need one," she said confidently. "This is an active ritual right now. Standing on those points means you're plugged into it, which means you can modify it with your soul like a Skill. Don't do that yet. We need to get the others in position." She started giving instructions to the others, setting them up in various parts of the room. Once they were there, she nodded to Callie first. "Alright. Calliope. I want you to close your eyes, focus on the energy running through you from the runes. Then I want you to flex your soul like you're modifying a Skill and focus on switching those two symbols."

Callie nodded, closing her eyes, and I felt the strain on her soul as... something happened. Looking down at her feet, I saw two of the glowing symbols flicker and switch places. Yvette nodded. "Excellent. Gabriel, now you. Calliope, reposition yourself over there." She sent her over to another spot, and Gabriel swapped the two runes. She ran us all around in circles, having us stop and switch out runes periodically, and between all of us managed to change about fifty symbols.

I could see what she was doing. She'd said we needed to do this slowly and methodically, and I couldn't think of a more methodical way than this. Sadly, the longer it went on, the dimmer the lights from the runes got. The energy left in the corpse of the undead was fading. Yvette didn't panic, and just started talking faster. She had us switch places a dozen times and was just finalizing the last rune as the glow finally winked out.

My relief was almost palpable as I saw that we'd made it. This temple had been reconfigured slightly, and while on its own that wouldn't do much, fourteen more of these would add up to the trigger we needed to prevent ourselves from being out-and-out murdered by an evil goddess when she finished resurrecting herself.

The fact that Yvette could do this at all was staggering. The Enchantments on this building were sprawling and extremely complex. Trying to rewrite them even minimally just by switching runes would be like trying to change the image on a scan box by switching a few pixels. And with the cascading nature of the changes (runes weren't pictures and had a ton of interactions that could cause untold ripples) it was amazing.

But then, that was probably why Yvette even existed. If you want something to calculate and alter a massive Enchantment by inches, a golem would be a good start. They were basically magic robots. Yvette had involved Benny and the others too, but I increasingly suspected that had just been to make them feel involved. Yvette was a tool that was custom built by the tower master for this exact purpose.

"That was… anticlimactic," Bethy said cheerfully. "I was expecting a big boom or a whoosh! Some crazy diagram of magical symbols appearing above us and rearranging itself. Switching a few symbols and then watching the lights go out is a bit of a letdown."

"What you are describing would have killed all of us," Yvette said helpfully. "We didn't want the system to notice the changes we made. I told you earlier, Suvaya built in multiple levels of redundancy. Triggering the fail-safe measures would have resulted in our horrifying and rather painful deaths."

"You're not a comforting person," Callie said conversationally. "In case you weren't aware."

"I am not a person at all," the golem replied. "I am a construct. Interaction is a secondary concern. I don't mean to be insensitive, but my first priority is the disassembly of the ritual and the prevention of the collapse of this subspace."

I shook my head. "That doesn't seem right. You *seem* like a person. You might be a golem, but racial traits are a thing. I guess you were made instead of born, but I wouldn't say you aren't a *person*. You don't need to be human to be a person. Bethy isn't."

The cheerful Vampire nodded. "He's right. I've never been human. What about after we stop Suvaya? You aren't just going to shut down, are you?"

Yvette paused. "Not to my knowledge. I was made to hold the key and aid in the destruction of the ritual and the prevention of Suvaya's ascension. Once that is done… I suppose I'm not sure what I'll do. Perhaps return to the tower? Keep watch over it."

"That sounds like a shitty life," I said bluntly. "I mean, if you want to be alone in a tower for eternity you do you, but if you're just doing it because you don't have any other options it seems like a waste. The tower master was a genius. You're the most complex golem I've ever seen, pretty much a literal work of art in terms of engineering. If nothing else, I refuse to believe anyone put that much work into making a person only for you to serve a single purpose."

Gabriel nodded. "She made you in her image, did she not? Perhaps you were a way for her to live on after this all ended. A legacy she left behind. If anything, you could probably consider her your mother in most ways. Parents don't want their children to suffer or waste away. They want them to live a full and exciting life. You could leave this place after we destroy the ritual. Maybe you can find her family."

I winced at that parent comment—it hit a bit close to home with all the shit about my mom lately. But he was right. "If you don't want to do that, you can still try to live your own life. Make friends. Find your own family. The point is, there's no reason to just hang it up and bow out of life because you accomplished your goal."

She looked… pensive. Yvette wasn't an emotive person. She made Celine look effusive. But despite that remoteness, it was easy to see what we'd said had at least given her food for thought. In the end, that was all we could do. It was her life—that was the point we were making to start with. It wasn't like we could force her to live it.

"Anyway," I said, clapping my hands, "we should head back to base camp. We need to find out our next target. Knowing Annelise and Benny, they probably sent a few of the other teams out for the next conduit once more of them checked in. Which is good, because we have zero chance of clearing them all out if we do them personally and one at a time."

Yvette nodded. "An accurate statement. I suspect we will need much larger groups for some of the more powerful conduits. As this one demonstrated, superior or even equivalent force of arms isn't always enough to offset certain advantages. I was pinned down in this case, and the hounds were able to attack the rest of you. If you had been less able, this could have ended very differently."

That was the nicest way anyone had ever overlooked my near death, which I was grateful for. I still felt sore, but she was right, we'd gotten lucky. Some of those fucking conduits were former S-rankers. With everyone's agreement we headed outside, taking off for the mountain, though our pace wasn't exactly top speed given my own recovery.

One down, fourteen to go. This had been rough, but the fun was just getting started. Gabriel had made a good point earlier, though—when the ritual was defused, did that mean this place would become open to the outside world? Without the Dew I wasn't sure how the Glade's people would integrate with the wider universe, though I doubted so many people with heightened Impact would be ignored.

It was a problem for later. For now, we had to make sure everyone survived.

Chapter Sixty

WE DIDN'T MAKE it back to the mountain. We called to check in with Benny, and he gave us the next temple. Yvette knew the order, but since we had other teams showing up, we ended up hitting them out of order. Yvette had given him all the alteration patterns to pass to the other teams, and he was sending out groups of twenty just to be safe. Bethy made sure each group was armed with a stake and one of her thralls. It was kind of a relief not to have to climb the damned mountain again at least.

Lucky for us, the next temple wasn't too far away, about a hundred miles, and we made our way directly there. When we arrived at the temple, we went about the same routine as the last time. Callie mapped the place with her shadows, and Bethy was ready to head in to take care of the cats. But to our surprise... there weren't any.

"There's no security at all?" I said skeptically as we stared at the squat building. "Because... why wouldn't there be? It just seems like a stupid sloppy move for someone who was... what, an A-ranker?" Yvette nodded. "Yeah I just don't see how this could be anything but a trap."

Callie shrugged. "I can see every inch of the place. No traps. No Night Pride. Just an open temple with none of the unnatural dark we've seen in the others."

"And you saw the undead?" I asked in disbelief. "Just... sitting there?"

"Yes," she said with consternation. "I know it doesn't make any sense. But she was just sitting on the ground with her arms around her knees. She doesn't look shriveled like the others we've seen. Whether that's because she was A-rank or some other reason, I don't know, but she doesn't look hostile. Just sad."

Yvette nodded. "Satala," she said solemnly. "Suvaya's daughter. She was the youngest of the priests. Perhaps that made a difference? Regardless, as her mother's only child, she was powerful. I do not know why she would allow us to approach—we should proceed with caution."

We all nodded. Yvette took up the front position since she was the sturdiest, and we all crept inside. The inside of the temple felt barren and empty, and the long stone halls echoed with the sounds of our passing. We never let down our guard. When we finished our trip inside, we found ourselves at the door to the same kind of chamber we'd seen in the other temples.

In the center of the room was a girl. Small, delicate, with silver hair and bright blue eyes, downcast in sorrow. She was hugging herself, and tears dripped down her cheeks. Based on the dust on her arms and legs she hadn't moved in quite a while. She twitched when we came in, but didn't look up.

"Hello," I said slowly. I wasn't sure what else to do. We couldn't just attack her. She wasn't offering anyone violence. She just looked sad and small and broken.

She kept staring at the floor, tears running down her cheeks and dripping onto her arms, leaving spots in the dust. "It wasn't supposed to be like this," she said quietly. "We didn't want to hurt anyone. We were kind to our people. Mother wouldn't have wanted this. Not the real her."

I cocked my head. "What do you mean? Suvaya is your mother, right? She was the one who created this whole ritual."

She let out a short, bitter laugh. "Her children were suffering. Her most loyal. Most faithful. They saw her as a danger, and so they came for her. She couldn't resist them. Not in such numbers. And my brothers and sisters, her flock, they cried out for her as she died. They lost everything. She just wanted to help them, to raise them up, to make something good out of it all. We thought it would only be you. Their heirs. Their descendants."

318

Her eyes finally came up to stare at us, and they looked haunted. "But our people stayed. They raised families and became part of this land. The ritual was flawed. The moonlight leaked, and our own began to partake of the poison. So many of them will die. My mother wouldn't want this. But there's nothing left of her. Just a ghost, obsessed with her grand work."

I once more considered the lack of security and shadowy cats. "You want us to kill you," I said in realization. "You know we're trying to stop it. You're going to let us do it."

"This is wrong," she snapped. "They don't deserve it. You don't even deserve it. Our time is over, and we should have accepted that. The hate has poisoned them. They're all so angry. It's her anger. It seeped into them. But she protected me. Even as a spirit. She always did love me best." She gave a sad smile.

"Don't you hate us?" I said. "For what our families did? They killed your mother. Ruined your lives, and for what? Fear? Power?" I felt sick. I'd never stopped to ask if the six killing off the vanished gods was the right thing to do. It was easy to paint myself as the hero, but I'd been ignoring something Zeke had been telling me for months. The universe wasn't nice, and it wasn't fair.

She shook her head. "I'm just tired. The world is so different now. My brothers and sisters are all mad or dead. My mother raised them all from infants. Even though they weren't blood, I still loved them like they were. Ralik, who would carry me on his shoulders as a girl so I could pick apples. Dara, who taught me how to braid my hair." Her tears picked up again, and she let out a choked sob.

"No," I said stonily. "This isn't right. I'm not going to kill an innocent person." I turned to Yvette. "Can't you help her? She's willing to come peacefully. Can't you use her life force to fuel the temple and switch the runes without killing her? That might even work better, right?"

The golem looked pensive. "Maybe," she mused aloud. "It would be quite painful, and if we tarried even a moment too long she would die. But it's possible."

I looked at the others. "I want to try at least," I said pleadingly. "She didn't do anything wrong. If she lets us continue altering the ritual... it sounds like after the changes she'll be weakened. She won't be a threat." I looked at her. "Satala, do you want to try? As an F-ranker there's no way the gods would bother with you. You never got strong enough to bother with—they probably don't even remember."

Not that I knew shit about the six, but this whole thing gave me the impression that they didn't really care much about the small stuff. They killed Suvaya and just… left her soul floating around. This whole thing was their fault. They wouldn't come after a former A-ranker who'd lost all her Impact. Zeke could keep an eye on her just in case.

Callie took my hand, nodding in determination. "Please let us try? We want to help you. You don't deserve to die alone in a stone room."

Satala could be lying to us. Could be manipulating us to get us to spare her. Maybe she would snap and attack at any second. I saw Abel ease into position for that, Gabriel taking up a stance on the other side, just in case. But I didn't change my mind. This wasn't right.

The universe might not be fair. It might be brutal and ruthless. The gods might attack other deities because they were potential threats. But Callie and I were heroes—or we were supposed to be. Just because something was easy didn't make it okay. Treating everyone with suspicion and trying to kill them before they killed me might be smart, but it also sounded sad.

Callie squeezed my hand, shooting me a smile of solidarity. She felt the same way. Gabriel looked approving. Bethy looked a little in awe. Abel looked like he wanted to smack us both, and Mel's mask kept me from seeing her expression.

Satala stared at us. "You ask me to put my life in your hands, though I have already done so. Even then… what do I have to live for? My mother is gone, and you seek to destroy what remains. My brothers and sisters are to be put down like animals, and I cannot even plead on their behalf. My very essence was drained away to fuel the ritual, and I will not recover. I assume I am to be severed from my connections to my old strength?" She aimed that at Yvette.

The golem nodded. "The modifications to the chamber will sever the links. I may have to alter them slightly, but they will do so. You will be greatly weakened by the process, and you will not recover. You may regain your former strength through the same means you acquired it in the first place, through cultivation, but the pieces of your legend thrown away will never return."

Oddly, that seemed to be almost a relief to her. But she still looked unde-cided. It was Bethy who found a response to give. "Your people are still here," she said. "Not the originals, but their descendants. Some people still worship your mother. Didn't you say you wanted to take care of them?"

Satala might not regain her A-rank abilities, but she *was* still rocking forty Impact and a peak F-rank power level. She could make a difference here. Hell, she was the same level as the king in Ladrigan. Plus her soul was probably *way* stronger.

She stared down at the ground for a minute, then nodded. "Very well. We shall attempt the process. Should I die… I suppose that is my fate."

She didn't exactly sound *happy* about the whole thing, but I'd take what I could get. The thought of murdering a helpless crying person in the middle of a dirty temple made me sick. That was the kind of thing the Cultists would do. Some kind of ritual sacrifice. I prepped myself to apply my healing burst if needed. I really wished we had Jessie here with us.

Despite the terrible situation, and the risk, I found myself smiling under my mask. I'd done a lot of things I didn't really like since I became an Ascendant. This wasn't going to make up for all of it, and I wasn't sure how much of it I *needed* to make up for, but at the very least, this would be a chance to prove to myself that I could do the right thing sometimes. That just because I accepted what the world demanded from me, I didn't need to bend.

I think that was the trick to being an Ascendant, really. To see the places where conventional wisdom failed and ignore them. I'd spent so much time learning to be more like all the others, learning to accept what I was supposed to do and be a better Wishmaster Candidate. Maybe sometimes it had to be okay to say no. To decide to do things different. Maybe it was important to put down my enemies, or to be ruthless when I needed to be.

But even if that would grow my legend, that wasn't the only kind of person I wanted to be. I didn't want to be my dad, terrifying and effective. I wanted to write my own story. And if kindness was something that other people mocked me for, then that could just be one more story everyone told. Either way, it felt pretty damned good to try.

Chapter Sixty-One

"You sure this will work?" Callie asked anxiously as Yvette prepared. Rather than just slot in the coffin and turn it like before, the golem was actually carving new symbols onto the coffin itself. Since we'd killed all the other conduits and would probably kill the rest, they were automatically severed from their connections to their own Impact and the people who had ingested it.

Satala wasn't going to die (hopefully) which meant we had to manually sever the connections. That was part of why we weren't sure if she would survive. This was going to be dangerous and traumatic, and my heal bursts might not be enough to fix it, not to mention she'd be having her life force sucked out to fuel the temple.

"No," Yvette replied tersely, "just as I was not sure twenty minutes ago, and I will not be sure when I complete these adjustments. This was not part of my designated purpose, and I still believe it may be a foolish decision. However, I am willing to aid you in this endeavor since it will still result in the deactivation of the ritual."

"We have an advantage this time, don't we?" I pointed out. "Satala is willing to help. The other times we had to hurry and trigger the effects of the temple and the coffin because the dead bodies were losing energy by the second. With Satala taking an active role, we can actually study the necessary changes ahead of time and set up an efficient order and timing to get the changes over with as quickly as possible. That'll give her the best chance to survive."

She nodded without looking up. "This is true. But I urge you not to become complacent—there is still a good chance this may end in tragedy."

Bethy cleared her throat loudly. "She can hear you. We can *all* hear you. Come on Yvette, show a little compassion, will you? You're talking about her death." The Vampire had latched onto Satala and was sitting with the former A-ranker, trying to comfort her. Admittedly, Yvette's casual discussion of Satala's grisly, painful death wasn't exactly the most compassionate thing I'd ever heard.

The golem shrugged. "She wished for us to kill her. A minimal chance to live is still better than certain death."

"It's alright," the silver-haired girl said with a wan smile. "She's right. You're doing so much for me already. I don't mind her being realistic about my chances. It means so much that you're willing to take such a risk to help me. I know that your opinion of my lineage must be abominable."

To my surprise, Abel was the one who spoke up. "Not really. Sure, your mom did some terrible shit, but so did the six, or I guess the five at the time —I think this might have been before Unity Ascended."

I hadn't even considered that, but he was right. If it was that long ago, it might have been pre-Unity. I didn't know why, but for some reason that made me feel a bit better. I'd never met the Unity, but the god of the Conglomerate was the person I associated with the heroic organization to which I nominally belonged. The knowledge that he might not be involved in this was some small comfort.

Callie took my hand, squeezing it gently. She could feel my unease, and the discomfort I'd felt since we learned about what had happened. The worst part was that I couldn't really say that it was shocking to me. It sounded like something the factions would do. I could see where it might even seem necessary—I doubted most of the vanished gods were as friendly as Suvaya apparently had been. But it left a bad taste in my mouth all the same.

"It's ready," Yvette finally announced, slotting the coffin into the circle and then gesturing for Satala to get in. "Don't worry, we won't be starting just yet. I'm going to make instruction lists for the alterations. Solomon is right —we have more than enough time to do this properly, and preparation will make your survival all that much more likely."

Satala smiled at her gratefully and climbed into the open coffin. Most of the final changes to the device had been carved on the lid, and I understood precisely none of them. I'd lost my skill in Enchanting, and the little bit I did remember was nowhere close to this level of complexity.

Yvette passed out a series of papers to each of us with individual instructions on what to alter. Cutting out Yvette needing to verbally direct us would make it much faster. We were all powerful Ascendants with high Focus and Might. Being able to think and move so quickly meant listening for someone to manually call out the changes was highly inefficient. It wasn't something we could normally help because Yvette had to recalculate the ritual from a new starting point, needing access to the actual temple to give us the altered formulas, even if most of the prep work was done in advance.

Once we had the instructions all memorized, we took up position near our starting points and prepared as best we could. I triggered State of Grace as Yvette hefted the coffin lid back on with Satala still inside. As soon as the light flooded the room, we started to move.

I was almost shocked into stopping when she started screaming, but I powered through. I felt Callie's horror through the bond, but she kept focused too, following the instructions we were given in exacting detail, making sure we performed our parts at exactly the right time.

Listening to the muffled screaming from a girl I'd just met, I suddenly felt a lot worse about my stunt with the shield back at the fortress. Imagining Callie having to hear this from me made me feel sick. I didn't even know Satala and I was horrified. In movies, when people scream, it's usually just noise. Loud exhalations of surprise or fear. But screams from people who are in agony, from people suffering true torment, those sound different.

Despite the horror my girlfriend and I were both feeling at having essentially volunteered a person to be tortured for an uncertain chance at life, we pushed on. I blurred forward, touching a spot on the floor with each hand as the glow flared through the runes all over the temple. I shoved hard to switch the runes as I'd been instructed, then shifted my hands and swapped one of those two with another.

Ten feet and another three or four runes, then fifteen feet. I was using my overlay to avoid banging into the others as they blurred around the room, trying to get this finished as quickly as humanly possible. In the background, the screaming began to dim, and I knew not a single person here thought that was a good thing.

Finally, I finished, looking around and confirming that I wasn't the only one. "Everyone done?" I bellowed. At the affirmatives I dove forward, kicking the coffin lid and sending it flipping off into the air as I reached in to grab Satala and pull her out. The runes began to dim as they lost their power source, and I wasted no time at all.

Afterburner, heal burst. Five times I dumped an enhanced healing burst of life energy into the shuddering, tear-stained form of the silver-haired girl. Her skin was waxy, eyes sunken and unfocused, and she was twitching like electric shocks were wracking her body.

As the supercharged life energy roared through her, Bethy and Callie arrived by my side. My girlfriend was the most observant of us, and she noticed the seizure before it had a chance to really begin. She manifested a thick strap of shadows and jammed it into Satala's mouth as her jaws slammed shut, her back arching as her body became a battleground between the leaking sieve of her lost connections to her former power and the massive overload of life energy I'd dumped in.

Honestly, if she hadn't been literally about to die from energy bleed out and life consumption I would never have even tried it. Each of those charges was hundreds of points of Vitality, multiplied several times over by Afterburner and then stacked on top of each other. If one of those was like a healing energy drink, all five was like jump starting her heart with a regenerative car battery.

Bethy reached out and clamped down on her wrists, keeping the silver-haired girl pinned as Abel arrived and grabbed her feet with help from Gabriel. The green light bleeding from her eyes as her body seized was much more unnerving to see at this level of intensity. It took several minutes for her to stabilize, her body managing to repair the damage from the severed connections, which, while not physical, were more body-related than soul, being stat-based.

Through it all, the Vampire talked to Satala softly, telling her it was okay, and that she would be alright, and not to worry. Meaningless nonsense that was meant to comfort her and give her something to focus on, but kindness all the same.

Once she stopped jerking like she was being electrocuted, we were able to let her go, and Bethy cradled the still twitching girl and stroked her hair. Not in a romantic way, but just out of concern. I suspected our Vampire saw a bit of herself in the other girl's situation. Why that might be I had no idea, not having a firm grasp on Bethy on my best day, but at the very least I knew empathy when I saw it.

Finally, she was healed enough to sit up slowly. "Water," she croaked in a raspy, torn voice. Callie was closest and called a bottle from her ring to pass the other girl, who drank it slowly with a wince. Having recently screamed so loud I'd torn my own throat during my adventures in shielding, I recognized the signs there.

"I'm sorry," I said when Satala finished. "If I'd known it would be that bad..." I trailed off because I probably still would have suggested it. I hadn't wanted to murder her or let one of my friends do it.

She gave a tired smile. "It's a relief in some ways. Being free from the abomination that my mother's last desperate gambit became. Being free of all the things she made me. I still love her, but the Impact and stats harvested from me were twisted up in the harming of a great many innocents. Having to start over isn't so bad, really."

"Weird question," Abel began, "but why aren't you like... old now? Maybe not dead, but you must be thousands of years old to be an A-ranker, even independent of how long you were in that coffin. Now that you're an F-ranker your lifespan should be like four thousand years."

She giggled. "The coffins kept us in stasis, but I'm only about thirty years old aside from that. My mother was a goddess. Accruing renown and gathering resources were hardly an imposition for my family."

I hadn't known it worked like that, but I guessed it made sense. The children of gods would be massively renowned and by that token would grow absurdly fast. A-rank in thirty years. I wondered if that was some kind of record. "Well," I said with a sigh, "good to know we didn't waste the effort at least. Now, let's get back to base camp. I need to rest up, and then we have to figure out how we're going to help Satala."

Saving her had been the easy part. Now we had to deal with the fallout.

Chapter Sixty-Two

"I'm just saying I don't get why we have to tell everyone!" Bethy protested as we approached base camp. "Why can't we just hide her or something? There's no reason to call a big meeting and put her in front of the group like she's on trial. She's so weak right now—it's a huge risk." She gestured at Satala, who was currently being pushed in a shadow construct wheelchair.

"It's our only option," I repeated in exasperation. "We already decided as a group to minimize the involvement of the locals. The chances of there being hidden loyalists embedded is too high. Since we agreed to that, how the hell do we explain where she came from?" I pointed to the ethereal, silver-haired girl. "Oh, this is my cousin Suzie, her parents sent her to study in this *isolated dungeon space?* Or do you think they just wouldn't notice us coming back with a new team member?"

Callie sighed. "He's right, Bethy. Besides, like we said, it's not as dangerous as it sounds. We don't just represent the thirty people on our teams, we also represent all our allies and other groups from our factions. Templeton will probably try to mobilize those opposed to try to squeeze us for resources, but there's no way the majority of people will be stupid enough to kick off a civil war amongst the only group we have that can stop the ritual."

"The Church represents a solid third of the current outsiders," Gabriel said soothingly. "They'll side with us, and the WCP factions and those related will side with Shane and Natalie. Shane is right. If we do it this way, we can leverage our majority to have her actually protected instead of having to hide her away. She'll ultimately be safer."

We'd even discussed sending her to the locals, but the thing was, while some of them might be loyalists and willing to shelter her, most people didn't worship Suvaya anymore and would probably resent the assumption of authority. Not to mention by siding with us and helping she was effectively turning against her mother, so even the loyalists would probably want her dead. Once Suvaya was gone, we could work on smoothing things over, but at the moment we didn't have the time.

"Bethany," Satala murmured, "it's alright. I owe you all so much already. If Shane and Gabriel think this is for the best, I trust them. Besides, I'm sure you wouldn't let the others hurt me after going to so much trouble to save me, would you, Shane?"

"Of course not," I said with a wave. "This is all a formality, but an important one to establish a precedent we can refer to after the defenses on the dungeon collapse. This place will be crawling with high rankers trying to figure out what's going on. As the only agents on scene, the current lineup of outsiders are acting on behalf of their factions. If we get the green light from them you'll be safe from the higher ups."

I didn't think there was any threat there, given she was effectively crippled now, but it was best to take thinking out of the equation.

Bethy looked skeptical. "You don't honestly think the factions will honor what their heirs say? My daddy wouldn't let what I said bind him to anything." She paused. "Unless he felt like it. Then he probably would."

"Your dad is the strongest S-ranker in the universe," I said bluntly. "He's also mostly independent, which puts him in a good spot to ignore what people think. Factions have political agendas with lots of agreements and contracts between them. Involving this many forces mean tons of red tape, and unless the gods bother to get actively involved, chances are good they'll keep this a local problem." I glanced at Callie. "At least that's my read."

She nodded. "Agreed. Any big sweeping moves against public interest would piss off way too many people. Better to let sleeping dogs lie. This is, of course, dependent on us stopping the ritual. If a bunch of high-ranking faction members get their Impact ripped out and die of soul collapse, the six will probably glass this whole planet."

Which begged the question of how Suvaya planned to survive her ascension at all, but that was her problem. Mine was making sure *we* survived it.

"Templeton is our main issue," I said with a grimace, turning to Gabriel. "His weird power makes him a nightmare to negotiate with. What do you think he'll try to get out of us?"

"Anything he can," he said, sighing. "I suspect the details will depend on exactly how the sides play out. If it's close to fifty-fifty in his favor, he'll have more capital to squeeze us. If it swings more in our favor, he'll have less leverage. He'll take a mile for every inch we give him, but less inches means less miles."

I nodded. "Well, fair enough. We can make a binding contract for everyone to sign with a wish. I can get one from Nat or Alistair. I'm already going over some possible legalese to shield us from any of the higher-ups as much as possible. I'll probably mention my mom and dad too. Having the shadow of two A-rankers behind me will probably help." I glanced at Gabriel. "You willing to back me up about my mom, or are you still not sure?"

He shook his head. "It's not that I don't trust you. It's just that you're asking me to put my reputation on the line for hearsay. I can stay silent, which is an endorsement of its own, but I won't forswear myself. It isn't in my nature."

"Close enough," I said with a shrug. "Now everyone, put your game faces on—we're about there. This will be much more crowded than last time based on what Benny said on our call. Be prepared for an audience." I looked at Satala warily. "About the other thing... Are you really willing to help Yvette dismantle your mother's ritual?"

Not approving of her mother killing off the descendants of their worshippers was one thing, but actively helping us prevent her mom from coming back... I was worried that was too much to ask.

She wore a sad smile. "My mother is already gone. Her spirit has been soaking in hatred and malice for millennia, just like my brothers and sisters. Moreso, even, because I truly believe she was shielding me from my own portion of that influence. I believe the person she was before wouldn't want to see this twisted approximation reach divinity. Not at this cost. This is my responsibility, and I will see it through."

My heart broke for her. Not the least because of my own family's role in all this. But I could tell she was being honest. My divination class had very few tangible benefits, but I'd been able to sense honesty a time or two. Having stepped onto a Path, I was even more in tune with my role as a Fatewalker, and given the importance of Satala's help, this was very much a turning point in a great many fates.

It felt weird, sort of like my fate sense, but like... the other hand? A secondary ability I wasn't used to using. I could feel that this was more in tune with what I should be doing with my Path, not just stabbing things.

As we approached the base camp, I noticed the density of powerful Ascendants and couldn't help but tense. They watched us go. Some I knew, most I didn't, but they didn't speak, didn't glare—they just waited. Templeton stood in the center of a ring of people, and he raised a brow imperiously as we approached.

"Was it necessary to call us together like this?" he drawled. "We've all of us important work to do if we wish to survive. Too many of our own have partaken of this poison. Now you call us away from our work for the sake of the enemy?" The attention from his side of the circle seemed to redouble, and I felt ranks close behind us. There seemed to be a line in the sand, our side versus his, and to my delight we were edging him out.

Of course, that could change if we didn't present a strong case. Callie had been extremely clear that conclaves like this were fickle. Momentum mattered—if opinion started to swing too far to one side it could snowball, and we would be in trouble if that happened. Bethy wasn't going to let anyone hurt Satala, and neither was I. She'd trusted us, was still trusting us, and I could feel how important she would be.

"We've come across new information," I said solemnly. "Information, and a new ally." Satala had agreed to let me talk. She had good reasons to hate the factions and getting her involved in the politicking when someone like Templeton was arguing for the other side was a bad idea.

I gestured to Satala and filled them in on a simplified but still technically accurate version of events. I'd been tweaking my retelling the whole walk back, just to make sure not to give Templeton any openings. I wasn't clear on his exact relationship with truth and lies, but I suspected spewing bullshit during this little negotiation would be a mistake. Whether this was my Path, my fate sense, or just my gut I had no idea, but it didn't hurt to be careful.

My biggest priority was making Satala sound like an asset. She was, of course, but I needed to highlight the upsides and minimize the risks. My mind wandered back to a lesson with my dad as a boy. I asked him why anyone would ever sign an uneven contract. If it wasn't fair, what was there to be gained? I knew why the person who came out on top would sign, but why would anyone sign a contract that benefited the other person more?

He'd told me something I hadn't really remembered until recently. "Contracts are a manifestation of compromise, and compromise means both parties get what they want. The trick is to convince the other person that the things that you want are the things that they want."

I didn't need to convince these people to help me protect Satala. I needed to convince them it was the best way to help themselves.

After I said my piece, the group called up Yvette to testify as to Satala's usefulness, and I realized that this little argument had devolved into a legitimate trial. That was fine. We'd considered that possibility. Templeton wanted to wring some benefits out of us, which meant he needed to put us on the defensive. We didn't need to talk to him, we needed to talk to the others.

Templeton opened his mouth again, but to my surprise, Annalise cut him off. "Enough from both you and Shane. This isn't some casual decision. We're not idiots. If we come to a quorum here, it will represent the will of all our factions if we survive this. You've said your pieces. Let us talk amongst ourselves. Regardless of the decision, it's clear we'll need to document it."

She glanced at Nat, who nodded. No one here had the contract Skill at Intermediate as far as I knew, and even if they did, a lot of the teams seemed to have partaken of the Dew. A normal Intermediate contract wouldn't work. If we were going to come to an accord here, we'd need a contract with a powerful geas. A wish was the best way to manage that.

No one seemed put out by that, but we hadn't figured they would be. After all, we were going into battle against a goddess together for the sake of our joint survival. Having everything spelled out as a real binding agreement would put everyone at ease.

This wasn't just about Satala anymore. This had just become a competition to accrue influence over who would draft the agreement that would set the stage for the rest of our time here.

I groaned internally. This was why I hated fucking politics.

Chapter Sixty-Three

Of course, they didn't stick us in a corner and make us watch the others deliberate. This was a full-on conclave now, and everyone was mixing and discussing, including Templeton and me. That was something to worry about, honestly, but the people here were all monsters—I bet that they knew what the slippery bastard could do better than I did and probably had defenses against it that I didn't.

I was kind of lost and wasn't sure who to appeal to. Despite the new stakes (and I could *feel* them now), this was still mainly about Satala for me. Sure, this was definitely a turning point in history, and the senses I'd been developing as a Fatewalker were buzzing like there was a swarm of bees in my brain, but that would be the case regardless of the outcome.

This meeting had spiraled pretty far out of control, which meant there *was* a possibility Satala might end up as collateral. While we'd figured this would be a formality, the fact that the negotiations would have such huge repercussions meant there was a non-zero chance they'd want to make an example of her to set the tone.

A contract like this wouldn't just set the tone for our cooperation, it would also represent one of the biggest joint undertakings anyone had ever heard of. I hadn't understood the exact scale of this kind of compact, but hearing everyone talking about it really drove home exactly what we were doing. Politically we would be setting the possible tone for interactions between the factions for our entire generation, interactions that could affect policy even in the current faction leaderships.

Which made it important to be careful. Despite many of us being important members of our respective factions, we weren't *really* important. Not every faction picked their leaders by trial like the WCP. Our cuckoo bird strategy was fairly novel among the big factions. The result there was that nepotism and power concentration were rampant. No one here was a core member of the younger generation of a major faction, which meant everyone from one of the big six had to represent their faction fairly and without making too many waves.

Theoretically this freed up people from S-ranked factions and clans to be more aggressive, but not being part of a larger machine also meant they had less separation from their respective overlords. If a member of an S-ranked clan did something their family's founder disapproved of, they might just get killed.

That said, *not* taking part would also be unacceptable. It was insane to miss out on an opportunity to network like this, not just because of missed chances to make connections, but because this would be a *historic* accord, and the people involved would be winning renown from their factions in general and the universe at large if it was well received.

My head was hurting just listening to all the muttering, but that might just be the buzzing from my damned Path. Callie took my elbow deftly and walked us both casually off to one side, making sure no one could tell how much pain I was in. Must be my Path, then—politics might make my head hurt, but it wasn't usually this literal. My girlfriend's steadying touch was helping though.

"This has gotten out of hand," she said quietly. "I was expecting things to escalate a bit when we all got together, but this has turned into something bigger than I think any of us could have anticipated. We might have made a mistake."

She was right. We'd lit a match and tossed it on a pile of sticks, but we'd missed that they were soaked in gasoline. "How much of this was Templeton, do you think?" I asked in annoyance. His power was complicated and hard to understand, but it might be possible for him to pivot a large-scale meeting into something like this.

"Doesn't matter," she said with a shrug. "We need to get out there and start swaying people to our side. The final decision here is going to affect the balance of power in the actual team that helps draft the agreement. We're pretty much doubling down at this point."

I knew that. I knew exactly what was happening. My Path was trying to take it all in, trying to push me slightly. This was what being a Fatewalker was about, even more than battle—changing the course of destiny. And suddenly, several different things about the current situation just... clicked. I didn't magically get an answer, but I felt a hard shove that aimed me right at a specific group of people.

The devil girl I'd seen in one of the starting teams was talking to a tall, purple-skinned man with curling ram horns, and I could feel that I needed to talk to him too. I started walking before I figured out what I was going to say. I stopped in front of him and held out my hand, my Path pushing me to introduce myself a certain way. "Hi there, Shane Wyndham, son of Elijah."

I knew my dad had become a devil from Zeke, though I had no clue what the circumstances were. From the widening of the purple-skinned demon's slitted orange eyes, he definitely did. "Elijah... Wyndham?" he said slowly.

"Yeah," I said with a chuckle. "I know he's got some connections in the devil world." Which I didn't know for sure, but it was easy to assume. Not just because of the push from my ability, but because there really weren't that many A-rankers out there in the grand scheme of things, and I knew my dad had made the shift to being a devil to break out of B-rank. "You know of him I take it?"

He adopted an inscrutable expression. "What do you know of how the devil leadership is arranged?" He was watching me intently. From what I'd seen of the devil girl, she was leaning to Templeton's side, and since they were friendly he might have been too, but he seemed to be hanging on my every word here, so it might be possible to pivot him to our camp.

"I heard you guys are kind of like fae? Though I'm not clear on the differences." A fae had mentioned it to me once, but it hadn't made much sense.

He waved me off. "It's not important. For the purposes of this conversation you can treat us as a subset of the fae. We live in a territory of the Faerieland technically speaking, but it's mostly its own area. Being the nearest god, the Faerie Queen nominally holds dominion over us, but we're ruled by a council of nine princes, all high in the S-rank and their generals, who are all A-rank."

"And my dad is one of the generals?" I asked, seeing where this was probably going.

"My family falls under the purview of the demon prince Adramalech, and the Wish Devil is his most recent general," he said helpfully. "He's considered a unique resource and has been extremely helpful to the prince. As his son, you could be considered half a member of the Adramalech faction, and you have my support." He glanced at the devil girl. "Nasha, can you convince your team leader as well?"

She nodded. "Probably. It's close enough not to have any serious repercussions either way right now." She shot me a winning smile. "Just try to mention me to your dad next time you see him."

That was unlikely to happen anytime soon, but since I was wearing a mask my grimace went unnoticed. "Sure thing," I said lightly. "I'll mention you both." I cocked my head at the taller demon. "I don't think you mentioned your name?" I wouldn't be a dick about this. I'd try to remember to mention them to my dad if I saw him, after I finished telling him what an asshole he was.

"Markoth," he said, bowing his head slightly. "My father is Lieutenant-General in the prince's army, Malkor. It's an honor to be of assistance to the son of the Wish Devil." The way he said that made me incredibly curious what my dad had been doing in devil territory. I knew he was an A-ranker, but the reverence in Markoth's voice implied a certain level of fame. Or infamy.

To my surprise, Markoth headed off to speak to others on my behalf almost immediately, as did Nasha, and our political sway seemed to pretty much triple. Whoever Malkor was, he was clearly impressive in whatever circles he ran in. I wondered if he was considered an invincible B-ranker like Zeke. Then again, I'd already noted these weren't core members of the major factions. Maybe Markoth's dad was just local or was well known in local circles.

My Path didn't push me in any new or useful directions after that. In fact, it seemed to drain off after that conversation. I guessed my divination was only strong enough to influence events slightly. Hopefully that would be enough.

Finally, after what seemed like both far too long and not nearly enough time, the conversation seemed to wind down. I couldn't have said how it happened. There was no indication, no one called things to a head, everyone just kind of... knew.

Templeton took up the role of spokesperson again, once more making me suspicious he'd steered things to this point.

With everyone already quiet, it was simple for him to make himself heard. "You've all discussed this," he said solemnly. "You know the importance of this decision. We are at the mercy of the masses. Should we decide to put down the interloper, I will do my best to represent the interests of all of us when I craft the document on which this alliance will be built." He said it with a slight smile, as if he was discussing Sunday brunch.

Bethy was glaring at him from her place next to Satala, and as he met her burning ruby gaze, I saw him flinch a bit. It was hard not to smile at the sight of that. I looked around. "All in favor of letting our new friend aid us in this important task?" I resisted the urge to try to subtly slip in some references to how necessary she was for our survival.

Hands went up. Lots of them. I counted slowly and let out a loud sigh of relief as I confirmed that we'd pulled out ahead. About sixty percent. Not as big a margin as I'd hoped. Templeton was more convincing than I'd given him credit for. Ignoring the snarl on the bastard's face, I turned to Satala with a smile. "Then I suppose it falls on me to welcome you to our alliance."

Of course, Satala would have to sign the accord we came up with. Not only would this ensure her safety, it would ensure ours. I might be optimistic and fairly sure of my abilities, but I wasn't stupid. Insurance was necessary to make certain we were all protected.

Turning to Nat, who was waiting nearby, I grinned. "Now, since we need to get started on the drafting process, I wish for a binding geas in paper form, suitable for the purpose of a large-scale alliance agreement. I offer as payment first pick of the spoils upon our defeat of the goddess Suvaya." There were plenty of winces, but no one objected. This was an important step for all of us, so we should all pay. Of course, Nat was on my team, so I'd be keeping the potential windfall in the family, but the opportunity was big enough to be worth the wish at least.

There was the usual lightshow that only we could see, and Nat passed me a piece of paper rolled up in a scroll. Nodding somberly, I turned and glanced at Annalise, Gabriel, Bethy, Markoth, and my other allies. "Now, if you might help me hammer out the terms, we can arrange a beneficial accord that will carry us through this battle and together into a brighter future."

And with that, our true work began with the drafting of the Pact of the Fist.

Chapter Sixty-Four

THE CODIFICATION of the terms of the Pact of the Fist (Benny named it, and he'd been so helpful with all of this that no one argued) took about a full day. We were short on time, but no one was willing to move forward with the missions until we'd hammered everything out. With the entire group of nearly a thousand outsiders gathered, there were too many interests represented for any of us to feel at ease leaving things to chance. Because of all the information wishes, Annalise helped immensely, allowing us to swing some of the terms in our favor we might otherwise not have managed.

The numerous bindings on betrayal (ostensibly for everyone) that were thrown in to make sure Satala didn't screw us took the longest. Templeton and his goons had to make them vague enough to be technically applicable to all of us but also not restrictive enough to box in anyone but her. Still, there were several provisions for protections from family and factions for all involved parties that would be useful to us as well as them.

Finally, at about noon the next day we finished writing it all out, and everyone got in line to sign the agreement. One by one, we put our names down, and I felt the temporary draw of Impact in the same way I did when Enchanting. It wasn't just me, either—everyone gave some up from the look of it.

The paper that the geas was written on collected power as we went until finally the last signature was put down and the thing burst into purple flame. The electric current I associated with wish-granting shot out from the blaze and slammed into us all, tightly binding us to the agreement we'd just signed, and I for one felt both much better and a bit worried to have it over with.

The geas fell heavy on us all too. Nearly a thousand F-rankers, most of whom had gotten ahold of the Dew, contributed to the binding, and the damned thing was pretty sturdy for all the help. Once it was done, we all gathered around Yvette and Satala, both of whom were, while signatories, *not* involved in the crafting of the accord and had plenty of time to work on the calculations for the ritual shutdown.

In fact, Satala was familiar enough with her mother's abilities and personality that she was able to streamline the alteration process, cutting down on the time the temples needed to be active during the changes, and making it much easier for us to manage them in the allotted time.

It was incredibly useful, considering that based on that and her own understanding of the conduits, they were able to set up a plan for us to evenly distribute our forces and complete the alterations within one more round of missions. Satala in particular seemed pleased about this, filling us in on her reasoning without any hesitation.

"Basically, the sooner we trigger the ritual, the less prepared my mother's spirit will be," the silver-haired girl said. "Theoretically, doing it the day before is fine, but if we can manifest her soul body weeks in advance, she'll be much less coherent and much less dangerous to all of you."

Yvette nodded. "That isn't in doubt." She gestured to the ground, where she'd sketched a complicated diagram. "I've been able to refine my process considerably, and along with the information Satala has shared about the conduits and their names and traits, I've been able to work up guides similar to the one we used at her temple for each of them."

"Which means we can dispatch teams to each of the conduit temples directly," I said. "All at once. With so many of us here, we can even assemble teams best suited for each fight. But will that trigger her descent immediately? Because somehow I feel like that would be a mistake." Suvaya was a goddess. Fallen or not, weakened or not, deprived of her body or not, she was a threat that not a single one of us would survive alone. We needed to fight her as a group.

"Of course," Yvette said. "We've arranged things to account for that. It'll take a day for the ritual to cycle once it's been activated. The last conduit will complete the script and trigger the reroute, but we've built in buffers to slow down the process. Once you've completed your assignment, you'll regroup with the rest of us outside the main temple to prepare for the final battle."

I sighed with relief, then held out a hand for the little booklet she'd prepared for my team specifically. Honestly, moving the timetable up like this was better. I hadn't been excited about spending a month sitting around picking off scary targets while checking in constantly back here. This place freaked me out, and if it wasn't the only landmark that would work from a distance, I'd have been happy to avoid it.

Which reminded me. "How did we get everyone back here for the meeting? I get Templeton pushed for it, but did he have some method of contacting them we didn't?" I looked at Benny.

"Alistair," my friend said in distaste. "He doesn't seem to have the same problems with Templeton as everyone else. I'd have assumed he would be more... I don't know, loyal to the team? Isn't he like your second cousin or something? He's a relative at least."

"Nothing that close," I said, shaking my head. "He's from another branch, which means literally the closest relative we probably share is a great-grandparent. My grandfather is branch elder for ours, and I know for a fact that there's competition. Family politics means that siding with us earlier is probably about the most support we can expect from the guy."

Benny whistled. "I'm *so* glad I'm not related to you. No offense. Your family is seriously dysfunctional. And I thought Maria's bad taste in boyfriends was family drama."

"Yeah, I'm not a fan of all the backstabbing either." I paused. "Though I guess with the whole competition thing it's more frontstabbing. At least they're direct about it."

I opened the booklet and flipped through. "Oh hey, nice. We've got Gabriel, Abel, and Bethy again, plus a bunch of backup. Willow is coming along—she can definitely help." The girl scared me more than Abel did, so having her on our team was pretty cool. "Twenty-man team. That makes me feel a lot better about this next..." I trailed off, closing my eyes with a sigh.

"What?" Benny said, raising his eyebrow. "Twenty people seems... Shit." He stared at the page on the booklet. S-rank. We were going after Pallax, a former high priest of Suvaya, or in the parlance of current religious organizations, a Pope. Sure, he was stripped of most of his power, but based on the serious danger we'd faced fighting the last guy...

"Hey," I said consolingly. "At least we aren't going in blind. We don't just have a general idea of his abilities—Satala put together a whole package on him. Skills, techniques, habits—if we have to fight a complete monster at least we get to do it prepared. And with twenty people we can do a *lot* of preparing. Imagine the invocations we can manage, especially with someone like Yvette acting as a focus. She's got so much Impact."

He nodded slowly. "I could actually see that working. I mean, we have to talk to the others and get a list of their tricks, but a huge invocation would be a great way to level the playing field."

I wasn't sure it would be *quite* that easy, but it was definitely a direction to work toward. "Hey, Abel! Bethy! Gabe!" I called the three strongest members of my team verbally and reached out for Callie through our bond. She noticed immediately and headed over, plucking the booklet from Benny's hands without bothering to ask for it.

My snicker at that might not have been the most diplomatic response, but my friend's expression was funny. Celine also stepped up, followed by Jessie, and both of them were with us, so that worked out for the best. Callie whistled as she read the booklet. "We have a good lineup, but they sent us after a tough son of a bitch."

"Guess that's what we get for being the best." Abel said with a shrug. "What do we have..." He grabbed the booklet and flipped through it. "Gold manipulation? Transmutation too. That doesn't seem so..." He trailed off as he started reading some of the technique descriptions. "Oh. Never mind. Well, that just seems excessive."

He passed it to Mel, who scanned it with a visible wince, and then started passing it around. We all had pretty high Focus, so it wasn't like we needed to read it more than once. "We were talking about possible invocations to deal with the conduit. With so many people plus Yvette coming along, we can really cut loose. She has so much Impact she should be able to leverage that much power easily."

Gabriel nodded. "Maybe. The conduit himself will have plenty of Impact, and don't forget there are other options for dealing with attacks than just tanking them. We have to land the hit in order for it to be effective. Still, it's a good strategy for dealing with a powerful enemy."

"I don't think we should attack," Callie mused. "We have functional attack methods already. His Impact is the same as the others—it's his capabilities that are a problem. We should find out if anyone on the team has binding abilities. A powerful binding would probably serve us well in this instance. If we can pin him down, Gabriel, Shane, and Bethy can lay into him with their respective weapons."

"Nasha can do that," said a voice off to one side. I wasn't surprised to see Markoth approach. He was listed among our allies, though I didn't know how strong he was. Since the devils seemed to be considered fairly impressive on a large scale, I was hoping he'd have some useful abilities to contribute. Racial traits could be pretty scary as I'd seen with Bethy.

The demon girl waved cheerfully, offering us a bright smile. "My main Skill is Unholy Binding. Not only should it be pretty helpful for pinning him down, it counters divine energy to an extent. Is that going to be a problem for you, Crusader?"

Gabriel shook his head. "Unlikely. I just need to avoid being bound myself. As for the other aspects of it, while I know some members of my faith dislike your people, the devils aren't considered proscribed by our Lord. I'm happy to have you working alongside us." He offered his hand, and Markoth and Nasha shook it in turn.

"For sure," chirped Bethy. "Devils can be super strong. You guys work for Prince Drama right? Daddy says he has a fine understanding of the importance of presentation."

Both devils flinched when she said that, and I had to hold back a laugh. Only Bethy would reference an S-ranker by the embarrassing nickname her father used for him. I doubted Adramalech was going to start a war with the Vampire over something so mundane, so I guessed she would get away with it.

"Well then, seems like it's time for us to get started planning." I flipped back through the booklet. "Alright, I've got a list of everyone we need, you guys want to have a meeting before we go? Or we can talk while we walk. I really want to get off this fucking mountain forever as soon as possible."

That got a laugh and a round of agreements from my friends, so we rounded up our group so we could head out. It would be a bit of a trip this time. Pallax's sub-temple wasn't close, but this would be the last one. Once we finished this, we could group up and prepare for the descent of Suvaya.

After that... Well, I couldn't wait to get off this fucking planet.

Chapter Sixty-Five

WE MADE PRETTY good time getting to the temple, but we didn't head in immediately. "Callie, can you scope this place out for us? Satala says this priest guy doesn't like the Night Pride, and he shouldn't have any guarding him. With her dossier on his techniques, and your information gathering ability, we can definitely avoid any casualties." Speaking of which— "Bethy, how many stakes did you bring?"

The tiny Vampire beamed and withdrew a pair of them. "These are my last two. I sent some with Aida and Tracey too, just to keep them safe, but these two should be more than enough. You want to carry them? Your neat little armor bypassing trick worked really well with them last time."

I took one, waving off her attempt to pass me the other. "Better to have two points of attack in there. Will they still work?"

She waggled a hand. "Yes, but not as well. That guy's soul is probably monstrous, and with enough soul power you can resist a lot. It won't be enough to save him, but he might be able to force himself to move still."

"It's fine. Nasha, you ready with your binding Skill?" Her Unholy Binding should keep him still long enough for us to put him down, which would save us so much trouble here. I had a plan for taking him out if we could get the shot, and it was a pretty good one, but it all depended on opportunity.

The demoness looked troubled. "Yes, but I'll need him to stand still long enough to actually use it. We need to pin him down with attacks before I can lock him down with my Skill."

"That won't be a problem," Abel said confidently. "I'll make sure he keeps still. Gabe and I should be able to distract him, especially in combination with the invocation teams. I'm like... sixty percent sure no one is going to be mummified alive in a living coffin of molten gold!"

I winced. That particular technique had bothered me too. Nasha didn't look particularly reassured.

Callie glared at our mentor. "Can you be serious for once?"

"I am being serious," he said in a wounded voice. "I really think we might all survive this."

Mel smacked him in the back of the head. "She's unhappy with the implication that there's a forty percent chance we might *not* all survive. You're not supposed to talk about possible fatalities before a raid. It's bad for morale. No one here wants to think about all the terrible ways some of us are probably going to die!"

I palmed the forehead of my mask with a sigh, and she winced, apologizing quickly as she decided to stop talking. "We'll be fine, guys," I cut in. "We're insanely prepared for this. Plus we have Yvette to leverage our power into a strong invocation."

"Yeah, about that," Benny interjected. "I thought invocations were based on soul strength. Shouldn't we be letting Abel do this?"

"Kind of," I hedged. "If you think of an invocation like a lever, the soul is the material, and Impact is the fulcrum. Better Impact lets you pull off more powerful invocations without as much soul strain. At least that's how it was explained to me. Yvette is our best bet for pulling this off. She has as much Impact as Pallax himself, so she should definitely be able to bring some serious power to bear."

There was a loud roar as Randall, who was nearby, stood up on his back legs and crowed in triumph. Jessie, who was standing next to him, pinched the bridge of her nose. "That's not what that means Randy. It's just an expression." The bear paused, cocking its head and issuing a confused growl. "No, I don't know why they phrase it that way." She rolled her eyes. "Yes, bears are very powerful."

Bethy, who was standing nearby the two, was trying desperately to hold in her giggles. "Your teddy bear is pretty funny!" she said, grinning at Jessie. "You've gotta teach me how to train my kitties like that."

My blonde team member nodded smugly. "I am an expert in animal training. I have tons of experience."

"You're basically an animal puppet master," Benny said incredulously. "You just shove life force into them and use it to make them do what you want until it sticks."

She shrugged. "It works, doesn't it? How many giant animals have *you* trained?"

He shot me a smirk. "Just the one. Though to be fair, yours smells better. Plus, they don't hog all the hot water with absurdly long showers. I don't even think mine knows any tricks."

I sneered at him. "Well I can do magic." Then I flipped him off. "Look, a bird." Callie cleared her throat over the sounds of Jessie and Bethy choking back laughter. I schooled my expression. "Anyway, Randall will be incredibly useful in this fight. Though we'll need Abel's help to get him inside. He can just ride him."

"You want me to ride into an ancient forgotten temple to kill the high priest of a vanished god on the back of a giant supernatural bear?" Abel said slowly.

"Yeah. Why, is that a problem?" I hadn't expected him to mind, honestly.

He reached up and pinched the skin of one of his arms. "No," he said absently. "I just needed to make sure I was awake. I legitimately have no idea when my life got this awesome."

"If it helps, remember that you might suffocate to death on molten gold as it boils your lungs from the inside," Mel chimed in helpfully. We all threw up our hands, giving her a *what the fuck* look, and she winced. "Oh, I said that out loud, didn't I? Right, bad for morale."

"I thought it was informative," Abel said charitably, and we all just rolled our eyes at their antics.

"So, what do we have?" I asked Callie. "You get a good look at the inside of the temple? I'm betting there are some traps laid out for us."

"You could say that," she said helplessly. "He coated the entire place with gold. Every inch of the walls and floor is plated with the stuff. If we set foot in there we'll basically be walking right into his hands. I couldn't tell exactly from the shadows, but I'm pretty sure it's all forty Impact gold. Which means it's much more durable than any normal F-rank metal, and if he turns it on us we're screwed."

I cursed. "Not what I wanted to hear, but I guess it's better to know at least." With that bit of information, we got down to the serious business of planning a raid.

After an hour, we considered ourselves officially prepared and moved into the temple as a group. We had several defensive ability users on the team, and by grouping them all up we'd put together a first line of defense in case Pallax tried to ambush us. Despite the preparations, once we entered the golden halls of the temple, nothing happened. We peacefully headed into the heart of the place.

When we arrived, we found a golden-haired man sitting at a golden table, drinking tea from a golden pot. When he saw us, he smiled lightly, took one last sip from his golden cup, and then set the teacup down. "Ah," he said warmly. "You must be the current generation sent by the false gods. I take it you're here to kill me?"

Despite the words, Pallax seemed perfectly at ease, and I stepped forward to speak for everyone, a bit of hope kindling in my chest. Maybe this was another person like Satala, who couldn't bear to kill their own people. "We are. I'm Solomon, one of the potential heirs of the Wish Curse Palace. Are you Pallax?"

The golden-haired man smiled sadly. "I am. I'm surprised you're willing to talk. Are you hoping to resolve things peacefully?"

"We are," I confirmed. I didn't even need to ask my allies. If we didn't have to fight the former S-ranker, we shouldn't. That just seemed like common sense. "We've already helped one of your own, Satala, break her ties to the ritual. She couldn't bear the thought of killing so many descendants of your worshippers."

"That sounds like her," he said with a fond chuckle. "The little princess was always the kindest of us all. I can understand why she would take that path as well. I too find the thought of killing the descendants of our flock sickening. I've only recently become aware of the leakage, and I would

348

mourn their loss."

I let out a relieved breath. "I'm glad. I thought you might hate us for what happened. I know that malice has infected most of your fellow conduits."

"I'm sure," he said easily. "But no. I hold no hatred in my heart for any of you. Not just you—I don't even blame your ancestors. All things must end. My brothers and sisters were always far too easily swayed. I've felt our mother's madness for centuries, and I know she has strayed from her path."

This was going perfectly. "So you'll help us put a stop to this? Make sure that no one else gets hurt? Because I have to say I'm incredibly relieved by how reasonable you're being about this."

"No," Pallax said, flashing a bitter smile. "I'm afraid that isn't the case. I'm going to finish my tea, and then I'm going to kill you all. It's nothing personal, of course, simply my duty. If you remain still, I can at least make it quick. There's no reason for unnecessary suffering."

My smile froze. "What?" I just blinked at him. "But you just said you don't hate us, that you know your goddess has gone crazy, and that the thought of your worshippers and their descendants dying is sickening to you."

"All of that is true," he said. "It is also irrelevant. I am a priest. It is not my place to question, or reason, or cajole. I am not an advisor. I am an instrument of my lady's will, Her divine judgement made manifest. Madness, fear, vengeance—I act on her designs. If you hoped to negotiate with me, you've gravely misjudged this situation. I bear you no ill will, and that will continue to be true even as your lungs fill with my moongold."

There was a slight rumble, and I watched in horror as the walls and floor began to vibrate. No, not vibrate. Superheat. The gold glowed as he used his control over it to accelerate the internal kinetic energy, heating it to a molten state even as we stood inside.

Cursing, I triggered Moonlit Night. Fog filled the room rapidly, and I felt the stealth-imbued water clash against the heat and counter it slightly, steam filling the room as our defensive team triggered their invocation. A massive transparent turtle shell came into being above us, a membrane manifesting below, and Yvette winced as the gold on the walls and floor exploded downward in a massive omnidirectional wave.

However, with Moonlit Night up, the attack was off center. More of the gold hit the back side of the shell than the front, and the force sent the

349

whole defensive construct rocketing out of the mist and away from the golden deluge, revealing the normal dark stone walls of the chamber appearing before us as the gold formed into a massive serpent that shot after us, emerging from the steam and fog.

Which was when a fist materialized from the air and smashed right into the snake's golden face. Abel had stepped up as an alternate for the invocation teams to offset the disadvantage. The snake was made of a *lot* of condensed gold, but Abel's punch was superimposed multiple times, enough to leave a small dent.

Sadly, that was all it did. I had a feeling this fight wasn't going to go as smoothly as the last few.

Chapter Sixty-Six

THE SIGHT of the giant golden snake made all of us pale. This technique was one of the ones mentioned by Satala, but it was on a totally different scale. According to her briefing, it took time to transmute things into gold, and the materials used mattered. Coating the walls and floors must have taken him ages, and a not insignificant amount of soul power. By condensing the gold, he made it stronger, and was able to effectively make a low-level enchanted weapon.

"Huh," Benny said as he looked up at the serpent through the transparent turtle shell. "Guys. I think this might be a trap."

We all turned to glare at him, and Celine pinched her nose. "Yes, love. We knew that when we came in here. Also, in case the walls made of gold didn't give it away, the whole building coming alive and trying to kill us made that quite clear."

He shrugged. "That's fair. I wasn't really paying attention, honestly. You guys talk a lot, and I sort of drift in and out. I was working on ideas for new inventions." He squinted up at the snake. "I wonder what I could make out of that thing. Actually, I'm going to use that. Dibs."

"You can't call *dibs* on the giant golden snake weapon," I protested. "If anyone gets dibs it's Nat—we're contractually obligated to give her first pick."

"Can you two *please* focus," Callie snapped. "We're about to be eaten by a giant construct monster."

"I don't think it's going to eat us," I said uneasily. "Look at its mouth." The snake's jaws opened, revealing a terrifying glow. That explained why Pallax had superheated the walls before making the construct. Shit. "Brace for impact!" I shouted, channeling Mountain Stance while placing a hand on Adrian, the thin, long-haired man channeling the turtle shell shield that surrounded us.

The snake reared back and struck, not biting, but throwing its whole body forward like a whip as it vomited forth a torrent of glowing golden metal.

"Oh shit!" Benny yelped. "It can breathe molten gold? I didn't know it could do that. Did anyone *else* know it could do that?" His voice was high and panicked, which I understood as I grimaced under the force of the blow to the turtle shell.

If I was shaken, that was nothing compared to Adrian. As the golden deluge hit the shield, he vomited blood, doubling over, and the shell began to crack. I saw the burning metal seep through the cracks with an acidic hiss, and realized the snake had somehow made the gold fucking poisonous. Or venomous? It wasn't a real snake so I wasn't sure. Regardless it was eating through the shell and Adrian was failing fast.

"Drop it!" barked Abel, and I nodded to the other man, still doubled over. Adrian dropped the shield and Abel lashed out with a hand, making a waving motion and creating an arc of lubricated space that diverted the gold.

Then he lashed out with a phantom hand and slapped the snake away. I looked around. Bethy and Gabriel had split up to hammer attacks into Pallax while Yvette held his attention. Sadly, the binding plan was on hold because the golden-haired priest was very mobile, even while operating his fucking giant snake.

"Does that thing look smaller to you?" I called hopefully to the others still in our group. A chunk of them had split off to help pin down Pallax with invocations, but we still had ten with us, counting Adrian who admittedly wasn't in great shape.

"Probably," Jessie said distractedly as she appeared next to him, laying on hands and pumping in life energy while Benny laid a palm on his shoulder to channel spiritual calming. "That gold had to come from somewhere, and condensing it only gets you so far." She grimaced as she stood up. "That's all I can do. Most of the damage wasn't physical. Benny will be more help for the soul stuff."

Abel stepped up next to her. "That works. Mel is off trying to help the Vampire and the choir boy. I need a partner for this next part. I have an idea if you trust me. I need you to get Randall within touching distance."

"Sure." Her bear companion was close by, acting as a shield against the snake that was still recovering, either from Abel's attack or from vomiting up half its mass. I was concerned the gold might have either been part of or be damaging the temple, but at a glance it was clear some of the enchantments were defensive. They did *not* want this place broken.

Randall shuffled back, and Abel put a hand on Jessie's shoulder and one on Randall's flank. He grinned like a lunatic as he screamed, "Bear witness!"

With a massive heave of power, he pulled them into the invocation, leveraging his powerful soul to handle it. In the air above them manifested a *massive* image of a fucking *bear* made of green energy, glaring right at the snake as it roared in defiance, sweeping its paws up and around to create a series of afterimages just like the six-arm attack stance Abel used in combat.

The snake froze, staring in bewilderment at the huge green animal before Abel's bear construct started raining down a torrent of slaps on the golden monster. The impact of each blow was only enough to make slight dents like before, but the rain of smacks was knocking the snake around like a sock in a windstorm.

We all just stood there and stared at the giant green energy bear. "Well," I said faintly, "that's something you don't see every day." The bear was absolutely ruining the snake's day. Randall's massive Might, Jessie's life force to keep up the output, and Ragam to tie it all in a bow—the combination made the damned construct an absolute machine of destruction.

"They've got this!" Callie shouted in my ear, trying to be heard over the noise. "We need to help the others with Pallax!"

She was right. Tapping the others, we bolted over to where the battle with the priest was still going strong. Gabriel's charger was dashing in circles trying to circle around the blonde man, and Yvette was hurling herself in front of attacks to prevent him from smashing the others. Bethy had her cats out and was flashing back and forth trying to exploit weaknesses, using them to attack when she had him distracted and vice versa, though with minimal success.

Pallax, for his part, looked mostly serene as he shuttled across the stone, hurling wobbling orbs and whips of molten gold to control the battlefield. I lashed out with a hand, triggering Pit of Despair, and he cursed as the ground dissolved into dust under him, catching himself with a golden claw.

I made sure the ground reformed once he was free. I was surprised that even worked, but I didn't want to damage any important enchantment portions. The distraction forced him to sit still though, and Gabriel's lance smashed into his exposed shoulder with a bellow of, "Rubrum gloria!"

The priest soaked the damage as he was thrown backwards and landed gracefully, glaring at the crusader. He'd finally gotten upset at the situation, but it was too late. There was a blaze of dark energy, and the ground beneath him opened up as a pair of flaming green skeletal hands reached up and snagged a wrist each. I saw Nasha sway, Markoth propping her up as a bunch of the others funneled stats into the invocation.

"Bethy!" I bellowed at the top of my lungs. "Tee me up! On his back!" She seemed confused for a second, then looked down at her stake and realized my plan. She slashed her wrist, bleeding on the weapon as she dove at his back, slamming the stake into it and grimacing as it stopped at only a few inches in. But I didn't mind that at all. I'd expected it in fact.

Double Trouble. Afterburner. Marked for Death. Mercy Kill. Triple-strength density-shifted attack. Touch of Tears. Consecration of Flame. A full power swing from my staff and all the death energy stored in it. I put every ounce of power in my body into the strike as I swung my E-ranked weapon in one of the forms Willow had shown me to maximize sudden power.

The staff came down with a terrifying force… right on top of the exposed end of the stake that Bethy had yanked her hand away from and left stuck in Pallax's back. The raw force of my blow hit the end of the stake like a hammer driving a nail into a plank of wood. The massive stacked attack drove it right through his back and into his heart, the death energy being carried through it by the power of all my subskills.

Unfortunately for Pallax, the stake wasn't made to be smashed in with an E-rank bludgeon, and once the staff completed its arc it fucking *exploded* in a shower of flaming green poisony death right inside his back. He threw back his head and howled, but he wasn't down for the count. I snagged my own stake from my belt and yelled, "Gabe!" as I hurled it end-over-end to the crusader.

He reached up and snatched it from the air, tying it to the end of his lance in a way I suspected wouldn't have worked for any non-Ascendant. Pallax roared, yanking back and forth against the Nasha's bindings. The skeletal hands started to crack and the demoness screamed in agony.

"Hurry the hells up!" Markoth roared.

Gabriel mounted his charger, and I could feel the air shift as his Path infused his lance, his steed, and his whole being. His eyes blazed with divine light as he blurred forward, an avalanche of unstoppable force and fury as he repeated his battle cry of "Rubrum gloria!" at the top of his lungs. Path, ability, weapon, and faith merged into a gleaming comet of shining glorious death as the lance hit Pallax head-on and speared the stake right into his heart.

The priest threw back his head and roared in pain and despair as a torrent of white light poured out of his body, the merged attack funneled through the stake exploding inside him as blazing faith-powered Adamant strength shone from eyes, nose, mouth and ears.

Nasha released her hold with a wail and fell to the ground, Markoth catching her as Benny blurred over to help with his spiritual calming. Almost in slow motion, Pallax's body toppled to the floor, eyes charred out, limply sprawled on the dark stone as his massive snake construct lost its animating force and crashed to the ground.

I triggered a pair of my heal bursts on myself, and walked over to use one more on Nasha, hoping to help with the last of my Afterburner buff. "Everyone alright?" I croaked as the weakness tore through me, mixing with the vital energy to create an extremely nauseating cocktail of sensations.

Almost two dozen voices called their affirmative, and I slumped to the ground, exhausted and panting. We'd made it. Our last mission before the biggest fight of our lives and no one died in the attempt.

I groaned and got to my feet. "Alright. Places everybody. We need to get that bastard in the coffin and adjust the ritual before all the life in his body fades."

After that though, I was gonna take a fucking nap.

Chapter Sixty-Seven

WE ARRIVED at the rendezvous point the next morning. Most of the other teams had beaten us there, probably because they had much weaker priests to deal with and mostly larger teams. We'd been expected to make do because of the concentration of elites we had.

Sadly, the major issue we discovered when we arrived wasn't related to our fellow outsiders, it was related to something... worse. Specifically, the *massive* army of undead cultists shambling around in the plane outside the central temple.

"Okay," I said slowly. "I feel like considering how many of those look like they used to be local worshippers, not involving the locals was the right call. Thankfully they're zombies, because I doubt we could stop the other teams from straight up murdering them to get to that central temple. They don't look so tough, and I'm not too worried about scything through a few thousand random corpses."

"That's because you're not paying attention," spat a nearby voice. I turned to find Templeton glaring down at the field of zombies. "They aren't there to slow us down, they're there to soak up damage and force us to use our energy before we reach our target. Soul strain and energy depletion might be minimal for one or two of those, but there are about twenty thousand down there. More than a dozen a piece even if we had our full complement of a thousand."

Which made sense. Shit. "Meat shields," I sneered. "Classy." I looked around for our resident expert, who was with us by virtue of us abandoning Fist Mountain for this location. I spotted her telltale silver hair and waved her over. "Satala!" I called as I made my gesture. When she got close enough, I nodded down to the shambling corpses. "Any idea where these things came from?"

She nodded. "If I had to guess, probably the temple. They're most likely people that have tried break in over the centuries, with maybe some cultists mixed in." She frowned down at the bodies. "I can't believe my mother would disrespect her faithful in such a way. To have fallen so low, she must truly be suffering."

I personally felt like the mass murder of tens of thousands of Ascendants throughout the known universe was a pretty good indicator of dickishness. Still, it was her mom, so I didn't say that. I just sighed.

Callie stepped up beside me, staring down into the valley where the massive black stone temple was housed. It reminded me of all the sub-temples, but bigger, though there was some space warping going on from what I could see of the zombies' walking patterns.

"This is going to suck," Callie said matter-of-factly. "It won't be as simple as twenty or thirty a piece. A lot of us don't have the skillset for mass carnage. We need to carve through them in the most efficient way possible, but without burning up our energy." She paused, thinking it over. "I think our best bet is physical combat. Rely on weapons to tear through them as quickly as we can."

In the end, we decided to charge the horde and wipe them out manually on the way inside. Jessie agreed to refresh everyone as they entered, effectively erasing any physical drain and undoing the damage from the trap. Of course, this was all predicated on no one getting injured in the fight, but it wasn't like we could wait. The ritual would trigger in a few hours and we needed some time to set up.

Yvette had some last-minute alterations she wanted to make to the temple to minimize Suvaya's power when she manifested, something she hadn't expected to have time to do. Satala's information about the ritual had been invaluable.

So, with that said, we made our way down into the horde as a group, spreading out to present a single long front with plenty of room between groups so we could clean the undead up. I spun my staff up as we approached. "Is it just me, or are you kind of excited about this?" I asked my girlfriend casually.

She chuckled. "This part? Yeah. We haven't been in a real fight as a team like this in a while. The whole godslaying thing is a bit intimidating, but the coming fight should be good." As she spoke, a small subsection of the horde broke off and started to surround us.

Offering my hand, I grinned at her. "Well then, may I have this dance?" She lay her hand daintily in mine and I pulled, spinning her into a twirl. As she slid behind me, she dropped into my shadow, vanishing from the field of battle. With a bellow of joy, I waded into the melee. As a regular mechanism of her ability, her shadow portaling didn't strain her much over short distances, so using it for positioning was fine.

Waiting for the zombies to clumsily stumble into range, I saw Callie appear inside a group with her daggers. I lashed out in the low-high combo move I'd learned earlier, sprawling one corpse into two others as Callie neatly severed their spines at the neck and the tendons behind their knees. A follow-up smash pulped their heads after she disabled them and she moved on to the next one.

I'd forgotten how nice it was to fight like this, the bond feeding me everything I needed to know alongside my understanding of my partner, entering the flow of battle as I blended seamlessly into her combat style and she into mine. Even with the new additions to our fighting styles we had Balam as a common element. Combined with the bond, we were easily able to keep up with each other.

Zombies aren't particularly smart, so we didn't need to do anything but play meat grinder. I could see Gabriel's people riding through the crowd, literally herding them toward us so we could cut them down. A few of the other groups that had proven particularly effective took up the same position, while the less slaughter-oriented waited at the edges of the melees to pick off stragglers.

Step, shift, backspin. Attack, defend, counter. The forms that Willow had shown me were useful and versatile, and stupid clumsy zombies were an ideal training mechanism to improve. One would think that trying to learn complex patterns of attack while working around my girlfriend would be tough, but in fact it made it easier for me to comprehend the style.

Not only did I have my own experience and senses, but our combat styles were intertwining perfectly. Through the bond I could feel her reactions to the moves I was making and even sense her own responses before she made them, allowing me to adjust small imperfections in my combat flow. Callie's daggers worked with her Balam mastery surprisingly well too, the circular patterns of Balam not contradicting the striking maneuvers my girlfriend had learned.

The biggest benefit of the fight though was Callie's perspective allowing me to feel out what Willow meant about leverage. Every attack, every defense, all of them were vectors of force, acting on someone or something. With my staff I had a level that could enable me to act on those forces. Not energy, at least not yet, but physical forces and forms. A stab of the staff into the ground and then a snap could redirect a zombie into another, or into the path of a blow.

As I fought, I activated my overlay, and I felt all the disparate elements of my combat style congeal into one whole. My staff art, my stats, my experience, my instincts—all merged into one big tapestry of information, and as I saw it, I found a Path forward. Striding through battle, slightly shifting the tide of battle for maximum effect. Fatewalker. This was possible because I was at an important point in history, granted, and even outside this battle I was involved in a historic task, but at this moment, I was *all* the way in.

My Path shifted and so did the overlay, and suddenly it was guiding me, showing me the way. I took two steps and then slammed my staff into the dirt, leveraging a chunk of earth up into the face of a zombie as the end came up and over, splitting one's head. Then the back end slammed in reverse, smashing in the nasal bone as my next blow shattered an ankle.

The zombie with the ankle toppled over and tripped another that fell into the backswing of my attack as Callie shredded one coming at my back without me ever needing to turn around. Callie wasn't on my Path, but she was keeping up with my movements at least.

Eventually, when I turned to smash another opponent, all I caught was empty air. I panted, surveying the killing field for movement.

"We're through," Gabriel called from across the field of bodies. "Let's go everyone, time is wasting."

I blinked. We'd really demolished all of them. Granted, they were garbage-tier undead, but still, I'd expected it to take more than a few seconds.

I grinned as I came down from the weirdly charged state I'd been in, then inhaled sharply as I checked on my progress. While there was no stat gain, my soul had progressed a full four percent during that fight. I was up to twenty-three percent of the way through orange.

I made a mental note to check with Zeke and possibly Abel about this later. If the Path was helpful for soul strengthening, I needed to know about it. This wasn't like just aimlessly training—my soul didn't feel strained right now, it felt *energized*. It might be hard to enter that enlightened state, but if it let me train longer and more efficiently I should definitely look into this Path thing more. It explained how Abel's soul was so strong, too.

"Shane!" Callie exclaimed as she grabbed my hand, jarring me from my thoughts. "Come on, we need to get inside. Satala said that when we start tinkering with the ritual, the shields on the central temple will go up. If we don't get there in time, we'll be stuck out here while the others are left to fight Suvaya alone."

We raced into the temple, finding Yvette poised outside the door to a room similar to the conduit rooms, except instead of a coffin, there was an altar underneath a skylight. It was partially ringed by mirrors made of the rare silver we'd found in the mining complex, all aimed through a smoky and unusual lens that overlooked the room.

Around us, the symbols on the ground glowed a blazing silver-white, and Yvette stepped forward with a grim look. "The buffers didn't last as long as we calculated—we only have a short time to finish the final alterations. Everyone, I need you to do exactly as I say. If you follow instructions, we can finish this in time to prevent ourselves from being killed."

My battle joy from earlier faded, replaced by resolve. Yvette pointed out spots where we needed to be, positioning dozens of us for this one last push. As she did, those not involved took up their own positions, readying invocations to use to slow down the monstrous entity we were helping bring into the world.

Weakened, disoriented, unprepared—we'd made sure to arrange every possible obstacle we could in Suvaya's path. We needed to manifest and kill her before she tapped into the energy still in the ritual to create a proper body, or worse got to the mountain and used that. If she fully manifested, she could use the severed connections in the ritual to link up to everyone who had gotten any of the Moonglow Dew and then she'd be on her way back to full power and we'd be dead.

But hey, no pressure, right?

Chapter Sixty-Eight

"ALRIGHT!" Gabriel called. "Is everyone in position?" We'd finished altering the final aspect of the ritual, just managing to get it done in time. Now the ritual's power was being rerouted and was about to climax, and we were all tense and readying ourselves for this fight.

Nasha called out from her spot towards the back of the temple. "Binding team one is ready!"

"Binding team two is ready!" shouted a voice from the back I didn't recognize. It was echoed by two more, four binding teams for four limbs. Despite her stats being roughly the same as ours, Suvaya had been a god. We had no idea what kind of beneficial effects that would bring. Even without her own flesh to craft her body, her soul was bound to be freakishly powerful.

Our only potential saving grace was that her Impact couldn't withstand a soul that was so much more powerful. Two ranks was the hard limit for base level Impact, but she'd been a god, which meant she was likely going to be at *least* Master Candidate level with *every skill*. She would be like Abel on steroids.

"We've got incoming!" Bethy bellowed.

I grimaced and triggered my poison fire, readying my staff. Callie drew her daggers and took up a position at my side, both of us turned slightly to protect each other's blind spots. As we watched, the light from the lens condensed, shooting right down to the altar in the center of the room.

The white, milky stone absorbed the light and began to glow with an unearthly radiance. As we watched, lightning began to play along the runes on the floor, jumping back and forth in short arcs. As it climbed the walls, the runes increased in power, as did the electricity, until it hit the rim of the lens and condensed into an eye of lightning above the altar.

A beam of condensed electricity slammed down into the glowing stone, and the power coursed through the rock, bouncing back and forth and increasing in strength. I saw a lot of the power arc off, though, and it was obvious that not having her body to work from and having to use the backup was costing her most of the stats she'd saved up from the conduits.

Despite the leakage, I saw the stone begin to flake and crumble, bits of it falling off and chipping away with each arc until it was all gone and all that remained was a female body. The electricity condensed into a set of flowing silver robes and then hair, and with an explosion of power, Suvaya, Goddess of the Moon, stood and took her first breath in the mortal world for thousands of years.

Eyes still closed, she tilted her head back, exhaling the same silvery mist that condensed over the Lightblooms. As she did, her skin shifted, changing to become actual flesh from the stone it had been. Her eyes opened, swirling silver orbs that seemed to focus on all of us and none of us.

"Blood of my destroyers," she purred, her head cocking to one side like a hungry cat. "You've robbed me of my flesh." She glanced down at herself. "This form is... weak. You've killed my chosen. Or at least, most of them. Is that my own daughter I see behind you?"

Satala flinched but took a deep breath and pulled herself up straight. "Yes, mother. It is. This ritual was wrong. Our own people were going to be harvested. The descendants of those we swore to protect. I understand your anger, but I refuse to allow this."

"You... understand my anger?" the goddess said coldly. "You understand *nothing!*" Her eyes were wide with rage as she hissed at her daughter. "You accomplished nothing in your life I didn't give you. I *created* you. And now you side with our enemies over some thin-blooded descendants of the sheep who fawned over us?"

Satala looked wounded. "Mother, you taught me guarding our flock was our most important duty. That we needed to protect them above all else."

Suvaya laughed, a harsh, brittle sound. "Our flock? Tell me, do you think the inhabitants of this barren rock are all the descendants of those who worshipped me? Do you think I became a goddess on the belief of a few thousand or even a few million adherents? Where are the rest, Satala? Where are the prayers, the devotions, where are the beliefs? Why are the only worshippers I sense a few hidden cultists caught in this trap of my own devising?"

Seeing her daughter at a loss, the goddess smiled cruelly. "They're gone. All of them. Not dead, not at first. Defected. I was cast down, and they all turned their backs. Only a few of them made their way to this place when I called, before I was able to erect the distortions keeping the dungeon hidden. The rest turned their adoration to others, to the very gods that killed me. Tell me, then, what care I should show them? What duty do I have?"

"But the ones who came were your most faithful!" Satala protested. "They stood by you through the worst. Their descendants deserve our respect and loyalty."

"Their descendants deserve *nothing!*" roared the maddened goddess. "Simpering cowards too weak to make their way without me. Did they speak up when the others left? Did they spread the word of their goddess? Look at the state of them. A fringe cult hidden inside a population of millions, barely any worship to speak of."

I decided pointing out how hypocritical it was being equally pissed at the ones who betrayed her and the ones that didn't wasn't a great idea, so I kept quiet, but my hand tightened around my staff as I readied for combat.

Satala shook her head sadly. "You've lost your way. I refuse to stand by while you do this. I won't attack you, mother, I could never, but I stand with our people. Take that as you will." Her tone was blunt and forceful, and her jaw was clenched stubbornly as she spoke. It was clear she meant every word of it. Which was a good distraction for the skeletal hand that erupted from the floor to grab onto Suvaya's left arm.

The goddess's silver eyes narrowed in rage, but before she could react, a massive root ripped out of the ground and encircled her leg up to the knee, then a golden chain encircled her other leg, while the tail of a massive ethereal fox grabbed her remaining wrist. All four binding teams had moved like a well-oiled machine to lock her down.

Bethy stepped forward, ripping open her palms and splattering her blood on the floor. As the blood touched the stone, a transformation rippled across the ground. Grass grew, the earth shifted, and we watched in shock as a hill under a blood-red sky manifested in the real world.

Our usually jovial and flighty Vampire friend was glaring at the goddess, her eyes blood red all the way through, no iris or pupil, even as blood dripped from her tear ducts. Despite the sky, there was no moon, with the red light beaming from behind the clouds and illuminating the hillside.

"Domain," I murmured in shock. That made a bit of sense, considering all the stories about the Vampire, but it opened up so many more questions. Those would have to wait though, because it was clear Bethy couldn't hold this for long.

Above us, a green bear with six arms roared in defiance as Abel and Jessie pulled their new trick, and several other groups triggered invocations, lashing out at the restrained former deity. Fists, blades, animals, poison— every one of us let loose at her. I triggered Double Trouble, slamming the butt of my staff into the base of her skull with Mercy Kill, Marked for Death, Flurry of Blows, and any other useful ability I could tack on.

Her head jerked forward with a hiss and she whirled to glare at me, tearing through the skeletal binding and the root as she dove for me. There was a rush of darkness and cold as Callie yanked me through my own shadow, pulling me out of the way as the goddess's fist slammed into the air where I'd been so hard that the shockwave cracked the stone. Abel's condensed green punch smashed into the back of her head, pitching her forward, even as Gabriel's lance slammed into her kidney.

Snarling, she stomped down hard, tearing away the last two bindings with an explosion of force as she cratered the stone beneath herself and unleashed a wave of white flame that threw everyone back and off their feet. Abel, Jessie, Randall, and Benny, who were trying to recover, would have been sitting ducks for that burst except Valk erected a shield of blue gel in front of them to soak up the fire, though it started melting on contact.

Callie hissed in distress as she looked around. "Shit!" she cursed. "We lost all four binding teams and like eight of the attack teams."

"Gods, are they dead?" I asked in horror. "And thanks for saving me there Cal. If my head had still been there you'd have had to hose me off the walls."

"Of course," she said with a wan smile. "And no, not dead as far as I can tell—the breaking of the bindings soaked up a lot of the damage. Unconscious though, and not in good shape. I managed to pick up which were the worst when I was in the shadows, and Jessie is already on it. We need someone to pin Suvaya down while we get situated again. If we can't catch our breath, we're *screwed.*"

Suvaya spun in circles, staring at the blood-colored light and washed-out grass until she finally found Bethy. Our Vampire friend was still up, though she was nursing a broken and burned leg. Yvette appeared in front of her, along with Satala.

The goddess sneered at her daughter. "I thought you couldn't bear to harm me?"

"I can't," the silver-haired girl sadly. "But I can't let you hurt my friend, either. Bethany has been nothing but kind to me. I can't just stand by while you harm her."

While she stalled, I was trying to get my head on straight. This temple was big, but we'd decided early on that trying to mob Suvaya would just result in casualties. Most of the weaker members of the raid had been sorted into the teams, tens or more of them helping fuel invocations to minimize the attack vectors. Unfortunately, the attack that had crushed so many of those manifestations had knocked out a ton of people.

I caught Gabriel's eye, and he gestured for me to come over. Snagging Callie I triggered Double Trouble, appearing behind him without covering the intervening space. "What the hell do we do?" I asked the crusader tensely. "This is a fucking train wreck. We've got dozens of wounded and potentially a few dead. We planned this out to the most minute detail and it still wasn't enough."

Looking to where Yvette had engaged Suvaya with Satala supporting defensively to protect Bethy, I grimaced at the image of them getting knocked around. Bethy's Domain was weakening the fallen goddess, and it still wasn't enough to offset the advantage. Not in raw power, but in sheer skill level.

Gabriel grimaced, then looked to me and then Abel. He frowned slightly, then nodded. "Alright. I think I have an idea. We need to get over to where Apollyon is. We might have a way to offset her advantage, but it's going to be tough to pull off, and I'm going to need to teach you both some more about Paths."

Chapter Sixty-Nine

"You're sure this will work?" I asked Gabriel suspiciously. "Because…
I feel like it probably shouldn't based on everything I've heard about Paths
so far." From what I could tell, Paths were a deeply personal and unique
thing that made it possible for Ascendants to climb to a higher level after
becoming a Master. That last bit was conjecture, of course, but it lined up
with the obscure 'something else' Zeke had mentioned needing to advance
to D-rank.

"Not at all," he said bluntly. "I wouldn't even suggest trying it if we weren't
both about to die and in possession of these." He held up a hand with a
pair of glowing rings on it. "I took the opportunity afforded by our
comrades' distraction to approach Alistair and wish for the catalysts that I
believe will allow us to pull this off."

"What did you pay him for them?" I said, picking one of the rings up to
marvel at the delicate craftsmanship and the surreal glowing metal.

He gave me a flat look. "His life. I said we would save him if he gave them
to me. He seemed to think it was a fair deal. Wouldn't have worked with
you or Natalie, since you're friends and I planned on doing that in any
case, but I find Alistair repugnant at best, and his death wouldn't be particularly sad for me."

"Huh," I said with a nod. "Makes sense. What happens if you fail to save
him though?"

The big Crusader just shrugged. "Well, we'll most likely all be dead, so probably not much. But that seems like a problem for future Gabriel."

I laughed and slipped a ring on. "Fair enough. Let's do this then." I turned to my mentor, who had been unusually quiet. "You capable of this Abel? Honestly, I wouldn't blame you if you're not. I have no clue how I access my Path most of the time. These Resonance Rings will do the job, but we have to supply the fuel. I'm honestly shocked an F-ranked Wishmaster Candidate could make something like this."

"It's single use," Gabriel clarified. "They both are. They're linked to me because my Path seems to be the one best suited for this. Not that the both of you aren't going to be an important part."

I waved him off. "I get it, don't sweat that part. You'll be the one to finish this—I have no issues teeing up a winning shot."

That said, the rings were... weird. I wasn't sure how I felt about using them. Gabriel had warned us that the magic items could have some odd side effects for a bit. The necessary mechanism for pulling off the Crusader's plan was going to make this deeply unpleasant to experience.

When Abel finally nodded, now focused on losing himself in his own Path in preparation, I decided to cut the chatter too. I stepped back as Gabriel mounted his starlight charger, bringing his lance to bear. I wanted to stack a bunch of skills and abilities on it, but I knew that wasn't going to be helpful. Not for this. I'd need every ounce of soul strength I had to use these rings. Especially given they would be breaking down even as we formed the connection.

Unfortunately, this wouldn't be a quick process, at least not based on what Gabriel said. We needed time, which meant we needed a distraction. Yvette was doing her best, but the golem wasn't up to handling Suvaya. Despite being made of magical stones like the former goddess's new body, Yvette didn't have all the overpowered Skills and the terrifying soul the moon goddess could bring to bear.

That said, the golem was doing better than I had feared. Her blurring form and fluid movements allowed her to at least attempt to keep up with the silver-haired beast she was fighting. Satala was trying to cut in to prevent Yvette from becoming too damaged, but she was also guarding Bethy, whose Domain was hamstringing her mother enough for any of us to survive this.

For every blow that Suvaya took, Yvette took two, and they did more damage. Luckily for us, most of the teams were still in the game. A massive black flaming demon avatar manifested above Suvaya with a howl, and I saw Markoth standing over Nasha protectively with several other people joining hands to fuel his construct.

The turtle shell we'd used to escape Pallax came into shape around Satala and Bethy, and I spotted one of the Dew users with higher Impact channeling that one, alongside what looked like a twin to share the burden, supported by a crowd of Ascendants helping power the invocation.

Our second wind came as all the teams who hadn't been knocked flat in the first wave came together to help pin the vengeful deity while we got ready. Exhaling loudly, I closed my eyes, feeling Callie take up a protective position next to me as I let myself drift down the connection to the ring.

It was... weird. The sensation of being two people and also one person and then suddenly three people when Abel joined was strange. This had been the plan—the Resonance Rings were unique as far as we knew, and if they hadn't been single use and basically disposable quality trash they probably would have been too expensive to wish for.

The ones we'd gotten made us do the heavy lifting, but that was fine. I felt my place in our shared head, Gabriel's head, and Abel's as well. Gabriel was the momentum, the power and the force. I was the understanding, the guiding hand that lit the way, and Abel was the determination, the unflinching force of will.

Gabriel was a brilliant fighter with a lot of momentum, but he wasn't Abel. Being invincible might be good for confidence, but Abel's personality was tough as diamonds. The combination, guided by my Fatewalker instincts and the overlay, would be a winning one—if we could pull this off.

The world in front of me superimposed itself as my mind joined with Gabriel's and Abel's. I saw the temple from atop a starlight charger, staring down at my enemies from my invincible perch. Pushing with my soul, I triggered my overlay, and I saw the world resolve into a series of golden arrows. As we focused, I also felt a deep upwelling of fierce violent determination, like blood welling up from a puncture, and Abel was there besides us.

We had to adjust for a second—three souls weren't meant to exist in one body. I felt my soul begin to groan under the pressure as the ring on my hand cracked and spat, coming apart violently and threatening to drag me back into my own head. I pushed myself back down the link despite the blood I could feel leaking from my eyes, ears and nose.

I made a mental note. Just because wishes *can* let you do something doesn't mean you *should* do it. This wasn't natural. It was wrong and it was killing me. Still, it was already happening, and I shoved the damage and pain to the side, just as Abel did. Gabriel was mostly fine, thankfully, so the host body was holding up.

As one, the three of us threw back our heads, roaring out in defiance. "Rubrum gloria!"

Then, we charged. The sound of starlight hooves on black stone was like thunder carrying us to victory. The lance shone with a blinding golden light, and our full, combined power propelled us to glory. An Invincible spear guided by Fate and propelled by Blood slammed into the formerly stone body of the goddess and sent her into a spin as we rode past.

Swinging around at the end of our charge, we saw the damage it had done. Blood gushed from the hole in Suvaya's shoulder and she glared at us. "Insipid children! What is this abomination? You're tearing yourselves apart. To pervert the natural order in such a way is blasphemy."

We didn't bother responding. We charged. The feeling of being spurred on by the momentum of every victory, like a snowball rolling downhill and gathering speed, was intoxicating, and pushing it forward was the unbreakable will to do battle at any cost, my mentor's lust for blood and combat accelerating us. Three Paths superimposed on top of each other, and I could feel my soul about to collapse with the sheer power of it.

She was right—this was unnatural. But I didn't care. I wasn't going to let her hurt my friends, wasn't going to let her take anyone I loved from me. I'd had enough of ineffable forces snatching away people I loved without my permission. The WCP waves a hand and my dad leaves, my dad decides she should go and my mom leaves. I wasn't letting someone take away anyone else. Not Benny, not Jessie, and certainly not Callie.

The second pass slammed right into her chest, the glowing lance crashing into her sternum, lifting her off the ground and carrying her back. She howled in rage, hands going up and conjuring a giant spectral moon behind her, bringing it slamming down on our heads like a boulder.

Before it could hit though, a swarm of bats flooded the air above us, overwhelming the image and holding it back. Not just bats though—silver bats. I glanced over at Bethy (with my own normal bloody eyes somehow) and saw her latched onto Satala, drinking from her wrist with her eyes blazing the same blood red, except this time with silver irises.

I was jarred back to the present by the impact against the wall as the lance slammed through Suvaya's chest and heart, pinning her against the black stone. She snarled in rage, and she started to actually pull herself down the lance an inch at a time trying to get to us.

My soul was cracked and nearing shattering. I had nothing left in me, and the damned overlay faded but the rings were still holding on, leaving me trapped in Gabriel's body. I wasn't sure what would happen to us if we got killed in here, but I doubted it'd be good. Gabriel couldn't move, having channeled too much power himself tapping into the Paths all at once, and Abel had nothing left in him.

I watched the mad face of the enraged goddess draw closer and closer to us, teeth pulled back in a rictus of hate as she reached for us with deceptively small hands, ready to crush us into pulp.

And then a black staff smashed down on the goddess' head with a crack. I felt my bond with Callie manifest more strongly as I realized she'd taken my staff and was using our connection to wield it.

There was no style to it, no form or martial arts. Just rage and frustration as she hauled off like she was beating a pinata and slammed the staff down on Suvaya's skull over and over again. "Don't." Slam. "Touch." Slam. "My." Slam. "Fucking boyfriend!" That last smash included every ounce of death energy stored up in the staff since the fight with Pallax, including all the energy it had just harvested from Suvaya herself.

By the time Callie was done, the goddess's skull was shattered and her head was basically pulp. Callie stood over her, panting as she gripped the staff and stared down at the body of the fallen goddess.

I grinned as the ring finally shattered, catapulting me back into my body along with Abel. Callie, who had stepped into the shadows as she felt me revert through the bond, caught me and lowered me to the ground.

I was still smiling in relief as the world faded to black. It was all over.

Chapter Seventy

I woke up with my head killing me. Which was pretty nostalgic, because I'd managed to avoid knocking myself out from overexertion for quite some time. I groaned without opening my eyes. "Did anyone get the number of that planet-sized truck that hit me?"

"Pretty sure that's just the feeling of being blindsided by your own stupidity," drawled a familiar voice that I hadn't heard in what felt like forever.

I bolted upright in bed, eyes flying open as I twisted to find my uncle draped across a couch, quaffing a relatively large bottle of liquor. "Zeke!" I exclaimed. "You're here! That must mean..."

"The distortion is gone? Yep. It collapsed when the moon cracked. You missed quite a show." He scanned me over, obviously checking for damage. "Though you put a pretty decent one on yourself. That was pretty shocking —I was almost impressed."

My grin was smug. "Because I killed a god? I bet you've never done that. Well... Callie killed a god actually. Is she okay? She must be worried sick. I tried to keep the damage isolated from her."

He smirked. "I'm impressed that you managed to accidentally stumble upon the stupidest and most dangerous possible way to get yourself out of that situation. Did it not occur to you that there might be a *reason* people don't Path Stack?"

"I... thought we invented it?" I said with a wince. "Plus it was so damned useful. We never could have beat her without it."

He pinched his nose. "You may have homebrewed your Skill and stumbled on a Path early, but you're a ways off from reinventing the wheel, kid. Path Stacking is a known phenomenon, it's just considered reckless and dangerous and no one does it. Dying is the *best* of the possible bad outcomes. I've heard of path stackers fracturing their souls in such a way that they all mix, becoming a distorted mashup soul with qualities from all three and no sense of self."

"Oh," I said faintly. "I... was not aware that was a possibility." Note to self, no more Path Stacking.

That got me an eye roll. "The things you don't know could fill a planet of libraries. But it worked out. Smart using a wish as a buffer. They can pull off some crazy shit. Speaking of crazy shit, how's your soul doing? Bet you got quite a bump off a stunt like that."

Closing my eyes, I focused inward, blinking in surprise. "Thirty three percent of the way through Orange. That's a ten percent bump." The shield had given me a decent boost, but not *that* decent, and the further you refined a soul the harder it was to affect it, at least based on my observations.

"Very nice," Zeke said appreciatively. "Bet you have plenty of stats incoming, too. This mess isn't quite sorted, so the points are delayed, but you made a big difference in that fight. Of course, you didn't *finish* it, so you won't be getting most of the credit. Your girl is in for a hell of a boost."

I grinned at that. "I'm glad. She saved our asses out there. I thought Suvaya was going to kill us for a second." It also might help Callie pull further ahead and let her feel like more of an asset to the team. I was more worried about her downtrodden mood lately than getting credit for godslaying. I could always get the points through wishes later. Besides, she deserved to be treated like a hero—she really had come through in a big way. Even on the verge of death Suvaya was a massive threat. No one else had the guts to take the final shot. I was proud of her.

Zeke, who knew me better than anyone, just rolled his eyes. "Anyway. With all this over, several *very* powerful people are on the way. Luckily the contract you all signed will act as a template for this interaction. Smart move getting them all locked into an agreement in those circumstances.

Given their positions they all had emergency powers that make that kind of thing feasible."

That actually reminded me. "What about Satala?" I was worried they might decide to just ignore the contract and kill her just in case.

"You're concerned they might just ignore the terms and do whatever they want?" he asked archly. At my nod, his expression became a grin. "As well you should be. If one of the gods showed up, any agreement you made would have fallen apart. In the end, power is the only real currency in our universe. Luckily for your tinsel-topped project, the baby Vampire got attached. Lark is on his way apparently, and no one is going to tangle with his baby girl over a crippled former A-ranker."

"The Vampire is coming *here?*" I said in shock. "Are we going to meet him?"

"What are you, stupid?" my uncle asked in horror. "No, we aren't going to *meet* him. We're fucking leaving. He's not the only S-ranker coming, and we aren't going to be here when they all arrive. This planet is their problem now. Though it would be a good idea to pick up as much Dew as we can before we leave. With Suvaya dead the mechanism to condense it is gone, but Impact doesn't just vanish. All the Dew already on the planet is still here and after a quick once-over has been confirmed to be safe."

"Nat should be able to pick some up for us," I said in relief. "Part of the terms of the contract when we wished for the document we all signed."

"I saw," he said with a smirk. "You did a decent job on that thing. Eli would be proud. However much Dew you can get, I would do so. It's a nonrenewable resource. Still, don't spend too much time on haggling or searching. Like I said, I want to be gone when all those terrifying geezers hit the atmosphere. Shouldn't be more than a day or two, so do with that what you will. Once this is done we'll head for the Ruined Soul Temple."

I wasn't sure how long it would be until the trials. I didn't remember getting an exact date, but Zeke was the expert so I'd leave the travel arrangements to him if I could get away with it. As I had that thought, the door opened and Callie came blurring in, tackling me onto the bed. "Ow. Ow. Ribs!" I croaked as she squeezed me.

"Oh my gods," she said in dismay. "Did your ribs get injured in the battle?"

"No," I said with a chuckle. "Just when you squeezed me like an old tube of toothpaste. You're a godslayer now, honey—you'll need to be careful with all that muscle."

She rolled her eyes, but her lips quirked into a smile. "Oh please, I haven't even gotten my points yet. Seems like it'll be delayed a bit until the meeting. We're doing the ceremony thing again. Still not sure how that works, but Bethy knows how to delay the stats until they can hit all at once."

"Still," I said happily, "you're going to be famous for sure. No way it isn't going to get out. The first godslayer in... what, centuries?"

Zeke nodded. "At least. Probably longer. Closest we got recently was the Vampire's fight with Unity. I hear that was a hell of a dust up. Still, even then it didn't actually devolve too close to a deathmatch. There's a big difference between a mortal and a god." He grinned at Callie. "You're going places, kid. I'd start preparing for the stat drop, because it's going to be *rough.*"

Her face went slack. "Oh gods, I forgot about the pain from bulk stat gains. It's percentage based right? What do you think I'll be getting? A few hundred? Like a fifty percent bump tops probably, right?"

We both gave her a pitying look, and she slumped against me. I smiled and kissed the top of her head. "I'll try to offset some of the pain with the bond. I played a big part but I didn't finish her off. Plus my stats are crazy evenly distributed so chances are good I won't have too much in one spot."

"Alright, enough of your cuddling," my uncle said with a laugh. "You can gaze lovingly into each other's eyes later. None of the rest of us have time for that. Besides which, you have visitors, Shane."

Raising an eyebrow, I looked up to see Cass barrel into the room and throw herself bodily at me and Callie. We caught the little girl easily enough, and she dissolved into giggles as we did. Cark stepped in with a laugh. "Cass, you're supposed to be gentle with sick people, not smash into them at terminal velocity."

"She's fine," I said with a wave. "It's good to see you guys. Hope your time up there wasn't too boring? Was Zeke able to teach you anything?"

Cass completely ignored where I was looking, chirping, "Tony got beat up a whole bunch! It was really funny. I did all my forums just like Master taught me before he left. Why are you so sick, Shane? Did you eat something bad? You don't look like you got hurt so I think that must be it."

Zeke groaned. "It's *forms* Cassidy, and I told you not to call that brat Master. He isn't even close."

"Hey!" Abel objected from the door, where he was leaning against the frame looking nearly dead. "I'm definitely close. I'm an Expert. Don't be a snob you washed-up theater kid."

Cass's eyes widened and she jumped down and ran over to tackle-hug Abel, who apparently she hadn't gotten to see yet.

Zeke rolled his eyes. "I'm being mocked by babies now. Oh, how the mighty have fallen. Shouldn't you be in bed like he is?"

Mel, who was standing behind her boyfriend anxiously, nodded. "Yes, he *should*. Unfortunately, along with common sense and taste in music, he completely lacks any self-preservation instincts." With a huff, she smiled at Callie and me. "Good to see you two up and awake. Plenty of people have been hoping to talk to you."

"Me?" I said with a laugh. "I think you mean *her*. I was just riding shotgun with Abel and Gabe. I didn't put Suvaya down for good."

"You *literally* staked her out for me to kill," Callie said in annoyance. "I refused to talk to anyone until you woke up, and we've been holding off the stat gains. Zeke said not to do it before you, Abel, and Gabe woke up. The soul strain was bad—a big stat influx might have killed you."

I nodded in understanding. "Good call. I'm firmly against my own death. I'm surprised you aren't berating me for the risk to be honest."

She rolled her eyes. "I'm not insane. We all would have died if it wasn't for you three. I'm against you taking stupid risks when you don't think them through. This wasn't a stupid risk, it was a necessary one, so I'm not going to complain." She buried her head in my chest. "I'm just... so glad you're okay."

I squeezed her tight. "Only thanks to you, Cal. She'd have killed us for sure. In any case, I'm awake now, so let's get the meeting shit out of the way. I want to get the stats and start collecting as much Dew as possible before we have to leave. We have to be gone before all the S-rankers show up." I was just glad they were taking their time getting here. Then again, this whole mess was still a bit below their level.

Callie grinned and hopped off the bed, pulling me to my feet and throwing my arm over her shoulder. I wondered how many of the others were waiting. I hoped it wasn't all of them.

Chapter Seventy-One

"SHANE!" Benny said as he barreled into me, lifting me into a crushing hug. "You're up. I'm so glad you didn't scramble your egg by accident. Also, I want priority on wishes for a while. Seriously, between Jessie's bond with Randall and now all this shit, I'm lagging behind."

"Thanks for your concern, ass," I said with a chuckle. "But I'll see what I can do." I looked around and spotted Gabriel, Bethy, Satala, Markoth, and a bunch of the other people from the raid. "Hey guys, thanks for waiting— I heard we have a meeting to attend. We don't have to do this up on the mountain do we?"

Abel snorted. "Like they would leave that where it was. The first wave of seniors from the various factions snatched that up. Not sure who got it, but it's long gone."

"Valak Dante," Zeke said with a grimace. "A-ranker from the Labyrinth Lord's clan. Sneaky fucker. I'd have fought him for it if he wasn't so slippery." That was a stark reminder that Zeke wasn't a normal B-ranker, though I was guessing this Dante guy wasn't a combat focused A-ranker. I'd just gotten a clear lesson on how rough it was trying to punch up.

To my relief, the meeting happened in a nearby clearing. Apparently someone had texted everyone when I woke up, because the whole crew was there when I arrived. Well, the ones who were left. Which was apparently about eight hundred and fifty of us. I looked around, and the only person missing I knew was Chad, the team leader I'd met at the party back at the Bazaar.

It was rough to realize we'd lost so many people. I thought we'd all made it. Some of those unconscious people had never woken up. It was a stark reminder of the kind of danger we'd all been in.

Once we arrived, Callie got called up to address the group. She made a nice speech about using the contract we'd signed as a foundation for future cooperation, some comments that implied she might try to recruit some of them into my faction, and then officially called the task of defeating Suvaya to a close.

I'd positioned myself behind her, and when she collapsed, I caught her easily. Or at least, I would have if my own brain wasn't basically imploding from the pain. Not just my own pain either, but her pain as well. She was getting it much worse than me and I was glad I could offset some of her agony.

Once it was done, I lowered her to the ground, vision blurry, as I checked my own stats.

Wishmaster Candidate Status: F-rank.

Ability: Intermediate Wish—Six times a day, grant an Intermediate wish in return for proper compensation. Wish must be feasibly achievable by the candidate's own efforts within a three-day period with current statistics.

Might: 475 (+200)
Impact: 33
Fantasy: 500 (+200)
Vitality: 220
Focus: 220 (+52)
Perception: 204 (+24)
Creation: 180
Progress to next rank: 1832/10000

Soul Strength: Orange 33%

Stored: 7 shadow attacks, 7 shadow jumps, 10 Stealth charges, 5 triple-strength density shifted attacks, 9 spider leg attacks, 10 heal bursts (10 in reserve), 4 gravity attacks, 3 shadow clones, 21 scan heals (I-rank)

Pet: Wolf named Jin

Skills: Intermediate Path of the Doom Sovereign, Lesser Valtek Mastery, Lesser Cooking Mastery, Lesser Inventing Mastery, Minor Piano Mastery, Minor Guitar Mastery, Lesser Balam Mastery, Minor First Aid Mastery, Lesser Paired Dueling

Path of the Doom Sovereign:
Monk: Stone Limb, Moonlit Night, Consecration of Flame, Ripple Running, State of Grace, Steam Arrow, Afterburner, Pit of Despair, Mountain Stance

Rogue: Mercy Kill, Double Trouble, Touch of Tears, Flurry of Blows, Heavy Hands, Marked for Death

Diviner: Overlay, Song of the Soil, Rhythm of the Wild, Eye of Revelation, Danger Sense

Two hundred points of Might and two hundred points of Fantasy. That had been rough. The pain was based on percentage, and luckily I hadn't doubled either stat, so I wasn't *quite* fried out of my head, but Callie's boost had been much bigger than mine, and she'd gotten it bad. I rested her head on my lap, cleaning the blood off her nose and waiting for her to wake up. "Hey," I said with a smile as she eventually came around. "How are you feeling?"

She groaned. "I don't think this can be considered pain anymore. I need to invent a new word. I feel like bees made of molten bleach are colonizing my brain stem. My eyebrows hurt." I laughed and helped her up. "How about you? I know you took some of that for me. How are you still so… lucid?"

I shrugged. "My brain is pretty used to pain at this point. The Path Stacking was pretty much just as bad. So, how did you make out? I got four hundred points across two stats. Surprised it was so focused, but I guess my main impression was Might and Fantasy. Crazy impressive lightshow and big stabbing."

She giggled, then winced. "Ow. Stop making me laugh. Laughing hurts. Anyway, I think I did okay. Honestly, better than okay—I'm blown away."

Calliope Reynolds: F-rank.

Ability: Intermediate Abyssal Infiltration—Enter the shadows and emerge where you will within range. Shape the darkness to your call, moving it as if it were part of your body, and even extend your senses through the shadows to spy on your enemies.

Might: 1050 (+832)
Impact: 33
Vitality: 342 (+200)
Fantasy: 550 (+400)
Focus: 108 (+50)
Perception: 875 (+500)
Creation: 405 (+300)
Progress to next rank: 3443/10000

Soul Strength: Orange 14%

Pet: Wolf named Rellia

Skills: Minor Tracking, Minor Dual Dagger Mastery, Beginner Stealth, Beginner Trap Mastery, Beginner Disguise, Lesser Balam Mastery, Beginner Shadow Manipulation Mastery, Lesser Paired Dueling

"Holy Shit!" I gaped at her. "That's... so fucking many stat points. Eight hundred and thirty-two might? Five hundred Perception? Four hundred Fantasy? Three hundred Creation? I know you killed a god but *damn.* No wonder it hurt so fucking much. Over two thousand points. You almost literally tripled your total. And congrats on the increase in your soul strength. I know you've been working on that. Five percent is a nice jump." The bump to Focus was probably just the natural drift from her being higher ranked. Lagging stats tended to creep up naturally.

"Your staff mastery jumped up a rank though," she pointed out brightly. "And your soul is *way* more advanced."

"Hey, I'm not complaining," I said with a grin. "I'm used to chasing after you. I just need to step up my game a bit. You're pulling ahead again." I frowned. "I'm honestly surprised it was only this much. For slaying a god I'd have figured you'd have hit E-rank or something."

"Not a chance," Zeke said with a laugh. "There are limits to bulk drops of renown. She'll get a steady income over time for this, but remember, just like you need stats to withstand Impact bestowal on rank up, you need Impact to withstand mass stat dumps. It's cyclical and builds on itself. That's why we improve one step at a time. Don't worry, though—the story is only just getting started disseminating. She's bound to keep riding that rocket through F-rank at least. Probably further."

I grinned at her. "See! You're in the fast lane. Now I'm going to be playing catchup." She squealed and reached up to wrap her arms around me, but Zeke caught her.

"Whoa there," he said sternly. "Let's not pulp the nephew. Your Might just pretty much quadrupled. You need time to adjust so you don't accidentally murder people when patting them on the back. One of the downsides to fast growth. We'll have plenty of time for you to train on the way to the Ruined Soul Temple. We're taking the long way since we have some time. Which is good—you'll all need some serious training before the trials."

"After we pick up some more Dew," I stated. "An Impact advantage isn't something we can give up. But before we do that, I want to check with everyone else. I bet they got some pretty solid boosts."

I stood on shaky legs, helping Callie up, and we made our way over to Gabriel and Bethy, who were seated with legs crossed, having apparently been way better prepared for this than we had. Why hadn't I decided to sit down? Rookie mistake.

Gabriel nodded as we approached. "Shane, Callie. You look like you had decent returns. Especially you, Callie. I imagine as the final victor you've gotten quite a boost. Your condition certainly suggests that."

Bethy nodded cheerfully. "He's right! You look terrible! I did pretty well I think. My Domain helped out a lot, and people saw me tank that moon attack for you guys at the end. Still, I think aside from Callie you three are the big winners. I bet you'll get some more points off this over time."

Gabriel shrugged. "I'm approaching E-rank, and once I cross the dividing line, those trickling stats will be far less of a benefit. As big of an ordeal as this has been, it's still just an unusual dungeon run. It's a big universe, and strange things happen every day. I doubt this will carry us as far as you might expect."

"Boo! Hiss!" Bethy jeered, literally saying the word hiss instead of hissing. "Don't be such a buzzkill, Gabe. Don't you know frowning ages you? Speaking of, you guys totally have to meet my daddy when he shows up! He'll be so excited to meet my friends."

We all flinched, and Callie offered her a weak smile. "Oh, sorry Bethy, we can't stick around. We have those trials in the Ruined Soul Temple coming up. Have to head out so we can make it on time. We're taking the long way apparently." I had zero idea what the long way even *was*, but I didn't let that stop me from using it as an excuse. Having seen Bethy in full Vamp mode, I didn't want to meet her dad, who was the person who *created* that state of being.

She pouted. "Oh, fine." Then her face lit up. "Ooh, I can come to the trials too! Daddy says it's really important to reach the peak of green soul in F-rank. If you wait longer, you'll be behind once your soul solidifies at D-rank. He says achieving that edge of blue soul quality is called the 'Azure Soul Body' and that it's a necessity for anyone who wants to become a god."

I hadn't known about the name, though I knew the rest of it. Still, scary dad aside I welcomed Bethy. The more friends we had in the trials the better... probably. I still wasn't sure what they were exactly, but I wasn't complaining either way. Before we headed off to search for Dew though, I pulled Gabriel aside. "Alright. You were being vague earlier. Faction secrets, whatever, but you know something about my mom, and I want to know what it is."

He stared at me with a complicated expression for a minute, then nodded. "You're right. We've been through quite a bit together. I've seen into your soul from a certain viewpoint, and I trust you. This isn't common knowledge, so I hesitated to speak on it earlier. I only know about it because I met her. It concerns the reason that the Star Queen will be at the Ruined Soul Temple to begin with."

I frowned. "That's a good point—why is an elite A-ranker being sent to babysit a bunch of kids? Important or not, that seems like it would be beneath her."

"It would be," Gabriel said, his face blank, "except for one small factor. The Star Queen isn't going to the Temple to babysit a bunch of kids. She's going there to babysit her own. She's attending the trials to bring along her daughter." He gave me a sympathetic look. "I don't suppose you know about it, based on your earlier comments, so I suppose I'll be the first to inform you. Apparently you have a sister."

Chapter Seventy-Two

I ADMIT, my mind was a mess after finding out about my sister. My mom had another kid. Was she Dad's? Did Mom have a new family? Was that why she left us? But what role did Dad play in that? I'd come to the conclusion from things Zeke hadn't said that Dad had chased Mom off or at least was involved in her leaving.

Callie sat next to me, holding my hand and looking worried. I appreciated the concern, but I forced down the bad feelings. I was going to see my mom soon and could ask her this in person. I wasn't going to let it ruin my time with my friends. Family drama could wait. I looked up at Benny, who was nearby, waiting quietly with Celine. Clearing my throat, I forcibly changed the subject. "So, Ben, how did you do?"

Gabriel had long since left, and we'd retreated so I could get my head on straight, grouping up in a clearing. My best friend looked surprised but also relieved to have the out. "Pretty well, honestly. I was kind of worried since I didn't play a big part in the final battle, but I guess all the calculations and mapping I did during the hunt for the conduits left an impression, even after Yvette showed up."

Benicio Cortez: F-rank.

Ability: Intermediate Mechanical Embodiment—Allows

the integration of existing inventions into the user's body for the purposes of strengthening and enhancing them.

Might: 405
Impact: 32
Fantasy: 56 (+40)
Vitality: 41 (+10)
Focus: 683 (+220)
Perception: 82 (+40)
Creation: 71 (+40)
Progress to next rank: 1370/10000

Soul Strength: Orange 19%

Pet: Wolf named Rolf

Current integrated tech: 9/10.
Torso: G-ranked intangibility for short bursts.
Right fist: triple punch.
Left forearm: F-ranked energy barrier or variable shape.
Left fist: minor slow-acting tranquilizer effect.
Right foot: density shifting to create heavier kicks and more powerful jumps.
Left foot: momentum neutralization to allow stopping instantly.
Head: slight cognitive boost to allow more thinking time.
Back: ability to grow a shell to tank damage.
Chest: pair of golden G-rank spider legs that arch up from the shoulders.
Waist: belt of spiritual calming

Skills: Minor Cooking Mastery, Intermediate Inventing Mastery, Minor Haggling Mastery, Minor Stealth Mastery

"Not a massive bump compared to you guys," he said after sharing, "but two hundred twenty points in Focus as well as some natural creep in most of my other stats isn't bad at all." He glanced over at our resident healer, who had been extremely quiet, clearly as worried about me as the others. "How about you, Jess? Bet you did pretty well, considering not only did you heal most of the wounded, you also helped Abel make that crazy bear construct."

She brightened a bit, looking excited. "Yeah, that helped a ton I think. As usual, technically everything I do leans mostly to Vitality. I got a bit of general creep, and some Might, but I got a *lot* of Vitality."

Jessica Evans: F-rank.

Ability: Intermediate Lifeweaving—Infuse living things with life itself and direct their actions while the user's power flows through them. Control has limited effect on sapient entities. Prolonged exposure to life energy may cause lasting effects in controlled subjects.

Might: 375 (+225)
Impact: 32
Fantasy: 78 (+50)
Vitality: 1292 (+530)
Focus: 55 (+30)
Perception: 65 (+50)
Creation: 58 (+50)
Progress to next rank: 1955/10000

Soul Strength: Orange 14%

Pet: Wolf named Lily and bear named Randall (Beginner Beast Bond)

Skills: Beginner Horticulture, Beginner First Aid, Minor Herbalism, Minor Flower Arrangement, Minor Beast Taming Mastery, Beginner Beast Bonding, Intermediate Shape of the Wild

"Five hundred thirty points of Vitality, two hundred twenty-five of Might, plus various bumps to lower stats," she said proudly. "I'm right on the edge of two thousand total. Plus my soul is up to fourteen percent. Benny's got his spiritual calming so he jumped higher there, but my bond with Randall is a steady and consistent stress on my soul. I think it's really helping."

"How the hell did you get so much?" demanded Benny in flabbergasted amazement. "You barely even *did* anything! You got more than Shane!"

She sniffed haughtily. "I healed a bunch of people, and obviously they talked. My influence had a big and noticeable impact on the battle, and people love to gush about healers. Shane got less of the renown because he landed a non-finishing blow. People love to exaggerate and twist retellings, and talking about how Callie single-handedly killed a goddess is a much better story than saying she did it with help."

Benny grimaced. "At this rate you'll keep getting further and further ahead of me. Am I ever going to have the chance to catch you?"

Seeing it laid out like that I realized Benny was right—he was lagging behind. Sure his Focus was a huge help here, but he hadn't been in the fight as directly. He needed my focus for the next few months until we could catch him up. Not to mention his soul improving at the temple meant he might be able to push up to Expert in Inventing and exert more control over what he made.

"Well, sounds like we all made progress," I said cheerfully, hoping to redirect some of my friend's bad mood. "Now, why don't we talk about getting some more Dew before we leave. Now that Suvaya is gone it's just free-floating impact. Think we can buy some off Ladrigan or some of the other outsiders? We still have plenty of things worth trading for. The metals from the mining complex and the spellbooks we got from the wizard's tower."

"You want to trade those?" Callie said in shock. "I thought for sure the idea of learning magic would have been too big a temptation to pass up."

I shrugged. "It normally would, but in the end, more Skills are just going to pull focus. Sure, I could merge them into my DS Mastery, but honestly I need to learn to use the Skill as it is—complicating it more won't help. Meanwhile Impact is a method to pull ahead of our competitors and keep ourselves safe. It's kind of a no brainer."

She shrugged. "You're not wrong. It's a solid plan; I was just surprised. I can call up Anna-Marie and set a meeting if you want. There must have been other teams that arrived after we left, at least before this whole mess, plus they had native forces searching. With the dungeon open to the world again, Impact is going to be less valuable to the locals than support from larger organizations."

I nodded. "I could see that. Any random E-ranker should be able to take on the king, and if not one, then two. Being exposed to the whole universe like this, they're better off finding a backer. No way they can hoard all that Impact for themselves. If they don't sell to us, chances are good someone less pleasant will just take it by force."

"That's a good point," she said with a wince. "In the meantime, we should definitely talk to some of the others. Gabriel mentioned finding some Dew didn't he? I'm not sure he'd trade it normally, but the spellbooks we found are rare and hard to get too. I'd bet we have some options that would fit well with some of his people." She grimaced. "I wish we could just ask Zeke to find the stuff for us, but that would definitely violate his geas."

"True," I said with a nod. "But with so many people showing up, I'd bet we could arrange for some Dew another way." I glanced over at Nat. "Twelve wishes. Think we can get some of the teams from the other factions to do our work for us?" Between the wishes, the metals, the spellbooks, and Nat's first dibs on materials, I was betting we could scrounge up enough of the Dew to get some for everyone.

My cousin's eyes sparkled. "That's a fantastic idea. Most of the smaller faction members won't be able to hold onto their Dew anyway when the big boys start arriving. Better to sell it off for something as incredibly valuable as a wish. I'll go talk to some of the other teams about the wishes and the spellbooks while Callie reaches out to the locals." She gave me an encouraging smile. "You just buck up, okay?"

My groan of exasperation got a chuckle from Benny as everyone scattered, Jessie heading off to try to feel out some of the people she healed while Celine went with Nat. Abel was around somewhere, probably nursing a headache after the soul damage plus the stats.

I sighed, looking at Benny. "You gonna give me the 'it's okay pal' treatment too?"

He shrugged. "Honestly, I don't think having a sister is as bad as it seems to you right now. Sure, it's not ideal to find out like this, but you and Maria always got along great. Doesn't it seem like it might be kind of cool having one? Sure you don't know her, but you can change that. Did Gabriel tell you her name?"

"Chelsea," I said matter-of-factly. "Her name is Chelsea and she's eighteen. My mom took her away for some reason when I was two, not that I remember her. Hell, I barely remember Mom. She clearly cares a lot about her since she's taking up the chaperone position on this trial. Based on what I've heard, she isn't the type to babysit. She's supposed to be my grandfather's iron fist."

I tried not to be jealous, but the thought of my sister living the life I could have had… raised by mom, considered a princess by the Church and taken care of with the best of her generation… Well, it was difficult not to resent that a bit.

Benny nodded sympathetically. "Have you talked to Zeke about all this?"

"What's the point?" I asked with a shrug. "He can't tell me anything. I'd imagine the reason the geas tightens up so much when my mom comes up is specifically because my dad didn't want me to know about my sister. Gods only know why, but then, who knows why my dad does anything."

He shook his head. "Your family is a mess, man. But hey, at least you've got Nat and Zeke. Plus your sister might be cool, and you can still try to talk things out with your mom."

"I will. For now, let's go check in with Bethy and Satala, see how they're doing after all this." The silver-haired girl had been present for her mother's gruesome death, so I wanted to make sure she was okay. Plus Bethy was going to be leaving much later than the rest of us since she was waiting for her dad. I wanted to say goodbye at least.

We found her easily enough. She had Donuts and Poptarts both out, and they seemed okay. Whatever damage being out of Bethy's shadow had done to Donuts at the beginning, apparently it could be staved off under the right circumstances. When she saw us, she squealed and clapped her hands. "Shane! Benny! It's good to see you guys. I was just helping Tala pick her new clothes. She's decided to stay on as one of my thralls!"

She gestured grandly to where the former A-ranker was standing shyly, wearing a pair of dark blue pants covered in buckles, a white tank top with a silver snowflake on it, and some lilac sleeves that weren't attached to anything. The finishing touch was a dark blue beret sitting askew on her head. She seemed… better than I expected. A bit lost, but not as upset as I'd have figured.

Despite that, I could see Bethy was trying hard to distract her, and of course the Vampire fashionista had decided to dress her new thrall up. I smiled and waved at her. "Hey Satala, haven't seen you since the fight. Hope things are okay."

"Of *course* they are!" Bethy squealed energetically. "Tala is going to stay and keep an eye on this place. Daddy says he's going to claim it and give it to me as a present. It's only F-rank so no one is going to fight him too much on it, though he says he's going to have to let them take some of the Dew. Cost of doing business and all."

I just gaped at her, having not expected *that* even if I probably should have. Then I chuckled, shaking my head, and Benny and I sat down to catch up with the both of them. Good for Bethy—it was nice to know this place would be taken care of at least. Satala obviously cared about it a lot.

Until Lark's arrival, I'd leave the others to work on sourcing that Dew. If they couldn't get enough we could ask Bethy for some before we left. For now, I'd just enjoy spending time with friends.

Chapter Seventy-Three

"ALRIGHT, SO HOW DID WE DO?" I asked my group as everyone gathered up to submit all the Dew they'd gathered. "Remember, Zeke wants us gone before the Vampire gets here, so to be safe this is our last day on planet. Nat and I managed to gather thirty-six drops total between us, three per wish. Plus another twenty-seven on her part gathered as first dibs." Thankfully we'd already used some, so the subjective value was lower.

Callie grinned. "Between the metals and the spellbooks we managed to swing fifty-two." She seemed pretty happy with the haul. "Anna-Marie came around to our way of thinking easily enough. Since there was little chance they could keep any stockpiled drops, they figured it was a better idea to trade it for future favors and wring as much value out of it as possible, especially since the king has already reached full saturation."

"More than a hundred then," I said with a grin. "We'll give the excess to the group members who didn't get any before, fully distributed we should be looking at enough to get us each to about thirty five Impact. It's not forty, but that was never going to happen on a large scale." I glanced over at Zeke. "You sure we can't stay and compete for more?"

"Nope," he said cheerfully. "I've already arranged our ride out of here. Cashed in a favor with an old friend and caught passage on a transport ship. Like I said, we're taking the long way to the temple. The trial won't be starting for a few months still, and sitting around there waiting won't accomplish much. Better to spend the time improving and getting used to your new abilities."

That made sense. "So, where is this ship then? Do we need to find a way back up to the Bazaar to get on?" I was kind of excited. Teleporting was great, but I was going to be getting on an actual spaceship. Flying through *actual* space. Despite having crossed a galaxy, I hadn't really had a chance to enjoy that kind of travel. Now I was going to become a real citizen of the universe.

He shook his head. "They're coming to pick up some of their own kids, so they'll be providing a shuttle. The ship itself is too big, so it'll be parked in orbit. The shuttle should arrive in a few hours, so take the time to say your goodbyes and use up that Dew. Carrying it onto a huge ship full of strangers would be pretty stupid."

We distributed the Dew, and each of us secluded ourselves to take it, prepared for the insanity to come and wanting to minimize exposure. As for goodbyes, we really only had a few friends here. Bethy and Gabriel were both planning to attend the trials (the Crusader was going to be hitching a ride) so we'd see them there. We hadn't gotten too close to anyone else.

Satala would be staying to govern the planet in Bethy's stead, so we would need to say our farewells to her, and Yvette was sticking around to help her, so that was one more person to see us off. We also had to visit Anna-Marie and wish her well—she'd been a good friend to us since we'd been here.

Despite how busy we were, the time flew by surprisingly fast. I took the drops slowly, letting my soul process them since I was still a bit injured. With the improvements, though, it wasn't too big of a problem. Still, I was pretty sure thirty-five Impact was the limit of what my friends could handle, anyway, given their soul strength. I could probably have managed thirty-seven if we'd had the Dew for it, but it was more important to get all of us on a similar level.

Once everyone had gotten caught up and said their goodbyes where needed, we all filed out to a large open field to wait for the shuttle. To my surprise, the 'kids' that were getting picked up were Annalise and her team, and we waved to the fae girl as we settled in to wait.

It didn't take long before the shuttle (a monstrous open-sided ship made of black iron that glowed with runework) descended. The enchantments were tiny but carved in spiraling designs that enhanced the ferocious image of the shuttle, making the jagged dark edges look even more imposing.

Callie bumped me with her elbow. "We totally need to get one of those. I bet I could even imbue it with shadow energy!"

Normally I worried about her driving, but since the sky was basically infinite, if she could literally merge into the shadows it should be fine. Actually, given her ability to view things through the dark, I was betting with access to a shadow-imbued vehicle she'd be a flawless driver now, or at least much better able to avoid accidents. Still, in my head I couldn't shake the image of all the dings on her bike. Best to let Jessie do the driving.

I made a noncommittal noise as we headed for the shuttle and got a suspicious glare as she picked up my emotions through the bond. Once we were on board we sat down on the padded leather couch, taking advantage of the spacious interior (bigger on the inside) while we settled in to wait for the trip to be over.

My own mind was kind of blown when no doors or anything closed. The shields kept the air inside, and we got to watch in real time as the shuttle rose, the ground falling away as the planet started to recede. I gave a bittersweet smile as I looked down at it.

I'd been through a lot since becoming an Ascendant, but the Moonsong Glade had been a special experience. No Zeke, no family nonsense really, just crazy Ascendant bullshit I hadn't expected and had to adapt to. We'd made friends, fought battles, and established even more of a reputation than we'd had before. Now we were heading back out into the universe stronger than we'd ever been and ready to take on whatever came next.

We saw the jungle spanning the core, the massive mountain range of the ring… and then the Glade fell away and we were staring out into the perfect dark of outer fucking space. I put an arm around Callie and just stared in awe and wonder at the emptiness of space firsthand. The Bazaar had been huge, so it had just been like looking at the night sky, but actually being out here was… amazing.

"It's so… dark," Callie murmured in a daze. "I've seen dark before, but that's nothing compared to this. Shadow is only the absence of light, but this… it's like it's swallowing everything. Like a bottomless abyss." Her tone was soft and shocked, like she was being hypnotized. I could feel through the bond she was in a weird state, but before I could shake her out of it, Zeke put a hand on my shoulder.

"Whoa kid, hold up. She's gaining enlightenment." He seemed genuinely amazed. "That's extremely rare, especially at lower ranks. Might be because of all the renown she's gained recently pushing her forward. She might be on the edge of discovering a Path, or at least the nascent version of one."

"Is that a big deal?" I asked, raising my eyebrow. "I mean, Abel and I both have a Path, and so does Gabriel. I mean, it's good that she might step onto one, but it's not like it's some crazy thing."

Zeke rolled his eyes. "Kid, you need a Path to advance to D-rank. It's one of the requirements for Mastery. Plenty of people *never* develop one, and the ones who do usually do it at the peak of E when their souls are notably higher quality and they have a lot more raw stats to stack up for it. Abel is a freak, and so is that Gabriel kid, and you just happened to get stupidly lucky."

I'd kind of figured that D-rank thing out from what he'd said about it before, but it was nice to have confirmation. Since it was a rare opportunity, I went ahead and left Callie to contemplate her possible Path and went back to staring out at the vast expanse of nothingness in front of us.

At least... it was nothing to start. Then we reached the right height and turned, and suddenly my vision was absolutely filled with a metal behemoth of a vehicle. Dark metal plating sprawled for miles below us as it loomed over the Moonsong Glade like a specter of death.

"That," Zeke said with a grin, "is the Necromedes, the current flagship of Killian Zayne, the Black Arbiter. Kill and I go way back. His father was actually the one who taught me the Soul Dissection Skill that I used to create my Voltomancy ability. He and Eli and I went on plenty of adventures together. He was the second of our little group to hit A-rank actually. But I don't count it because the Zayne clan is old as dirt." He cut off with a wince—the geas.

I was fascinated by the idea that my parents had once been in a group like mine. The geas triggering meant that Killian Zayne might know more about my mom and dad, too. I'd definitely ask him about it if I got the chance.

As we approached the ship, the form of the Necromedes loomed larger in my sight, consuming the whole of my view as we approached a small open bay that seemed to be protected by a similar shield to the one keeping us all from being sucked out into space.

Touching down, I turned to check on Callie, who was still in a bit of a daze. Taking her arm in mine, I led her off the shuttle, leaving her to process whatever she'd gained from the view. The whole thing made me incredibly curious about how things like renown and the soul played into Path formation. It made sense it would all be intertwined, but I wasn't sure how.

The bay around us was completely empty, with only some other shuttles around. Zeke gave a whistle. "Man, Kill's taste is as bad as ever. These things look like they were hammered together out of scrap."

"At least I don't paint porcelain masks like a weirdo," bit out a voice from behind us. Turning, we saw a tall, thin man, his pale chest exposed by his long red velvet coat, which lay open down to the ankles of his leather pants. His eyes were a swirling mix of red and black and his hair was black and white, split right down the middle. It should have been too much honestly, but weirdly he pulled it off.

Zeke grinned at him. "You might want to invest. Your face is pretty terrifying—a few nice masks to put people at ease could only help. I can't imagine the scare you get when you look in the mirror."

The tall man laughed, stepping up to hug my uncle and clapping him on the back before pulling away to nod at us. "This is Eli and Sasha's kid, huh?" he said with interest. "Poor kid takes after his dad far too much. Oh well. Welcome to the Necromedes, everyone. I guess I should probably show you around."

And with that, he turned and strode off, leaving us all to stare after him for a second before following. Man, why were all the high rankers I knew so weird?

Chapter Seventy-Four

THE NECROMEDES WAS both huge and fascinating. As expected, it was bigger on the inside, but aside from the outer layers where the docking bay had been, the interior was wide and open like a floating city. There was even a sky, presumably made through enchantments.

Rather than being all dark and depressing, the interior felt like we were standing on a mountain peak, cold, chill air wrapping around us. Killian looked pretty proud to show everything off. "We tend to use the flagship for VIP transport when possible. The favors and payments we extract are always useful, and unlike most clans, the Zaynes have no stable location to defend. We're spacefaring, so don't need to worry about being attacked so easily. It's a win-win."

"I still say it's not the same," disagreed Zeke. "Something about having real, hard dirt under your feet is just… different. Fake it as well as you want, but I'll take planetary living any day of the week."

Killian shrugged. "Yeah, but you're a snobby artist. I still can't believe you took my family's soul stitching Skill and turned it into arts and crafts. My ghost binding talent is so much more useful, which is obvious since you still haven't hit A-rank with your ridiculous clown faces."

"Empty shells," sneered Zeke. "They keep their stats but lose their ability. What's the difference between that and using golems? Sure you can have way more of them, but an army of generic ghosts can't compete with my capacity to use more than a dozen different abilities."

This sounded like an old argument, so I jumped in, cutting them off before they could get sucked in. "So, your whole family lives in space?"

Killian refocused on me. "Oh sure. My son Blake is around here somewhere. And my wife Cara. My whole branch is on this ship." That didn't fit with what I knew of branches, and my confusion seemed to be easily visible, even behind my mask, because he laughed and elaborated. "S-rankers start branches of god factions, or their own clans, but S-ranked clans with only one S-ranker can benefit from branches as well. In those cases, A-rankers are allowed to branch off."

"Forgive me for saying so, but you don't… seem like an A-ranker." I'd half expected him to be a hundred feet tall and breath fire, considering what A-rankers were capable of.

He just chuckled. "I consider that a compliment. Only weaklings and incompetents flex their power unconsciously. Restraint is an important component to success. I'm sure you've long since realized that Zeke doesn't let out most of his strength when he's around you. It would be massively inconvenient to smash everyone you meet into gibbering paste just by your sheer presence."

We chatted for a while as we walked, learning more about the Zayne family and the Necromedes itself, until we finally came to a wide-open area with a massive white stone building. Killian stopped. "This is our training hall. Lots of cutting-edge equipment in there. Some high-Impact exercise gear for training, targets for practicing dangerous abilities, and even sparring golems that can be set to variable levels for both combat skill and raw power."

Zeke sniffed. "It's a bit low-tech, but it's not like we can't make do." He kept his haughty expression for a second, then winked. "Kidding, thanks for the help." His eyes drifted to me. "This is already as close to overt help as I can give you on this. Technically speaking I just happened to ask a friend for a ride to ensure our safety. Him allowing you to use his training hall is a coincidence. That said, I won't be able to do anything to help directly."

"It's fine," I said with a chuckle. "I'm grateful you managed to find us a place to improve. We've probably got a lot more points coming in the next few months, and having somewhere to acclimate and work on our combat abilities will be important if we want to do well at the trials. Speaking of which, what *are* the trials? Like do you have any hints you can give on passing them?" I glanced at Killian. "Either of you?"

They shook their heads, our host answering for both of them. "Nope. They actually change, so we can't give specifics, really. Not to mention the trials don't take place on the physical plane. The Ruined Soul Temple is a spiritual space, and almost all of the memories you make there get left behind when you emerge. I've been myself, and so has Zeke, but we only have a vague understanding of what's there."

I cursed. "Damn. Well, thanks for telling me what you could at least. How about the timeframe? How long do we have on here? Zeke said we're taking the long way."

"Yup. Lady Valsara, the fae who contracted us for the pickup of her daughter Annalise, is also planning to do some training before arriving at the temple." He winked at me. "We get paid more this way, so I don't mind. It'll be about three months. If I were you, I'd use it on soul tempering. Having a higher soul will give you a huge advantage in the Temple. The better your soul the higher your starting point. Even if we forgot most of it, that much is easy to remember."

Abel grinned at that. His soul was at the peak of yellow, having been boosted a full grade on rank-up just like the rest of us, and having already reached the peak of orange in G-rank. Training the soul past one full rank ahead (Master Candidate status) required special resources and techniques, or places like the Ruined Soul Temple. Hearing that he'd have an advantage in the trials had to be pleasant for him.

Of course, I was betting there would be plenty of other Master Candidates showing up to this if that was the case, and probably even monsters whose souls had advanced to a level close to the two-grade-higher limit. Since the Ruined Soul Temple trials gave prizes, some of those clan heirs who had trained on their family's own inheritance would probably make an appearance to try and sweep the rewards.

The thought of fighting more people like Abel was... kind of exciting. And I had three full months of training against Abel himself to hone those skills. My mentor had beaten me before, but that had been a while ago. And I'd come damned close to winning. I'd advanced quite a bit since then in terms of combat fundamentals.

I felt Callie start next to me and glanced over to check on her. She looked pretty intense, glancing around wide-eyed as if she had no idea where she was, but I could tell from the bond that she was excited. Apparently she'd had some success with whatever comprehension of her Path she was working on. I wanted to ask about it, but now definitely wasn't the time.

So we followed Killian, enjoying the tour and listening to his stories for an hour or two, until finally the A-ranker was called away and left us to head to the dining hall to grab something to eat. It had been most of the day since my last meal, so I for one was pretty damned hungry.

Sitting down at a table, we all ordered food from one of the waiters they apparently had on staff here full time, and then I gave my girlfriend a curious glance. She shook her head, giving me a quick 'later' gesture, and then asked me to fill her in on what she'd missed during her downtime.

"Huh. This place is pretty cool," she said in wonder, glancing around the dining hall to try to see something interesting. Of course, we were in a building so she didn't see anything but tables and food, but for my girl-friend, the latter would always be the most important thing in the room. "Also those steaks smell *amazing.*" She grinned at me. "Honey…"

"No," I said flatly. "You got an eighteen-ounce ribeye and like four sides. I'm not sharing.

"But I'm so *hungry,*" she moaned, letting her head slump to the table dramatically. "I used so much energy on my epiphany, I need sustenance."

I glanced at her suspiciously, then over to Zeke. "Is that actually a thing? Do epiphanies make you hungry?"

"I'm pretty sure *breathing* makes her hungry," he said wryly. "But I guess it's possible soul strain from working on a potential Path would drain stamina? Theoretically? Seems like a stretch, but you might as well just give up on your steak and order another one."

I rolled my eyes with a sigh, nodding my head and eliciting a squeal of delight from Callie, who threw herself on me in a crushing hug. I smiled under my mask where no one could see, closing my eyes and enjoying the warmth of us all being together.

In the background, Cass, who had been unusually quiet from her spot riding on Randall, started to chatter excitedly to Jessie, who laughed as she entertained the smaller girl. Nat's guardian, Selka, was haranguing my cousin, asking her rapid-fire questions since she had only been allowed to join up with us at the last minute. I thought her being so worried was sweet, but Nat mostly just seemed annoyed. Benny was sitting next to me, and as the food arrived and I gave mine to Callie and ordered more, he rolled his eyes and cut half a steak and dropped it on my plate.

"Thanks," I said with a solemn nod, which he returned. I wasn't just talking about the food, and he knew it. Benny had been there through the whole dungeon mess, often relegated to the back line, and he'd come through for us every time it mattered. He'd been patient and helpful if slightly annoying, ready to do anything he could to turn things around.

Jessie and Callie were both mostly taken care of in terms of growth, and that left Benny to help out. I owed him—not just for being there during this, but for my whole life, and I was going to pay it back tenfold.

Three months of stats was enough to explosively boost his abilities, and since I should be getting some rollover renown from the godslaying (if not as much as Callie would) I could dedicate most of my wishes to that. Some of them would go to improving my own power, of course, but Benny had some great attacks to pay with, and I knew I'd be using them consistently in training, so that was a win-win.

A hand closed around mine, Callie grasping my fingers and giving them a light squeeze as she speared a steak with a fork and started chomping into it from one side, much to my amusement. I felt a surge of warmth from her through the bond, and I returned it wholeheartedly as I looked around.

Family. I was going to look for my mom, meet my sister, and eventually get answers from my dad. I was going to change the way kids grew up in the family and make my name ring through the whole universe. I was going to do that for *family*. Not just my parents or relatives, but *this* family, the one I'd made.

I'd taken a step with this whole dungeon episode, a step out onto the wider stage. People would be hearing my name, would know who I was. I'd officially joined the wider universe, even if, based on what Zeke said, I was competing with enough ridiculous shit that I wasn't likely to stand out at first. It was still progress, still a story that other people would tell.

I'd written the first chapter of my legend, of *our* legend, and I couldn't wait to write the next.

About the Author

Malcolm Tent is, in fact, smarter than a fifth grader. He enjoys reading, writing, and spending time with his dogs. He's lycanthrophobic and addicted to Cajun food.

Author website:

About Timeless Wind Publishing

Founded in late 2020 by Lorne Ryburn and Silas Sontag, Timeless Wind Publishing is an up-and-coming indie publishing house. We love sci-fi and fantasy—progression fantasy, power fantasy, LitRPG, time loops, cultivation, system apocalypse—genre fiction of all kinds! We're prolific readers within these genres and endeavor to bring awesome books into the limelight.

We look forward to helping authors (aspiring and published alike) develop and expand an audience of readers who believe in their vision.

Our logo is an exotic cat from a Palmyrene ruin. The word along its back roughly translates to, "Alas!" or "What a shame!" This word is present on all gravestones in Palmyra. It's a recognition that all things come to an end… even the best people and stories. Alas!

We hope our readers will have "alas" moments when they finish our books.

Connect with Timeless Wind Publishing
TimelessWind.com
Facebook.com/timelesswind
Twitter.com/timeless_wind
Instagram.com/timelesswindpub

www.ingramcontent.com/pod-product-compliance
Lightning Source LLC
Chambersburg PA
CBHW030802260626
47169CB00001B/152